STARBORN

Lucy Hounsom

STARBORN

The Worldmaker Trilogy:
Book One

✳

TOR

First published 2015 by Tor,
an imprint of Pan Macmillan, a division of Macmillan Publishers Limited
Pan Macmillan, 20 New Wharf Road, London N1 9RR
Basingstoke and Oxford
Associated companies throughout the world
www.panmacmillan.com

ISBN 978-1-4472-6845-1 (HB)
ISBN 978-1-4472-6852-9 (TPB)

Typeset by Ellipsis Digital Limited, Glasgow
Printed and bound by CPI Group (UK) Ltd, Croydon, CR0 4YY

For my parents, Dee and Terry, and my sister, Laura:
the best story is the one we've written together.

ACKNOWLEDGEMENTS

This book would not exist without the support of two exceptional people. Huge thanks to my agent and earliest champion, Veronique Baxter – your initial enthusiasm and professional guidance set me on the path of my dreams. And to my editor, Bella Pagan – not only did you take a chance on a new author, but you worked tirelessly to make *Starborn* the best book it could be. Thank you for your trust and for sharing your vision with me.

Many thanks to everyone at Team Tor and Pan Macmillan – you've made this the ride of my life and I'm so grateful for all that you've done. From design to rights to copyediting, you've been behind me and my book every step of the way.

I've met many new faces on this journey, both online and in person, and all of them have been supportive, encouraging and ever willing to share advice with a newbie. Thanks to fellow Tor author Liz de Jager for being an informative whirlwind of fun, to Jen Williams and Max Edwards for laughs, Edward Cox for hugs and Ewa and Nazia for showing me the ropes.

Thank you to those people who read all or part of *Starborn* in one of its previous lives and provided me with feedback. Since this was undoubtedly a painful experience, I'd like to acknowledge Cheryl Coppell, Alashiya Gordes, Mikey Gwilliams, M. J. Starling, and the brilliant writers on my Creative Writing MA: Emma Chapman, Tom Feltham, Liz Gifford, Carolina Gonzalez-Carvajal, Kat Gordon, Liza Klaussmann and Rebecca Lloyd James. Thanks also to those Royal Holloway tutors who pointed me in the right direction: Adam Roberts, Susanna Jones and Andrew Motion.

I'll soon have been indulging my literary obsession at Waterstones for five years – and five years is far too short a time to work among such excellent and admirable folk. To my colleagues at Exeter Roman Gate: don't go changing. Special thanks to Paul, account sales partner-in-crime, for his musical education and for laughs as plentiful as Papa's coffees. Warmest thanks to all of Waterstones for supporting me and my writing.

This is my first book and I'd be remiss not to mention the authors who inspired me as a teenager and continue to inspire me still: you filled my head with possibilities and transported me to realms far beyond my ability to reach alone. Because of you, I never needed a Relic to show me my calling. And if you've kept with me so far, dear reader, this one's for you: thank you for choosing to enter my world. I hope I manage to tempt you out of yours for a time, and that when you return, you'll have stories of your own to tell.

Finally, thank you to my family: you have known me the longest and have stood beside me at the helm through all weathers. Here's to the voyages we've yet to make.

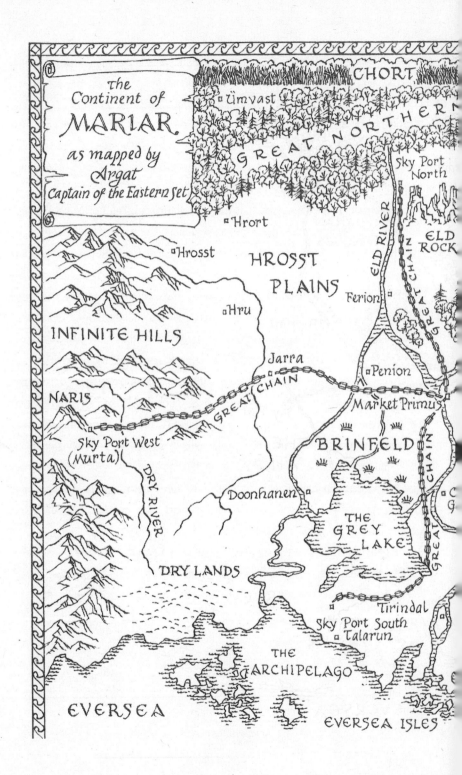

The
Continent of
MARIAR
as mapped by
Argat
Captain of the Eastern Set

CHORT

Úmvast

GREAT NORTHERN

Sky Port
North

Hrort

HROSST
PLAINS

ELD
ROCK

ELD RIVER

GREAT CHAIN

Hrosst

Ferion

Hru

INFINITE HILLS

Jarra

Penion

GREAT CHAIN

NARIS

Market Primus

BRINFELD

Sky Port West
(Murta)

DRY RIVER

Doonhanen

THE
GREY
LAKE

GREAT CHAIN

DRY LANDS

Tirindal
Sky Port South
Talarun

EVERSEA

THE
ARCHIPELAGO

EVERSEA ISLES

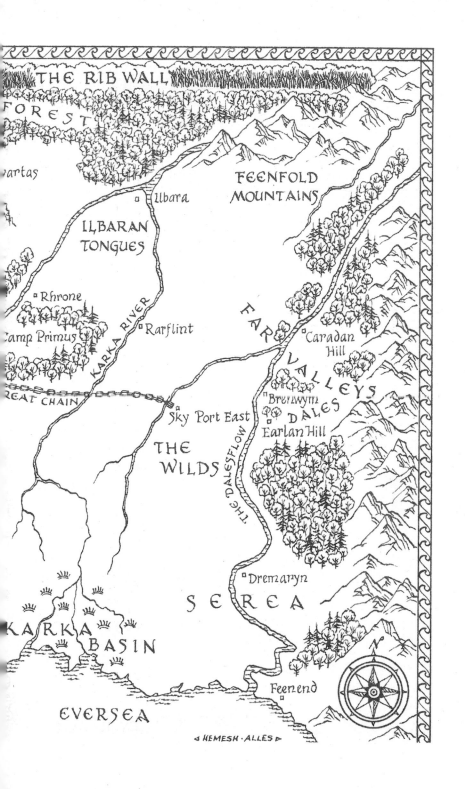

THE RIB WALL

FOREST

artas

FEENFOLD
MOUNTAINS

▫ Ilbara

ILBARAN
TONGUES

▫ Rhrone

FAR

Camp Primus

KARKA RIVER

▫ Rarflint

▫ Caradan
Hill

VALLEYS

GREAT CHAIN

▫ Brenwyn

DALES

Sky Port East

Earlan Hill

THE
WILDS

THE DALESFLOW

SEREA

▫ Dremaryn

KARKA

BASIN

Feenend

EVERSEA

◁ HEMESH · ALLES ▷

But in the process of the centuries the mountain is levelled and the river will change its course, empires experience mutation and havoc and the configuration of the stars varies. There is change in the firmament.

'The God's Script'
Jorge Luis Borges

Some say that gleams of a remoter world
Visit the soul in sleep . . .

'Mont Blanc'
Percy Bysshe Shelley

Acre: Tales of the Lost World

Solinaris is widely regarded as the most magnificent structure in all Acre. It is home to the Wielders, a people able to harness the energies of sun and moon. Such is the power these magic-users have at their command that the glass of their citadel has stood without crack for seven centuries. Human-like servants called the Yadin walk these halls, clothed in purest white. Created by the powers they serve, they would willingly lay down their lives for their masters. Solinaris stands on the western edge of Rairam, a large, varied continent whose natural beauty and resources make it one of Acre's richest lands.

The Wielders of Solinaris term their power 'cosmosethic energy', claiming it derives from the cosmos itself. To the minds of Acrean technicians, this assertion is unverifiable. Their own logic pales against the fearsome power employed by those in Solinaris. How may a Wielder channel the sun's heat? How access the moon's reflected glory? These things lie beyond rational comprehension, yet none denies their existence, or their might.

Solinaris is governed by an autonomous group comprising all

Wielders who have graduated to full status. This ensures a fair ruling on every issue considered and is widely thought to be among the most advanced political systems in the world.

The Estreyan Mountains are rumoured to be the home of the dragon people, those who call themselves Lleu-yelin. Little is known about this fierce, silent race, from whose wrists and ankles stream the sinuous tendons of their mounts.

Cymenza and the Raucus Cities are famed for their towers, built to withstand any attack – though nothing sharper than the arrows of peace has rained against their stones in all of a hundred years. Under moonlight, they take on the hue of their moats, so that to an easily fooled human eye, they could be mere reflections trapped in the heart of the water.

And those feared most are they whose names are twinned with the stars', for their grave countenances bear only a semblance of humanity, and in their hands lies the undoing of worlds.

PART ONE

I

When Kyndra awoke on the day of the Ceremony, she believed – for one dream-tangled instant – that it was her last.

She sat up, gasping. Beneath her shift, her heart hurtled through its beats, and she pressed a sweaty palm against her chest. She couldn't remember the dream now. Only the vaguest sense remained; like a threat, urging her to flee.

I don't run.

Kyndra rubbed the sleep from her eyes. As her blood cooled, so did the sweat on her body, and she pulled the woollen blanket back up. *The Ceremony is my Inheritance*, she reminded herself. It marked the start of her adult life. She had counted the years until this morning, savoured the ripening sense of anticipation.

But an hour later, returning home from a walk through Brenwym's muddy streets, Kyndra realized it wasn't just the cold that peppered her arms in gooseflesh. Each breath took her closer to the Ceremony, closer to her fate. She glanced up. The sky was a mass of dirty white clouds, and the rain flattened both her hair and spirits. She didn't want to see her mother's look of strained pride, the sad inflection in her voice that plainly said she was losing her child. Today

Kyndra would become a woman and her town would put her to use.

As long as we don't drown first. She grimaced. The spring blossom had brought only clouds and, two wet weeks later, petals fell to settle like snow on a town underwater. Kyndra thought of being dry with a wistful sigh. Her shirt stuck to her skin and her woollen trousers clung horribly. The rest of her clothes hung from a rafter in the attic at home and were only slightly less damp. She'd have to wear a dress for the Ceremony, she realized sourly. Even in this rain.

Kyndra brushed the wet hair off her forehead and wrinkled her nose. The town smelled of rotten green and people packed into a space too small to contain them. Brenwym provided the only haven within easy reach for families flooded out of their homes in the lower dales. And now of course the rest of the Valleys had arrived for this year's Inheritance Ceremony.

Kyndra stopped short. Her chosen route home led through the main square, which had become a lake overnight. Its surface mimicked the bloated sky and around its edges, rubbish piled up against cottages and shops. She allowed herself one unenthusiastic sigh before shrugging and wading in. After a moment, the cold water came creeping across her toes and Kyndra gritted her teeth. Her boots would never dry by this afternoon's Ceremony and she'd outgrown her mother's. Maybe a walk to clear her head hadn't been the best of ideas either. She shivered, catching her reflection in a window. The cheap glass blurred her face into a pale, disgruntled oval.

Teeth chattering, Kyndra increased her pace. Her mother's inn would seem welcoming after this, even filled as it was with the stale smell of drink. The wind picked up, so that she heard the shutters of The Nomos before she saw them. Chinks of firelight spilled out into the street and she fought her way around the side of the building to the back door.

'. . . Wish you'd make more of an effort, Jarand. Sometimes I don't think you care.' Kyndra's mother, Reena, turned to throw out a sack and caught sight of Kyndra dripping on the step. 'What are you doing?' she gasped. Jarand winked at Kyndra over her shoulder.

'I went for a walk.'

'I thought you had gone—' The sack slipped from Reena's hand. She didn't seem to notice.

'Mother?'

Reena stared at her for a few, stunned moments, then swallowed and shook her head. 'Never mind,' she said. 'I . . . I just thought you were upstairs getting ready.'

Kyndra frowned. 'What's the matter?'

But Reena stepped back inside and deftly took down a towel. 'Boots off.' She thrust the ragged cloth at Kyndra. 'You'll have to wear mine.'

Kyndra shook her head. 'They don't fit.'

'I'm not having mud traipsed over everything.' Reena's voice hardened and chased some of the blood back into her face. 'People are paying good money to stay here.'

Irritated, Kyndra rubbed the towel over her head. 'Is it always about money? Even today?'

Reena tucked a curl of hair more red than Kyndra's back under her kerchief. 'You want to eat, don't you?'

Kyndra didn't reply, but broke the awkward silence by kicking her boots onto the mat. A thick swell of heat and smoke welcomed her into the hall, and she battled to close the door against the wind that blew through the backstreet.

'It took the families from Caradan Hill a week to get here,' Reena said, as she watched Kyndra's struggle with the door.

'Really,' Kyndra said without interest. The door latched shut and she leaned against it. Jarand had disappeared. He always did when a foul mood puffed out Reena's chest. Kyndra didn't care. Her wet clothes chafed and all she wanted was to escape upstairs. 'Why are you so worried about impressing visitors?' she said. 'They'll never come back.'

Her mother's face darkened. 'You are about to become a woman of this town, Kyndra. Whatever future you're shown, you will find it in Brenwym.' Reena paused. 'This is your home.'

She was right. Brenwym *was* her home. Kyndra had never been outside the Valleys. *And I'm not likely to either*, she thought despondently.

'Go and clean yourself up,' Reena sighed. 'I managed to dry out some of your underclothes. They're on the bed.' To Kyndra's trouser-clad legs, she added, 'I've always thought that blue dress looks nice on you.'

The blue dress was ready and waiting. Kyndra scowled at it. Moving slowly, she filled a basin, peeled off her sodden clothes and scrubbed her skin clean. The water was cold and quickly turned brown. She shivered. The rain sounded more like hammers up here, a relentless pounding that threatened to split the rafters. She shared the garret with Reena and Jarand, her mother's husband. A thin partition split the space in two.

Once she was dry, Kyndra wriggled reluctantly into the dress. Its tight sleeves stopped her from raising her arms and twice she tripped over the skirt whilst hunting for her mother's boots. She tugged at it fiercely, but stopped when she remembered that Reena had paid for it. Flushed and ready at last,

Kyndra dropped onto the bed and laid the backs of her hands against her cheeks.

What had her mother seen during her own Inheritance Ceremony? Kyndra assumed something to do with an inn, or Reena wouldn't be here running The Nomos. Jarand was an outsider, from Dremaryn to the south, so he didn't count. He had only become an innkeeper when he married Reena.

Kyndra let her feet carry her to a small mirror set in the corner of the room. 'It will be fine,' she told herself. An uncertain face looked back, framed by dark red hair that ended untidily just above her shoulders.

She picked up a comb and tapped it against her palm. The Inheritance lay at the heart of Valleys life. The first survivors of the Acrean wars to settle here had brought the Relic with them: an artefact that revealed a person's true name and calling. The Inheritance Ceremony had taken place every year since, five centuries of young people looking into the Relic and seeing their future in its depths.

Kyndra dragged the comb through her hair and then twisted the damp strands into a knot. She had longed for this day as much as her friends had. Now she dreaded it. The full force of those centuries bore down upon her, thousands of lives lived as the Relic intended. Its power reached into your soul, people said. It showed you the truth of yourself. To stray from the calling it gave you was not only unheard of, but it was also a sin.

What if it gives me a future I don't want?

Kyndra spun away from her reflection, threw open the door and stalked downstairs. Her fear clung as close as her own shadow.

The common room was packed with people and pipe smoke. Dark varnish coated the walls, obscuring the kind of stains an inn racked up over the years. Patrons crowded between tables, idly keeping an eye out for empty places. The spectre of rain hung over everything and Kyndra couldn't suppress a smirk when she recalled her mother's words about the floor. Mud smeared the usually spotless boards.

A finger jabbed painfully into Kyndra's ribs. She flinched and looked down. The woman sitting there studied her crookedly, lips stretched in a leer. 'So, girl, your day has arrived,' Ashley Gigg said. 'But bud or blossom, you'll always be a chit to me.'

There were stifled guffaws and Kyndra's face grew hot. *Ashley's rude to everyone*, she reminded herself. *And you did push that tinker's weasel through her bedroom window. She probably hasn't forgotten.* Kyndra pressed her lips together. She hadn't played that trick alone. Her best friend Jhren had been a willing accomplice.

'Don't you listen, Kyn.' Hanna leaned over her bench. She was a plump, fair-haired woman with slightly large teeth. 'We know how much you've looked forward to this day. Me an' Havan have come up specially to see Jhren's Inheritance.' Her dimpled cheeks were flushed with the heat.

Kyndra grinned and muttered thanks. Jhren's aunt and uncle were traders and Kyndra had sat up many a night, listening to tales of a world beyond Brenwym. Those candlelit evenings seemed far away now. Nodding to Havan, she slipped past, eager to get away.

She pushed through the crowd to an unshuttered window and cleared a patch of condensation with her sleeve. The rain continued to swell the streets into brown rivers. Idly, she drew a pattern on the glass; a star with only three points.

'Blue suits you.'

10

She jumped, hearing him laugh softly. Jhren stood behind her, so close she could feel his breath on the exposed skin of her neck.

Kyndra spun and punched him lightly on the arm. 'It doesn't. And don't creep up on me.'

'Ow,' Jhren protested. Then, seeing her frown deepen, he added, 'All right, I take it back. You look awful in blue.'

'Better.'

Jhren's bright smile faded a little. 'It is a nice dress though, Kyn. You should wear it more often.'

'And what about *my* dress?'

Colta appeared beside Jhren, arms folded, lips pursed. She looked as lovely as ever. A red ribbon held back her curls and at the same time somehow sent them tumbling over her shoulder. They were dark, like her eyes.

Obediently, Jhren turned to look. Kyndra watched his gaze rake across Colta's neckline and, despite her best efforts, felt a flash of annoyance. Colta's dress hugged her form and fell in attractive folds to the floor. Pretty woven sandals peeped from beneath its hem.

A little smile curled Colta's lips. She laughed. 'I didn't sleep a bit last night,' she told them. 'I'm just too excited.'

If that were true, Colta showed no sign of it. Her face had none of a sleepless night's shadows, but was fresh and bright. A scent clung to her. *Rose*, Kyndra thought.

'How do you like my outfit, Kyndra?' Colta asked her. 'Gerda made it especially for today. The shoes too.' She eyed Kyndra's dress with just a hint of disparagement. 'You should have asked her to make yours.'

'I know what Gerda charges,' Kyndra said. 'Why pay so much for something I'll only wear once?'

'She's the best dressmaker in town.' Colta stroked her skirt defensively. 'She can charge whatever she wants.' Giving up on Kyndra, she said to Jhren, 'I really wanted the bodice cut lower. But you know Gerda.' She rolled her eyes and smiled a dimpled smile. 'She has such old-fashioned ideas.'

'Shouldn't you put some boots on?' Kyndra said a touch more harshly than she'd intended. 'It's raining. You'll spoil those shoes.'

'I know it's raining, Kyndra,' Colta snapped. 'But we all become adults today and I intend to look the part.'

'There's more to growing up than looking the part,' Kyndra said before she could stop herself. She tried to stuff her hands in her pockets and then realized that she didn't have any.

Colta gave her a pitying look that made Kyndra grind her teeth. 'If you'd had some made yourself, you wouldn't have to be jealous,' the other girl said sweetly. She turned to Jhren. 'See you later. I've still got lots to do.' With a bat of her lashes, Colta swept off.

'Don't mind her,' Jhren said. 'She's probably nervous.'

'She really looked it.'

'What's that supposed to mean?'

Kyndra waved a hand. 'Forget it. I'm not in the mood to argue.'

'Me neither.' Jhren grinned at her and Kyndra felt her frown disappear.

They stood side by side at the window. Frequent gusts of cold air announced each new patron and lifted Jhren's blond fringe. 'Busy,' Kyndra remarked.

Jhren glanced at her. 'How many do you think are in town?'

'I don't know. Not everyone has come for the Ceremony.'

'You mean the flood in the lower dales.'

12

Kyndra nodded. 'There isn't enough room here. They'll have to go home eventually.'

'It's weird,' Jhren said. 'Aunt Hanna told us the weather's only bad in the area around Brenwym.'

'What do you think's causing it?' Kyndra watched the points of her star leak, tear-like, down the glass. 'I can't remember there ever being a spring this wet.'

Somewhere in the inn, a low bell chimed. 'Is that the time?' Jhren gasped, leaping away from the window. 'I'm supposed to be home for lunch. Mother's roasted a pig in my honour.' He grinned. 'See you on the green, I guess.' Then his face grew serious. 'I can't believe it, Kyn. *This is it.*'

Kyndra tried to ignore the butterflies in her stomach. 'I know.' She watched her friend open the door, coat held over his head as a pathetic shield against the rain. Jhren winked once and then he was gone.

Wondering how Jhren could face lunch, Kyndra headed unobtrusively for her window seat. Hidden by the curtain, she settled herself on a long cushion that ran the length of the casement. It was here that she sat through dark, winter after-noons when Jarand was too preoccupied to find chores for her. She'd read for hours. Her favourite stories were about Acre, a lost world of Wielders and magic, dragon-riders, soaring cities full of people beyond counting.

Acre: Tales of the Lost World were really just that: tales. But, sandwiched between two pages, Kyndra had found a scrap of parchment, badly preserved and almost illegible. On it was an alphabet. And under each letter someone had faithfully trans-scribed its equivalent in Mariar's common tongue. The find restored Kyndra's hope: that once upon a time, Acre had existed.

Kyndra peered around the curtain. Her mother didn't seem to have noticed her absence. She was probably too busy. Kyndra propped a cushion behind her head and leaned back. The Inheritance was not to begin for another two hours and perhaps she could snatch a few minutes of the rest this morning's dreams had stolen. With a sigh, she closed her eyes and the clamour of the inn dimmed.

. . . *A burning valley spreads at her feet, bloody earth bare of life. A light blazes at one end like noon sun on glass. She flies through the air, its dry pressure hot on her cheeks. Something takes shape within the light: a building, tall as a mountain. The shine she imagines is sun on glass is indeed that: glass so fine, she wonders how the wind doesn't shatter it. Crystal towers spin dizzily into the sky.*

And then she sees the man. Behind him, the glorious building crumbles and falls and all the light is gone. The man's face beneath his white hood is strong-boned and harsh. His eyes are black like crows' feathers. His mouth opens, lips start to frame a word: Kyndra . . .

'Kyndra, wake up!'

Blearily, Kyndra opened her eyes, struggling out of sleep, but it clung to her, weighing her down.

'Kyndra!'

She realized her eyes had closed again. Fighting the impulse to sleep, she tried to hold them open.

'What's wrong?' Jarand asked, as he held the curtain back. His gaze was worried. 'You look awful.'

'I *feel* awful,' Kyndra groaned. She raised a hand to her forehead, trying to relieve its throbbing. There was something she needed to remember, but the dream kept getting in the way. Just thinking about it made her eyelids heavy.

'Kyndra!'

She frowned at Jarand, still massaging her forehead. 'Stop shouting, Jarand. What is it?'

Jarand stared at her, mouth open. 'What's the matter with you? You were supposed to be at the green half an hour ago.'

For a long moment, Kyndra gazed at him. Then, 'The Ceremony!' she cried, springing to her feet.

'Steady,' Jarand said. He retrieved the cushion that Kyndra had kicked off in her haste. 'They haven't started yet. Reena thought you'd already left, but I spotted your coat upstairs.'

'Thanks, Jarand.' Kyndra took it and rushed for the door. The common room was all but empty now. How could she have forgotten?

'Good luck!'

Kyndra waved and bolted outside. Forcing her arms into the coat's sleeves proved impossible in her dress. She thrust it under her arm and scooped up her skirt to leap puddles and potholes, running as fast as she dared towards the green. She arrived out of breath, ankles spattered with mud.

It looked like everyone in the Valleys was present. Kyndra edged through the crowd and made what she hoped was an inconspicuous dash to the group in the centre. Miraculously the rain had stopped, although vast, murky pools swamped the area. The earth was so wet that water oozed over her cramped boot toes.

'What kept you?'

Jhren appeared beside her, dressed in his formal clothes. 'I overslept,' Kyndra said shortly, ignoring her friend's startled laugh. She took a quick glance around. The Inheritors' families stood in a semi-circle surrounding their sons and daughters. There were probably a few curious spectators here too, Kyndra thought, come to witness a local custom. Everyone's gaze was fixed on a high-peaked tent in the centre of the green. The Relic Keeper stood in front of it, speaking, hands clasped on the waist of his robes.

'. . . We receive these young people in the Ceremony of Inheritance, gifted us by our most precious artefact, a wonder of the ancient world. In this we honour the Relic!'

Cheers rang out among the watching people, accompanied by clapping and the slushy stamping of children's feet. As the Keeper hoisted up his sodden robes and disappeared inside the tent, Kyndra's fellow Inheritors mumbled, 'We honour the Relic, the illuminator of our paths. We are thankful for its guidance.' Kyndra opened her mouth to speak the words along with them, but her throat was strangely dry and nothing came out.

A sturdy man, in garb more practical than the Keeper's, organized the Inheritors into an alphabetical line. Then he stood back and consulted his parchment. 'Jane Abthal,' he called.

A nervous girl Kyndra didn't know shuffled her way to the tent. The man greeted her solemnly. With a last look over her shoulder, she slipped inside. It was only a few minutes before she emerged, pale-faced but smiling. She waved at the crowd. They cheered her, and the girl went to stand with some people Kyndra supposed were her family. She looked relieved.

The Inheritance continued in much the same way. As she moved slowly up the line towards the tent, Kyndra wondered why she hadn't spoken the devotion. Perhaps Reena had not been as zealous as some parents in her attempts to make her understand the Relic's importance, but she'd still grown up here. She had watched past Ceremonies with a child's trusting eyes, standing in the safety of the crowd. She had copied the mumbled devotion out on paper when Jarand had taught her the letters. So why now – on the day it mattered most – had she not been able to speak it?

Kyndra tried to distract herself by searching for Jhren, but the press of Inheritors blocked her view. Glancing over her shoulder, she spotted Colta a few people behind. The girl waved when she saw Kyndra looking, but as the Ceremony progressed, Kyndra noticed that she chewed on her lower lip and her hands trembled.

'Jhren Farr.'

Kyndra started at Jhren's name and squinted at the tent just in time to see the blond boy flash an exultant smile. She waited nervously for Jhren to return, twisting one of the buttons on her coat.

The button came away in her hand and Kyndra hastily shoved it in a pocket. The noise of the crowd lifted. She raised her head to see her friend emerging from the tent.

'I am Huran!'

Jhren yelled out his true name, his eyes brighter than ever, and the crowd shouted their pleasure. Kyndra could see Hanna and Havan right in the front. They stretched out their arms and clasped their nephew's hands. Jhren met Kyndra's eyes and Kyndra found she couldn't bear the look of triumph on her friend's face. Why did it all feel so wrong? Hadn't she wanted this as much as Jhren?

With only nerves for company, Kyndra resigned herself to waiting. The Ceremony and the dream fought for dominance in her mind. Her fear might influence the Relic. Dreams were odd creatures, Jarand said; they usually told you things you already knew. Would her mother insist she accept her calling? She looked for her in the crowd. Reena's red hair stood out against the drab mass of coats, but her face was wan. She looked as worried as Kyndra felt. Her eyes lifted to find her daughter in the dwindling group of Inheritors. She smiled and Kyndra did her best to smile back.

'Eram Tyler.'

Kyndra found herself at the front of the line and wiped her hands on her coat. There were only nine Inheritors left. She kept her eyes on the tent entrance into which the last boy had just vanished. When the boy returned several minutes later, wearing a rather sick smile, Kyndra tried to slow her thundering heart.

'Kyndra Vale.'

Kyndra took a deep breath and walked towards the tent. She felt the stares collect on her back. When she reached the entrance, she turned to look over her shoulder. The faces of the crowd merged, until they became a blurred mass of watchers. A strange thrill coursed through her and she looked closer. There was one face that remained separate, one face in the whole crowd whose features were clear. The breath froze in her lungs. Dark, almost pupil-less eyes found hers, burning beneath the shadow of a white cowl. Kyndra stared, mesmerized. None of her limbs would move. The man from the dream smiled then, a surprised stretching of his lips. He nodded once and, between moments, was gone.

'Girl?'

The Keeper's assistant was speaking to her. The crowd gazed at her curiously. Kyndra tore her eyes away and stumbled into the tent. Her heart pounded. *I must have imagined it*, she thought, staring numbly at her surroundings. The tent's canvas walls stretched up to a pointed dome, supported by poles at each corner. The Keeper sat behind a small table, which held only one object. Kyndra looked at the Relic.

It was a bowl – shallow and wide, as rumour alleged, but nothing like as wonderful. To Kyndra's eyes, the Relic appeared distinctly ordinary, sitting there full of water.

'Come, come.' The Keeper gestured her to the stool in front of the Relic and Kyndra sat down. Sweat slicked her palms, but the tips of her fingers were cold.

'As I said at the beginning of the Ceremony, I am Iljin, the current Relic Keeper. No doubt you have heard of me . . .?'

Kyndra nodded slowly, throat still too dry to speak.

'When the Relic senses your approach, its appearance changes,' the Keeper explained. 'Through time spent in close proximity, I am able to witness this alteration.' A pompous light brightened his face. 'The Relic has been thirty-five years in my keeping and I am considerably experienced in its use. You must place your hands on either side. Do not let go until I tell you. I shall interpret the water's riddles.'

The Keeper looked from the grey bowl to Kyndra's eyes. 'Perhaps it's a good omen that I have never seen the Relic adopt this likeness before.'

Kyndra frowned. Was that the truth? The dull bowl looked as grim to her as the leaden sky outside and a sense of foreboding arose, so strong that she began to believe she should not touch it. She drew back.

'There is no need to be afraid,' the Keeper assured her. 'You will not be harmed.' He clasped his weathered hands. There was nothing else to do. Kyndra reached out and took hold of the Relic.

It felt insubstantial and icy cold. She lifted it off the table without meaning to do so. A hum built in her ears, low at first, but growing higher and louder with every second. Was this supposed to happen? She saw the Keeper frown. The bowl darkened, becoming so unbearably cold that she let out a grunt of pain, but when she tried to drop it, she couldn't pull her hands away. The water inside hissed and for a moment she saw a thousand pinpricks of light reflected in its depths. Then it hardened into crystals of steaming ice.

'No!' The Keeper threw himself forward, but it was too late. With a sharp *crack*, the great Relic shattered. Shards of ice ricocheted off the tent walls.

The pieces fell wetly from Kyndra's stinging hands. Covered in chill fragments, she stared at them, unmoving. The silence that ensued, when the last reverberation of the hum had died away, stretched for endless moments. Then the old man gave a whimpering cry. His eyes shone with unshed tears.

'What have you done?' he wailed at Kyndra. *'What have you done?'*

2

A drum beat steadily in her veins. The Relic had broken into three uneven pieces. One lay in her lap; the other fragments had fallen onto the rush matting. Water had begun to ooze up from beneath and a damp smell filled the tent.

Kyndra felt as if she had been sitting on the hard stool for hours, staring at the remnants of the Relic. She couldn't hear the crowd and thought for one wild moment everyone had gone. Something moved at the top of her vision. She looked up to see Iljin lowering himself onto hands and knees. Bones clicked and the old man winced. Kyndra watched him gather the two fragments slowly into his arms. Their shallow curves glistened wetly. The old man hugged the pieces, ignoring the moisture that seeped into his robes.

Kyndra slipped from the stool to kneel beside him. Small, half-smothered sobs came from the old man's throat, his head bowed low over the broken bowl. Kyndra gingerly held out the fragment that had been in her lap. 'Here,' she muttered and thrust it forward. 'I . . . I'm sorry.'

'You're sorry?' Iljin lifted his head. Beneath the tear stains, his skin was corpse white.

Kyndra laid the fragment at the old man's knees and backed away, hands coming up in front of her. 'I didn't mean it.'

Iljin looked from the spilled ice to Kyndra's face and for a moment his eyes burned with suspicion. Then, 'Stupid child!' he cried, breaking the stare. 'Why should you be sorry? How can I blame you for this?'

Kyndra said nothing.

'What am I supposed to tell everyone? That a girl broke something made with the old powers? The Relic that has weathered five hundred years?' He stumbled to his feet, cradling the fragments. 'It's inconceivable, impossible.' His nose ran, but the old man didn't seem to notice. He stared at Kyndra, mouthing uselessly. Then he began to stagger around the tent, until he found a large velvet pouch that had fallen under the table. The mouthing became a barely audible gabble. Iljin placed each piece of the Relic gently inside the bag.

Kyndra's body began to shake. Her head felt light, just like the time she'd stayed out in the sun too long. She had skipped her chores to play with her friends, splashing in the streams that spilled out of the hills above Brenwym. The memory made her wish for a glass of icy water and she blearily thought of the crystals that had formed in the bowl before it broke. Maybe one was still lying around.

'You –' Iljin gripped Kyndra's arm. The old man was surprisingly strong. 'You are to say *nothing* about what happened here. Do you hear me? Not a word.' He shook Kyndra until she nodded and pulled her arm free. The effort seemed to exhaust Iljin, who swayed then and grabbed at one of the tent poles.

'I should have known,' the old man whispered. His face slackened and Kyndra watched the blue eyes turn inward. 'The

Relic was ancient. I should have seen it coming . . . that grey colour a warning, and I missed it.'

She would never receive her life's calling, Kyndra realized numbly. She would never know her true name. She felt a pang as she remembered Jhren's happy shouts, Hanna's wide smile as she welcomed her nephew into adulthood.

Kyndra bit her lip too hard and tasted blood. Roughly, she wiped her mouth on the back of her hand. She'd been so worried about what the Relic might tell her, and now it would never speak again.

There were noises outside the tent. Someone raised their voice in a muffled question and Kyndra remembered the other Inheritors. They'd never receive their true names either. A cold sorrow settled in her stomach. Colta was one of them. Kyndra thought of the other girl's excitement, of the way she had touched her dress. She thought of the anticipation that had brought light to her dark eyes. Colta could be difficult sometimes, but she was still Kyndra's friend. She didn't deserve this. 'Can the Relic be mended?' Kyndra asked hesitantly.

Iljin puffed out his chest and she braced herself for another tirade. 'You can't,' the old man began angrily, but then he deflated. 'I don't know,' he confessed in a broken voice. 'I don't believe so. Its power has probably leaked away.'

Moments passed in which it seemed to Kyndra that the old man would never move again. He leaned against the tent wall, clutching the velvet pouch, his eyes watery and distant. The noise of the crowd grew louder and finally Iljin straightened. 'What am I going to do?' he asked.

Before Kyndra had a chance to answer, the old man began to ramble. 'I must tell them that the Relic was fragile. Yes. That I could sense its power waning, but didn't realize it would break so soon. They have to believe there was nothing anyone could do.'

Iljin shuffled to the tent flap. He dragged a hand across his nose and looked at Kyndra. 'Go out the back way. You must not call attention to yourself.'

'What about the other Inheritors?' Kyndra blurted, but Iljin swiftly pulled the canvas aside and stepped out.

Kyndra retreated. She hadn't noticed the back flap, hidden behind the old man's chair. She shoved the chair to one side and quickly undid the strings that held the canvas closed. Her fingers fumbled on the knots.

Outside, the sky was forbidding. It began to rain again. Large drops spattered Kyndra's cheeks, but she ignored them, carefully peering around the side of the tent.

Although most families had left to escape the weather, there were at least fifty people still watching. Iljin seemed to be speaking, but Kyndra was on the wrong side of the wind and couldn't hear.

Guilt dug at her. She felt its claws despite the old man's claims about the Relic being old. What ill luck had chosen her to witness its destruction? To be the one holding it when it broke? She began to walk quickly, heading for the line of trees that marked the far edge of the green.

The past week's anxiety suddenly resembled childish worry. She felt no relief at escaping the possibility of a future she didn't want. The Inheritance was dead. The young people of the Valleys would have to be content with their birth names. They would have to choose their calling without the Relic's guidance.

What if it *was* her fault?

Kyndra had almost reached the trees when a shout went up

from the crowd. She quickened her pace. How long would it be before they realized it was her? Would anyone believe Iljin's claim that the Relic had broken on its own?

It was no drier under the trees. The wind-shaken branches lashed her with old rain. Kyndra ploughed on until she caught sight of the road that curved back to town. Then she sat on a wet log and leaned against the tree behind. Though the wood felt damp through her dress, she dropped her coat on the ground and left it there.

Weeks of rain had melted the road into a wide, muddy track. Kyndra stared at the sodden ruts and felt an awful gloom seep into her. She watched the puddles deepen and let the minutes pass. She didn't want to go back to the inn. She didn't want to answer the inevitable questions.

A slapping, sucking sound made her look up. Kyndra wiped the rain from her face and peered through the murk. The sound came again, regular, growing louder. It was hoof beats, she realized. Someone was on the road.

She scrambled off the log and stepped back into the trees, but her movement had caught the rider's attention. A male voice murmured and the hoof beats stopped. With a sinking feeling in the pit of her stomach, Kyndra stepped out onto the road.

Two horses stood side by side. She had only expected one. The riders had their cloaks pulled tight and heavy cowls hid their faces. One of the figures sat lower in the saddle and, after exchanging a whisper with the other, drew back her hood. Her companion threw off his own cowl. He seemed tall, though slightly built, with ragged dark hair.

The woman turned and Kyndra sucked in a breath. Her gaze was blank and unseeing, a winter-sky white. 'Girl,' she said imperiously and Kyndra jumped, 'the town Brenwym is how far from here?'

'A mile . . . half a mile or so down the road,' Kyndra stammered. The woman's answering smile contained little warmth and she continued to pin Kyndra with her white, pupil-less eyes. They seemed to glow against the backdrop of dim woodland.

Then without another word, she heeled her mount, drawing the hood back over her pale hair. The man nodded at Kyndra, whispered a word of command to his own dappled horse and trotted slowly off. Mud sucked at the animals' hooves, causing the odd sound Kyndra had heard earlier. Uneasily, she watched them leave. It was not a good time for strangers.

The wind wailed, urging her home before the riders arrived in town. Kyndra snatched her coat and picked up her pace, jogging alongside the swollen river and through a curtain of willows. A gloomy twilight shadowed Brenwym. The old boots pinched her toes and the blue dress stifled her like a shroud. Mist crept over the riverbank and Kyndra broke into a clumsy run.

She was soaked by the time she reached the back door of the inn. Kyndra slipped into the hall, hoping no one was there. Water dripped from the hem of her dress. Shivering, she headed for the stairs.

'Kyndra!'

Kyndra groaned silently. Not Jhren, not now.

'I've been searching all over for you.'

She turned. Jhren looked as wet as she did. Rain beaded on the fine wool of his trousers and his hair lay flat against his head.

'You were in the tent when it happened,' he said, as if he couldn't bring himself to mention the Relic by name.

Kyndra stared at him, wondering what to say. If Jhren told Colta, and he would, then every young person would know within the hour. It was inevitable. She sighed and dropped down to sit on the rough boards of the stairs. Jhren came to sit beside her.

'There isn't much to tell,' she began, avoiding her friend's eyes. 'I just did what the Keeper told me to . . . and then it broke.'

'Surely there's more,' Jhren said, and Kyndra caught a strange hint of desperation in his voice. 'What did it look like? Were there cracks in it?'

'No.' Kyndra kept her voice low. 'It was plain, kind of ordinary. The Keeper told me to put my hands on it, but when I did, I couldn't let go.' The memory of that awful hum came back to her and she swallowed, aware that Jhren was hanging on her every word. 'The water inside turned to ice,' she whispered, 'and it broke. The Keeper said it can't be mended.'

Her hands trembled, perhaps remembering the pain of the chilled Relic. However, they were unmarked. Jhren was very still beside her. She knew he was watching her; she could feel the intensity of his gaze.

'It broke when you were holding it?'

Kyndra winced. 'The Keeper thought it was weakening,' she said quickly. 'It was just an unlucky coincidence.'

Jhren was silent. She thought she sensed a change in him but when he spoke, his voice was level. 'So you never received your Inheritance?'

Kyndra glanced at him. 'No,' she answered shortly. 'Listen, Jhren. How many people know it was me?'

Jhren shook his head, as if stirring from a reverie. 'Everyone started shouting, so it's hard to say. I saw Reena.' He paused. 'It was weird, Kyn, her face. Almost as if she'd expected something to happen – or dreaded it.'

'Great,' Kyndra said roughly. She stood, intending to go upstairs, but Jhren caught her hand. Startled, she turned to look at him as he rose.

'You'll never know your true name,' he said with a strange catch in his voice. 'You'll never know what you were born to do.'

Kyndra frowned at him. 'Colta won't either.'

'I don't care about Colta.'

His hand was hot on hers. She shifted uncomfortably. 'Jhren, I—'

'I don't understand you, Kyn. Aren't you upset? Worried? What are you going to do?'

She stared at him, her frown deepening. 'I don't know. Of course I'm worried. But I don't want to think about it just now. I want to go upstairs—'

'And do what? Pretend nothing's happened?' Jhren's grip tightened. A flush rose up in his cheeks like flame. 'I don't want you to be alone, Kyn. You need people around you at a time like this. You need your friends. You need me.'

Kyndra snatched her hand away. 'I don't need you,' she said fiercely. 'I don't need anyone. I'm fine.'

Her rebuff only served to encourage him, for Jhren seized both of her arms and pulled her down a step. Unprepared, Kyndra gasped and fell against him. 'Shush,' she heard him say, close to her ear. 'Just listen a moment.'

'Let go, Jhren.'

'Please, Kyn. I . . .' He released her arms and stood there, breathing heavily. Kyndra retreated, her own wild heartbeat in her ears. What was wrong with him?

'I'm sorry,' Jhren said. He took a deep breath. 'It's just that
. . . I want you to know you can always rely on me, that I'll
always be here for you.' He made as if to touch her face, but
she jerked back. Jhren dropped his hand. 'You don't have a
name, or a future. I do. I can support us both—'

'Stop.' His words woke a cold fury in her. 'I *do* have a name.
It's Kyndra. And I have a future. I may not know what it is yet,
but an old, broken bowl isn't going to take it away from me!
And neither are you.'

Jhren stiffened. 'Don't be stupid, Kyn. I'm not trying to take
your future. I'm trying to give you one.'

'I don't want your future!' she shouted at him and watched
the words hit like a slap. Without waiting for his response, she
turned and ran up the stairs, her dress catching under her
heels. Just before she reached the top, the material snagged on
a nail and she felt the hem tear. With a dry sob, she hurled
herself into the attic. Jhren was still standing where she'd left
him when she turned to slam the door.

Clenching her teeth against a howl, Kyndra threw the bolt
and then all but ripped off the dress. She yanked a shirt and
trousers down from the rafters. They were damp. She put them
on and then lay on her bed, fighting the whirl of feelings in her
chest. That Jhren could think . . . that he would ask— No, she
wouldn't spend another minute on him. Nostalgia, sharp and
wistful, seized her and she yearned for those lost years when
they were both just children, running over the fields. How had
everything gone so wrong?

She let her thoughts drift to the rhythm of the rain and
slowly they calmed. Her clothes warmed. The Ceremony had
driven this afternoon's dream right out of her mind, she realized. Now it rushed back, vivid and compelling. It *beckoned*.

Her eyelids grew heavy. She didn't want to close them in case the man with the black gaze returned. To think she'd seen him in the crowd . . .

Kyndra struggled to focus on the solid wooden beam above her head. The rain pounded and her heart beat, twin drums whose rhythm set a pace for her walk up the hill.

. . . She doesn't know where to go. The air is blinding; light shines behind her, above her, all around. She can't get away from it, so she walks up the hill, watching red earth pass beneath her feet. The light hounds her to the crest and, instead of the village in the next valley, she sees a towering citadel, a fortress of sun. Its spires are bright fingers pointing skyward . . .

'Kyndra!'

The wooden beam was back. Kyndra jerked upright.

'Are you up there?'

'Yes!' she called and then gasped and clutched her head, trying to halt its spinning. When she heard footsteps on the stairs, she stood up unsteadily and unbolted the door. Jarand came in.

They stared at each other for a few moments before Jarand awkwardly moved to grasp her shoulder. 'I'm sorry about your Inheritance,' he said, his voice strained. 'Reena told me you never left the tent. No one could have guessed that the Relic would fail after all these years.'

The words sounded rehearsed and Kyndra didn't have a reply. Jarand sighed and took his hand away. 'It's going to be crowded tonight,' he said apologetically. 'We could really use your help downstairs, but if you need to be alone . . .'

You need people around you at a time like this. You need your friends. You need me –

'It's fine, Jarand,' she said quickly. 'I'll only think about it if I stay up here.'

Jarand smiled faintly. 'I promise we'll make time to talk. But for now –' he shrugged – 'business must go on. I was wondering whether you'd help me bring in those cider casks outside the back door.'

Kyndra pulled on her own high boots, now mercifully drier, and followed Jarand downstairs. He was doing his best to understand, she thought, but she knew he didn't. No outsider could understand the Relic and what its absence would do to the Valleys. Not even Jarand.

When she reached the bottom, her head swam and she grabbed at the wall.

'Are you all right?' Jarand studied her. 'You're pale.'

Kyndra nodded. 'Just overtired, I guess.'

'We won't keep you late.'

She went outside, Jarand on her heels. The chill air of evening felt good on her skin and Kyndra slowly exhaled. How much could change in a few hours. Even though she had no true name and no certain path ahead of her, she felt her childhood slipping away.

Wiping the sweat from her forehead, Kyndra shifted the last cask into place and straightened with a groan. She dusted down her hands and climbed the stone steps that led to the brightly lit kitchen. It was heavy with the aroma of roasting meat and her stomach rumbled.

Halfway across the room, one of the two cooks who worked the kitchen on busy nights swooped down on her, an apron dangling from stained fingers. Kyndra sighed and took it. A long evening of waiting tables loomed ahead. *So no dinner yet,* she thought glumly. She looked through the archway that led into the common room and saw with dread that the place was full.

'Kyndra.'

Reena stood beside her, balancing a tray on the palm of one hand. She gently touched Kyndra's face with the other. 'I am so sorry.'

Kyndra looked away. 'It's all right.'

'No, it isn't,' her mother said. Damp strands of hair clung to her cheek. 'I always hoped this day would turn out right for you.' Her eyes were distant and Kyndra abruptly remembered Jhren's words about Reena expecting something to happen at the Ceremony.

'I hoped . . .' Reena blinked and shifted her fingers on the tray. 'We'll talk about it, you, me and Jarand. We'll talk as soon as the night is done.'

'There's nothing to say.'

Reena's eyes were kind. 'Yes there is,' she said and Kyndra had a sudden urge to bury her face in her mother's neck, as she had done as a child.

Reena smiled at her. 'Things will work out.' She turned away then, but not before Kyndra heard her mutter, 'Perhaps it's for the best.'

Before Kyndra could ask what she meant, Reena nodded her head at the common room. 'I see a few people waiting to order.' She stepped back to let a cook add another plate to her tray.

Kyndra nodded. Now wasn't the time to discuss it. Her mother moved off and she followed in her wake, taking orders for food and juggling plates and cups. She immersed herself in the familiar routine and tried to put the Relic from her thoughts.

On top of her serving and clearing duties, Reena encouraged her to sell wine by the cask wherever she could. Over the last few years, Kyndra had developed an eye for spotting likely customers. She remembered one occasion several months ago when they'd over-ordered on Serean Red, a wine made in the sour lands south of the Valleys. Nobody had shown much interest in buying or trading for it, so Kyndra had simply removed its label and pretended it came from somewhere more unusual. Even when customers asked to taste it, the deception had worked surprisingly well.

Although her mother was grateful for the extra coins when business was slow, Kyndra hoped Reena never found out exactly how she'd earned them. Now, as she scanned the heaving room, looking for likely customers, Kyndra spotted her mother returning from a table in the corner. Hands full with steaming bowls, she beckoned Kyndra over with a jerk of her chin.

'Kyndra, could you serve those people their drinks?' she said briskly, balancing the food. 'That small table there. They want wine.' She paused, eyeing the table she'd mentioned. 'Fetch goblets,' she said quietly, 'and choose something nice. They're strangers here.'

Kyndra found the goblets and dusted them off. They were cut-glass and only ever used for special occasions. She chose their best white wine from the cold cellar and hurried back to the common room. As she approached the dim table, she noticed that one of the strangers had pulled up their cloak, despite the heat from the fire. The man sitting opposite was uncloaked, but faced away. A prickling began on Kyndra's skin.

'Wine?' Her voice sounded loud in the silence surrounding the strangers.

The man nodded, but didn't look up. A couple of coins already lay on the tabletop, more than enough to cover the wine. Wondering whether she should just pour it and go, Kyndra's curiosity got the better of her. She only wanted to see their faces.

Her eyes alighted on the flask she held. It was risky. She couldn't trust the strangers not to have visited some of the places she usually claimed her wine was from, so she chose another city and smiled, knowing they would not have heard of this one.

'We keep a good lot of wine and ale here,' she said casually, 'all of which is for sale by the cask.' She paused, but neither stranger moved. 'I thought you might be interested in this?' She proffered the flask. 'It's one of our best, distilled in the golden vineyards of Calmarac.' Calmarac was a city she'd discovered in a book about Acre.

The table's silence grew to surround Kyndra and so too, it seemed, did its circle of darkness. The cloaked figure looked up and for the second time that day, white eyes pierced her.

The man turned. 'Calmarac?' The beginnings of a smile pulled at his mouth.

Kyndra felt like a rabbit caught in a predator's stare. The blind woman held her and she could not seem to move. 'Now,' the man said. He held a shabby volume in one hand and shook it at Kyndra's canvas-wrapped flask. 'If that wine were truly Calmaracian, I'd eat this book.'

3

Kyndra watched, stunned, as the stranger leaned forward and took the flask from her hands. He popped out the stopper and splashed wine into his goblet.

'Not bad,' he said, after a sip, 'even if it *is* only Ilbaran.' His voice was like music, or barely restrained laughter. Kyndra winced, thinking of the Ilbaran stamp on the crate downstairs. She felt her cheeks redden.

'What is your name, girl?'

The woman's tone was quiet, but this didn't disguise the iron that laced it. She placed a hand on the tabletop. Kyndra stared at it in an effort to avoid her gaze. 'Kyndra,' she said. The hand was slim without being delicate and the nails bore a peculiar silvery sheen.

'Kyndra,' the man repeated and she looked up at him. He had the greenest eyes she had ever seen, like a shady, summer forest. 'I am called Nediah and the lady you see is Brégenne. We are . . . historians, you see.' He quirked his lips in a smile.

Historians. Kyndra groaned silently. *Just my luck.*

'Will you sit for a few minutes?' the woman asked politely. 'We don't meet many young people interested in Acre.'

Kyndra sat down warily, wondering whether she detected

condescension. There was a kind of stern beauty about Brégenne, though her smile barely crinkled her eyes. They glowed faintly too, like snow under night sky. With her white-blond hair, she looked like a ghost.

'Jarand's a historian – my stepfather,' Kyndra said to break the fresh silence. Jarand was an innkeeper, but Kyndra was sure he'd be a historian if he had the means. Acre fascinated them both.

'Ah,' Brégenne said, 'and is he well-schooled in the history of your land?'

She *was* mocking her. 'Jarand owns the oldest text anywhere in the Valleys,' Kyndra said irritably. She didn't care whether this was true; the strangers wouldn't know.

'And that would be . . .?' the man prompted, peering into her face.

'My book on Acre.'

'*Your* book?' Nediah raised an eyebrow and Kyndra's cheeks grew hotter.

'Well, Jarand doesn't have much time to read these days, so I do his reading for him.' When neither stranger replied, she admitted reluctantly, 'It's not exactly history. More . . . stories. But a few of the words are in the language of Acre.'

'Acrean?' Brégenne sat up straighter. 'You can read it?'

'Only a little,' Kyndra replied. She probably shouldn't have said anything. She didn't know these people and she certainly didn't trust them, yet there was something compelling about Brégenne and her white, haunted eyes.

'Might I ask a favour?' Brégenne said, leaning back in her chair. 'I understand that you do not know us, nor can you place your trust in our discretion. But our principal interest is our work and if you have a remnant of a text, a detail on some part of Acre, we would very much like to see it.'

Kyndra looked from her to Nediah. She'd never spoken to anyone about Acre except Jarand. Nobody was interested. For the first time, she wondered how much her book was worth. It had no value in Brenwym, but she knew next to nothing about the rest of the world. Perhaps it was rare.

'All right,' she decided. Her head felt a bit light from all the pipe smoke and it would be good to sit down a while. She rose from the bench.

'Thank you.' Nediah smiled at her. 'I promise we won't keep you long from your work.'

Kyndra glanced back at their table as she headed for the window seat and saw Brégenne whispering into Nediah's ear. The man's eyes widened.

Wondering what they were saying, Kyndra ducked behind the curtain. Her boots snagged on its fraying threads. Muttering, she ripped them free. The cushions were sun-faded and fraying too. She pushed several out of the way to reveal the wood beneath, streaked with old varnish. Shielded by the curtain, she began to brush the tips of her fingers over the seat, searching for the loose panel.

Lifting it up, she fumbled for the book in which she kept the old alphabet parchment. Her hand closed on its spine and she wiggled it free from amongst her other possessions: a smooth black pebble, a bunch of letters from Jhren's aunt and uncle, an abnormally long feather that Colta had found last year. She cradled the book in one hand and replaced the panel with the other. Then, trying to appear as unobtrusive as possible, she slipped back to the table in the corner.

The strangers watched her come. With a furtive look over

her shoulder, Kyndra sat down. She knew she was needed in the kitchen, but curiosity pressed her to stay. Outside, the wind tossed itself against the inn and she imagined dark wings swooping between the chimney pots.

'This bit is the oldest. It's an alphabet.' She opened the book and laid the ancient parchment in front of Brégenne, remembering too late that the woman wouldn't be able to see it. She shifted uncomfortably as Nediah reached out and scanned the half-faded text. Kyndra expected him to describe it to his companion, but the man continued to read to himself and when he had finished, returned the parchment to the table. He took a sip of his wine.

'How did you know the vineyards of Calmarac produced golden grapes at the height of their time?'

The sharp question caught her off guard. 'I must have read a story about them,' she said, tapping her book, though she couldn't remember which one. 'How do *you* know?' she asked Nediah.

The man smiled good-naturedly, but another question lurked in his eyes. 'We belong to a select order. Part of our job is to search out relics of the lost world.'

'So Acre *is* real,' Kyndra murmured to herself. Then, realizing what the man had said, she looked up. 'There are actually people devoted to finding out about it?'

'It may seem small compared to the old world, Kyndra, but Mariar is still a very large place. Many others share your interest.'

Although Nediah spoke kindly, the flush returned to Kyndra's face. She looked down at her knees. Resentment for the Dales flashed through her. Suddenly she hated the inn, the people crowded into it, the small, pointless talk about farms and cattle and bad weather. How she longed, just for a moment, not to be one of them. She wondered where Brégenne and Nediah came from and where they were going.

While the strangers watched her, the noise of the common room rose up around their table. The front door banged against the wall. Kyndra turned to look and a gust of wind lifted the hair off her forehead. Another sodden man stumbled in, quickly swallowed by the crowd.

She looked back at the strangers. They were still silent, still staring. Brégenne hadn't said anything for a long time.

'Well.' Kyndra sought to fill the quiet. 'I don't suppose *you* know why it won't stop raining?' She gave a short laugh and quoted, "Water, water, disappear, never bring the Breaking here."'

Brégenne did not smile. 'Perhaps you've answered your own question.'

'What?' Kyndra gaped at her. 'That's just a children's rhyme. And I was joking.' She tried to suppress that small flicker of superstition.

'There's always truth to children's rhymes,' the white-eyed woman said. 'And the Breaking can strike anywhere.'

Kyndra shook her head. 'Not here.'

'No one can predict it,' Nediah said, 'but excessive rain has long been a warning sign. It might be safest to start moving people out of the town.'

Kyndra glowered at him. 'Send everyone away who doesn't live here?'

'*And* those who do,' Brégenne added coolly.

'You can't,' Kyndra snapped. 'People came here because their own houses were flooded. They'd have nowhere to go. Nor would we!' Her hands balled into fists on the tabletop.

What gave either of these people a right to come here and frighten her town with threats of the Breaking?

'You don't understand,' Brégenne said sharply. 'If people remain here and ignore the warnings, they could die.'

'Why are you telling *me*?' Kyndra made herself meet the white eyes. 'If you really believe we're in danger, why haven't you told the town elders?'

'We tried to,' Nediah said, 'but they were meeting to discuss a crisis.' Both strangers studied Kyndra with an intensity that burned. Her tongue stuck to the roof of her mouth.

A crash shook the common room. Before Kyndra could turn, a gust of cold air hit her, sweeping Nediah's goblet off the table. A cry rose up above the sound of breaking glass. The inn's door bounced against the wall, allowing the rain inside. A woman stood in the entrance, water dripping from her clothes. She wasn't wearing a coat and mud caked her slippers. Her face was red with cold and tears, but Kyndra recognized it. Tessa was one of her mother's friends.

The nearest townspeople rushed to her side, but Tessa shouted over their heads, reaching towards a large man sitting at a nearby table. 'Benj!' The blacksmith leapt to his feet. 'Help me – my husband, it's my husband.' Tessa gulped and swallowed. 'He was on the roof, and I told him not to go, I said the leak could be fixed in the morning when people would be around to help, when the rain stopped, but he wouldn't listen to reason—'

'Where is he now, Tessa?' The blacksmith kept his voice slow and clear.

Tessa blinked through a fresh roll of tears. 'The roof fell in.'

'Weylan, Drew,' the blacksmith called. 'Come with me.' The two men named jumped from their chairs and followed Benj through the door.

They weren't the only ones. Most of the inn left their drinks and hurried outside, despite the freezing rain. Kyndra was no exception. As she passed Tessa – in the arms of another woman – she noticed her nails were torn and bleeding. Not only that, but an ugly mark marred her cheek like a spread hand. The sight turned Kyndra cold.

Rain pounded Kyndra's shoulders, soaking her shirt in seconds. She wrapped her arms around herself and followed the bobbing lanterns that formed havens in a dark sea. The rain became hail. It stung her face, pelting from the sky, as if thrown by some colossal fist. Warmth leaked from her body and the flame in the nearest lamp danced wildly before a gust snuffed it out.

They hurried through the town's swollen streets. The cobbles were slick beneath Kyndra's feet and she slipped more than once. With muddy hands, she pushed her fringe out of her eyes, leaving streaks across her forehead.

Faces looked out of windows. Lamps flickered to life in dark rooms and doors creaked open. The people inside reached for coats and boots and then joined the growing crowd. Did they come for Tessa's husband Fedrin, or just out of curiosity? Kyndra wondered. A silent flash bared the town and thunder arrived a moment later. The houses looked frail beneath the lightning; a toy village ready to be flattened by the wind.

The lanterns were no longer moving, but had congregated in an oily glow some twenty feet in front of her. Another flash of lightning stopped Kyndra in her tracks. A shattered silhouette reared up: a house, its roof gone, the tops of broken walls jagged against the sky.

People gathered around the open door, which, remarkably, was intact. Kyndra caught a glimpse into the rest of the house.

It was a mess of broken furniture, beams and plaster. Her boot encountered something soft, a chunk of thatch torn free by the wind.

'Make way there! Make room!'

Three men staggered out of the front door, carrying a long, coat-wrapped form. They lowered it to the ground and Kyndra recognized Tessa's husband. Fedrin had taught her how to fish. She remembered sunny days at the stream with Jhren, Colta and the other children, learning how to hold a rod and how to fix the bait.

With a lump in her throat, Kyndra pushed closer. Fedrin's hands looked worse than Tessa's. He'd torn his nails, as if he had tried to use them like claws. An awful wheezing came from his throat and when the next flash arrived, Kyndra saw a trickle of blood oozing from the corner of his mouth. It slid down his neck and soaked into his collar.

The scene grew brighter. There were enough lanterns now to illuminate the people gathered in the street, which looked like most of the town. The townsfolk stared at the devastated house and Kyndra could see her own shock reflected in their faces. Blankets were brought and eased beneath Fedrin. People shouted for Ashley Gigg, the bad-tempered herbalist, who seemed to be the only one not present. Kyndra saw everything through a grey haze. Water poured mercilessly from the sky and there was no shelter for anyone. She scanned the crowd for Reena or Jarand, but saw neither.

Perhaps she noticed the strangers because they lurked at the very edge of the light. They stood close together, whispering furiously. Kyndra watched Nediah point repeatedly at Fedrin. He clutched Brégenne's hands as if in adjuration, but the woman stood adamant. Kyndra used the cover of the crowd to get nearer. Once on the fringes, she left the shelter of people and hid in the shadows. She was as close as she dared go.

'Listen to me.' Brégenne ground out each word, her voice like steel. 'Naris has remained hidden for five hundred years and it is not for us to choose when and where to uncover its secrets.'

'I'm not saying we should tell them who we are!' Nediah flung at her. 'I'm only asking you to help the man.'

'And you know very well what it will take for me to do that.'

Nediah did not reply. He stared deeply into the eyes that Kyndra could hardly bear to meet. A long moment passed before he straightened and stepped away. 'Then I shall do it myself,' he said, his tone so quiet that Kyndra strained to hear him.

Shock flitted across Brégenne's face. The anger faded. She stared at Nediah and her expression softened. 'You know you can't, Nediah. It's cold and dark. Where is your sun?'

Kyndra's heart thundered, a counterpoint to the storm above.

Nediah stood looking into the night. His gaze passed over the wreckage and the townspeople gathered around the man on the blankets. His shoulders slumped and his face fell into shadow. 'Of course. I'm sorry.'

Brégenne nodded and, smiling, laid her hand on her companion's arm. Nediah turned away from her and looked directly at Kyndra.

Kyndra didn't know who was more surprised. She saw Nediah's eyes widen, his mouth opening . . .

She dived into the crowd. She'd heard something she shouldn't have, of that she was certain. She didn't care to guess whether the strangers were angry. Who were they, knowing what they did about Acre and the Breaking, about a detail as insignificant as the colour of long-perished grapes? Kyndra wasn't sure she wanted to find out.

She emerged on the far side of the crowd, close to Fedrin. Ashley Gigg hunched over the man, running her hands across his body, lifting a drooping eyelid, listening to his breathing. She straightened from this last act and turned to face the crowd, holding up a hand for quiet. Beneath the thudding of the rain, Kyndra heard the air gurgling in and out of Fedrin's lungs, wet as the water that threatened to drown them all.

'This man has seen his last sunrise.'

There were shouts of protest. Ashley wiped her hands on a rag and simply waited until the noise subsided.

'He has bruises no salve will mend. His lungs are crushed, perhaps further organs are ruptured, I cannot say. The damage is too serious to rectify.'

Tessa let out a wail and collapsed beside Fedrin. Her knees landed in a puddle inches deep, but she ignored the water welling into her lap. 'Fedrin, oh no, oh please.' The last two words were meant for Ashley, who shook her head, her expression not without pity. Tessa's face crumpled and she laid her arms across her husband, burying her face in his chest. Sobs shook her body.

Some of the women hurried over, but seemed unsure how to console her. One laid a hand on her shoulder. Tessa shrugged it off.

Kyndra became aware of the muttering that filled the night. She heard the word *Relic* hissed more than once and tried to make herself smaller. The muttering grew. Individual voices piped up amid the general unrest. 'It's our punishment,' one man said. 'The Inheritance is gone. We have broken the Relic entrusted to us.'

'Aye, it's the bad luck. We'll lose an honest man tonight,' a woman agreed. Kyndra recognized her. She was in her sixties and often came to her mother for the spirits she favoured. Reena disapproved of her addiction, but not of the coin she received in exchange.

More voices joined the dissent. 'It can't be a coincidence,' added a voice Kyndra knew well. It was Colta. Some people turned to look at her. Kyndra's friend stood tall, a cloak pulled tight across her shoulders, drenched hair framing her face. 'The day the Relic breaks, a man dies.'

Why was she doing this? What had Jhren said to her? Kyndra felt the first stirrings of panic. Surely Colta wouldn't tell everyone, wouldn't betray her. They'd been friends for years. Distantly she heard the town's elders trying to restore order, but their commands for silence drowned in the tide of discontent that swept through the Dales folk. Where had this anger come from?

Kyndra blinked rain out of her eyes, no longer on the edge of the crowd. They closed up around her and carried her forward as a shocked cry from Tessa rang through the night. Kyndra saw at once what had caused the commotion. Fedrin was sitting up, supported by Benj.

Before Tessa could fling her arms back around her husband, Ashley Gigg seized them. Tessa tried to shake the woman off, but Ashley held on, her knobbly knuckles white on the woman's sleeves. 'Wait,' she hissed.

Unlike the elders' shouts, Fedrin's movement effectively silenced the crowd. They pressed in closer, forcing Kyndra with them. There was something strange about the man's eyes. They were unfocused, as if staring at the space between raindrops.

Words bubbled out of his throat. 'Breaking,' he said, unmistakably clear. Nobody spoke, though eyes began to fill with unease.

Fedrin's gaze shifted and he stared directly at Kyndra. 'You will destroy us all.'

He died then, eyes still fixed on Kyndra. Slowly, as if in a dream, the townspeople turned to follow Fedrin's final gaze. A circle cleared rapidly around Kyndra. She watched it happen, her mind as frozen as the dead man's face. She saw accusation in their stares, even fear.

'That's her.' Colta pushed her way through the crowd. 'She was the one who broke our Relic.'

'No!' And Jarand was there, struggling to reach her too. Unlike Colta, he met a wall of arms. 'No!' he shouted again. 'This is madness. It wasn't her fault!'

'She broke it,' Colta said, and there was a coldness in her tone Kyndra had never heard before. She didn't understand. What could make Colta hate her so much?

Colta came right up to her. 'I will never know my true name because of you,' she said, but loudly enough that everyone could hear. 'Because of you, my calling is hidden from me.' She leaned in closer, so that her next words fell on Kyndra's ears alone. 'Jhren was ready to give you everything.' Her face contorted, as tears and rain gathered in her eyes. '*Everything*. You don't deserve him. You never did.' A sob broke from her and she turned, elbowing her way back through the crowd.

'Colta!' Kyndra shouted, but the dark-haired girl didn't look back.

Kyndra swayed, dizzied from the scene. There were torches in the crowd where only lanterns had been before. The noise was rising. 'Do you deny it?' someone shouted.

'No, I—'

46

A roar rumbled through the people, gaining strength as it swept towards her. 'I didn't mean to!' she cried. 'I promise I didn't mean it!' No one seemed to hear. Jarand screamed her name, but the crowd drowned out his voice.

'A life for a life!' It was taken up, chanted, and there was no escape. Kyndra couldn't focus. Faces she knew, faces which had smiled at her, were contorted with hatred. It could be a nightmare, except for her own panicked heartbeat in her ears. She looked for a way out, but the wall of people stopped her as effectively as it stopped Jarand. They were loath to touch her, though. Their hands pushed at her when she tried to run, but only to keep her penned. The townspeople held her at arm's length, as if she were a foul thing.

'She should have been taken instead of Fedrin!' Tessa's wild shriek cut through the tide. 'A life for a life. She destroyed the Relic, destroyed our children's futures – she's hidden their true names from them forever!'

'And do you not believe that is the way it should be?'

Brégenne's voice boomed in the night like an echo of the thunder. She stood beside Kyndra, hooded, arms spread wide. The crowd blinked at her, stunned into silence.

'Who are you?' someone demanded finally. Brégenne turned towards the voice, her white eyes frosty.

'That is none of your concern. Why are you so ready to persecute this girl?'

'She destroyed it!' a man yelled, sharpening the edge of hysteria in the crowd. 'She brought this doom upon us all. You heard Fedrin. She took away our heritage.'

'You foolish man. The rain is a warning you have all ignored. The Breaking is here.'

Brégenne's words drew gasps from the night. Amidst denials and cries of fear, one of the elders shouted, 'Then it is Reena's bastard's doing! Must we all suffer for her crime?'

The insult slammed Kyndra back into her body. At her sides, her hands curled into fists.

'The Breaking has nothing to do with that,' Brégenne shouted over the roar caused by the elder's words. Her icy gaze roamed over everyone gathered. 'It cannot be stopped or controlled. If you don't get out of this town, many will perish. Forget this thing you call the Relic. It was recovered from a world you cannot hope to understand.'

'It was a gift,' the elder said stoically. Kyndra looked at him. The man's beard dripped over his chin and his elder's robes were stained with mud. Still, fervour gleamed in his eyes.

'It was an abdication of responsibility,' the blind woman snapped, 'and is better off destroyed.'

Fury steamed from the crowd. Nediah now stood at Brégenne's side, exasperation tightening the skin beneath his eyes. The closest townspeople made to charge Brégenne, but the woman raised her arms, threw back her head and screamed.

Kyndra clapped her hands over her ears. People dropped their torches to do the same and the light in the crowd dimmed by half. The scream went on forever, its notes tearing the air above the town. Kyndra thought of a midnight lake and a wilderness beneath an unforgiving sky. Through her palms, she heard other sounds: the cries of black beasts, the paws of a wolf, the triumphant shriek of a hunting owl. Each creature was part of night's song and behind Kyndra's closed eyelids, the moon shone.

When she opened them, the moon shone still. It pooled on Brégenne, silent now, in a silver shaft that reached to the parted clouds. The woman was brilliant, a shining pillar of frost. Her skin glowed, as if light welled from beneath it. Her eyes struck Kyndra, blazing white. With a wrench she felt to her bones, Kyndra pulled her gaze away.

The crowd stumbled. 'Witch!' someone cried, part-way between accusation and dread. They retreated to a safer distance, leaving Kyndra alone with Brégenne. Nediah stared at his companion. Pride and something that might have been sadness kindled his eyes.

'They will think you in league with us now,' Brégenne said to Kyndra and indeed the people pointed as they backed away, hurling accusations of crimes she had never committed.

'You saved my life,' Kyndra said. Her voice shook badly. Her own people had turned against her. Her own people wanted to kill her. It was senseless.

The shaft connecting Brégenne to the sky faded. Her skin still glowed, but the wonder she had been was lost. 'And for that I am sorry,' she said.

'I don't understand.'

Nediah put a hand on Kyndra's shoulder. 'Now that the Breaking has begun, there is no hope for this town.'

4

'You're wrong!' Kyndra shouted at Nediah. The sympathy in the stranger's eyes only made her angry. She wouldn't believe it. She turned her back on them both and had only taken a step when a blinding flash made her stumble and cry out. Fire cracked across the sky and the lightning stabbed the roof of a house. Its thatch burst into flame. Straw fell smouldering to the wet street and part of the roof collapsed with a roar. The mob finally broke and ran, and the night filled with screams.

A man dodged the flaming debris and wrenched open the door of the house. After a few moments, he returned with two children. The little girl at his side dashed to one of the waiting women and threw her arms about her waist. The boy in the man's arms didn't move. Small legs hung limply from his body and one of his feet was bare. The man cradled his son to his chest and howled at the black sky.

'We must leave. I'll call the horses.'

Kyndra couldn't take her eyes off the grieving man. The child's body flopped grotesquely; each flash lit up the pale, smudged skin of his arms and legs.

'Good. I thought we had more time, but it's the same here

as it was in the Karka Basin. The Breaking is growing stronger and gives fewer warnings.'

The strangers' words abruptly broke through Kyndra's shock. 'You're just going to leave us?' she demanded, rounding on them. 'Surely you can do something!'

Brégenne regarded her coolly. 'Your town is beyond help.'

'How can you say that? What have we done wrong?'

The three of them stood in an island of relative calm. People ran haphazardly, crying to one another, scooping children up from the crowd. Lightning struck houses at random; more roofs caught alight. Hail bounced off the cobbles, doing nothing to douse the fires. How could waterlogged wood burn so fiercely? Kyndra thought, feeling the heat of the flames against her face. It wasn't natural.

'Not all will perish,' Brégenne told her. 'It's not the Breaking's way.'

Kyndra stared at her, wide-eyed. Then she gave a strangled cry and darted past the strangers, dashing back towards the burning houses and the inn beyond, smoke thickening around her.

Her body slammed into something. Dazed, Kyndra looked for the obstruction, but there wasn't one. She put her hands up in front of her, feeling the invisible barrier. 'Let me go!' she screamed and pushed forward, kicking and punching. The force captured her limbs and held them, one leg outstretched, arms frozen mid-swing.

'No,' Brégenne said. 'I won't let you throw your life away.'

'It's my home!' Kyndra yelled. She pushed against the force that held her and felt it give a fraction of an inch. Brégenne grunted, as if in surprise, and Kyndra turned to look at her. The woman's face was pale and her mouth slightly open. After a snatched glance at Nediah, she waved a hand and the force released Kyndra.

'You *must* come with us,' she said.

Kyndra sucked smoke into her lungs and coughed fiercely. It was getting hard to see. Brégenne moved closer to her and extended a hand. 'Come with us,' she said again. 'We can help you, Kyndra.'

Kyndra stared at that slim, outstretched hand. 'Never,' she said and threw herself down the street. She expected to feel the force encircle her again, but it didn't. She ran into the night, leaving the strangers in the storm.

'Mother!' she called. 'Jarand!' Her voice joined the chorus of those searching for their families and friends, cries that mingled to become one panicked refrain. Smoke from the burning buildings rolled over the rooftops and Kyndra wiped a sleeve across her watering eyes.

In the hellish light, she ran headlong into Reena. Her mother cried out and threw her arms around her. 'I found you!' she choked. Her face was smoke-stained, hair wild and wet on her shoulders.

'Have you seen Jarand?' Kyndra shouted over the roar of wind and fire.

Reena shook her head. 'I saw Tessa,' she said, and her voice was dazed. 'She went back into the house, after Fedrin died . . . and she stayed there. It was burning. I couldn't get her to come out.' Tears ran down her mother's face and Kyndra hugged her again. She tried not to think about Tessa's fate.

'Why has this happened?' Reena asked the thick air. 'What did we do to deserve it?'

'We need to find Jarand.'

'I haven't seen him since he tried to reach you. How could

they . . .?' Her words died, but Kyndra knew what she meant to say. How could the people of Brenwym turn on her? How could Colta betray her after all the years they had been friends?

Kyndra pulled her mother in the direction of the inn, slipping on the wet cobbles and dodging debris torn from houses to either side. They turned down lanes where the water came up to their shins. Reena ploughed on beside her, white lips pressed together. Fear was in her eyes and Kyndra hoped Jarand had had the sense to go back to The Nomos to wait for them.

When they reached the inn, its roof was ablaze. Reena shrieked and Kyndra held on to her firmly. The garret where they lived would be an inferno. All their clothes, their possessions . . .

'My book!' Kyndra gasped. She must've left it lying on the table in the corner. It wouldn't be long until the fire found it. 'I have to get it,' she told Reena. 'You stay here – don't move!' and before her mother could stop her, Kyndra flung herself through the inn's door.

The common room looked almost normal, except for thick curls of smoke that hung in the air. Kyndra darted between tables, kicking abandoned tankards out of her path. The flask of wine still sat on the strangers' table along with one empty goblet. The book was gone.

'They took it when you left.'

Kyndra whirled. The common room was empty.

'I had my eye on them soon as they came through the door.' The voice was harsh, choked, but Kyndra recognized it. 'I'm sorry,' Jarand said. He lay slumped against the back wall. In one hand he held his customary bar rag, stained a shocking red. The other clutched a shaft of wood buried in his chest.

'Oh no, Jarand . . .' Blood stained Jarand's shirt and the hand curled almost protectively around the shaft was slick with it. Kyndra had never seen that much blood. Her mouth opened, but she couldn't push any words past the lump in her throat.

'I'm glad you're safe.' Jarand's eyes were different, as if some spark were leaving them. 'I tried to reach you.'

'Mother's outside,' Kyndra managed to say. 'She's fine. She's looking for you. I'll—'

'I don't want her – to see me like this. It'll be over soon.'

'No.' Kyndra's eyes felt dry and scratchy. 'Don't say that. You'll be fine.'

The ceiling creaked a warning and they both looked up. 'It isn't safe for you here,' Jarand said. 'I came back . . . when I lost you in the crowd. But . . .' His eyes dropped to the awful wound in his chest.

Kyndra shook her head. 'I'm not leaving you.'

I'm only asking you to help the man. Kyndra drew in a startled breath. That's what Nediah had said when Fedrin was dying. Perhaps Brégenne could – 'That woman,' she said. 'What if she could help you?'

'*No*,' Jarand said harshly. 'She'll have a price, Kyndra.' He coughed and cried out. Fresh blood flowed around the wood. A trickle oozed from the corner of his mouth.

'I'll pay it, then,' Kyndra cried and dashed to the door. There wasn't time to consider. There was barely enough time to find the strangers.

'I was coming in for you!' Reena gasped when Kyndra burst outside. She darted frantic glances at the roof. 'It'll come down any minute.'

'Jarand's in there,' Kyndra said shortly. Where could she

find the strangers? Somehow she knew they were still in town. *They won't leave without me.*

'What?'

'He's dying,' Kyndra said and blinked at the unbelievable word as it left her mouth. 'I'm going for help. Don't go in there, it's too dangerous.'

'No!' Reena cried, her eyes wild. She ran to the inn. The smoke rolling out of it had grown thicker.

'Mother!'

Reena ignored her and dashed inside. Kyndra spun to stare at the dark. Where were the strangers? What if they *had* left? No, they wouldn't go without her. She'd overheard them talking about that place . . . Naris. It was obviously a secret. The strangers would want to make sure she didn't tell anyone. Perhaps Brégenne had let her escape deliberately. Perhaps she knew Kyndra would come back begging for her help.

As if called by that very thought, the blind woman walked out of the smoke. Despite her small stature, she looked oddly impressive silhouetted against the fiery night. Nediah stood at her shoulder.

Kyndra stared at her. She tried to swallow the fear and the anger that bubbled just beneath it. 'Jarand is hurt. Will you help him?'

'You shall come with us,' Brégenne said, white eyes shining starkly amid the shadows of her face.

A life for a life, Kyndra thought. For a moment she was so afraid, she couldn't speak. Then she pictured Jarand, as the blood drained out of him. She imagined her mother, heard her ravaged cries as clearly as if Jarand were already dead.

'Yes,' she whispered and led the way into the inn.

Brégenne coughed in the smoke clouding the common

room. Barely five minutes had passed since Kyndra first found Jarand, but the heat had spiralled unbearably. Reena crouched on the floor, holding her husband. Tears glinted on her cheeks, but her face was set. She looked at Brégenne with a mixture of hope and distrust. Jarand's eyes were closed, every breath he drew laboured.

'Step away from him,' Brégenne said and Kyndra's mother reluctantly let Jarand rest against the wall.

Brégenne's skin became moonlight. It shone through every pore, as if there were a hundred moons inside her. Silver ran like veins down her forearms and concentrated in her fingertips. She glanced once at Nediah and something seemed to pass between them. Then Brégenne nodded and placed her glowing hands on the injured man's chest. Jarand opened his eyes. The look he gave Kyndra was full of sadness. Then he screamed.

Before Kyndra could leap forward, Nediah grabbed her arms. A gush of blood pushed the wood up out of Jarand's chest. A pearlescent sheen hovered over his exposed skin. It spread to the ragged hole the shaft had left and welled into it like quicksilver, cauterizing the edges as it went and knitting the torn flesh. Jarand's scream of agony cut off and he shuddered and groaned. Awe mingled with fear on Reena's face. She gripped the apron she still wore with white fingers.

Brégenne removed her hands and stepped back. Although weariness darkened the skin around her eyes, she seemed taller. A faint aura outlined her body and Kyndra caught an echo of the night song she'd heard earlier.

Jarand sat up and placed a wondering hand on his chest. The gaping wound had become an ugly red scar.

'My healing skill is rudimentary compared to Nediah's,' Brégenne said. 'If you strain yourself, the wound will reopen. You've lost a lot of blood.'

'Jarand!' Reena gasped. She tried to embrace him, but Jarand held her back.

'We have to get out of here,' he said roughly. His face was bleak.

A crash shook the inn. Cracks spread through the ceiling above their heads. Kyndra and her mother each seized one of Jarand's arms and helped him to the door. The strangers had already moved outside.

The five of them stood and watched the flames race over the building. Kyndra felt oddly detached. The roof of her child-hood home caved in, its sturdy beams eaten by fire. Her possessions were burning, everything she had ever owned. Per-haps her trove would survive, concealed beneath the window seat. She hadn't even thought of rescuing it.

She wanted to cry for what she had lost: her Inheritance, her friend, her home. She'd almost lost Jarand. But, as always, the tears would not come. She'd never cried once in her life, not even as a child.

Kyndra turned at a light touch on her shoulder. Nediah stood there. He whistled and the strangers' horses trotted obediently into view, tranquil despite the fires that raged all around them. Brégenne caught the reins of hers and swung smoothly into the saddle. Kyndra turned to her family. Uncer-tain, she opened her mouth.

'You're going with them,' Jarand said in the same bleak voice. Rain ran down his cheeks and soaked into his short, dark beard.

'What?' One of Reena's arms lifted, as if to take hold of Kyndra, but then she crossed them over her chest in a pose

Kyndra had long grown to recognize. 'What's this?' she demanded. 'What do you mean?'

'I made a promise,' Kyndra said, trying to smother her fear. 'She saved Jarand's life.'

'Nonsense!' Reena said, a dangerous light coming into her eyes. 'You are not leaving. You owe these people nothing!' Her voice wavered on the verge of hysteria and Jarand put a weary hand on her arm. Reena must have sensed something in the touch for she gaped at her husband. 'You're not agreeing with this?' she asked him, eyes blurring with tears. 'We don't even know these people. We can't trust them!'

'Rest assured your daughter will be safe with us,' Nediah said. Kyndra looked at him, wondering whether the words were a lie.

'What could you possibly want with her?' Reena asked. 'This is her home. I'm her mother. She belongs here.'

Brégenne tilted her head to one side, as if to regard Reena. The white gaze was penetrating and Kyndra's mother shifted uncomfortably beneath it. She didn't look away, though, which somehow seemed to matter very much to Kyndra.

Brégenne had to raise her voice over the roar of the storm. 'Do you truly believe that?'

Perhaps it was only the lightning that brightened the next moment, but Kyndra thought her mother's face drained of colour. Reena's anger faded and she seemed suddenly uncertain.

'Time is short,' Brégenne continued. 'I would advise you both to get out of this town.' She turned her head towards Jarand. 'Will you waste your second chance at life?'

'But where are you taking her?' Reena cried. 'I don't understand. When can she come back?'

Brégenne's face was impassive. 'When she is ready,' she said cryptically.

'No!' Reena screamed, her grey-blue eyes widening, as if she had seen something in the blind woman's face. 'You can't take her, you can't!'

'Mother.' Kyndra caught up her hands. 'If these people want me to go with them, I don't have any choice. They saved Jarand. How can we ever repay that?' She tried to swallow the tremor in her voice.

'It's foolishness,' Reena sobbed. She looked up at Brégenne. 'Ask for something else, witch, anything. Money – we can pay you.'

'I think not,' Brégenne said coldly. It was evident that she didn't appreciate being referred to as a witch. She inclined her head towards the burning inn. 'It seems to me that you have nothing left to offer.'

In that moment, Kyndra hated her.

Reena's hands clenched. 'I will come back,' Kyndra promised.

'It's not safe for your daughter here,' Nediah said and all four turned to look at him. 'Tomorrow, people will remember what happened. They'll look for someone to blame.'

'They wouldn't blame Kyndra,' Reena said weakly, but Jarand's face hardened. Kyndra relinquished her mother's hands and Jarand turned her around to face him.

'I saw them, Reena,' he said. 'They were seconds away from attacking her. First the Relic and then the Breaking. It's easy to link disasters together and people need someone to blame.'

Reena shook her head, but the fight had gone out of her. She addressed her next words to Nediah. 'You will keep her safe?'

Nediah's rain-washed face was sober. 'I swear to do so, as does my companion.'

'I will only take your word, sir.'

Nediah bowed his head.

'I'll come back,' Kyndra said again. She couldn't bear the look on her mother's face.

Reena clasped her fiercely, and as her wet hair pressed against Kyndra's cheek, Kyndra felt a terrible surge of sorrow. When Reena finally let go, Jarand took Kyndra's hands in his and then hugged her tight.

Kyndra stepped away from her family and let Nediah help her up onto his horse. She sat behind him and gazed down from the animal's greater height. Reena and Jarand looked fragile against the backdrop of fire and smoke. 'Please get to safety,' Kyndra told them.

She didn't mean for those to be her last words, but Brégenne's mare leapt away and Nediah's mount followed. Kyndra flung her arms about Nediah's waist. She had one glimpse of Reena and Jarand before rain blocked them from her sight.

Nediah's horse raced through the night, much faster than Kyndra thought it safe to go. It seemed to be following Brégenne's mare, but woman and horse were rarely in sight. Kyndra tried to work out which road they had taken, but once they had left Brenwym's sulphurous light behind, there was nothing to illuminate their way. They raced through the darkness and the horses ran as if the fire itself licked at their heels.

Maybe it was the motion of the horse, or the terror of the last few hours, but Kyndra felt herself drifting. Shapes reared out of the night, born of weariness and imagination. She was flying, walking in the sky between the stars. There was a black road and she took it, following as it wound through wind and fire and thick red earth. Light welled up before her. It was the fortress again, its glass-spun minarets catching the sun's beams and feeding them into the structure beneath. The night was behind her now.

Kyndra opened her eyes to a muddy morning, as the horses began to slow. Brégenne was only a few paces ahead, her mare making for a small rise in the land, where she halted. The terrain here was flatter than Kyndra had ever seen it. Her home in the Valleys was steep and hilly, and Brenwym's fields stretched to the Feenfold Mountains. They marked the edge of the world as she knew it. Those who ventured there returned with stories of endless peaks, capped with snow all year round.

For the first time in her life, Kyndra gazed at the landscape and didn't see mountains. She was on a vast plain, a grassland sea that rolled away from their little knoll towards a horizon indistinguishable from the sky. How much ground had the horses covered last night? Nediah's mount huffed as it came to a standstill and he hopped down energetically. He offered his hand to Brégenne and the woman dismounted. Kyndra tried for the same elegance, but her numb legs got tangled in the stirrups and she fell.

'Where are we?' she asked, brushing dry stems from her trousers. The horses looked very pleased to find themselves surrounded by grass. Nediah removed their saddles and left them to graze.

'The Wilds,' Brégenne said. She folded a blanket on the ground and sat down. It struck Kyndra how ordinary she looked, a blind woman dressed in traveller's browns. She found it hard to equate her with the shining being she had been last night.

Brégenne's words abruptly hit home. 'The Wilds?' Kyndra gasped. 'But that's leagues from Brenwym!'

'Twelve, to be precise,' Nediah said. He emerged from behind the horses with two saddlebags over his shoulder.

Kyndra looked sidelong at the horses. Both placidly cropped the grass that grew on the rise. They seemed fine and not unduly tired. Wondering at them, she rubbed her lower back. The long ride had left her muscles aching. She'd barely slept in twenty-four hours and the pounding in her head was getting worse.

Nediah's smile offended her. Had the man forgotten the horror from which they'd run? Daylight had brought out the gold in his green eyes and he whistled happily as he unbuckled the bags. Brégenne listened with a long-suffering expression.

Kyndra thought of her home. What did it look like this morning? Perhaps the fires had subsided and the rain hissed on ruined houses that smoked under this same pallid sky. How many lives had the Breaking claimed? Where would Reena and Jarand go to find shelter?

'Are you hungry?' The voice was Brégenne's. Kyndra looked over at her, surprised to hear kindness. So far, she'd seemed as distant as the moon itself.

'Yes,' she admitted.

'We'll rest the horses here a while.' Nediah produced a loaf of bread and a flat, folded packet. His whistle changed to a hum.

'Will you stop that,' Brégenne said testily.

Nediah's song halted, but as he broke the loaf into three pieces and unfolded the packet, Kyndra heard the tune well up once more. Brégenne turned her face away.

The greased paper concealed several strips of pork. Kyndra's stomach rumbled. Earlier she'd sworn privately not to eat any food offered her, but she had none of her own. And anyway, she couldn't attempt escape on an empty stomach. She had no intention of going along with whatever the strangers planned for her. Kyndra felt a flicker of dread. What *did* they have in mind? Where were they taking her?

Nediah smiled at the pork. Then he separated the strips and laid them side by side on the paper.

'Nediah,' Brégenne said with a note of warning in her voice. 'I know what you're doing. Nothing hot.'

Nediah raised an eyebrow, but instead of rewrapping the pork, he glanced at the sky. For a moment it seemed the sun brightened behind its coverlet of clouds. Light glowed at Nediah's fingertips and Kyndra heard the crackle of fire. She yelled and jerked back as golden flames burst to life around the pork. Nediah quirked a finger at the meat, which lifted and started to turn in the flames. Instead of burning, the pork sizzled. Nediah watched his floating meal with a look of intense satisfaction.

'It is fortunate that the safety of Naris does not rest solely on your shoulders,' Brégenne snapped. 'You betray our secrets for the most trivial of wants.'

'She's seen enough to know she cannot go back,' Nediah replied mildly, and Kyndra felt a chill. 'I think your display in front of a whole town poses more of a risk.'

A flicker of unease tightened Brégenne's face. 'The town was under the Breaking,' she said. 'And you know I had my reasons.'

'I do.' Nediah nodded. 'But you didn't have to heal the innkeeper.' He didn't look at Kyndra.

Brégenne pursed her lips and said nothing. Nediah calmly prodded the pork. A small smile returned to his face.

When it was done, Kyndra studied her meat in a way that would have made Reena cross.

'It's not poisoned,' Nediah said, sounding exasperated. 'If I wanted to harm you, I'd have done it under cover of the Breaking.' He wrapped some bread around his pork and took a bite. After a few more moments of scrutiny, Kyndra did the same. The meat was salty on her tongue and tasted of the smokehouse. Nediah watched her, amusement in the glint of his eyes.

It was good to eat hot food. She devoured her makeshift sandwich and then looked on as Nediah peeled strips of fat off his pork. The man handed them to Brégenne, who accepted his offerings in silence.

'Never liked it,' he explained when he finished his greasy work. Brégenne laid the fat on her bread and ate it. Nediah winced.

Kyndra knew it was only weariness that blanketed her fear and shock. So many unbelievable things had happened in the last day that a part of her was convinced she must have dreamed them. She gazed at the strangers. Neither seemed the same as the previous night. A few hours ago, Nediah had turned to Brégenne for guidance, but he seemed surer of himself this morning. That didn't stop Kyndra from thinking Brégenne was in charge – she looked at least ten years older than her companion, despite the strange, smooth quality that graced both their faces.

Nediah wiped his hands on the dewy grass and Kyndra found herself staring. The man's fingertips no longer glowed. They looked normal, except for an odd golden sheen to his nails.

'Where are you taking me?' she asked abruptly, failing to keep a tremor from her voice.

Brégenne pulled her cloak tighter so that her body was all but hidden in its dark folds. 'Once you have heard the name of Naris, you cannot unhear it,' she said.

5

The day passed by in a greyish procession. Mist swathed the land like a vaporous lake and no matter which way Kyndra looked, the view was the same.

Now that they travelled at a more sedate pace, she wasn't entirely sure what to do with her hands. She settled for gripping the saddle's wide rim, but her fingers cramped in the cold. Whenever the horse stumbled on a rough patch of ground, she found herself clutching at Nediah's waist. Cheeks red, she quickly let go and mumbled when the man asked if she was all right.

Reena and Jarand were never far from her thoughts and Kyndra hoped desperately that they were safe. She hoped, too, that Jhren and his family had managed to escape the town. Guilt was beginning to hound her over the way she'd treated her oldest friend. *Jhren was ready to give you everything*, Colta had said. Kyndra remembered the tears in the other girl's eyes, the hurt in her voice, and felt even worse.

She dug her nails into her palms. Why was everything so messed up? Yesterday morning she'd woken thinking only of the Ceremony, worrying what it would show her. That fear now seemed small and insignificant against the backdrop of last night. Kyndra gazed at the changeless plain and wondered what she was doing here. Every so often, she saw her friends' faces in the waving grass and blinked them quickly away.

Nediah drooped as evening fell, his energy seeming to set with the sun. Brégenne looked happier. She stroked her horse's neck and Kyndra heard her whisper thanks. The horse snorted, nostrils huffing. Kyndra watched the animal's breath dissipate and shivered in the chill air.

When night climbed out of the folds in the land, Nediah reined in. The day's clouds veiled the stars and only a lighter patch of sky hinted that the moon had risen. Brégenne tipped her head back, her white eyes faintly glowing. Nediah dismounted with none of his earlier grace. He didn't speak as he lit a small lantern, spread a tarpaulin over the ground and handed out blankets from the saddlebag. Kyndra accepted hers in matching silence. She had barely spoken all day.

'It will be good to get off these plains,' Brégenne said, her voice abrupt in the night.

Nediah made a sound of agreement. He sorted through the bag on Brégenne's horse, pulling out another loaf, a few bits of dried meat and a wheel of cheese. Kyndra was ready for something hot. She ached from the unfamiliar motion of the horse and her mist-damp clothes stuck clammily to her skin.

Nediah laid the rations on a blue cloth he produced from his pocket and sat back on his heels. Kyndra watched him expectantly, but the man didn't move to heat the food. Brégenne seated herself opposite and started to tear off chunks of bread. 'Is there nothing hot?' Kyndra asked.

Nediah snorted. 'Ask Brégenne. I doubt she will oblige you.'

'This is adequate,' Brégenne said, gesturing with a slice of cheese.

Kyndra continued to stare at Nediah. 'But earlier you—'

'Don't rile him.' Brégenne picked her cheese apart. 'He's scarcely manageable as it is.'

'I'm not,' Kyndra protested. 'I just wondered why—'

'I can't,' Nediah said shortly. He reached out and took one of the pieces of bread Brégenne had torn off. 'Only in daylight.' His voice was very quiet.

Something clicked into place. Kyndra had only ever seen Brégenne use her power at night; Nediah was the opposite. She thought of the stories and her eyes widened. 'You're Wielders,' she gasped without thinking. 'Sorcerers from the old world.'

The strangers regarded her in silence. Brégenne's face was stony.

'We are not from the old world,' Nediah said finally. 'We are from *this* world.' The lantern light cast him half in shadow.

'But the Wielders were killed five hundred years ago, at the end of the war.' Kyndra felt the pulse quicken in her throat. 'How is it possible?'

'This is not to be repeated,' Brégenne said. Her voice was low and hard. 'You will tell no one who or what we are. Breathe a word and you will regret it. Do you understand?'

Numbly, Kyndra nodded. Brégenne studied her, dinner forgotten in her lap. 'Not all the Wielders perished in the Deliverance,' she said. 'A handful survived, but they were young, little more than children, and without leaders. So they hid from the world, deep in the tunnels below the ruins of Solinaris. For better or worse, we became a secret people. And now it has to stay that way.' She nodded at Kyndra. 'You saw how the folk of your town reacted last night. The world has forgotten that the Wielders gave their lives to halt the war.'

Kyndra privately thought that Brenwym's reaction was only to be expected, but she kept her mouth shut.

'It's the same with the Breaking,' Brégenne continued. 'It was once accepted as the price of freedom, a necessary consequence of the power used to save Mariar from its enemies. Now it's the subject of children's rhymes, dismissed and disbelieved.'

Kyndra shifted uncomfortably. 'We don't disbelieve it. It's just that the Breaking is something that happens in other places.'

The strangers regarded her silently and Kyndra wished she could take the words back. In the face of her situation, they were absurd.

'Attitudes like that cause unnecessary deaths,' Brégenne said finally. 'Especially since the Breaking is growing worse. What used to behave like a simple, albeit dangerous storm is now a force capable of wiping out whole settlements.'

Kyndra looked into the night, seeing again the killing fire that had broken open the sky. She remembered the screams and cries of pain on what usually would have been a day of celebration. 'Why?' she asked.

'We don't know,' Nediah said. 'We've just come from the Karka Basin, some leagues to the south-west. The Breaking struck there only a month ago.' His eyes were sober. 'Few live in the Basin. The ground is swampy and difficult to build on, so the Breaking did little harm.'

The unspoken comparison with Brenwym left Kyndra cold, as did the sympathy in Nediah's voice. She doubted the strangers really cared about her town, or how many of her neighbours and their children lay dead.

'Nediah and I were tracking the Breaking when we arrived in Brenwym,' Brégenne said. The expression she turned on Kyndra was calculating. 'I never imagined I would have to intervene to save your life.'

'It wouldn't have come to that,' Kyndra said swiftly. She thought back to last night, remembering Fedrin's last words, Colta's accusations. The crowd had taken her up, closing ranks, but surely they would not have—

'They would have killed you.'

'No,' Kyndra protested. 'I've lived there for seventeen years, all my life. They know me.'

Then it is Reena's bastard's doing. Must we all suffer for her crime?

The elder's words returned to her abruptly, and she felt a surge of anger. Yes, Brenwym knew her, just as they knew Kyndra had no father to claim her. Whose crime, she wondered suddenly, had the elder been referring to? Reena's for producing a child outside wedlock, or her own for breaking the Relic?

Reena's bastard's doing.

She remembered a time when, as a little girl, she had run to her mother, ears full of that poisonous word. It was uglier when it came from the unknowing mouths of children.

What does it matter, Kyn? Reena had said. *You are who you are, and you are my daughter.*

And years later, with a lump in her throat, Kyndra had asked, *Don't you regret it? You know what they say about you. Don't you regret ever having me?*

Reena had studied her a long time before answering. *The man who was your father gave me two things – my courage and you. I have never regretted either.*

Surrounded by the empty grasslands, Kyndra again felt a lump in her throat and she swallowed. That was all her mother had ever said about her birth.

'We have seen it before, Kyndra,' Nediah told her quietly. He shifted position on the tarpaulin. 'We have seen what fear and superstition can do to a community.'

'The Far Valleys should never have been allowed to keep a relic of Acre,' Brégenne said. 'Even ones that seem innocuous should be treated with caution. I didn't like the influence it had over so many people.'

'But it broke,' Kyndra said, shivering at the memory. 'Why did it break after five hundred years?'

Brégenne gave her a speculative look that made Kyndra's skin prickle. 'Why indeed,' she said. The shadows cast by the lantern did not touch her silvery eyes.

Later Kyndra lay in a blanket, stomach hollow after the small meal, and considered Brégenne's words. The woman had refused to say anything else. If she was honest with herself, Kyndra wanted to know more about them, about how they used their power, but Brégenne had made it clear that the subject was none of her business. *And anyway*, Kyndra thought, *I need to figure out a way to escape.* She didn't believe for one moment that the strangers had taken her to save her life.

A bitter night wind scoured the plain. Kyndra huddled deeper in her blanket. Although she'd caught only a few hours' sleep that morning and felt the weariness in her bones, her mind wouldn't stop turning. She imagined warming her hands at The Nomos' hearth, and realized with a jolt that the inn had gone.

Dawn came slowly, sluggish on the heels of night. Half the sky was still dark when Kyndra raised her head a fraction. Someone was standing with their back to her, silent at the edge of a rise. The silhouette was tall and slim: Nediah. He faced

71

east, watching the sky pale. Kyndra stayed still while above her, pink spread into yellow and orange. Then the sun broke free from the horizon.

The man on the hill blazed gold. His bare forearms were molten, dipped in brilliance, and heat radiated from his body, rolling over Kyndra like the tropical wind that blew in the south. Instead of the night song, she heard a roar, as if a thousand voices spoke at once. The roar was dry, desert light and the abiding blue of the sky. It was green and golden, the rush of hooves through trees, the afternoon flight of a hawk. It was everything the sun touched. It was the vast growth of living things. And yet Kyndra sensed a balance between song and roar. They were aspects of life itself.

Kyndra caught a small movement – she was not the only one watching. Knees on the wet grass, Brégenne crouched in her blanket, an unfamiliar tenderness on her face. She stared at Nediah, her lips slightly open, the fading glow in her eyes made golden.

As if he sensed her gaze, Nediah turned and the brightness failed. 'It's morning,' he said unnecessarily.

Brégenne's expression dissolved. 'We had better be going,' she said. 'If we're to buy another horse, I'd like to reach the—'

'What's that?' Kyndra interrupted. She'd turned to look at the grey shadows that still clung to the west. Ground mist shifted, parted, reformed. Nediah narrowed his eyes, body tensed. No sound reached them.

Then a silver beast trotted out of the morning gloom. Instinctively, Kyndra took a step back. It had the look of a wolf, but its shoulders and haunches were grotesquely muscled. Despite this, it moved with surprising grace, eyes a luminous blaze of white gold. 'Brégenne,' Nediah said sharply, 'it's an envoi.'

The wolf-thing passed from shadow into sun and its form blurred. The body shrank, legs lengthened into wings. Soon a golden bird hovered before Kyndra's eyes, its brilliance blinding her.

Wordlessly, Nediah held up his arm. The bird flew to it and, as it perched on his wrist, its form melted again to run like molten metal over Nediah's skin. The man drew in a sharp breath, face tight with pain. 'They're not pleased,' he said grimly.

Brégenne didn't ask who *they* were. As Kyndra gazed in astonishment, the sheen over Nediah's hand and wrist sharpened into glimmering words. Nediah read them silently. He glanced once at Kyndra and then his gaze strayed to the west.

'What is it?' Kyndra asked. Now that the message had been read, the words faded until Nediah's hand was once again his own.

'An envoi,' Nediah said. 'A messenger.'

'Who from?'

'They *know*, Brégenne,' Nediah said, ignoring Kyndra's question. Kyndra looked at the small woman. Brégenne's face had paled ever so slightly. 'We're to return as soon as possible,' Nediah continued. 'And we're to take a ship.'

Kyndra frowned. Ship? They were hundreds of leagues from the nearest coast.

'So be it.'

'Return where?' she tried. 'What's wrong?'

Nediah spared her a glance. 'Brégenne broke a law when she rescued you in Brenwym, one of our strictest.' His voice dropped. 'How did they find out so quickly?'

'Who?'

'The envoi's senders,' Nediah said.

73

'You're not going to tell me, are you?'

'This message must have been crafted by more than one of them,' Nediah said to Brégenne. 'It's been travelling by day *and* night.'

Brégenne merely nodded. 'How much coin do we have?' she asked quietly.

'Enough.'

Breakfast was cold and rapid. Kyndra watched as Nediah led Brégenne to her horse, placing her hands on the saddle. Brégenne nodded her thanks, but climbed up without aid. Nediah hovered nearby in case she needed steadying, and only went to his own horse once she was settled. Kyndra watched her fumbling with the reins and frowned to herself. Last night, Brégenne had behaved as if she could see perfectly well. This morning, however, it was clear she could not.

'How does an envoi work?' she asked Nediah's back once they were underway.

'It's a construct,' the man answered, 'with a single purpose. The message is actually imprinted in the energy used to create the messenger and can only be read by its intended recipients.'

Kyndra blinked. '. . . Right. What did you mean when you said it's been travelling by day *and* night?'

'Envois are usually created from either Solar or Lunar energy, so they can only travel during the hours that energy is active. The one we received was made with both. It reached us much faster. And it had a lot of power behind it,' Nediah added uneasily.

'Did it hurt when it melted on you like that?'

'Well-constructed envois are capable of conveying simple emotion.' Nediah paused. 'I was meant to feel the anger in that one.'

Kyndra shivered.

The day brightened until a wide band of forget-me-not sky opened along the horizon. The sunshine lifted Kyndra's spirits, but when she glanced back the way they had come, she saw only a thick wall of grey cloud. Stuck on the back of Nediah's mount, she had little else to do except stare at the scenery and contemplate escape.

The longer she thought about it, the more problems she encountered. As far as money was concerned, she had only coppers to her name: a tip she'd been given at the inn on her last night in Brenwym. Even if she managed to evade the strangers, how would she get home? She doubted she could steal one of their horses undetected, which meant a whole lot of walking. And she'd never be able to afford enough food to see her back to Brenwym. Kyndra grimaced. She would have to lie low for a couple of weeks, pretend to go along with the strangers, and wait for an opportunity. Perhaps she could earn some coin once she managed to get away from them.

Less than happy with her plan, Kyndra lapsed into brooding, and it wasn't until the tail end of afternoon that something snapped her out of it. About half a league away, smoke curled lazily into the sky. She stared at it, gripped by a peculiar excitement.

'Sky Port East,' Nediah said.

The smoke puffed from a cluster of chimneys, and although distant, the town looked ramshackle. None of the buildings were whitewashed like those in Brenwym. Half the chimneys perched on the slant of their roof, seemingly ready to slip down the side as Kyndra watched. She sniffed the air. Whatever they were burning, it wasn't the wood so widely used in the Dales.

This smoke was heavy and black. It drifted slowly upwards until it was high enough to ride the breeze.

As they moved nearer, an amazing structure began to materialize above the houses. At first it looked like scaffolding, but, narrowing her eyes, Kyndra saw a web of circular platforms connected by rope bridges. It was an airborne archipelago that swayed in the wind. The great twisted ropes groaned against every gust until she thought they must snap under the strain. And here and there, thick poles rooted the larger platforms to the earth. It was a gypsy collection, each platform a different size and colour. The sky port rambled twenty feet above the rooftops, the wind blowing a tenor note through the gaps in its boards.

'Why is it called a port?' Kyndra asked of the creaking structure. 'There's no sea.'

Nediah pointed westward. The setting sun gleamed on a huge chain raised high in the air. Supported by posts at regular intervals, it stretched into the distance. Kyndra frowned. 'What's that?'

'It should be here soon.'

'What should?'

'You'll see.' Nediah turned his head to look at Kyndra, a smile on his lips. Then he steered their horse towards a small mound. The extra height afforded a better view of the chain, as it disappeared into the westward plains. Kyndra shielded her eyes against the setting sun and listened to the muttering of the grass as they waited.

There was a squeal of metal on metal. Out of the sun came a monstrous shadow, straining against the huge chain that tethered it to earth. Two paddles spun at its rear, cutting the sunset into orange segments, and a vast inflated sack bulged above it in the smoky wind. Kyndra gaped at the craft as it whirred into port. There were figures on its deck, one holding an anchor chain ready to throw.

'Can we go closer?' she asked Nediah.

The man said nothing, but urged his horse into a trot until they were beneath the dock. Kyndra craned her neck, watching as the craft lumbered to a halt. Two men vaulted its rail. They moored the craft to a huge iron ring set in the wooden platform and then the rear paddles slowed and stilled.

Passengers shouted jovially as they disembarked. Men caught the hands of others who waited on the dock. A motley troupe of girls and boys scampered aboard and disappeared down a ramp into the craft's belly. Each returned with a small crate. The boxes began to pile up on the dock and were stamped and briefly inspected by a man in a hat that was forever slipping down the side of his head.

It was almost a pattern, Kyndra thought, unable to tear her eyes from the spectacle. When the dock master's hat fell to the right, he pursed his lips and quickly put the lid back on the crate. When it fell to the left, the corners of his eyes crinkled and he lingered over the contents. The children continued their ferrying until every crate was unloaded. Then each held out their hand to receive a coin that gleamed in the last of the light. Having bitten it, they scampered away as swiftly as they'd come and the craft lay quiet, its crew dispersed into the aerial town. A few climbed down ladders and lost themselves amongst the buildings on the ground.

'This is amazing,' Kyndra said, unable to help herself. Her neck ached from looking up and she raised one hand to massage it. Brégenne's mare ambled into view, cropping at the long grass. There was no sign of the small woman. Kyndra frowned. 'Where's Brégenne?'

'She's securing our transport for tomorrow,' Nediah said. He glanced at the darkening sky and sighed. 'I suppose we'd better find something to eat.'

Although Kyndra's stomach contracted at the word *transport*, it was also aching with hunger. Brégenne's rations had been none too generous. She nodded.

Nediah dismounted, leaving Kyndra in the saddle, and gathered up the reins of Brégenne's horse. Then they started down the half-paved road into town.

Night fell quickly. Lamps bloomed in the sky port above, strung on poles that swayed in the wind. It was like magic, the balls of light seemingly unharnessed in space. The wind brought music too; the wicked lows of an organ flute thrummed to male voices and the occasional peak of a soprano. The day's clouds had dispersed, leaving the sky clear, and Kyndra tipped back her head to stare at the stars. They were so distant, so cold.

The music ended and a shiver ran over her body. The thin cloak Nediah had lent her did little to keep out the night.

Nediah stopped outside a tavern. Peeling letters named it The Shipper's Hole. Kyndra looked at the battered door with a certain professional disdain.

'Why don't you go in and find a table?' Nediah suggested. 'I'll stable the horses.' He gave Kyndra a searching look. 'We're strangers here and we want to remain strangers. Understand?'

Kyndra nodded and slipped off the animal. Her legs and rear ached abysmally. She rubbed them, staring at the tavern. Whereas The Nomos was welcoming, its shutters painted blue against whitewashed walls, this place was stolid and dark. Almost all the shutters were closed to the night, but chatter and warm light spilled through their chinks. 'Go on, then,'

Nediah said, and Kyndra had no choice but to open the door and step inside.

The latch clanked loudly and a few people raised their heads. When they saw Kyndra standing there alone, more heads turned and she tried to ignore the stares. The common room was large with an oversized fire blazing in one corner. The rough tables were about three-quarters full and a dozen people lined a long, chest-high counter. Servers in aprons stood on the other side, filling tankards from silver-tapped casks.

Kyndra hadn't seen anything like it; customers in The Nomos sat at tables and waited to be served. The people at the counter just stood there chatting, drinking and then waving their empty cups at the staff. These were refilled and coin changed hands.

More heads turned to look at her, most of them male. Kyndra hastily shut the door and made her way towards the counter. 'What can I get you?' asked a big man in a brown shirt. He wiped his hands on a grimy apron and stared unabashedly at her body. She suddenly felt very exposed standing there in her shirt without jerkin or jacket.

'Um . . .' she stammered. 'Do you have any Dales—?'

'No,' the man said. He thumped down a foaming mug with enough force to send froth over the sides. 'You'll like this better. Six coppers.'

'I've only got—' Kyndra began, but a brisk female voice overrode her.

'Here's ten coppers and give me a shot of your strongest. Keep the change.'

The man seized a tiny cup and measured out some clear liquid. The stranger tipped her head back and threw the contents down her throat. She slammed some coins on the counter top.

'You didn't have to do that,' Kyndra said, clutching her ale. The tankard was heavy and worn from countless lips. She sipped it. The taste was a little malty, but it made her think of home.

'You looked thirsty,' the woman said. She stepped away from the long counter, giving Kyndra a moment to study her features. She had a pointed chin, pale above a scruffy collar. The rest of her face was pale as well, except for two spots of colour high on her cheekbones. Almond eyes regarded Kyndra coolly. She wore a dark coat buttoned down to her knees, where leather boots met its fraying hem. Her hair was straight and brown and very long. 'So,' she said, 'shall we sit down?'

The woman led her to a table near the one unshuttered window. It was too dark to see out now and Kyndra watched her own face framed by the fire. It looked young and slightly scared. She took a deep breath and sat opposite the woman, trying to seem at home.

'Well now,' the woman said, with a small smile. 'You seemed a little lost up there.' She nodded at the counter. 'First time in Sky Port East?'

'No – yes, I mean . . .' The woman's eyes were teasing. 'I guess so,' Kyndra finished weakly.

The woman flashed a smile across the room and the same man came over with another small cup of liquid and a leer for Kyndra. The woman nursed this new drink, rolling it slowly between her hands. 'I see. Where are you from?'

'Who are you?' Kyndra blurted and then worried it had sounded rude. 'I mean—'

'My name is Kait,' the woman said. She sipped her drink and considered her. 'You look like someone with a story worth hearing.'

Kyndra didn't know what to say, so she drank some more ale. 'I'll get you another,' the woman said, and, to her surprise, Kyndra realized that her tankard was almost empty. Before she could stop her, Kait had slithered from her seat and made towards the counter.

Kyndra tried to pull herself together. Where was Nediah? She couldn't work out how long it had been since they'd parted and looked suspiciously at her tankard. She was used to ale, but this was a lot stronger than the pale drink they brewed in the Valleys.

'I grew up in an inn,' she said, as Kait placed another tankard in front of her.

Kait smiled. 'And where might that be?'

These tankards *were* larger than the ones back home. The taste she'd earlier found strange was now quite pleasant. Talk washed up around Kyndra and her head felt light. She smiled back at Kait. 'The Valleys. But I had to leave.'

'Why?'

She was aware of a sensation in the back of her mind urging her to keep quiet. Kyndra swallowed it in another gulp of ale. 'I broke something,' she said, wiping her mouth. 'Something valuable.'

'Is that all? Things can be replaced—'

'No. This couldn't. It made people angry.'

Something intense sparked in Kait's eyes and her red lips were slightly parted. Kyndra remembered Brégenne's impassive face and drew back slightly. Kait re-crossed her legs and took a sip of her drink. 'How did you escape?'

'I had help,' Kyndra said evasively.

'A man in white? With black eyes?'

Kyndra choked on her mouthful of ale. 'What?'

'The man. Did he speak to you?'

'No,' Kyndra said, unnerved by the fire in the woman's voice.

'Listen,' Kait said urgently. 'If you value your life, stay away from him.' She ground the last four words between her teeth. 'If he can, he will—' She looked up, startled by something behind Kyndra's chair. Then, between one breath and the next, she disappeared. Kyndra just caught the ends of her long coat whipping through a side door before a hand clamped down on her shoulder.

'There you are,' Nediah said, his voice falsely bright.

6

'Who were you talking to?' Brégenne demanded. Kyndra blinked at her, shocked at Kait's sudden departure. The blind woman's eyes glowed silver in the dim tavern. She'd pulled up her hood to cover them.

'No one. A woman bought me a drink.'

Brégenne rounded on Nediah. 'You let her come in here on her own?'

'She hasn't been alone very long.'

Was Brégenne worried about her, Kyndra wondered, or about what she might say? Heads were beginning to turn again and Nediah made swiftly for the counter. Brégenne regarded the chair Kait had just vacated with some suspicion. Then, muttering under her breath, she sat down and fixed her glowing eyes on Kyndra.

Kyndra tried to clear her mind. The ale had fogged it to the point where everything seemed exaggerated. She wasn't sure what would come out of her mouth if she opened it.

'This port ale's strong stuff.' Nediah put two tankards on the splintered tabletop. Kyndra was a little relieved to see that she had been left out of the round. She'd probably had too much. Then, in one smooth motion, Nediah placed a cup of wine in front of Brégenne, hooked a leg over the bench and pushed one of the tankards towards Kyndra. 'Careful,' he warned. 'It's probably more than you're used to.'

What did it matter? Kyndra thought, picking up the tankard and taking a long swallow. She was starting to like it here. The light seemed warmer, lending the room a red cosiness. The fire crackled affably and people were laughing. One man leapt off his bench to perform a drunken quickstep before collapsing forearms first onto the table. A snorted gale of mirth hid him from view. She smiled.

'What a pleasant place this is,' Nediah said, avoiding Brégenne's gaze. 'Ah, thank you.'

A woman set three bowls of stew on their table and waited while Nediah retrieved some coins from his pocket. Kyndra ate a few mouthfuls and grimaced. The best she could say for the food was that it was hot. She took another swig of ale to banish the taste.

'I think I should decide where we eat from now on,' Brégenne grumbled, stirring her stew unenthusiastically. 'You have an unerring instinct for the disreputable.'

'I thought we weren't supposed to draw attention to ourselves,' Nediah said blandly. He blew on his steaming spoonful. 'There are certain places where it's not a good idea to announce you have money to spend.'

Brégenne pursed her lips. 'Be that as it may, I'm getting a bit tired of dirty floors and nameless chunks of meat.' She prodded just such a chunk with her spoon.

'Who picked The Nomos, then?' Kyndra asked.

'I did, actually,' Nediah said. 'Shame we didn't have a chance to sample the food.'

'What were you saying?' Brégenne asked abruptly. She'd

given up on her stew and slowly sipped her drink instead. When Kyndra looked confused, she added, 'You were talking to that woman. Who was she?'

'Why do you want to know?' Kyndra finished her ale and looked with disappointment into the empty tankard. Maybe Nediah would buy her another.

'. . . could be important,' Brégenne was saying. 'Are you listening to me?'

Kyndra sighed and waved a hand. 'She was only asking me where I was from.'

'What did you tell her?'

'Not much. You chased her off.'

Brégenne's lips turned as white as her eyes. 'I warned you not to say anything about us.'

'She was interested in me, not you. She bought me a drink.'

'Don't be stupid,' Brégenne snapped. 'She was after something.'

The ale in Kyndra's stomach turned to cold embarrassment. She shouldn't have told Kait as much as she had. At least she hadn't mentioned her name.

Brégenne set her wine down. 'This isn't a game, girl.'

'What isn't?' Kyndra said loudly. Several people glanced her way. 'I didn't ask to go with you. You took me!'

'We didn't *take* you. You agreed.'

'I didn't have a choice. Jarand would have died if I hadn't promised to go with you!'

Nediah leaned forward. 'You don't understand the danger you were in, Kyndra. You want to believe the best of your town, and that's commendable. But a man had died and people were scared.'

'So you did it to save me?' Kyndra felt a profound anger.

The strangers had forced her to leave Reena and Jarand when they needed her most. She had ridden away while her home burned, and neither Brégenne nor Nediah had lifted a finger to help.

'I don't believe you,' she cried, unheeding of the heads that turned towards her. Brégenne's face darkened, but Kyndra couldn't stop. 'You did this for your own selfish reasons. You've no right to take me anywhere or tell me who I can and can't talk to!'

Nediah's eyes were flinty, but when he spoke, his voice was composed, even sympathetic. 'Don't shout at us, Kyndra. You're making a fool of yourself. If you want answers, you must prove responsible enough to deserve them.'

'I'm going home,' Kyndra growled. She jumped to her feet and swayed, the inn sliding sideways in her vision. She made a grab for the table, but it wasn't where it should have been. Her stomach roiled and everything looked wrong. Faces turned to her, all featureless and blurred. Her knees hit something hard. Why was she sitting on the floor? She managed to get her legs beneath her and tried but failed to stand up.

Rhythmic banging invaded Kyndra's ears, rousing her from a thick sleep. Her body felt fragile and her head ached.

'You had some of the drink last night.'

Kyndra jerked up. Her stomach lurched and she groaned. There was an awful taste in her mouth and her tongue felt dry and hot. She retched.

'No point. It all came up earlier.' The banging continued.

Mortified, Kyndra sniffed at her clothes, recognizing the stale odour for what it was. *Stupid,* she thought, *stupid. Anything could have happened.* Trying and failing to remember last night, she held her flushed cheeks and desperately wanted to cry.

'Women can't hold their drink,' the voice told her amiably.

Kyndra felt too sick to argue. She sat under an awning like a three-sided tent. Blinking out at the bright sunlight, she saw a man there, dressed in short trousers and a vest. His bare calves were muscular and he had large wide-toed feet that gripped the wooden planks as if he expected them to rock beneath him.

'Where am I?' Kyndra swallowed, trying to ignore the sour taste in her mouth. 'I don't remember coming here.'

'Not surprised,' the man said. 'Your friends brought you. Slept here they did too, just opposite.'

'You mean Bré— the woman and the tall man?'

'Aye that's them.'

'But where are they now?'

The man scratched at the patchy hair retreating across his scalp. 'Don't know about the woman. Your other friend's over there buying passage on the *Eastern Set*. He'll be done soon enough.'

'The what?' Kyndra got to her knees and crawled through a pile of rugs to peer out. She was on a large aerial platform like those they'd seen last night. This one was painted green and looked rather like a giant lily pad.

'*Eastern Set*,' the man said patiently, coiling a rope. Kyndra inched her way outside, squinting as the sunlight bit into her eyes. Then she gasped.

'I saw one of those yesterday, but not as big!'

'Ah, you mean that old plodder.' The man jerked his chin to the right and Kyndra spotted the craft she'd seen yesterday evening, still moored to its dock. 'She moves like a cartwheel through snow. *Eastern Set*'s no barge. She's an airship and the finest on the southern circuit.'

It really was a ship, Kyndra saw. Its decks gleamed under the sun, rails carved from silky wood. Nediah stood on the dock beside it, his back to her. He seemed to be haggling with some sort of quartermaster. Her eyes drifted back to the airship. Smoke puffed from a tube-like opening set in the sternward hull. There were two decks, and apparatus cluttered part of the lower one. Grappling hooks and canvas sacks peeped out from a tarpaulin, secured with ropes at each corner. By contrast, the top deck was neat and tidy and a round golden device faced with glass stood in place of a ship's wheel. Kyndra squinted and saw a hand like that on a clock hovering over a background of constellations, each star a shining dot of white ink.

A prickle ran over her skin and she shuddered. Jhren called the feeling 'grave-shivers' – the echoes of future feet passing over your resting place.

Silly, Kyndra chided herself, and she turned her gaze outwards once more. A great windlass dominated the middle of the lower deck. The chain wound around it fed through a hole in the floor and had links as thick as her forearm. Two huge balloons floated either side of the airship in the blue air, and two circular paddles turned lazily at the rear.

'They're the means of propulsion,' the man said, seeing where her gaze had strayed. 'And the balloons do the lift. You see there?' He pointed at the huge airborne chain she'd noticed the day before. 'That's the safety line. Ships are hooked onto it at launch so they don't escape into the sky.'

'They can't control how high they go?'

'It's the law,' the man said gruffly. 'If it were up to me, I'd unhook and fly to the stars.' He grinned, showing unusually white teeth. 'But the Trade Assembly that rules in Market Primus won't risk it. It owns all the ships and the workshop in Jarra, and by limiting access to the sky ports through the capital, they cream off the best of the trade.' He tucked the end of his rope through the centre of the coil and dropped it into a crate stamped 'E.S.'.

Kyndra stared at the gently bobbing airship. The posts that supported the safety line here were of a height with the aerial platforms of Sky Port East, but they increased in size as they moved away west. She guessed that the ship was connected to the safety line through the hole in its deck. 'It works like a sea anchor,' she said aloud, and when the man grunted agreement, she asked, 'Where does the line go?'

'There are four sky ports,' the man said, ticking them off on his fingers. 'Northern one links to the area around Svartas, the southern port to Talarun and the Eversea Isles. Sky Port East is for Serea and the Valleys and the west port's for Murta.' He paused. 'We've been trying to get a connection up near Ümvast, but those barbarians come out at night and cut down our posts.'

'Why would they do that?'

The man shrugged. 'Probably don't want the Trade Assembly getting its hands on the far north.' His gaze sharpened. 'There's money to be made up there. Mining, lumber – the Great Northern Forest is vast. They say it stretches to the bounds of the earth.' He chuckled darkly. 'Though no one's ever come back to prove it.'

Kyndra's mind filled with visions of distant lands and she felt small. Airships had never featured in Jhren's aunt's and uncle's tales. In the young Kyndra's imagination, Hanna and Havan were explorers: grand adventurers in pursuit of fabulous goods, living an exciting – even dangerous – life. Now, with the stranger's words ringing in her ears, Kyndra realized why Hanna and Havan had never told her about the airships. Trading across Serea and the east, they'd probably never seen one. She tried to swallow her disappointment.

'So you work on the *Eastern Set*?' she asked the man, who was now banging down crate lids.

The man's eyes glittered. 'Aye.'

'And is every sky port like this one?'

The hammering paused. 'All are stilt-towns, if that's what you mean. Except Sky Port West. There's only a dock there.'

'Why's that?' Kyndra asked. She waited, but the man was absorbed in his nails and didn't answer. She repeated the question, but still the man worked on, as if he couldn't hear her. She raised her voice. 'I said, why is—'

'I heard you.' He looked up, hammer clutched in his fist. 'Sky Port West is only there to serve Murta. It wouldn't be there at all if the place didn't import so much.'

'What's at Murta?' Kyndra asked carefully. She could tell by the man's tone and the uncomfortable slant of his shoulders that the subject was not one he wanted to discuss.

'It's just a town,' the man said finally, 'but it lies in the shadow of the mountains. I've heard some strange talk come out of there. People must be crazy to live so close to those monsters.' When Kyndra raised her eyebrow questioningly, the man clarified, 'Mountains.' He gazed into the middle distance. 'Saw them the one and only time I docked at Sky Port West. Black giants, they are, reaching up higher than anything into the sky. And they cover Mariar's western rim with never a break for a thousand leagues. North to south, and they reach all the way to the sea.'

'I wonder what's beyond them?' Kyndra mused, her mind still teeming with thoughts of the places she had yet to see.

'Nothing,' the man said softly.

There was a bucket of water in the tent. Kyndra cupped her hands and sipped it slowly to settle her stomach. Then she splashed her face and neck, all the while wishing fervently for a bath. She was still wearing the clothes she'd put on after the Ceremony. Mud crusted her trousers and her pale shirt showed the sooty fingers of fire.

When she came back out, clutching a heel of bread, the talkative stranger had gone. She could still see Nediah. His negotiations had perhaps taken a turn for the worse, since he now accompanied his speech with increasingly vehement gestures. Kyndra stared at him for a few moments, until her bruised senses caught up.

No one was watching her. For these scant few moments, she was alone.

Diving back into the shelter, she snatched up the rest of the bread and wrapped it in a cloth. At least that was something. Kyndra grinned to herself. This was her chance to get away. If Nediah was buying passage on an airship, it could be her only chance.

Keeping a close eye on him, she crept out of the tent. Half a loaf wouldn't get her very far, she reasoned, especially on foot. Kyndra squinted at the sky. It was almost midday. If she was careful, perhaps she could find a market with food too old to sell.

She took a bridge that led her swiftly away from Nediah. At

first, she bent low and scurried, until common sense hissed, *Stand up. You look suspicious.* Kyndra slowed and straightened. The last thing she needed to look like was a thief. Walking steadily now, she headed for a cluster of platforms spanned by myriad bridges. Some were little more than rope and wood, while others were solid enough to admit small carts.

The market was easy to spot, a stripy swarm of bustling tents. Fruit and vegetables sweated under the canvas and the place was noisy with the sounds of half-struck bargains. Kyndra drifted through the haggling people, entranced. She stopped at a stall, looking longingly at apples and bunches of berries. There was plenty of fruit she didn't recognize, including a long yellow thing bent almost into a horseshoe and a root with start-lingly orange flesh. Most peculiar of all was a fruit so stuck with spines that she wondered how anyone could eat it.

'What can I get you?' the stall owner asked, smiling briskly.

Kyndra looked up. 'Um . . . do you have anything you can't sell? I don't really have any money.'

The woman's smile vanished. 'I run a business not an alms-house,' she snapped. 'Get going.'

'Please,' Kyndra said, shooting a worried glance over her shoulder. 'I'll take anything.'

The woman's eyes narrowed. She bent and began to rum-mage beneath some canvas. When she straightened, Kyndra balked at the thing in her arms. It was definitely one of the spiky fruits, but its skin sagged like a poor man's purse. She could tell it had lost over a third of its original volume. 'What is it?'

'Want it or not?'

Kyndra took it hastily and wrapped it in the cloak Nediah had lent her. She could still feel the spines.

'Now clear off.' The stall owner pointed a finger. 'You're blocking my trade.'

'Thanks,' Kyndra muttered, though she wasn't sure the woman deserved it.

The crowd propelled her to a platform hung with colourful fabrics. There were scarves and skirts, shirts and jerkins. Kyndra eyed the new clothes hungrily, wishing she had money for a tunic to cover her stained shirt. She was attracting several disparaging glances just by standing there. The stall's owner, a prim, elegant man, watched her smudged hands like a bird of prey. When she reached out to touch a green jerkin, his mouth opened and Kyndra let her fingers fall before he told her off.

At the next stall along, a dress swung from a peg clipped to the awning. It was such a sheer and useless garment that Kyndra couldn't imagine how anyone would pay the asking price. Nobody in Brenwym had money to spare for clothes like that, but Colta would have liked it.

She turned quickly and caught sight of a basket of wool labelled 'Far Valleys'. Kyndra swallowed. Whenever she thought about Brenwym, it was with a creeping sense of guilt that only grew stronger the further away she went. She couldn't bring herself to imagine it as a burned-out shell, only as the dreary farming town she had called home. The wool here would shoot up in price when the news reached them. If Brenwym's storehouses had burned, there'd be no income and no way of rebuilding the town. Reena and Jarand had nothing without the inn. Maybe they could make it to Earlan Hill where Kyndra's aunt lived, but many would be making the same journey and what if the Breaking came again?

She shook herself. Worrying would not get her home. Her encounter with the fruit woman had yielded such poor pickings that she doubted there was any point in trying another stall. Things obviously worked differently here. No one in Brenwym would have let a penniless stranger starve.

Feeling hard done by, Kyndra pushed out of the crowd, stealing guarded glances over her shoulder. She would have to get back to the ground if she was to stand any chance of evading Nediah.

Angling away from the centre of town, Kyndra chose a narrow bridge that led towards the inn they had visited the previous night. From this height, its slanted roof and stained walls were easy to make out. *There's a ladder around here*, she thought, and tried to remember exactly where she'd seen it. The sun was hot on her back and the spiny fruit pricked her through its covering of cloak.

Kyndra caught sight of the ladder's wooden posts and felt her pulse quicken. She hadn't decided what to do once she was on the ground, and half a loaf and a shrivelled fruit weren't going to see her back to Brenwym without a horse. Perhaps she could find a wagoner heading east. *They'll want paying*, a voice in her head said pragmatically. Kyndra ignored it.

She turned to descend the ladder, feeling for the first rung with her foot.

'Kyndra!'

Curses, Kyndra thought, and quickly started climbing, buffeted by gusts of wind. In her haste, and with her eyes smarting from the breeze, she fumbled the fourth rung. Her boot slipped and she fell hard against the ladder, clutching it desperately with both hands. Bread and fruit tumbled away. She only just managed to keep hold of the cloak.

Then, out of nowhere, an arm reached down, gripped her under the armpit and hoisted her back onto the platform.

Kyndra dashed the wind-mist from her eyes and saw Nediah hurrying over a bridge that swung drunkenly at every step. She'd missed her chance.

Her rescuer released her arm and Kyndra turned to look at him. Everything he wore was white, even his leather gloves. His clothes were like some sort of uniform: long coat over parted robes, leather boots and a wide belt. Bizarrely out of place, a flute hung in a pouch at his waist. A heavy cowl hid much of his face, save for a chin shaded dark with stubble.

Kyndra stopping breathing. *Listen. If you value your life, stay away from him.*

Nediah stepped onto the platform, leaving the bridge to dance in his wake. He spread his feet and stood tensed as if for a fight. The stranger smiled, or at least his mouth did. Kyndra watched them both, weighed down with Kait's warning.

'Medavle,' Nediah said. He didn't move.

The cold greeting only warmed the stranger's smile. 'Hello, Nediah,' he replied, as if the two were old friends. 'It's been some time.'

'Kyndra,' Nediah said sternly. 'What are you doing here?'

Kyndra fidgeted, doing her best to ignore the fact that her rations had just plunged to their doom. 'I was . . . exploring.'

'Looks like she was trying to give you the slip,' the stranger commented and Kyndra winced.

'That's enough.'

'Not quite.' Medavle reached into his coat and pulled out a faded piece of paper looped through the cord of a small, worn pouch. He studied the little bag for a moment before grimacing and returning it to his pocket. Then he offered the folded paper to Kyndra. 'This is for you.'

Kyndra blinked and took it. Nediah, she noticed, looked ready to snatch the note and burn it.

'Read it later,' the man named Medavle said and for the first time Kyndra heard a deep, desperate authority in his voice. When he next spoke, however, it was gone. 'I can't say it's been fun, Nediah-ad-Sollas. You're not the person I remember.' He tilted his head at Kyndra. 'And you had better keep a sterner eye on your young friend here.'

Nediah glowered, but before he could reply, Medavle jumped onto the thin wooden railing, balanced like a cat. Kyndra's stomach clenched. It was a long way down. As if in a parting gesture, a mischievous wind swept back the white hood.

There were the midnight eyes Kyndra remembered. They had pierced her twice already, once in a dream and once upon waking. They burned in the deep sockets that had frozen her at the Inheritance, when even her mother's features had appeared indistinct.

Medavle looked at her and there was a roaring in Kyndra's mind, an exultation like the soaring of many voices. The man bowed his head to her. 'Blessings.' And he stepped into space. Kyndra gasped and ran to the place he'd been standing. Instead of plummeting to the distant ground, Medavle seemed to be walking down an invisible staircase. He held the flute at his lips and Kyndra swore that with every note, a step coalesced under his feet.

Nediah made a sound in his throat and she twisted to look at him. He was frowning, his eyes troubled. 'Who is he?' Kyndra asked, turning back to watch Medavle's white form until it merged with the forest of poles below.

'His identity does not concern you,' a woman's voice said.

Brégenne stood on the near platform to their right. Kyndra didn't know how long she'd been there, or how much she'd heard. 'Nothing ever concerns me,' Kyndra replied.

Nediah went to Brégenne, took her arm and Kyndra thought he whispered something, but the words were lost in the wind. He guided Brégenne towards Kyndra's platform and when she reached it, the blind woman held out her hand expectantly. Kyndra stared at her.

'Give it to me.'

'What?'

'The note, girl.'

Kyndra frowned and clutched the paper more tightly. 'It's mine.'

Brégenne's face darkened. 'Now. I won't ask again.'

Anger flared. 'Why should I? He gave it to *me*.'

'You don't understand. Medavle is dangerous. He's not to be trusted or taken lightly. I want to know what he gave you and I want to know why.'

'Well, you're about to be disappointed. The note's mine.'

Brégenne's lips thinned. As if this were a signal, Nediah's hand shot out and snatched the paper from Kyndra. Kyndra shouted and made a wild grab for it, but found Nediah's other hand against her shoulder. Although it wasn't glowing, she felt the threat through her shirt. She froze.

Nediah seemed genuinely sorry, but Kyndra didn't care. She watched the man pocket the note and glared at him. 'I haven't even read it.'

'All the better,' Brégenne said and Kyndra felt a hot flash of frustration. She silently swore to get the page back at any cost. The possibility that it might be dangerous didn't trouble her – after all, what could it say? Her mind conjured a fleeting image of cursed words that brought death when read. Kyndra shrugged it off. She didn't want to think Brégenne and Nediah might be protecting her.

'Do you have everything?' Brégenne asked Nediah and, for the first time, Kyndra noticed a small sack at Nediah's feet.

'Yes.'

'Good. We had better get back. The airship sails in an hour.'

Kyndra's stomach dropped. 'Where are we going?'

'West,' Nediah said simply.

'To?'

'First to Market Primus. Then we'll have to argue with the captain.'

'About what?'

'Onward passage.' Nediah ran a hand through his dark hair, making a mess of it. 'Air is faster than road, but it's expensive. You don't have to bribe horses.'

Kyndra didn't really feel like speaking to Nediah after his theft of the note, but curiosity got the better of her. 'Where do bribes come into it?'

'Not many captains take their ships west.' Nediah sighed. 'He might agree to drop us at Jarra, but without a third horse, we'll struggle from there.' He looked mournfully at his purse. 'It's going to cost us a small fortune to dock at Murta.'

An ominous tingle ran down her neck. 'The sailor I spoke to this morning said some strange things about that place.'

Nediah snorted. 'Sailors are superstitious folk. The people of Murta don't much care for outsiders. I imagine they started many of the rumours themselves.'

'Rumours?'

'Are you two going to stand around and talk until the ship has left?' Brégenne turned her back and – reaching out to grasp the railing – started towards the area where Kyndra had woken that morning. Nediah picked up his sack and moved to take Brégenne's arm, but she shook him off. 'I can manage,' she said tersely.

With obvious reluctance, Nediah let her go on ahead. He looked at Kyndra. 'Come on.'

And Kyndra had no choice. She was disconcerted to be leaving the sky port so soon. Her plans for escape hadn't even had a chance to mature. Before she had taken five steps, however, Nediah bent and lowered his mouth to her ear.

'Medavle once tried to join a fanatical sect that lives in the roots of the mountain, far below Naris. The sect is led by a madman . . . but even they won't have anything to do with Medavle.' Nediah's green eyes were fierce. 'If he crosses your path again, be careful. He's not someone you'd want as your enemy.'

7

Nediah straightened. 'I've got some clothes for you,' he said tentatively and Kyndra thought she detected a peace offering. She looked away. 'We left in such a hurry,' Nediah continued. 'I'm sorry about that.'

Kyndra said nothing. She felt Medavle's dark eyes on her back and looked around, but the walkway was empty. Was the white-clad stranger really as dangerous as both Kait and Nediah intimated? And what was in that note?

They walked in silence for a minute or so, Nediah keeping an ever-vigilant eye on Brégenne up ahead. Kyndra watched the boards pass beneath her feet. 'Why are we going to Murta?' she asked.

Nediah gave her a wary glance. 'You saw the envoi. Brégenne and I must make our report.'

'Report to whom?'

'We can't talk here.'

'It's about the Breaking,' Kyndra said, hearing a tremor in her voice. She coughed to hide her weakness and added, 'You said you were tracking it.'

'Yes.' Nediah stopped and lowered the sack with a sigh. They stood on a blue platform little more than five feet across.

The *Eastern Set* was moored to their left, whirring in its dock. Sailors hurried to and fro, loading cargo and readying the airship. The dock master Kyndra had seen yesterday stood near the gangway, checking off each outbound item. The list he clutched hung to his knees.

'We'll be underway soon,' Nediah remarked. Kyndra nodded, watching the frenzied activity on the deck. The boards there looked pale from scrubbing, but the airship's hull gleamed like honey and sun sparked off the stern windows. *Those must be the captain's quarters*, Kyndra thought to herself. She gazed at the expensive panes, acutely aware of the three lonely coppers in her pocket.

Dales folk understood the need for money; it purchased luxuries to which they'd all grown accustomed. Ashley Gigg was always the first to pounce on visiting merchants, clamouring for herbs she couldn't find locally. But trading in physical goods still took precedence over the exchanging of coin. Her mother's inn was one of the only exceptions. However, the moment Kyndra had arrived in Sky Port East, she'd noticed how essential it was to have money. At home her coppers were enough to buy a decent meal, maybe even a bed for the night. Here they didn't amount to one drink.

A whinny of fright broke into her thoughts and Kyndra looked over to see Brégenne and Nediah's horses being winched up in a kind of lift. The men pulling on the ropes did not look pleased. Brégenne stood at the lift gate, her grey outfit turning her pale skin pallid in the sun. When the horses had completed their nervous ascent, she reached out with her arms until she found each horse's head. She stroked their necks as they were unloaded, making comforting sounds and offering a few small apples. The horses ate them with apprehensive eyes, clearly unhappy at being off the ground.

Nediah picked up his sack and he and Kyndra crossed over to Brégenne. 'How much did you give the captain before he'd agree to take our mounts?'

Brégenne turned at the question. 'He's concerned about his hold, naturally. But I threw in a gold piece on top of the price of our passage and that convinced him.' She smiled briefly and Kyndra glimpsed someone else, a stranger whose face was like the summer. When the smile faded, that person was gone and Brégenne stood stonily in her place.

The airship ground against its moorings, eager to be free. And once the reluctant horses were loaded, activity on deck began to subside. A sailor beckoned them over. Nediah took Brégenne's arm in his free hand and led her across the gangway. Kyndra followed with a flutter of uncertainty.

She felt the difference between solid dock and buoyant vessel immediately. The grinding changed to a rhythmic tugging on the boards beneath her. She watched three men haul in the wide gangway, muscles standing out in their arms. Another swung down from a rope tethered to one of the balloons. There was a fire-like *whoosh* and Kyndra glanced up. Flames flared in the braziers fixed beneath the taut canvas, and the balloons swelled, straining skyward.

The tugging grew stronger and Kyndra looked aft to see the circular paddles spinning even faster. A woman with a smoke-stained face and gloved to her elbows emerged from below decks. She signalled the men on the dock and they released the mooring lines. The craft lurched away.

Kyndra ran to the rail, watching Sky Port East recede. The airship rose steadily and a squeal of metal on metal reached her from below where the ship's chain slid along the greased length of the safety line.

Kyndra's eyes watered whenever she faced into the wind. It whipped up her hair and chilled her hands. When distance reduced the sky port to a smudge on the horizon, she tried not to feel as if her hopes for escape were fading with it.

Nediah beckoned her over to the opposite rail where he stood with Brégenne. The wind had reddened the woman's cheeks and pulled wisps of hair from the knot tied at the base of her neck. 'Exhilarating, isn't it?' Nediah said when he saw Kyndra. The tall man's eyes were bright. 'I haven't been on an airship in a long time. They're a lot faster than they used to be.'

'Didn't you come here on one?'

Nediah shook his head. 'We rode. Our horses are Hrosst purebreds. They excel at long distance across country. Not as fast as an airship, of course, but they're a good deal cheaper.'

'You'll be reimbursed,' Brégenne said. 'We're following orders.'

'I don't mind about that. It's the principle.' Nediah clicked his tongue in disgust. 'The Trade Assembly is already wealthy beyond imagining. I'm amazed that non-cartel merchants even use the ships, judging from the number of gold pieces I had to part with this morning.'

'It's the only real option for perishable cargoes,' Brégenne said absently. She had her back to them, her face tilted up to the sky. The sun was slowly sinking into a cloud bank on the western horizon.

Nediah glanced at the reddening sky and shifted uncomfortably. 'I dread the argument we're going to have with the captain when we reach Market Primus.'

'How far is that?' Kyndra asked.

'A hundred and twenty leagues or so. We'll be there in a few days.'

'A few days . . .' She watched the countryside fly by and marvelled at their speed. The airship raced towards the setting sun, bearing her with it.

Kyndra looked over her shoulder. Beyond the polished stern, grey twilight masked the way home.

Her cabin consisted of a narrow berth and a chest nailed down beneath the round window. At least the window had glass. Kyndra imagined it could get cold up here, especially at night. Being the only passengers – which was hardly surprising, Nediah had muttered darkly – they each had their own room.

'Yes, your clothes,' Nediah said, standing in Kyndra's doorway. 'They're the best I could do in the time.' He pulled a sack into the cabin and began to search it vigorously. Soon its contents were rolling all over the floor: cured meat in waxed paper, dried and fresh fruit, soap, a notched razor blade. 'That's mine.' Nediah snatched it up and threw it back into the sack, whereupon it promptly fell out again. 'I got us cheaper passage if I agreed to supply our own food.' Something black peeped out from the neck of the sack. Kyndra caught a glimpse of silk. 'They're here somewhere,' Nediah said loudly. He stuffed the garment swiftly out of sight and Kyndra suppressed a curious smile.

The clothes were found. Expecting a dress, she saw instead a linen tunic, tan jerkin and a pair of dark trousers made from thin, grainy cloth. It was wholly unlike the wool she wore at home. And they were too big. 'This will help,' Nediah said, handing over a belt. 'I know they're not a good fit, but we can get better ones at Murta. At least these are clean and you won't smell like a wet sheep when it rains.'

'Excuse me,' Kyndra said tartly, 'there wasn't ever a lot of choice back home.' She paused. 'Thanks for getting me something sensible.'

'Here,' Nediah said. He held out a tatty piece of paper.

A moment later, Kyndra realized it was the note Brégenne had demanded, the note given her by Medavle. She took it in disbelief. 'I don't understand.'

'I wouldn't get your hopes up,' Nediah said, as if the act of returning the paper embarrassed him. 'It looks like a fragment of poetry.'

'*Poetry?*'

Nediah smiled. 'I did say. And I'm as baffled as you are. However, Brégenne thought it was harmless, so I asked for it back.'

Kyndra unfolded the note. It was definitely a page from a book; she could see a faded number in the top corner. The paper smelled of spent centuries, but was thick and well-made. Perhaps that was why it had survived. Kyndra lowered her eyes and read:

> *Of times before the empire walked*
> *And tamed the soil as red as blood,*
> *My tongue will spin a marvelled tale*
> *To leave all listeners wondrous pale,*
> *To make all pulses thud.*
>
> *The cosmos then was full of light,*
> *But Starborn, they were dark and deep,*
> *In turn, each built a lonely hall*
> *And lived a life more cold than all*
> *The snow-ice on the steep.*

Lucy Hounsom

And yet came one who dreamed anew,
He dreamed that love unfroze his heart;
By day he chose a window high
To watch a rider swift and spry
Ascend on wings of art.

Her people were the Lleu-yelin –
A wild, remote and ancient race;
Her mount was scarlet, darkling hue
And ribbons on her wrist there flew
And sun shone on her face.

Such strength he saw in every line,
A savage charm her body made;
Her dragon eyes were ruby fire,
In him they sparked unknown desire
And found his soul waylaid.

She took him up upon her mount
And this before has never been,
For so are yelin maidens proud –
They would not pause to please the crowd –
And rarely are they seen.

He flew with her through Acre's lands
And danced on airs that seldom sleep,
Until he earned her given name
And shared in the embittered fame
That soon would make her weep.

Kyndra turned the page over, but it was blank. 'Is that it?'

'Seems so,' said Nediah.

'But it's not finished.'

Nediah raised an eyebrow. 'How do you know?'

'Well . . . it's a story. But it's not finished.' Kyndra glanced back at the poem. 'See, "shared in the embittered fame that soon would make her weep." But what fame?'

'I'd like to know why Medavle gave it to you.'

Kyndra bit her lip. Why *had* Medavle given it to her? The only names she recognized in the poem were Acre, Lleu-yelin and Starborn, and she didn't know much about any of them either.

'Perhaps Medavle has spent too long on his own,' Nediah said meaningfully.

'He called you something strange earlier.'

The man's brow crinkled briefly. 'Oh, ad-Sollas. It's an ancient title that means "of the sun". It's not used any more.'

The odd words were familiar, as if she'd seen them written down somewhere. Kyndra shrugged and looked at her feet. That Nediah cared enough to return the note both warmed and disturbed her. As much as she wanted to preserve her anger, Kyndra had to admit that perhaps Brégenne and Nediah intended something more for her. Buying her clothes and carrying her to bed didn't sound like the kind of things potential murderers did. They'd had every chance to dispose of her in the Wilds, where the words she'd overheard could be buried alongside her body.

'There's so much I don't know about you, about any of this,' she said painfully. 'And I think Brégenne wants to keep it that way.'

'She is only thinking of your safety,' Nediah replied. He

stood up and went to the window, leaving Kyndra to gaze at his back. Nediah placed a hand against the glass and let his fingers slide lightly down its surface. It was only then that Kyndra realized how dark the cabin had become. The sun had set.

There was a candle lamp nailed to the wall, so Kyndra struck one of the matches that lay on its bracket and warm light filled the room. Nediah looked smaller in the artificial glow.

She took a deep breath. 'I don't understand something.' She waited, but Nediah remained at the window, watching the dark. 'Is Brégenne . . . well, is she really blind?'

Nediah didn't reply straight away. 'Yes,' he said, his tone strangely expressionless. 'But she uses Lunar energy to help her see at night. It's not perfect. She can't see colour at all, I believe.'

'And so in daylight . . .'

'In daylight she has me.'

Kyndra suddenly wished she hadn't asked.

'Not like that.' A brittle edge sharpened Nediah's voice. He still faced his own dark reflection. 'We always travel with a Wielder of the opposite affinity. It's the rules.'

Before she could ask what he meant, Nediah turned. He brushed a hand across his mouth, as if to erase his self-mocking smile. 'Now, what do you say to dinner?'

They ate that night with the *Eastern Set*'s captain. Kyndra entered the saloon beside Nediah and gaped at the man sitting at the head of the table. It was the sailor she'd spoken to earlier. The workman's garb was gone, replaced by a waistcoat over a flowing white shirt. The waistcoat was blue and the front of it was busy with bronze buttons, each stamped with a different crest.

'You see I've done my share of deals,' the captain said when he caught Kyndra staring. 'Each button represents a different Trading Family, all master merchants. A crest is given to celebrate fifty successful contracts between merchant and captain. I get a share of whatever price the cargo fetches and it's up to me to find the markets where it'll go for the most.' He flashed those white teeth at Kyndra. 'The name's Argat. Surprised to find I'm a person of quality?'

Unsure what to say, Kyndra muttered an apology.

Captain Argat grinned. 'I do my share of the rough like any crew member. Only difference is I earn a lot more.' He laughed boisterously and rolled up his sleeves in preparation for dinner.

With the airship being just out of port, there was plenty of choice, though little was familiar. Kyndra avoided the extra-rare meat that Brégenne seemed to relish, and stuck with fruit, cheese and a bit of smoked fish that tasted of the salty waters of a coast she'd never seen. Ocean fish took too long to reach them in the Valleys and the cheese they made at home was softer than the yellow rind-less slab she found on her plate. When the table was clear, Argat proffered a decanter of amber liquid. Brégenne and Nediah accepted, but this morning's headache was still too close for Kyndra.

'Strange stories in the wind these days,' Argat said, leaning back. His eyes moved over Brégenne and Nediah. 'You from the west?'

'Talarun,' Brégenne said smoothly. 'But we're heading for the Hrosst plains.'

'Neither of you has the clan look. In fact, I'd bet my gold that he –' Argat nodded at Nediah – 'is an Islesman.'

'Your eyes are sharp, Captain.' Nediah smiled pleasantly. 'I was born there.'

'Comes from a life of sailing the chain. Only, as I say, one hears some odd stories. I thought perhaps you might have heard them too.'

'I'm afraid our business spares us little time for tales,' Brégenne said coldly.

'Of course.' Argat's smile barely dimpled his cheeks. 'But one does not hear of a mountain range crumbling into dust every day. Nor of the Breaking striking in two places at once.'

Although Brégenne and Nediah remained expressionless, the air between them seemed to stiffen. 'Who told you this?' Nediah asked.

'A customer, if you must know. He has farmsteads to the west of Sky Port North. It was a portion of the Infinite Hills, he said. Raised a dust cloud several days thick. His cows stopped giving milk, horses wouldn't step outside. Quite bizarre.'

'And what about the Breaking?'

'That news came up from the south. Apparently, the Breaking struck the Karka Basin *and* Tirindal on the same day, at the same time. The local cartel in Tirindal claimed it destroyed their entire shipment of garlic, which was why –' Argat's voice hardened – 'they said they couldn't pay me.'

'Perhaps it was just a bad spring storm,' Nediah suggested mildly. 'They blow in off the sea this time of year.'

'I'll wager it wasn't a spring storm that took down that mountain range, though,' Argat mused. He flicked dark eyes to Kyndra. 'You, girl, ever heard of such a thing?'

Kyndra caught Nediah's warning. 'No, Captain,' she said.

'What about the Breaking, then? Seen it where you live?'

Kyndra's mind filled with screams and fire, folk stumbling through the night, calling for loved ones. Tessa's swollen cheek, Fedrin's death. 'No,' she said quietly.

Perhaps Argat heard a shadow in that word, for he dropped the topic and the talk turned elsewhere. Yara, Argat's tall first mate, began a hard-to-follow discussion about airship mechanics. Kyndra recognized her as the smoke-stained woman from earlier.

'We're still running inefficiently,' Yara said, directing her words at Argat. 'Why use hot air to inflate the balloons when we've a boiler already in situ? Steam can be used to lift as well as propel.'

The captain stopped with a forkful of food raised halfway to his mouth. Slowly, he lowered it. 'Go on.'

'What we need,' Yara said, tapping her index finger rapidly against the tabletop, 'is a contraption capable of turning the paddles *and* inflating the balloons. We need a special kind of boiler, a kind of *engine*—'

'You think you could design this?' Argat said, his eyes gleaming. 'Could the boiler in the stern be modified? What kind of cost are we looking at?'

'The coin you'd spend on alterations would be offset many times over by the resulting cut in fuel,' Yara answered, her eyes now gleaming too. 'We'd have a faster ship that's less expensive to run.'

'And with a greater potential to unhook . . .'

While Argat and Yara traded ideas back and forth, Kyndra found her eyes roaming the saloon. The dining table only took up one end of the long room. Smaller tables dotted the rest of the floor, their flat tops crowded with miscellaneous objects. There were bottles filled with strange-coloured liquids, bones and teeth, books, maps and glass ornaments that refracted the lamplight. The more Kyndra looked, the more she noticed, and the more she wanted to touch. White sticks that looked like a petrified hand held a round stone. A foggy mirror cast endless reflections of the room, until she realized there was an identical mirror directly opposite. Faces leered from paintings propped in a corner, their huge eyes guarding a trio of wooden chests banded with metal.

'What do you think of my collection, then, girl?'

Kyndra's head snapped back to the table. The others were staring at her. 'It's . . . big,' she said lamely, disturbed by the unveiled warning in Argat's eyes. 'Where did you get it all?'

'Here and there.' The captain waved a thick hand. 'I have a passion for oddities. If I see something I want, I'll haggle to the death for it.'

Brégenne asked a polite but quiet question that Kyndra didn't catch. She was too busy thinking about the captain. Quite suddenly, she decided she didn't like him. What had happened since this morning to change Argat from friendly to sinister? The rough, talkative sailor was gone and in his place sat a shrewd stranger whose look was not so much companionable as suspicious. Kyndra didn't like the way Argat stared at her, as if trying to find the answer to an unpleasant question.

Yara finished her brandy and stood up. 'Been a fine evening, all, but I have duties to see to before I retire.'

Kyndra half expected Argat to wave her back to her seat, but he merely smiled and accepted the salute she gave him.

'We should retire as well,' Brégenne said. 'Thank you for your hospitality, Captain.'

'Don't mention it, my lady. You are, after all, paying me a handsome sum.' Argat smiled crookedly.

Brégenne's face tightened. She stood and pushed her chair in neatly. The glow in her eyes was so faint as to be barely discernible. Nediah took her arm and Kyndra realized they needed to maintain the charade of her blindness in front of the captain.

Argat's eyes were sharp in his reddened face. He held his glass at an angle so that the amber liquid came right to the lip and balanced there. 'I hope you enjoy your time aboard my *Set*,' he said. 'You're free to go where you will, of course.' He leaned back in his chair and his eyes met Kyndra's. 'Except this room. You will not come here.'

'We understand,' Nediah said and Argat smiled again, holding up his glass.

'May your dreams be ever of flying.'

As they reached the double doors, Kyndra glanced over her shoulder. The captain sat among his treasures, his eyes fixed on her.

'I wonder what he's keeping in there,' Nediah mused when they'd put some distance between themselves and the saloon. He glanced sidelong at Kyndra. 'He certainly doesn't trust *you*.'

'I didn't give him any reason to,' Kyndra answered, with what she hoped was a fair approximation of Argat's crooked smile.

Nediah chuckled and then looked at Brégenne. 'I think we might have more than a little trouble convincing this Argat to fly to Murta.'

'Hush.' Brégenne pulled her arm free of Nediah's and the tall man looked faintly disappointed. 'Don't go near that saloon,' she said to Kyndra. 'Nediah's right. He'll be tough to convince and we have to travel west without delay. Don't give him an excuse to strand us at Market Primus.'

'I'm not interested in his collection,' Kyndra lied stiffly. Brégenne gave her a dangerous frown. 'I'm not,' she insisted.

*

Kyndra spent the next couple of days up on deck, watching one foreign landscape change subtly into another and revelling in the constant wind that blew down the length of the ship. It did indeed feel like flying, as the captain was fond of telling her. Kyndra did her best to avoid the man, but Argat had other ideas.

Whenever she was alone at the prow, she'd inevitably hear the soft tread of the captain behind her. Argat would occasionally stand in silence, but more often he'd rattle off a series of anecdotes, most of which involved the acquisition of a new curio to sweeten his collection. The man talked of little else. His stories were diverting enough, but he never followed up on his promises to show Kyndra the skull of Mactoa or the horn that won a hundred battles. As far as she knew, there hadn't been a real battle since the Deliverance five hundred years ago, but she nodded politely. Despite her decision not to trust the captain, Kyndra couldn't help but be intrigued by his tales. Although they didn't involve Wielders, dragon-riders and towering citadels, they were a good way to pass the hours.

The rest of the time, Argat worked alongside his crew or shut himself in the saloon. They were not invited to eat there again and they made do with the galley. Kyndra steered clear of the saloon, as Brégenne had instructed, but she couldn't help but feel Argat's eyes following her wherever she went.

On the morning of the third day, they reached the capital, Market Primus. Kyndra leaned over the prow rail, enjoying the sun. It was a warm day – one of the balmy preludes to summer – and the rich breeze carried a hundred smells. When she breathed in, she caught a heavy tang of hot metal together with flowers and spices. Another breath brought a reek of warming rubbish and the musty odour of old stone walls. The city's open gates looked as if they had never been closed. Ivy and other climbing weeds had claimed them as part of their tangled colonies.

The thoroughfare was busy. A carriage stamped with the crest of the merchant cartel scattered a group of men bearing crates on their shoulders. Other men walked alone or with women, hauling on ropes tied to heavy-eyed oxen.

Kyndra was shocked at the size of it all. The only cities she'd seen were the ones she built in her head, the lost cities of Acre. Now she realized how many things she'd forgotten to imagine: the sheer noise of people, hooves and wheels, the baying of dogs and animals bound for market and the screeching and grinding that turns the gears of cities.

'Are you ready?'

Kyndra glanced over her shoulder to see Nediah strolling up the deck. 'For what?' she asked.

'It'll be a while before the ship leaves for Jarra. Brégenne and I have a few things to buy in the city.'

Kyndra's heart leapt at the thought of walking the busy streets. She smiled at Nediah. 'Yes, I'm ready.'

The approaching dock was twice the size of the one in Sky Port East. Kyndra watched three sailors vault deftly onto the wooden platform, bearing chains to secure the airship. On the ground, people swarmed between buildings, hauling produce, stacking barrels and loading horse-drawn carts to trundle their goods into the city.

'Nediah?'

Brégenne stood in the dwindling shade by the deckhouse door, arms wrapped around her body. Noon sun turned her into a grey and fragile figure. Nediah went to her instantly and took hold of her arm. With the other, he beckoned to Kyndra.

They disembarked and joined the throng of traffic heading into the city. Guards clad in leather, wearing white surcoats emblazoned with a set of scales, stood to either side of the gates. Their eyes slid over the crowd without interest. Peace had reigned here so long, Kyndra thought, that the guards must have forgotten what war looked like. These were just better-dressed versions of the lawmen in Brenwym, who dealt with drunkards and thieves. The Deliverance had ended Mariar's need for soldiers.

Once through the gates, the crowd began to thin. People splintered away down side streets, pushing handcarts or guiding mules by worn bridles. Those who continued up the main thoroughfare were generally better dressed: master craftsmen, merchants seeking an audience with the Trade Assembly, or rich ladies visiting friends in the capital.

'I've never seen so many people,' Kyndra said to Nediah, who only smiled in answer. Although he kept a close hold on Brégenne, the blind woman was rarely jostled. People veered away when they noticed her, darting glances at her white eyes. Brégenne pulled up her hood, as if she could sense their discomfort, and Kyndra felt a flicker of indignation until she remembered how uneasy she felt under that same stare.

The crowded streets put her in mind of Sky Port East and her failed escape attempt. *I haven't forgotten you*, she said to the smoke-stained faces of Reena and Jarand which floated accusingly to the front of her mind. *I will come back.* Since her encounter with Medavle, however, Nediah was being especially watchful. She wouldn't be allowed into any more taverns alone, either. Kyndra watched the city's menagerie pass before her eyes, and for a moment she was in one of her stories, strolling down the streets of some lost metropolis.

'We need another week's worth of food at least,' Nediah said, jolting Kyndra from her thoughts. They'd turned into a large square filled with sunlight and chatter. A market sprawled there, its stalls set up in horizontal and vertical lines like a gaming board. Kyndra took a deep breath, pulling the warm scent of baking into her nostrils. A nearby stall held fresh plaits of bread, seeded rolls and buns, all towering in wobbly stacks.

A woman wearing a white linen headscarf looked at them enquiringly. 'Five loaves,' Nediah said. 'Spelt, if you have it.'

Smiling, the woman wrapped the bread and passed it to Nediah, who dropped a silver coin into her palm.

As they continued through the market, Nediah added sausages, fruit, vegetables and cheese to his loaves until he needed a sack to carry it all. 'I think that might do us,' he said, ignoring the herbalist eyeing him hopefully from between two bunches of yarrow. 'What did you need, Brégenne?'

'Some ink,' she answered shortly. She'd barely spoken since they'd entered the city. While Nediah haggled with the scribing merchant, Kyndra watched her surreptitiously. Brégenne seemed distracted. Her head swivelled from side to side, as if she were searching for something. Occasionally, she would hold herself still, listening to the market's cries.

Barely audible under the throaty advertisements of a dozen tradesmen, Kyndra caught the regular sound of a kick wheel. She looked around for the potter and spied him right at the end of a row. The man was absorbed in his work. Frequently his hands would pause while one pumping foot restored the wheel's momentum. Kyndra found the steady rhythm soothing. It reminded her of home and she drifted closer.

The man worked a large lump of clay, breathing heavily from the effort of spinning the stone wheel. After a few minutes, a bowl began to take shape under his deft hands. Kyndra moved closer still, staring at it. The bowl grew shallow and wide. Water lay in the bottom, water that knew her true name and future path.

Kyndra sucked in a breath and shook her head to clear it. But when she opened her eyes, the water and the bowl-shaped Relic were still there, spinning and spinning. And then –

. . . she stands on a hill, the glass citadel to her left, watching an army advance up the valley. A hundred thousand men march beneath its banner and its siege weapons roll forward without the help of horses. Solinaris stands fragile against the bloody sunset. Tomorrow, it will fall. She has told them this, warned them countless times. Now it is too late.

She must do what she has come here to do. And quickly. She will clothe herself invisibly, the better to slip unseen between the crystal gates. She reaches . . .

Kyndra recoiled, stunned, as if she'd run full-tilt at a stone wall. The blow hit her mind with bone-breaking force. Pinpricks of light surrounded her, tried to fill her, but she wasn't ready. They were pain and power, and she wanted them and hated them.

Body trembling, head afire with agony, Kyndra found herself back in the market. The potter's wheel was broken, cracked right across the middle. The man himself sat in the wreckage of his stall, his wares smashed all to pieces. Dazed, Kyndra stumbled forward to help him. The man looked at her with eyes dim and unfocused. He ignored the hand she offered.

'What's going on here?'

Kyndra turned at the clipped question and found herself

face to face with a couple of city guards. Their gazes flicked between her and the potter's ruined stall and she could see them trying to fit the two together. She opened her mouth, a denial ready on her tongue, but then Nediah was there. He shot her a silencing frown.

'This gentleman needs help,' Nediah said. 'Is there a healer near?'

'All in good time,' the first guard interrupted. 'I want to know what happened here.'

'Are you responsible for this?' the second guard barked at Kyndra. Her white surcoat was blinding in the bright sun and Kyndra narrowed her eyes against the glare. Jerkily, she shook her head. Even that small movement sent the agony spiking up into her skull and she bit her lip to keep from crying out.

'We'll see.' The guard leaned down and, with her colleague's aid, heaved the potter to his feet. He swayed, but remained standing. 'What's your name?' she asked him briskly.

'M-Mardon,' he stammered after a few seconds. 'Jim Mardon. I have a shop in . . .' His eyes clouded then cleared. 'East District, I think.'

The guards exchanged a look. 'Must have hit his head,' the stubble-cheeked guardsman muttered and retrieved a notebook tucked behind his leather cuirass. Pencilling in the name, he addressed his next words to Nediah. 'Did you witness the incident, sir? This is some costly damage.' He indicated the wealth of broken pottery and cast Kyndra a suspicious glance.

Nediah nodded and began to spin them a story. Instead of listening, Kyndra stood hugging herself, trying to suppress the shudders that rolled through her body. She noticed Mardon's eyes sliding out of focus again. Blood dripped from a gash on his hand, spattering the carpet of shattered pots. He said nothing while Nediah talked, just stood there on drunken feet. Merchants and customers alike had turned from their business to watch him.

Kyndra's neck prickled and she looked around. Brégenne was staring at her, a small frown crinkling her brow. *No*, Kyndra corrected herself, *she can't see me*. But the way the woman tilted her head, the way that blank gaze was fixed on her . . . Kyndra shifted uneasily.

'Sorry you got caught in this, stranger,' the guard was now saying amiably to Nediah. 'Your help is appreciated.' He spared a glance for the man. 'Poor devil. I suppose we ought to get him home.'

'Shouldn't he see a healer first?' Nediah looked genuinely pained. 'Those cuts need cleaning at the very least.'

'I suppose you're right,' the woman said reluctantly. She sighed and beckoned her fellow guard. 'Let's get him to Willow Street.'

'I'd be happy to take him,' Nediah said quickly, causing both guards to stop in surprise. 'I feel somewhat responsible. If you'd be kind enough to give me directions, I can drop him off before I find my lodgings.'

'Well, if you're sure,' the unshaven guard said, looking hugely relieved. 'We ought to get this to the captain.' He flashed the notebook.

Nediah smiled confidently. 'He'll be safe with me.'

'My thanks,' the guard said with a nod. His colleague gave Nediah directions to the healers on Willow Street and they both turned to leave. The curious crowd began to disperse.

Nediah didn't ask Kyndra to help, but heaved the man up by himself. 'Are we really taking him to the healers?' she asked in a low voice, watching as Mardon stumbled and fell against Nediah, barely able to stand now.

Nediah just handed her the sack of food to carry. He touched Brégenne gently on the shoulder and the blind woman fell into step behind him. She'd have no trouble following them by ear, Kyndra thought. Mardon's boots dragged and scraped over the cobbles, filling the square with echoes. He leaned heavily on Nediah, who was beginning to sweat with the effort of holding him up.

They left the noise of the market behind and moved into a quieter district. Nediah did not stop until they came to a narrow passage created by the opposing buttresses of two buildings. With a swift look back, he dragged the man into the opening and propped him on a jut of stone.

'What are you doing?' Kyndra asked. Mardon sagged against the building, mouth opening and closing spasmodically. His eyes flicked from side to side, as if the unfamiliar stalked him. Kyndra wondered what he was seeing.

'Can you hear me?' Nediah asked him gently. When Mardon gave no sign that he'd understood, Nediah laid a hand on the man's head and closed his eyes. His face stilled. Only moments later, he gasped and cried out. Golden light blazed between his fingers, knocked the man away and Mardon's unprotesting body slid to the ground.

'Nediah!' Brégenne said urgently. She pushed past Kyndra and stretched out her hands until she found her companion's shoulders. 'Are you all right? What happened?'

Nediah opened eyes which were gold instead of green. He blinked rapidly and shed the light like a mist of tears. 'I'm fine, Brégenne,' he said in a raspy voice, 'but he isn't. I don't understand it. I was watching him back in the marketplace. He seemed fine at first, a bit concussed, perhaps, but by the time we left, his pupils were fixed and dilated. I thought he might have suffered internal bleeding, so I brought him here to check.'

Although Mardon lay sprawled where he had fallen, Nediah made no move to help him up. 'His mind is riddled with cracks,' he said softly. 'It's *dissolving*.' He wiped a hand across his face. 'I've never seen anything like it.'

'You are certain it's not natural?' Brégenne asked.

Nediah repressed a shudder. 'Yes. This wasn't caused by a fall.'

Kyndra's stomach began to churn. Her headache had eased enough to allow a memory through. It was a muddle of images: the glass citadel, a sunset, a valley full of armoured men. And then a force had hit her, flung her back from – somewhere. And not only her, but Mardon too. It had cracked the thick stone of his potter's wheel. How much had Nediah noticed?

'I won't examine him again,' Nediah said, eyeing Mardon nervously. 'Linking to his mind is too dangerous. Let's take him to the healers and get back to the airship.' He bent over Mardon, whose limbs had begun to shake violently. When he straightened, supporting the man, his eyes rested briefly on Kyndra. 'The sooner we get to Naris, the better.'

Kyndra didn't like that look. Perhaps Nediah *had* seen the wheel. She turned away from them all, from the sounds Mardon was making in his throat. The sunlight seemed weaker, the wind blowing more autumn than spring. She tried to convince herself that the potter's wheel had simply spun out of control and that she'd only imagined standing on the slopes of the valley. But she couldn't dismiss that feeling of collision, as if she had come up against a force capable of tearing a human mind apart.

8

When twilight veiled the walls of Market Primus, Kyndra turned away from the stern rail. She took the memory of Mardon's eyes with her. They'd left the man in the care of a kindly, soft-spoken healer, but Kyndra knew it was hopeless. Nediah could see no way of curing Mardon without putting himself at risk and conventional medicine would have little effect.

She shivered. Longing for warmth, Kyndra followed a lamp-lit passage down into the body of the airship, out of the evening wind. Gone was the excitement of seeing the capital. All she wanted now was to go home. Kyndra briefly closed her eyes. *You don't have a home any more.*

When she opened them, she found herself outside Argat's saloon. One of the doors stood ajar, allowing a chink of light to spill out onto the shadowy floor. The glow fell across her boot, stressing the creases in the leather. She listened. A distant chatter came from the galley where the sailors were finishing their meal, otherwise the corridors were silent. Brégenne was out on deck. She liked to stand under the moon, sometimes for hours at a time. As far as Kyndra knew, Nediah was in his cabin, still pondering the enigma of Mardon's affliction.

She put her eye to the gap, looking from side to side, but

there was no one in the slice of room that she could see. Holding her breath, she pushed open the door. It swung soundlessly.

The saloon was empty. Kyndra exhaled and stepped inside, easing the door shut behind her.

In the eerie quiet, warm lamplight fell across the dining table and gleamed on the panelling that lined the room. Each corner housed a towering shelf made to fit the contours of the airship. In the north corner stood a desk, a vast map unfurled across its polished surface. The inking was exquisite. Kyndra leaned over, running her eyes over a host of places she had never seen.

The Valleys grew from a green nib, tucked away on the right. The letters looked unimaginatively narrow compared to the crimson copperplate that proclaimed the names of the larger settlements. A horse with a violently inked mane pranced next to Hrosst, a city surrounded by plains three times the size of the Wilds. A grim march of trees presided over the mountainous territory in the north. Ümvast lay somewhere beyond those tangled branches, riven from the civilized world by the expanse of the Great Northern Forest.

Kyndra turned her eyes south. There the land was squeezed between the desert and Mariar's impassable sea. Numerous explorers had attempted a crossing, and if they returned, they returned unrewarded. They claimed the water was endless, a great shining sheet whose furthest waves had never known land. Kyndra inspected the archipelago just off the coast. A prickly fruit was inked there in ochre. It strongly resembled the one she'd acquired from Sky Port East.

Kyndra skirted several low tables, making for the opposite corner of the saloon. The shelves here were stacked with bizarre objects. One was a kind of snail shell, but huge and pearlescent. Its interior gleamed, as if it had borrowed the first flush of the dawn. Next to it rested a stone the shade of night beneath a forest canopy. Jagged edges showed where it had been hewn from some larger rock.

Other exhibits sat in glass boxes. It was a moving museum, constantly swelled by the *Eastern Set*'s adventures. How long had it taken Argat to accumulate these treasures? Some must be worth gold to merit protection behind such clear glass.

Fascinated, Kyndra crisscrossed the room. Arranged in macabre displays were several fish skeletons, tiny bird skulls, a rabbit's foot and a jar labelled *pickled sea-horses*. A horn much larger than a ram's hung above these gruesome offerings. It was broken, as if snapped off by a great impact. Cold violence leaked from it, or so Kyndra imagined.

She stepped away and bumped into a small table strewn with objects. A bright green feather fluttered to the floor. Kyndra made to catch it, but it slipped through her fingers. As she bent to retrieve it, a small leather bag caught her eye. Ignoring the feather, she straightened and reached for the bag instead. It was a pouch, somehow familiar, with a drawstring pulled tight around its top. Kyndra loosened the string. The inside of the bag was dark and at first it seemed as if nothing was there. She peered closer and something inside shifted with the tilt of her hand. Kyndra tipped the pouch over her open palm.

Red earth trickled onto her skin and immediately began to writhe as if alive. Frozen in shock, Kyndra stared at it, watching as the sand mounded into a red valley, capped by hills at each end. The living grains built a citadel on her palm. She'd seen it before: Solinaris, with its spires and parapets and its shining drawbridge. Figures climbed out of the valley floor. It was an army, set for a siege. Kyndra watched as they began to march on the citadel, tiny spears uplifted in challenge.

'I see you couldn't help yourself.'

Kyndra's hand jerked and the earth crumbled and spilled from her palm. She took a shuddering gasp and rubbed her hand furiously on her trousers, trying to rid herself of the feeling. Then strong hands seized her shoulders and spun her roughly around. Kyndra blinked up into Argat's angry face.

'I'm sorry,' she said. Her voice rasped and she coughed. 'I was only looking.'

'Those who *only look* sometimes see more than they'd like.' Argat's eyes were penetrating. He let go of her shoulders, took the pouch and scooped up the earth from the polished floor. The grains adhered as if drawn irresistibly together. Each one returned smoothly to the pouch, funnelled by the captain's hand. Kyndra watched it carefully, but it remained inanimate. Had Argat seen the valley and the army on her palm?

'I was interested in your collection,' she said quickly, Argat's silence unnerving her. Again she glimpsed the unanswered question that was always in the captain's eyes. Now there was more to it: alarm and a stark curiosity.

'I don't doubt,' Argat said finally. 'It is the work of many years and many journeys.' He pulled the drawstring tight and tucked the pouch into his shirt.

Kyndra watched the bag until it disappeared. She could still see the bloody hue of the earth. It haunted her, unnatural and alien. 'What was that?' she asked, not expecting an answer.

'Nothing of great value.' Argat looked down. 'An oddity. Like the rest of these things.' He swept up the green feather at his feet and presented it to her. 'Why don't you have this?'

Kyndra slowly took the feather. It was rather dirty, she saw now, with a dark smear at its base. She held it gingerly between forefinger and thumb and resolved to throw it away as soon as she could.

Argat observed her coolly. The pouch with the earth formed a bulge in his shirt. 'It's getting late,' he said, though Kyndra knew it could be no more than two hours to midnight. 'You don't seem well. Perhaps the sky doesn't agree with you.'

Kyndra wiped a hand across her brow and looked at the cold sheen on her fingers. 'Perhaps,' she said.

Captain Argat walked her to the door and held it open. 'Goodnight, girl.' His face was inscrutable.

Kyndra forced herself to leave unhurriedly. Only when the door clicked shut did she quicken her pace. She couldn't go back to her cabin. Nediah would hear her. If he came out to speak to her, he'd notice her pallid cheeks and the sweat on her brow. He would ask questions.

A dull throbbing began behind her eyes and Kyndra rubbed her forehead, digging in her fingers. Where could she go? As she stumbled through the airship's corridors, flickering night lamps cast their shadows across her path.

Four times she'd seen the fortress Solinaris and each time was different. She had dismissed the first two as dreams, but she couldn't do the same for the vision in the market. For one reeling moment, she'd been in another place: standing on that hill and watching the army close on the citadel. It was so real; she could remember the smell of heated air and the brush of the evening wind on her face. Rather than a vision, it was more like . . . a memory.

Kyndra took a few deep breaths. The earth had shown her the army too. Whose was it and why had it not appeared to Argat as well?

She found herself at the stairs to the deck and climbed them, holding tight to the rail, gulping down the breeze that gusted into the airship. The *Eastern Set* pulled on its anchor chain. Strong winds blew from the north tonight and she raised her collar against them. Her palm itched, as if it wanted to feel the red earth once more.

Kyndra wiped both hands on her trousers and leaned on the side of the ship. She gazed at the silent land sleeping beneath her feet, and though all was tranquil, she felt afraid. The airship was carrying her inexorably closer to the unknown and she couldn't help imagining that some unseen will directed her steps.

Isn't that what you wished for? her own voice asked her slyly. *A great adventure like the ones in your stories?* But none of those stories ever mentioned the fear, the uncertainty or the homesickness. She had left her family in a pit of fire and death, a pit she herself might have dug.

She wasn't in a story. Her own choices had led her here. Kyndra lowered her head to the rail and squeezed her eyes shut.

The headache kept her company until midnight. Kyndra had spent the time staring at the dark ground, letting her thoughts drift to the creaking of the ship. Finally she stepped away, body stiff from her long vigil, and headed for her cabin.

Nediah's door was slightly open and Kyndra heard talking. Although they spoke quietly, she recognized the voices. '. . . know about it,' Argat was saying. 'She's up on deck now. When I tell someone not to trespass, I mean it.'

'I'm sorry, Captain. She promised us she wouldn't.'

Kyndra's heart began to beat sickly. She hadn't considered that Argat would tell anyone.

'Where is the item in question?' Nediah asked.

'Locked in my chest.'

'How did you come by it?'

A pause. The door clicked shut and Kyndra swore silently. A short span of corridor separated her cabin from Nediah's, which was enough to ensure she wouldn't hear a thing in there. Then her gaze fell on Brégenne's door. Kyndra was certain that the woman was still on deck, as she'd seen her at the stern not half an hour ago, a small journal in hand. With any luck, her notes would keep her there. Palms slick, Kyndra tried the handle of Brégenne's door. It opened and she darted inside.

The room was much larger than hers, she saw with an itch of annoyance. Instead of a hanging berth, there was a proper bed, its feet nailed to the floor. A pile of black silk lay across the blanket. Kyndra blinked at it, recognizing the garment that had fallen out of Nediah's bag. Tearing her curious eyes away, she pressed her ear against the cool surface of the wall.

'No. I acquired it recently.'

'From whom?'

'That's my business.'

'Then why have you come to me?' Nediah asked bluntly.

Silence. 'The girl. Who is she?'

'She's our companion.'

'And nothing more?'

'I'm afraid I don't understand your meaning.'

'I think you do. I think you know why, out of all the hundreds of things in my saloon, she chose to pick up that bag.'

'Really, Argat,' Nediah said, frustration clear in his voice. 'I think you're reading too much into this. I'm sorry she trespassed. I'm sure she'll apologize in the morning if she hasn't already, but it's past midnight. Can we leave it be?'

More silence. Kyndra pressed her ear closer. 'Perhaps', Argat said coldly, 'I'm asking the wrong question.'

'What do you think you are doing?'

If the captain's voice was cold, Brégenne's was quiet ice. Kyndra leapt away from the wall as if stung, her heart pounding. She hadn't even heard the door open.

'Answer me.'

She desperately wanted Brégenne to be quiet, or Nediah would know at once that she'd been eavesdropping. She didn't know why that mattered to her, but it did. She sprang past Brégenne to slam the door shut. Then she whirled around and held up her hands in a placating gesture.

Brégenne's white eyes seemed portals to her outrage. They blazed in the dim room.

'Brégenne?' It was Nediah's voice outside the door. Kyndra shook her head, mouthed *please*. The woman didn't blink.

'Can I come in?'

'Not now, Nediah.'

'I need to talk to you. It's important.' Nediah sounded as anxious as Kyndra felt.

'It can wait, I'm sure. I have some things to sort out.'

'But—'

'No. Half an hour, Nediah, and I will be free to listen.'

They heard nothing from the man beyond the door and Kyndra was sorry for him.

'This had better be good,' Brégenne said softly. She folded her arms and – deliberately, it seemed – sat on the black silk. 'I am waiting.'

There was nothing Kyndra could say to justify her presence, except to tell the truth. Her blunder over the wine had taught her that. 'Nediah wants to talk to you about me,' she began.

Brégenne raised an eyebrow, but stayed silent. 'I came in here . . . to listen in on his conversation with Argat,' Kyndra said in a rush. She watched Brégenne's face carefully, but the woman showed no sign of approval or disapproval. She simply sat there, sphinx-still, her arms crossed beneath her breasts. 'I was in the captain's saloon.' She told Brégenne about the earth and the dreams she'd had back in Brenwym, but decided to leave out the vision she'd seen in the marketplace, frightened to think about what it meant. She described the citadel and the red valley and the headaches she suffered afterwards. 'The earth showed me the same things,' she finished, 'but it only worked for me, not for Argat. He might have glimpsed them over my shoulder, though.' Kyndra heard her voice tremble. 'I don't like them. I don't know how to stop seeing them.'

'They started on your Inheritance day?'

Kyndra nodded. 'I almost missed the Ceremony because of the first. I thought it was just a dream at the time.' She paused. 'Now I don't know what to think.'

Brégenne unfolded her arms. 'Thank you for telling me. It's more important than ever that we reach Naris swiftly.'

Any relief Kyndra had felt at being able to talk about the visions evaporated. 'Why?' she asked. 'What can they do there?'

Brégenne twined her hands together. 'I think we can help with the headaches. As for the visions, we have ways to examine a person's mind by means unavailable to others.'

'Examine a person's mind?' Kyndra repeated. She didn't like it. Just the thought of Brégenne poking around in her head was enough to trigger a nervous sweat. A new thought occurred to her and she shivered. 'You don't think I'm going mad like that man in the city?'

'Stopping the headaches may be enough,' Brégenne replied without answering Kyndra's question.

This *definitely* wasn't enough for Kyndra, since the subject Brégenne skirted round was her immediate future. She crossed her arms. 'Why are you taking me to Naris? There's something you're not telling me.'

'There is.' Brégenne stood up and moved towards the door. 'And the reason for my silence is simple. You wouldn't believe me.'

While Kyndra stared, slowly shaking her head, Brégenne jerked the handle of the door and pulled it open.

Nediah leapt back against the opposite wall, hitting his head on an extinguished lamp. He cursed quite inventively and then the dark flush that always lurked beneath his skin rose to the surface. It was too much for Kyndra. She laughed. Her fear of whatever Brégenne was keeping secret lent it a slightly desperate edge.

Brégenne did not laugh. She fixed her glowing eyes upon her companion. 'I take it *this* is the important subject you wished to discuss.' She nodded at Kyndra.

'Yes,' Nediah said, rubbing the back of his head. 'But I didn't think she would come to you.'

Kyndra shifted uncomfortably. Nediah was right; telling Brégenne about the visions was the last thing she'd have done, given the choice.

'She saw sense,' Brégenne said. Kyndra opened her mouth to protest, but the woman shot her a white glare and she closed it again. She owed her, and Brégenne knew it.

9

They arrived in Jarra near sundown. The *Eastern Set*'s stern paddles churned the air, speeding them through the late afternoon. The airship had maintained its impressive pace after leaving the capital, but Kyndra was already anxious to be off it. Not that she was looking forward to what would come next. Brégenne's words about Naris crouched in a fraught corner of her mind, tormenting her with images of her skull being opened by thin-fingered people.

It was hot on deck, so Kyndra shed her jerkin and rolled the sleeves of her shirt as high as they would go. Then, feeling reckless, she leapt onto the starboard rail. Grabbing one of the ropes, she leaned out, letting the wind blow the hair off her forehead. She grinned – now this was flying. From her vantage point, she could see down the whole length of the airship. Its body was like a gleaming animal, flesh dappled with cloud shadows. The oiled chain clanked, as the ground rushed below her. Everything was wind and world and hazy, rusting light.

A sailor's sharp word ended her flight and Kyndra jumped down. As if she'd left them on the deck, her fears flowed back to her chest where they clung like a winter fever. She snatched up her jerkin and put it on, pulling its laces tight. Suddenly the sun was too strong and the cooling wind too chill.

Kyndra wandered back to the cabins. Nediah, she saw, was repacking the saddlebags. 'How are the horses?' she asked him.

'Not happy. They've been cooped up for too long. But they'll get their wish to run soon enough.'

She frowned. 'What do you mean?'

Nediah's hands paused and he glanced up from where he sat on the floor. 'Thanks to your antics in the saloon, Argat told me he wants you off his ship the moment we reach Jarra.'

'But I—'

'It's his ship, Kyndra. His rules.'

Kyndra was silent, feeling guilty. Nediah shook out two shirts, laying one on the narrow berth.

'How are we going to reach Murta without another horse?' she asked.

'We'll think of something.' Nediah stowed the other shirt in the saddlebag and then gave her a crooked smile. 'You seem to have a talent for making enemies.'

Kyndra's protest shrivelled in her throat. She remembered the angry, frightened faces in Brenwym and the shouts of condemnation.

'Murta is near Naris, isn't it?' she said quietly. 'That's why we're going there.'

Nediah nodded, pulling the buckles tight on the saddlebag before rising and stashing it in a corner. Then he turned to remove his shirt, picking up the fresh one he'd laid out ready.

Kyndra blushed and was about to flee the room when she caught a flash of gold. Instead, she found herself staring. An intricate net of shining lines scored Nediah's back. They curved and plunged around each other, forming a great circle whose rays burst out like wings across the man's shoulders. Kyndra gazed raptly until the tattoo vanished under the clean shirt and Nediah turned to meet her eyes.

'The marks of my trade,' he said shortly. 'All Wielders bear them.'

Jarra was little more than an outpost in the west: a few buildings and two sturdy docks.

'Not many live here,' First Mate Yara told Kyndra, as the *Eastern Set* whirred to a halt. 'It's isolated and the soil's too poor to take crop. But the original workshops were built out here many years ago and the Assembly won't spend the gold it'll cost to relocate.'

'Yara!' a voice cried.

In one smooth movement, Yara gave her mooring line to a crewman and leapt the gap between airship and dock. She landed catlike on all fours. An equally tall woman with the same dark skin hurried to embrace her. When they parted, Kyndra saw that the stranger's face was a mirror of Yara's. Throwing a tumble of hair over her shoulder, she smoothed out the short scroll that Yara had squashed in her hug and looked expectantly at the first mate.

Yara shouted an order and crates soon began to arrive on the dock, carried up from the airship's hold. The woman Kyndra took for Yara's sister ticked them off, tucked the grubby quill pen behind her ear and then seized the first mate's hand. They slid down the ladder and – talking rapidly – disappeared into one of the whitewashed buildings on the ground.

Nediah appeared, loaded down with saddlebags, and Brégenne stood beyond him, characteristically hooded. She was speaking to the horses. As if they sensed their impending

135

freedom, the two stamped happily on the deck, attracting irritable looks from Captain Argat. Kyndra watched him approach with some trepidation, but the man addressed himself solely to Nediah.

'The rest of my fee.'

'Of course,' Nediah said smoothly. He dipped into a pocket and tipped a few small golden coins into Argat's hand.

The captain stared at them and then swiftly closed his fist. 'These are stamped with the Murtan sigil,' he hissed.

Nediah raised an eyebrow. 'Is that a problem? I have silver capitals if you prefer.'

An ugly look contorted Argat's face. 'Get off my ship,' he growled. Without looking once at Kyndra, he turned and strode away.

'What was that all about?' Kyndra asked once they and the horses were back on solid ground.

'Our Captain Argat's a superstitious fellow,' Nediah said, as they wandered towards the ramshackle town. 'I promised to pay him gold if he'd take us to Jarra. Unfortunately for him, he didn't specify what kind.'

'Gold is gold.'

'True enough, but he'll have a hard time spending those coins. There are few who'd accept them. Such is the power of rumour.' Nediah grinned. 'He'll have to trade them for half their value.'

Kyndra felt a peculiar pity for Argat. 'What's so bad about the Murtan sigil?' she asked.

Nediah gave her a sidelong glance. 'Although the coins are stamped in the town of Murta, the ore is mined in Naris and that results in a rather unusual effect. The coins show Murta against a backdrop of mountains.' His eyes grew distant. 'But some who look at the coins see another mountain, black and twisted, which throws its shadow across the town. A blink and it's gone. Enough people have seen the mountain in the coins to consider them cursed.'

The first stars were visible in the night sky. Kyndra stared up at them, hugging herself against the thought of the disfigured peak. She knew what was in the coins without needing to see one. It was the fortress of Solinaris – or what was left of it.

'I doubt we'll be able to find a third horse.'

Brégenne's words broke Kyndra's trance. Her head snapped down and she darted a guilty glance at the blind woman. Brégenne's white eyes glowed brighter now that they were away from the airship. 'I'll make a few enquiries,' she said, turning down one of the dirt roads that quartered Jarra.

Nediah started to follow her. 'Let me come with you.'

'No,' Brégenne said sharply over her shoulder. 'Stay with Kyndra. I won't be long.'

Nediah sighed as he watched her vanish into the shadow of a building. He motioned to Kyndra and the two of them looped the horses' reins around a tree and seated themselves on the rocky ground beneath.

'Is she angry with me?' Kyndra asked quietly.

'No.' Nediah propped his chin in his hands. At that moment, with his patched cloak gathered on his back, he looked nothing like one of the Wielders of legend.

'It's just that she's hardly spoken to me since I told her about the earth. And it's my fault we can't take the airship to Murta.'

'She's worried about the envoi,' Nediah said, his eyes searching the dark street that had swallowed Brégenne. 'Even if we do find a third horse, the journey will take three or four times as long.'

Kyndra nodded and they sat in silence for a few moments. Then she noticed the tavern that Yara and her sister had entered earlier. 'Can't we go in there?' It was a tall structure peppered with windows. The lowest ones were full of light and the sounds of gathered people leaked out to where they sat under the stars.

'I'm not making that mistake again,' Nediah said wryly, wiping a hand over his face. 'And it's a pleasant evening. I'd rather be outside to enjoy it while I can.'

Kyndra looked curiously at him. 'What do you mean?'

'We're almost home.'

She waited for more, but Nediah said nothing and his green eyes were remote. Kyndra realized he was gazing still further west at something as yet unseen.

'I don't understand,' she said softly. 'Aren't you glad to be going home?'

Nediah blinked. 'I suppose. But there'll be a hearing. Even if we come out of it well, Brégenne and I won't be able to leave the citadel any time soon.'

'You said you always travelled together,' Kyndra remembered. 'For safety.'

Nediah smiled. 'That's how a Solar–Lunar pairing works. It means we are never defenceless and can watch one another's back should events get out of hand. But any display is strictly prohibited unless the situation threatens our lives. When we return,' Nediah added, losing his smile, 'Brégenne will have to answer for breaking that law.'

Kyndra wondered whether she ought to feel guilty, but, after all, it wasn't *her* fault that Brégenne had used her powers in front of everyone in Brenwym.

More stars glimmered into view and a wind picked up,

blowing towards them out of the west. Kyndra pulled her cloak around her shoulders, gazing at the distant, twinkling lights. 'I thought there was another power,' she said. 'That poem mentioned it. The Starborn.' She hadn't thought about the poem for several days.

Nediah was a still shadow beside her. 'They are long gone.'

'What happened to them?'

The man's gaze wandered across the sky. 'They were rare in the first place. Only a few are recorded in Acrean history and none has appeared since the Deliverance.'

'There are stories.'

'Few.' Nediah took his hands from his pockets and rubbed them. 'They were greatly feared, for their power was born of the stars – all the countless suns separated from us by the frozen wastes of the void. It made them cold people, amoral even. They lived by their own laws.'

'But were they Wielders like you and Brégenne?'

'Not really. Their power was not restricted to day or night. It was universal, some said limitless, though I'm not sure I believe that. They kept to themselves and – according to some strange rule of the cosmos – no two were alive at the same time. That was something to be thankful for. Not even Solinaris could have withstood an alliance between two Starborn.'

'Why do you keep talking about Solinaris and Naris as if they're separate?' Kyndra asked. 'Aren't they the same place?'

'Yes and no.' Nediah lowered his face until his mouth was in shadow. The moon shone on his closed eyelids. 'Solinaris was destroyed in the Deliverance, at the end of the war. What remains is Naris – the dark mountain and my home.'

Such was the weight in his voice that Kyndra kept the rest of her questions to herself. The minutes passed and the moon rose higher and finally they heard footsteps coming out of the night.

'They won't sell,' Brégenne announced irritably, as she strode up to them.

'I'm not surprised,' Nediah said. He climbed to his feet. 'Any horse is worth its weight in gold out here.'

Brégenne gave her mare an apologetic pat. 'Sorry, girl.' She turned her moonlit eyes on the other two. 'There's no help for it. We'll have to do this the slow way.'

'Kyndra can ride with me like last time,' Nediah said. 'We'll go easy over the worst parts.'

'No.' Brégenne shook her head. 'I'll ride with you and Kyndra can have Myst.' She stroked the grey mare's mane. 'She'll look after her. She knows her way.'

Nediah's gaze flicked between the two women. 'I guess it makes sense,' he said. Kyndra was about to ask him just exactly *what* made sense, but the tart words died on her lips. She realized that she stood at least half a head taller than Brégenne. And the blind woman was slimmer too, she admitted. She'd be less of a burden on Nediah's mount.

'Uncle can cope,' Nediah said with an affectionate glance at his horse.

Kyndra stifled a laugh. 'Your horse is called *Uncle*?' She jumped at a burst of humid air huffed on the back of her neck. Nediah's stallion stared at her with large, liquid eyes.

'Yes,' Nediah said mildly, 'named in memory of the Hrosst breeder who tried to renege on our deal.'

'What happened to him?' Kyndra edged nervously away from the horse.

'Nicked himself with his own poisoned dagger.' Nediah's eyes narrowed. 'Quite tragic, really.'

*

The days that followed were as long and slow as Brégenne had intimated. Kyndra became used to Myst's rolling gait, though she inevitably fell asleep with aching muscles. Each hour of daylight found them further west. The terrain grew more rugged, the rarely used trail cluttered with rocks and pebbles. It stalked bluffs, ran down into chalk-choked valleys and out onto vast plateaux. Above them hung the elevated chain that marked the path of the airships, clankingly mocking their progress when the wind blew.

The strain of carrying two people over such mountainous terrain finally began to tell on Nediah's horse. They'd frequently have to dismount and walk – Kyndra included – until both mounts had recovered. The ground only grew worse as they moved west and Kyndra began to wonder what kind of people would willingly choose to live out here, surrounded by leagues of rock and shale. People who wanted to keep out the world or people the world wanted to keep out?

Water became hard to find. They would follow a stream for as long as they shared its course before filling each of their containers to the brim and parting ways with it. Their supplies grew scanty too. One morning, sixteen days west of Jarra, hard cheese and a couple of even harder loaves were all they had left.

'How much further to Murta?' Kyndra asked, eyeing her portion unenthusiastically.

'This will have to see us through another day,' Brégenne said, nibbling on a corner of cheese. Kyndra watched her make a face. 'By all the kingdoms, Nediah, where did you get this? I hope you didn't pay for it.'

Nediah chuckled. 'One of the *Set*'s crew gave it to me. She said it would keep for months.'

'This crew member wasn't Yara, by any chance?' Kyndra asked. When Nediah nodded, she groaned. 'And you believed her.'

Brégenne tore off a chunk of bread with her teeth and swallowed it grimly. 'Let's move on. I wouldn't mind being hungry if it meant I'd never have to eat that cheese again.'

Once they'd packed the food away and given the horses their dwindling ration of oats, Kyndra mounted Myst and Nediah helped Brégenne onto Uncle's back. When the small woman was settled and Nediah had mounted too, she wound her arms around his waist. Kyndra watched a blush redden Nediah's cheeks, as it had every morning since they'd left Jarra, and she smiled to herself. Then Uncle began picking his way through the rubble-strewn path and Myst followed obediently in his wake.

The long days of riding and walking had allowed Kyndra plenty of time to think. She still had trouble believing that Wielders lived at Naris. Although she'd glimpsed the power that Brégenne and Nediah commanded, she couldn't imagine an entire community gathered out here in secret. What did they do? Why had they hidden themselves from the world? In the stories she'd read, Wielders spent their time helping people.

They helped you.

She remembered the chant: a life for a life. The mob had wanted her dead in that moment and might have succeeded if it hadn't been for Brégenne.

It was past midday when Myst snorted and stopped, ears pricked. Uncle took her lead and paused beside her. 'What is it?' Nediah asked his horse. The afternoon was one of dusty silence. Heat shimmered across bare rock and the stunted trees stood perfectly still. Then Kyndra became aware of a whirring

— distant at first but growing louder the longer she listened. Myst turned and Nediah whirled Uncle around. Brégenne's hands contracted on his waist.

A huge shape swelled out of the eastern haze and a shrill screeching reached them, as of metal scraping over metal. An airship. It was darkly impressive, silhouetted against the sky. Its shadow could have belonged to a flying castle or a beast kept aloft on bulbous wings.

'Argat,' Nediah said grimly, eyes narrowed against the glare. 'It's the *Eastern Set*.'

'What?' Kyndra frowned. 'Why would he follow us out here?'

Nediah cast a speculative look over his shoulder. 'Brégenne?'

The small woman coloured, but said nothing.

Argat stood at the prow, Yara by his side. His bristling figure was now quite clear. At the sight of them, Argat's lips pulled back in a snarl and he shouted something. The airship began to slow.

'I don't like this,' Nediah murmured. 'Brégenne, get down. Change horses.'

'Nediah—'

'Now,' Nediah said firmly.

Brégenne closed her mouth and, without further argument, slipped off Uncle's back.

'Kyndra, make for the ridge,' Nediah said. 'Go carefully, it's steep. I'll handle this.'

'Are you sure?'

'Don't argue,' Nediah snapped and Kyndra swallowed her offer of help. Like Brégenne, she'd heard the warning in Nediah's voice. And what could she do anyway? What did Argat want?

The ship's rear paddles slowed and stopped. The craft shuddered. Before it had even come to a halt, Argat, Yara and three crew members – armed with blades and bows – seized ropes that hung ready at the rails. Kyndra gave a shocked gasp as they launched themselves off the airship.

The sun brightened Yara's knife to a yellow gold. She held it between her teeth, lips pulled back from the hot metal. For the first time, alarm coursed through Kyndra. Once they were safely on the ground, Argat's crew drew their weapons and broke into a run.

'Where is it, girl?' the captain howled as he sprinted towards them, a serrated blade in each fist. 'He gave it to me! It was meant for me!' The sweat of mania ran down his face and his eyes were wide with hatred.

The bowman in the *Set*'s crew nocked an arrow. Panicking, Kyndra threw herself sideways in the saddle, reaching for Brégenne's hand to pull her up, but the other woman tripped over a rock in her path. Missing Kyndra's fingers by inches, she fell to one knee. The bowman loosed his arrow.

Kyndra yelled and threw up both arms. There was a *boom* like silent thunder and the arrow burst into splinters. The ground in front of Kyndra shuddered and split. Chips of rock rolled into the gap and disappeared. A hundred yards from her, Argat's men skidded to a stop, staring aghast at the crack spidering towards them.

The pain was worse this time. Agony blotted out everything else. Kyndra lurched blindly for Brégenne's hand and caught it by sheer luck. With the last of her strength, she pulled the woman up behind her.

There was a voice roaring. Kyndra heard anger and shock and something much darker: fear. Blinking rapidly, she tried to focus. Nediah's mouth was open. The terrible sound rose from his throat. Then, without warning, both he and Uncle burst into flame. There were new screams. Caught between the earthquake and Nediah's hellish figure, Argat's crew retreated in the only direction they could: towards the airship, leaving their captain alone.

Kyndra stared, horrified. Clothed in white hot fire, even Nediah's skin was aflame. Uncle burned too with an awful majesty, hooves leaving flaming imprints on the rock. She could feel the heat rolling off the pair and smell the stench of Solar fumes. It was as if they'd stepped out of a nightmare.

Although fear showed in his face, Argat's gaze was shrewd and he gripped his blades with rage-stiffened fingers.

'Go!' Nediah yelled then and sent a tongue of flame to whip at Myst's flank. The horse leapt away. Kyndra sagged against Myst's neck and felt Brégenne reach around her to steady the reins. Her eyesight blurred and it was fortunate the horse knew the way. *Your riders are as blind as each other*, Kyndra thought and she began to giggle wildly, choking on her laughter.

'Kyndra,' Brégenne said urgently. It was the first time she'd spoken. 'Are you all right?'

Still slumped over Myst's neck, Kyndra realized her laughter had turned into shallow, pain-filled gasps. When they reached the ridge, she looked back and could just make out Nediah's fire as a smoking stain on the horizon. Then the steep downward trail hid it from view.

It could have been minutes or hours before the horse finally stopped and hands lifted her down. Nediah's skin was as unmarked as Myst's flank, the fire gone as if it had never been.

Kyndra dropped down to sit on a tree stump. Pine needles still lay in their rotting, winter piles and the scent of resin was sharp in her nose. She willed herself not to be sick. 'The arrow,' she mumbled.

'Hold still a moment.' A softer fire enveloped Nediah's hand, this time like liquid silk. When he placed it on Kyndra's brow, she felt warm and cool all at once. The painful fog in her head gave a last angry pulse and then subsided.

Nediah removed his hand and Kyndra saw him clearly. Words seemed to tremble in him, on the verge of speech, words that she had a sudden fear of hearing. But all Nediah said was: 'You saved her.'

Kyndra shook her head. In the absence of pain, she felt her confusion more keenly. 'I didn't do anything.'

'You stopped the arrow.'

'How could—'

'It's time to leave.' Brégenne stood just behind them, holding on to Myst's bridle. 'We can't be caught using power here, not this close to Naris. We're in enough trouble as it is.' When she paused and added quietly, 'Thank you, Kyndra,' Kyndra thought she detected a strange note of pleasure in the other woman's voice, as if something about the last few hours pleased Brégenne in unfathomable ways. Kyndra frowned, but allowed Nediah to pull her to her feet.

Once she was back in Myst's saddle, the horse's greater height awarded her an unobstructed view of the landscape. The line of the ridge fell away in a series of sharp trails and pines needled the slopes, spilling into the vast valley below. A black wall loomed in the distance: the mountains Argat so despised. They disappeared to north and south, an unbroken chain that barred the way west. She really had reached the end of the world.

Kyndra squinted. A town lay in the shadow cast by the

rocky leviathans and she thought she saw smoke curling up from its chimneys. Murta.

Without another word, they started down the ridge. Although Myst placed her hooves carefully, small stones still rolled beneath her, causing several heart-stopping moments where Kyndra thought she'd lose her balance. It was slow going and when finally they reached the valley floor, the sun balanced on the rim of the mountains.

Kyndra's thoughts turned from the mystery of the arrow to Argat. Why had the captain come so far out of his way? She remembered the mania in Argat's eyes, the snarl that curdled his lips. *What* was meant for him? And *who* had given it to him?

'Let her run,' Nediah called, startling Kyndra. 'It's the last chance she'll get for a while.' No sooner were the words out of his mouth than Uncle's stride lengthened into a ground-eating gallop. Myst leapt out joyfully to join him, her weariness temporarily forgotten. Kyndra couldn't help it; she smiled as the wind turned her cloak into a billowing wing. She could feel the horse's muscles bunching and stretching, the raw power in her stride.

Murta approached too swiftly and both horses slowed as they passed the town's unfortified boundary. Low buildings opened out on either side of Kyndra like the petals of a black flower. She turned her head to left and right, trying to take it all in.

Both the houses and shops were built of dark, veined stone. Murta's precise angles and odd, slated roofs discomfited Kyndra. The buildings she was used to sprawled around streets and squares, their mossy roofs soft with thatch. There was no sprawling here. Smooth roads neatly dissected the town, cutting it into squares.

Kyndra's skin began to prickle. Few people walked Murta's streets and all were dressed in black to match the stone. One woman fell back before their horses, wide eyes fixed on Brégenne and Nediah. She mouthed something unintelligible and stood with head bent until they'd passed.

The prickle on Kyndra's skin changed as they neared the far side of town. It thrummed through her, as if another heart beat in her chest. She rubbed her left side, uncomfortably aware of Nediah watching. The strange low houses grew further and further apart. Those on the outskirts had gardens and some were tiny farms. Chickens clucked, scratching in their tidy yards and white goats bleated. They were smaller than the black kind reared in the Valleys. Reena and Jarand had had six goats to provide for the inn and it had been Kyndra's job to feed them ever since she could remember. She watched the small goats frisking in their pens and felt a pang of homesickness.

When Kyndra raised her eyes to the mountains again, she saw a circular chasm which she could have sworn had been solid ground a moment before. A conical peak soared from its depths, black like its sisters, but folded and scarred. Its sides plunged into the chasm and she could see a series of shelves that spiralled down its length. Sheets of stone that shone like glass plated the summit.

Now that she stood in its shadow, Kyndra wondered how she could have missed it. She squinted at the crags that clawed earnestly at the sky and – just for a moment – saw battlements: a tapestry of towers and minarets, white-gold sills and windows that shone with a brilliant radiance. She couldn't take her eyes away; there were faces looking out at her, pale faces, carved as if from ice –

148

She blinked. The mountain stood dark and silent in the evening.

Nediah gazed at the peak with something close to trepidation. And Brégenne's face wore a tangle of feelings, until she stifled them. None of the people working on the farms spared a glance for the mountain. One man turned his gaze that way, but his eyes were unfocused, as if they looked at a distant landscape.

Kyndra heard the patter of disturbed stones and glanced back. One of the white goats had escaped its pen and was following them. Small hooves clopped over the bare rock that had superseded the cobbles of the town. The goat picked up its feet and overtook the walking horses, trotting placidly towards the chasm.

Kyndra whistled. The goat ignored her, as sure footed as its black-haired cousins. It effortlessly dodged boulders, heading for the cliff. She whistled again.

With a bleat of surprise, the animal stumbled and fell over the edge.

'No!' Kyndra cried. She stared disbelievingly at the place where the goat had disappeared. Goats never hurled themselves over cliffs. They were bred to dwell on the high slopes. Kyndra swallowed against the queasiness in her stomach. The little white animal simply hadn't seen the chasm. What had it seen instead?

Nediah reined in his horse. Both he and Brégenne turned their faces towards her. 'Why?' she asked them, hands slack on Myst's reins.

'Although the fortress of Naris casts its shadow over Murta,' Brégenne said, 'no ordinary human or animal can see it.' Her lips wore that strange spark of triumph Kyndra had seen earlier.

'In fact,' Nediah said, his eyes alight, 'the only people who can see Naris are Wielders.'

Kyndra looked back at them, feeling the mountain's heart pound in her chest. 'I can see it,' she said slowly.

PART TWO

10

'And you say you knew this from the start?'

'Almost immediately,' Brégenne replied. 'Gifted children are often found at the centre of dramatic events. Sometimes they are the cause.'

She stood in the Council's second-largest chamber, conscious of the stares she could not see. There were two men and one woman, she concluded, after hearing three sets of voices. And Brégenne knew exactly who they belonged to.

'But it's not a child you have brought us,' Lady Helira continued. 'She is – what?'

'Seventeen.'

'Too old to fit in easily. And you tell me she is wilful.'

'Stubborn . . . a little naïve perhaps. The Far Valleys are superstitious lands. If I didn't know better, I'd say they brought the Breaking on themselves.'

'The Breaking strikes by chance.' It was Lord Gend who spoke now, his voice husky from pipe smoke. 'Yet you felt it necessary to come to the girl's aid.'

Brégenne kept her voice level. 'I did.'

'You drew down Lunar power in front of an entire town.'

'I did,' she said again. 'I had to intervene. Kyndra would

153

have died that night at the hands of her own people. I couldn't let that happen.' She clenched her fists, holding them stiffly at her sides.

'Of course you apply your own rule of justice.'

Brégenne shivered at the honeyed voice and strove to keep her face impassive. Lord Loricus. She straightened her back. 'I did what I believed to be right.'

There was a sigh. 'You always do, Brégenne,' Helira said in a tone that betrayed her reproach.

'When will you test Kyndra?' Brégenne asked. 'You do believe she merits it?'

'Absolutely,' Loricus answered, but she sensed an undercurrent beneath the smooth word. 'Anyone who can see our city must be tested.'

'Thank you.'

'But your actions remain a cause for concern. I am surprised at you, Brégenne. I would never have marked you down as reckless.'

She could feel the rest of the Council's agreement. Chair legs creaked. She stayed silent, sensing the emptiness above and behind her. The chamber was long and narrow with an unusually high ceiling.

'Should you be mistaken in the girl's abilities,' Helira chimed in her clear, wintry voice, 'appropriate steps *will* be taken. Do you understand?'

Her breathing shallow, Brégenne nodded. 'But you will find, I'm sure—'

'That you are right? I hope so, Brégenne, for your sake.'

Chairs legs again, scraping over rock. The interview was over. 'Wait!' she called and the scraping paused. 'What about the man in Market Primus? Nediah examined him and found—'

'You should have concentrated your efforts on a swift return instead of wasting time in the capital,' Helira said. 'Not only are you weeks late, but you also failed to submit a comprehensive report.' She paused. 'I wonder, Brégenne, if you fully understand your situation. You and Nediah were dispatched to monitor the Breaking, to record its location, its intensity and the number of dead. I need not recount your list of responsibilities—'

'Potentials are found so rarely,' Brégenne interrupted. 'I thought their safe retrieval was more important than—'

'You thought wrong,' Helira said sharply. 'The Breaking is the one force in this world Naris cannot understand or control. That must change. Until it does, spilling our secrets to save one potential remains a most serious breach of conduct.'

The words brought with them a silence that closed around Brégenne, suffocating her. She tried to speak, but found nothing more to say.

'I urge you to give it some consideration,' Helira told her. 'In the meantime, you are dismissed.'

Silently fuming, Brégenne walked down the passageway, one hand on the stone wall. The Council didn't believe a case of such serious and unexplained injury in an ordinary person – however alarming – warranted their attention. She couldn't say she was surprised. From the moment she'd entered the chamber, every question had been about her actions in Brenwym. *And rightly so*, she reminded herself. *I knew what I was doing. I knew I was breaking the law.* But Kyndra's smoke-stained face was in her thoughts too, wild-eyed and disbelieving. If the girl had died that night and Brégenne could have stopped it, how would she have lived with herself?

She swallowed her irritation. Helira was right. She had shirked her duty and she fully deserved the reprimand. Brégenne shook her head and tried hard to forget the horror in Nediah's voice when he spoke of disintegrating minds.

She felt ahead with her right hand and found the sharp bend in the corridor that led to her quarters. After forty-six years, she knew the walls of Naris by touch. From the age of thirteen, the citadel had been her home and the centre of her life. If she'd never touched the Lunar, Brégenne reflected, she would be an old woman now. But power changed you and there was no going back. While she had the appearance of a woman in her thirties, her parents and childhood friends had died and aged without her. So many she had known growing up were now gone. When she had left for Naris, she had left that life behind.

Once she had shuffled through these corridors, clutching desperately at the black rock she couldn't see. Back then, vivid memories pierced every sightless moment. Summer skies, the brooch she had lost at Spring Dance, the rich green of woodland grass that left its dew like tears on her bare legs. She remembered the wind that blew across her homeland at dusk, the dawn that brought a pink stillness and the creases in her mother's face.

They used to make her cry, these thoughts. But one day she'd stopped crying and found herself unable to start again. She learned to see by moonlight, practising her own technique until she passed out from exhaustion. It wasn't the same. The moon bleached the colour from everything, turning it silver and shadowy. Still, it was sufficient to build her a mental map of the subterranean citadel they called Naris.

Her fingertips touched wood. Brégenne placed her palm against her door and it swung inwards. As soon as she stepped inside, she knew someone had been there. After her arrival, she'd barely had time to drop her belongings and wash her hands and face, before attending the Council's summons. But in the scant hour she'd been absent, somebody had come here.

Whoever it was had underestimated her. She knew this room and its few possessions as well as her own name. She had long ago devised a system to combat the unthinking cruelty of novices who borrowed her things. The first few times she'd searched the dormitory for hours, asking the same people whether they'd seen a hairbrush or that fossilized rock loaned from the archives. Her careful organization didn't stop them, but it did mean she knew when and what they had taken.

Brégenne shut the door and began to move deftly around, running her hands over familiar items: the tall vase she kept full of fresh flowers, the three-tiered bookcase that held her journals and a glass figurine of a wolf captured mid-leap, which Nediah had blown for her. The bed was neatly made with the ancient patchwork quilt she'd brought from home, her mother's scent fading over the years. *Sentimental*, Brégenne thought, knowing she would never part with it. Her feet sank into a carpet woven by the skilled fingers of the archipelago.

One of the wardrobe doors was open, only a fraction, but she knew immediately where the intruder had been. More alarming was the gap in her travel sack. Brégenne ran her fingers over the hooks that hadn't been fastened. The sack was another precaution. Two dozen closures disheartened even the most patient of thieves. Whether or not the intruder had deliberately failed to cover their tracks, Brégenne could only guess. There weren't many in Naris who'd have dared to enter here, let alone remove something from the room. Rank was seldom disrespected.

Brégenne knelt on the thick carpet. Nediah had described it to her: blue slashed with crescents of crimson, the edging looped chaotically in ribbons. The colour held no meaning for her, but her knees welcomed the soft threads.

She pulled the travel sack towards her, ran her fingers over its fastenings and slowly undid the rest of the buttons. She packed only what she needed in here – Nediah carried the rest – so the sack was almost empty. She was a poor target for thieves, Brégenne thought wryly, if they stopped to realize it.

As she searched, a prickling began to creep down her spine. By the time she'd pulled out everything except the item she sought, gooseflesh peppered her all over. Brégenne sat back on her heels and wished in that moment for light.

The pouch with the red earth was gone.

'So that's why Argat came after us,' Nediah said later, when evening had fallen. 'Why didn't you tell me you'd stolen it?'

'I'm telling you now,' Brégenne said testily. 'And how was I to know he'd follow us? I'm sure he has no idea what it is.'

'Well, neither do we.'

She frowned at the silvery shadow sitting in her chair. 'I know, Nediah. But someone does. Why else would they come here?' Her voice shook a little with the outrage she'd suppressed.

'What puzzles me,' Nediah said after a moment, 'is how they knew where to look.'

The question was one of the first Brégenne had asked herself. Who in Naris knew where they'd been and on which airship they'd travelled? How could they have known the captain of that ship had in his possession a small bag of earth? And, more to the point, how did they know she had taken it?

The moonlit figure that was Nediah uncrossed its legs and leaned forward. 'Brégenne, you need to be careful.'

She nodded absently, still absorbed in her host of questions.

'I mean it,' Nediah said. 'Not everyone in Naris can be trusted. There are factions that work for their own ends.'

Brégenne frowned. 'You can't mean the Nerian? They don't have one rational brain amongst them.'

Nediah didn't smile. 'Maybe so, but they have their own agenda.'

'Nediah, their *agenda* is born of a madman's ravings, which haven't an ounce of truth or sanity.'

'You know as well as I do that they wouldn't respect your rank. They would steal from Lord Gend, if he had something they wanted.'

Brégenne couldn't think of a reply. Nediah was right about the Nerian. It felt like the sect had always been there, eking out a stunted existence in the Deep – that labyrinth of tunnels far beneath the citadel. Their beliefs were heretical and ludicrous, and yet they had drawn away some of the citadel's best Wielders. Those who joined the Nerian lost their rank, their influence and their friends. And an exile to the Deep was forever. Apart from the occasional propaganda, the Nerian kept to themselves, their numbers too small to cause the Council any real concern.

'I can't see how this has anything to do with the Nerian,' she said aloud, 'but I won't rule out the possibility. I don't know what's in that bag and I don't like it that someone else does. We need to find out more about it.'

One of Nediah's silver-limned eyes flashed. 'Now that is something I can do.'

Brégenne smiled. 'I thought so. See if you can dig up any-thing in the archives. Don't ask Hebrin too many questions, though. He's sharper than he looks.'

Nediah grinned briefly. 'Where should I start?'

'Speak to Kyndra,' Brégenne said. 'She's the one who touched the earth. And ask her about the visions. It sounds like the two might be linked.'

Nediah looked at her and for a moment she was distracted by the shaded planes of his face, the dark fall of hair over his forehead. She shook herself and quickly rose to her feet.

Nediah stood up too. 'I'll go and see her now.' He paused. 'Do you remember what it was like when you first came here? The dark, echoing halls and heavy stone ceilings . . . All I could think about was sun and sea and the screeches of the cliff gulls I woke up to every morning as a child.'

Brégenne turned her face away. 'I tried not to think,' she said.

They'd put her in a room no bigger than the curtained alcove she'd liked to sit in at home. Kyndra perched on the narrow bed – the room's only piece of furniture – and wondered what was going to happen to her.

Earlier, she'd crossed the slim bridge that spanned the chasm, trying not to glimpse its terrible depths. A dozen or so people waited on the other side. They wore strange, parted robes, which left the legs free to move, girdled with various belts. Some were simple bands of leather while others were tooled in silver or gold. The robes were brown and spun from a common cloth. But as they led her through the gates of Naris, Kyndra spotted other observers dressed in robes of the richest gold or silver. Brégenne had already told her that garments in Naris were an indication of rank, that she should be polite and answer any question put to her.

Kyndra resented being given orders, but fear of the unknown kept her lips sealed. They left the horses in the care of a boy and moved on into a long hall full of floating fires. Kyndra watched them wide-eyed and edged away when any came too close.

She'd attracted quite a retinue by now, mostly comprising young men and women in brown. Brégenne and Nediah walked to either side of her, and their presence made Kyndra feel a little better. Beyond a second archway, the rough stone fell away and she found herself in a cavernous chamber – so vast that the far walls disappeared in a hazy light. Hundreds of small fires drifted through the air.

Kyndra blinked. As her eyes adjusted, she began to make out groups dotted around the chamber, the nearest of which had ceased its conversation to look at her. She felt each stare keenly, reminded of her walk to the tent during the Inheritance Ceremony. But there were no flaps here to duck beneath, no canvas to shield her from their eyes.

Brégenne and Nediah stopped and Kyndra came to a halt between them. Talk died completely. The followers in brown kept a respectful distance, for every person in the great chamber wore gold or silver.

'I see that you've not returned alone.'

Brégenne's head whipped towards the voice. A man of middling height in silver robes emerged from the haze. 'Alandred,' Brégenne said, and the man smiled.

'Your ears are as sharp as ever, Brégenne.' He came to stand in front of her and made a gesture that Brégenne performed a heartbeat later. 'We've missed you,' Alandred said quietly and Kyndra saw Nediah scowl.

'And *Master* Nediah too, of course,' the man in silver said, his smile growing wider. Nediah's face darkened and he opened his mouth.

'There will be time for pleasantries later,' Brégenne said.

Kyndra, watching the two men, suspected that the thunderclouds on Nediah's brow would lead to words which were not at all pleasant. He kept silent with a visible effort of will.

'Kyndra,' Brégenne said then, 'meet Master Alandred of the Lunar. He oversees the testing of those who show promise as Wielders.'

Numbly, Kyndra held out her hand. Alandred stared at the hand, as if confused, before laughing and shaking it. 'I forget how quaint these rustic greetings are,' he said, wiping a pretend tear from his eye.

Nediah gave Kyndra a tiny nod of sympathy.

'Kyndra, is it?' Alandred asked and she nodded, an even smaller movement than Nediah's.

'Excellent. I won't question Brégenne's judgement. If she says you show promise, then promise is what you show. We'll schedule a time for your test.'

Kyndra wrapped her arms around herself. 'What exactly does this test involve?'

'It's nothing to worry about,' Alandred said, waving a hand. 'You'll be given instruction before it's carried out.'

Whatever Nediah was about to say appeared to stick in his throat. A young man in brown had just hurried breathlessly up to Brégenne. His honorific gesture was so enthusiastic that it unbalanced him and he stumbled where he stood. 'Master Brégenne of the Lunar,' he panted. Brégenne turned her head towards him. 'You are summoned to an immediate audience.'

Although he didn't say with whom, Kyndra saw Brégenne's lips tighten. This was her only reaction.

Nediah looked far more concerned. The blood fled his cheeks, emphasizing his green eyes, and Brégenne seemed to sense his discomfort. 'Don't worry, Nediah,' she said. 'I'll speak with you later.'

Nediah did not look consoled and the messenger was still there, bobbing nervously in front of Brégenne. 'Please advise the Council that I will be with them shortly,' she told him, and the boy sped off. His belt bore a tiny silver thread, like a snake's tongue.

'Master Alandred will show you to a room, Kyndra,' Brégenne said and Kyndra's heart began to beat faster. She hadn't realized it before, but she found Brégenne's presence reassuring. The small woman had been there in Brenwym and she had seen Kyndra's home as it was before the Breaking. In this underground city, full of strange people with stranger powers, she and Nediah were the only ones who knew who Kyndra was and where she'd come from. Kyndra wasn't sure why this mattered, but it did. Distracted by the irony of this thought, she only realized she was alone with Alandred a few moments after Nediah's farewell pat on her shoulder.

Now Kyndra lay back on the bed, which wasn't especially comfortable, given its size, and stared at the black ceiling. Two hours had passed since Alandred had left her and she was beginning to feel the day catching up with her. There were no floating fires here to soften the dark stone. Instead, an old lamp hissed through its wick on the opposite wall, and by its spluttering light, Kyndra watched Wielders preparing for war.

. . . Gold- and silver-clad people hurry before her eyes, as she stands invisible amongst them. It's a feverish hurry that smells of fear. Carts roll through a small archway into the citadel, heaped for a siege with bags of oats, dried meat and fruit. A dozen young people in brown carry two pillars, which they position on either side of the great glass gates. There are markings in the marble floor that match the markings on each thick pole. After a moment, these runes begin to glow and the young people step back. Their faces are lit by the twin powers now activated in the wards.

The atrium blazes in the sun that streams through its crystal dome. And this glass curves right to the ground, so that all four walls are windows on the world. The floor portrays a night sky, studded here and there with gems.

An awful clarion note strikes the crystal and the Wielders halt as one, turning to the clear western wall. Beyond the glass, the land slopes away into a valley, its earth red as blood, as red as the armour of the force that advances, marching to that terrible horn. Their chants ring out in a counterpoint across the distance still to cross, to where the people of the fortress of the sun stand in horror – faces distorted behind their beautiful walls . . .

11

The door opened and the vision shattered into the rough black stone of her room. The space behind Kyndra's eyes filled with flame and she cried out, clutching her head. A click, footsteps over rock: someone was there. It felt like fire was falling from her eyes, scorching her cheeks.

'Hush, Kyndra, it's me, it's Nediah. You're safe.' The voice was a whisper, but she recognized it through the pain. She didn't want to open her eyes, or she'd see that great force marching implacably forward, bringing death with them.

Her face lay against something soft. She lifted her head, keeping her eyes closed. 'Where is the army?' she heard herself say.

'You were dreaming.'

Kyndra cracked open her eyes and Nediah flinched, as if he had seen something there to frighten him. 'I don't think it was a dream,' she said slowly.

'Another vision?' Nediah's green gaze was sharp with concern and something else; a question, perhaps. He let go of her shoulders and, suddenly awkward, Kyndra shuffled away.

'Maybe,' she replied. She didn't trust her legs to hold her, so she remained on the bed. Her eyes stung, as if from smoke. She rubbed them.

'Actually, I came to ask you about the visions,' Nediah said, 'but it can wait.'

'No.' Kyndra looked up. 'Go on.'

Nediah scrutinized her for several moments. Then he stood to lean against the wall and, for the first time, Kyndra noticed his clothes. 'You're wearing gold,' she said without thinking.

Nediah raised an eyebrow. 'And?'

'Well.' She hesitated. 'Brégenne made it sound like the people in gold and silver were . . . you know, much older.'

'How old do you think I am?' Nediah asked, sounding amused.

Kyndra blushed. 'I don't know,' she mumbled. 'Twenty-something?'

'Try twice that,' Nediah said and Kyndra failed to hide her astonishment. He smiled. 'Wielders age more slowly than other people,' he explained, 'and live longer. Perhaps because it takes a long time to learn how to use our power.'

Kyndra found herself smiling too. 'So how old is Brégenne?'

'It's rude to ask a lady's age,' Nediah said disapprovingly.

'You can ask mine.'

'I know yours.'

She glanced down. 'Unfair.'

'I was only raised to the gold last year,' Nediah confessed, plucking at the heavy robes. 'And it's still a bone of contention. Certain people like to forget it actually happened.'

Kyndra raised an eyebrow. 'Alandred?'

Nediah looked away. 'Always poking his nose into matters that don't concern him, talking to Brégenne as if he were her equal, as if—' He broke off, drew a breath and let it out slowly.

'Anyway, I came to ask about the earth you found in Argat's saloon.'

'Why?'

'Someone just stole it from Brégenne's quarters.'

Kyndra gaped at him. 'Brégenne took it from Argat? When? Why?'

'That doesn't matter.' Nediah ran a hand through his hair. 'What matters is that somebody here knew that she had it. And they gave her rank no thought before breaking into her rooms.'

'Her rank? Why would that stop them?'

Nediah folded his arms. 'You should know that Naris is governed by a strict hierarchical system. We earn our place through ability and deeds of merit. Brégenne is highly respected. She's found and brought many novices here and this theft is serious.'

'All right. But why did *she* steal it from Argat? No wonder he came after us.'

'Brégenne thinks the earth and your visions might be linked.'

Kyndra studied the palms of her hands. 'She never mentioned the earth. She was more interested in the headaches.'

'Yes,' Nediah said, and he began to pace as much as the tiny room allowed. 'That was because she suspected you were a potential. Those headaches are the result of trying to tap power that's not fully awakened.'

Kyndra said nothing. The idea that she could be a Wielder hadn't shocked her as much as it ought to have done, possibly because it was ludicrous. When she took their test, they'd discover that for themselves.

What will they do to you then? She tried to ignore the question that had crawled from one of the darker corners of her mind. *You've seen their city and learned their secrets. They'd be foolish to let you go.*

'What's wrong?'

'I don't think I'm a Wielder,' she said slowly. 'What happens to people who fail the test?'

'You won't fail,' Nediah said and came to sit next to her. 'Brégenne never makes a mistake. Some say she has a sixth sense when it comes to finding potentials.'

'I think she's made a mistake with me,' Kyndra insisted. 'I can't sense any of this Solar or Lunar energy you talk about. I don't even know what I'm looking for.'

'You've shown an aptitude for it twice already.'

She frowned. 'I have?'

'Remember in Brenwym?' Nediah asked and Kyndra nodded. 'You fought against Brégenne's binding when she tried to stop you running away. *And*,' he added significantly when she looked doubtful, 'you stopped that arrow today.'

Kyndra shook her head. 'That was the earthquake.'

'Earthquakes don't burst arrows in mid-flight.' Nediah gave her a penetrating look. 'And who's to say it was an earthquake?'

She let out an exasperated breath. 'How can I use a power I can't even feel? And it doesn't make sense,' she added. 'When Brégenne put that binding on me, it was night. The stuff with the arrow happened this afternoon. I thought you said Wielders are either Solar or Lunar.'

For a moment, Nediah looked uncertain, but then his face firmed. 'Cosmosethic energy first manifests itself as a force of will,' he said. 'Have faith in yourself. No one fails the test.' He looked away, but not before Kyndra snatched a glimpse of something he wasn't saying.

'You wanted to know about the earth,' she said to change the subject.

'Yes.' Nediah turned back to her. 'Can you tell me as much as you remember about it? I'm going to check the archives. And what did the bag look like?'

'I'll write it down, if you want,' Kyndra said. 'Is Brégenne absolutely sure it's gone? I mean, she might have missed—' She stopped at the glare on Nediah's face.

'She didn't miss anything,' the Wielder snapped and rose from the bed.

'Sorry.'

The apology didn't seem to touch Nediah. 'I'll be back with paper,' he said shortly and stalked out, shutting the door with more force than was necessary. Kyndra winced and decided it might not be wise to gainsay Brégenne in front of Nediah again.

The Wielder's exit had let in a burst of cold air. The lamp's flame guttered wildly over the stone, a dancer from a primitive time when the world was larger, and everything was possible. Kyndra looked away from the flickering wall. It was in those shadows that she'd seen the besieged citadel and she had no wish to return there. Instead she curled her feet up, rested her elbows on her knees and buried her face in her hands. Her palms prickled, as they always did when she thought about the earth. She closed her eyes, but the prickling followed her into the dark. Images came with it: a pennant snapping against the sky, a ridged wing, and always, always the glass citadel, flaming in the sun.

'Kyndra? Not another one so soon?'

Kyndra lifted her head too quickly and the room spun. When it righted itself, she saw Nediah standing in front her, clutching a sheaf of vellum, ink and an enamelled pen.

'No,' she said, waving away Nediah's concern. 'I was just trying to picture the earth.'

'I see.' Nediah seemed pleased. He dropped the items on the bed and stuffed his hands in his pockets, a gesture that didn't suit the stately robe. 'I'll leave you to it, then. Would you like some dinner?'

Kyndra's stomach rumbled at the mention of food and Nediah grinned. 'I'll bring you some.'

When the door had closed, Kyndra took the vellum and – in the absence of a desk – laid it on her knees. It was flawless, creamy and smooth, wholly unlike the parchment at home. The pen was beautiful too. It was blue and gold and held the ink neatly behind its shining nib.

Writing about the earth was oddly difficult. The rush of images it carried tried their best to manifest in the black letters Kyndra printed. Twice she scratched out lines she'd written, seeing the citadel there instead of the red soil. When she put down the pen and blew on the ink to dry it, she read:

> Bag made of dark brown leather with drawstring. No other markings.
> Earth – the empire has taken the valley, slopes running with fire, fingers sunk in the soil, wet like blood . . . it is their tears, hundreds in the city who resisted. But one came with the stars and he held a world in his fist – is red, coloured like blood. Dry and sandy, as if from a desert.

Kyndra turned cold. She stared at the lines written in her own hand, having no memory of anything between the thick black dashes. The citadel had crept in there, despite her best efforts. And it had not come alone. The whole paragraph was a jumble, incoherent and rambling. She couldn't show this to Nediah.

There was a knock on the door. Kyndra cursed and hid the pages under the bed's thin pillow. 'Just a moment!' She racked her brain for an excuse, but none came to mind. She just *couldn't* show Nediah that nonsense.

Kyndra opened the door, so busy wondering how to buy more time that the stranger in the corridor coughed nervously and took an uncertain step back. Kyndra blinked. 'Who are you?' she blurted.

The girl outside glanced over her shoulder and hissed, 'Can I come in?'

'All right,' Kyndra replied, eyeing the girl's brown robes and silver-threaded belt. She stepped aside.

The girl darted in. 'Please shut the door!'

Kyndra closed the door with a snap. As soon as the rectangle of wood obscured the corridor, her visitor relaxed and laughed a bit sheepishly. 'Sorry,' she said, her voice lighter now. 'I'm not supposed to be here.'

Kyndra stared at her. 'Why? What would happen if they found you?'

The girl's eyes were pale, almost colourless, and laughter lines dimpled the corners of her mouth. 'I'd rather not find out.' She smiled and the lines deepened.

Kyndra smiled too. 'So why risk coming?'

'Irilin,' the girl said, raising her hand, palm out. 'Iri for short. I wanted to be the first to meet you.' She flashed Kyndra some white, slightly crooked teeth.

'But how did you know I was here?' Kyndra asked. There was something immediately likable about Irilin. Her small features were set fairly wide apart, lending her face an appealing openness. She was shorter than Kyndra and seemed very young.

'Everyone knows. Potentials aren't found often. You're one of Master Brégenne's, aren't you?' Irilin asked and Kyndra nodded. 'Master Brégenne' sounded strange.

'You'll have to get used to calling her that,' the girl said firmly. 'Men and women are master alike and Wielders are mindful of status. Once you're into the habit, it comes naturally.'

'How old are you?' Kyndra asked curiously.

Irilin grinned. 'Getting used to that too? I'm twenty-one.'

'You don't look it.'

'I know,' Irilin sighed. 'Gareth says I'll look about ten years old forever.'

Kyndra laughed. 'My name's Kyndra, by the way.' She paused. 'Kyn for short.'

'Thought you'd forgotten to say,' Irilin said, her dimpled cheeks making her look even younger. 'Writing a letter home, are you?'

Kyndra froze and then remembered she'd pushed the offending paper under her pillow. The pen still lay on the bed, however, slowly oozing ink into the blanket. Before she could reply, Irilin said, 'I wouldn't bother. They won't let you send it.'

A whisker of cold stirred in Kyndra's blood. 'Why not?' she asked. 'I need to let my family know I'm safe. Can't letters reach here?'

The smile had slipped from the girl's face. She folded her arms and leaned back against the rough stone of the wall. 'Maybe, but nobody receives any. And it's too risky to send letters out. They could be opened and read. Naris is our home now. You'll learn that soon enough.'

'What if I don't want to learn it?' Kyndra said fiercely. No one was going to stop her contacting Reena and Jarand. She'd find a way.

Irilin gave a short laugh. 'I can see it's going to be fun with you here,' she said, though her smile wasn't quite as bright as before. 'Have you had any dinner?'

'Nediah's bringing it.'

'*Master* Nediah.'

'I can't imagine calling Nediah that. He's a friend.'

Irilin raised pale eyebrows. 'Is he? Well, I suppose he wouldn't mind if you didn't. He's only just a master.'

'I know. He said he was having problems with Alandred.'

Irilin made a face. 'No one likes Master Alandred. And of course he's been chasing after Master Brégenne for years,' she added offhandedly.

'What?'

'It's an open secret.' The girl's eyes twinkled. 'Everyone knows Master Brégenne wouldn't give him the time of day.' She grinned as if she had made a joke.

Kyndra realized her mouth was open. 'Brégenne? She's so . . . cold. It's just hard to imagine her—'

'That doesn't stop some people.'

Kyndra shook her head. 'So who likes who is a topic of conversation among the novices?'

'One of them,' Irilin said. 'Nothing escapes us.' She eyed Kyndra's outfit. 'Your trousers are too long, by the way.'

'Thanks, I know.' Kyndra hoisted them up. 'Can you tell me what the test is all about?'

'Have they scheduled it yet?'

Kyndra shook her head.

'The sooner the better, in my opinion.' Irilin cast the room a disparaging glance. 'Then you can move to a dormitory and—'

'Irilin Straa, what are you doing here?'

Irilin jumped. Nediah stood in the doorway, holding a tray. The smell of roast meat curled up from it enticingly.

Irilin scuffed a foot on the stone floor. 'I just came to say hello to the new potential.'

'Did you?' Nediah looked at Kyndra. 'I hope you found Irilin's visit educational because she's destined for the pinnacle this evening.'

The girl's face paled. 'No, not the pinnacle,' she whispered. 'Master Nediah, I was only up there last week.'

'I didn't realize you enjoyed it so much,' Nediah said, his eyes glittering. 'I'll have to arrange a few more excursions.'

'No, no more, I'll be good. Send me to the kitchens or down to the tombs, anything but the pinnacle.'

A grin flitted across Nediah's face. 'Very well,' he said. 'I'll think about it.'

Irilin opened her screwed-up eyes to look at Nediah. The difference in their heights was faintly absurd, Kyndra saw. With her long hair and delicate limbs, Irilin looked barely half her real age.

'You'd better hurry up or you'll miss dinner,' Nediah said pointedly.

'Oh! Yes, I'll go. Thank you, Master.' Irilin flashed Kyndra a smile and darted deer-like out of the room.

'What did she mean about the tombs?' Kyndra watched Nediah set the tray down on the bed. The accompanying cup of liquid teetered and she snatched it up before it added to the ink stain on the blanket.

'Exactly what it sounds like,' Nediah replied. 'We might live three or four human lifetimes, but we're not immortal. Where else do you think we'd bury our dead?'

'Oh.' Hundreds of decaying people right beneath her feet wasn't exactly a comforting thought. If visiting them was a punishment, Kyndra resolved to behave herself, at least until she managed to get out of here.

'So, do you have that description for me?' Nediah stood with arms folded.

Kyndra studied her potatoes. 'Not yet. That girl interrupted me almost as soon as you left.'

She felt more than saw Nediah's impatience. 'Could you see to it after you've eaten, please? It's important, Kyndra. I'd appreciate it if you took it seriously.'

Kyndra stared at her plate and nodded. 'I will, Nediah.'

'I'll make sure you're not troubled by other visitors,' the tall Wielder said, his hand on the door latch. After a pause he added, 'I'd eat that beef before it goes cold. Try the beans too. They're good.'

When Nediah had gone, Kyndra cut her meat into pieces just as she did at home, and pierced a little of everything on her fork before lifting it to her mouth. She ate slowly, despite her earlier hunger. The illusion of purpose she'd maintained during her days on the airship was starting to fade, its wide vistas narrowing to the four walls of this room.

She had found herself in Naris because it was Brégenne and Nediah's destination. Only now – sitting on the hairy blanket with a lump of meat poised on her fork – did Kyndra realize that Naris was *her* destination too, that Brégenne had intended it as such from the start.

She sank her teeth into the beef and wondered what Brégenne would say when she realized she was wrong.

*

Brégenne said nothing. She stared at Alandred, the midnight moon gilding each hair on his shaggy, grey beard. They were about the same age, she thought, though the years had been cruel to the Master of Novices. Except for those around her eyes, she knew her skin bore few lines, while the unforgiving moon gave Alandred a mountain's face, heavy with crags and shaded defiles.

'I thought perhaps you'd changed your mind.'

'Whatever gave you that idea?' Brégenne said dismissively. Alandred didn't respond and she sighed, adjusting the shawl around her shoulders.

'It's late, Alandred. I want to sleep.'

'No you don't,' he said and Brégenne opened her mouth in protest. 'Everyone knows you don't,' Alandred cut her off. 'I came because I knew you wouldn't be asleep. This is the only time I can talk to you privately since you're determined to keep that sycophantic hound at your side.'

'Leave him alone,' Brégenne snapped. A lock of hair fell out of its knot and she tucked it behind an ear. 'I don't see why you have any right to disturb me in the middle of the night, whatever habits I have.'

Alandred took a step closer and she dug her toes into the carpet, refusing to give an inch though instinct urged her back. She was acutely aware of her thin nightdress. Although it fell to her feet, the bodice was low, too low for comfort. She knew he was looking and cursed herself for not throwing the frivolous thing away. To make it worse, Alandred was only wearing a nightshirt over loose trousers and slippers. She needed to get rid of him.

Alandred made a sudden lurch towards her and she barely got a hand up before his arms enclosed her. Her body went rigid. His nearness disgusted her and she felt her heart flickering sickly in her chest.

'Perhaps this is what you want,' he breathed near her ear and she shuddered, turning her face away. She thought of the hand pressed against his chest and reached desperately for the moon that shone above Naris. Her fingers glowed.

With a crack like thunder, Alandred flew back and hit the door, denting the soft wood. He was on his feet immediately, silver bursting out of his skin, but she was too quick. A blazing rope snapped across the distance separating them, wrapped itself around his wrist and returned to her hand. The glow around Alandred vanished.

'A dirty trick,' he snarled. 'You won't be able to cut me off for long.'

'True,' Brégenne said coldly, drawing deep breaths. 'It would take a Solar to hold you properly. But we both know they are useless at night.'

Something in her words must have pleased him, for Alandred chuckled nastily. 'You'll come to my way of thinking, Brégenne. I can wait.'

Brégenne didn't reply. Against her better judgement, she let the Lunar block fade and Alandred opened the door. 'But I won't wait forever,' he said and left the room. With some degree of satisfaction, she watched him grope his way along the corridor, knowing that to him it was utterly dark.

She closed the door, added a second, more potent binding and retreated to her bed. The binding would unravel as soon as the sun rose, she knew, unless she strengthened it. A few moments passed and then her limbs started to tremble. She scowled at them, but they refused to respond. He could have come at her in the day, she found herself thinking, and what would she have done then?

Brégenne clenched her fists and forced her mind to quieten. It was more than she could stand. She would take this matter higher, as high as it took to stop Alandred in this foolish business. It had gone on far too long.

There was a knock at the door. The sound turned her cold before she pulled herself together and called, 'Who is it?'

'Nediah,' he said and, a moment later, she knew it was him. They were still paired through the Attunement, the rite that linked a Solar and Lunar Wielder together before they were permitted to leave the citadel. It allowed her to sense his presence when she concentrated. The muscles in her body uncurled and her breath left her lungs in one relieved rush. She lifted the binding from the door.

Nediah stood there, fully dressed. Lunar light limned the smooth crease of robe at his elbow and waist. She knew it was gold; only a master was permitted to wear silk. Seeing him in it still gave her a little shock, after so many years of coarse-woven brown. He stood over a head taller than her and his hair was an untidy mess, as if he'd run his hands through it several times tonight.

'. . . I cannot believe it. Are you listening, Brégenne?'

She shook herself, angry at her dreaming. 'Come in,' she said by way of apology. She stood aside so Nediah could move into the room, then she closed the door and leaned her back against it, hiding the dent left by Alandred.

'Are you all right?' Nediah turned his eyes on her. They were weary, she saw, but full of something he hadn't yet said. 'You don't seem yourself.'

'I'm fine,' she answered coolly, wondering how he always managed to sense her underlying mood. 'What is it?'

'Alandred's scheduled Kyndra's test for dawn.'

'What!' She realized her calm had slipped, but didn't bother to steady it. 'When, how?'

'Barely five minutes ago. It's gone up in the hall. There's no how to it. The Master of Novices doesn't need authorization for a test.'

'But he needs his volunteers. Most will be in bed by now and won't appreciate being woken to accommodate some whim of his.'

Nediah spread his hands. 'You know he has friends, Brégenne. He probably called in a few favours. He can do it.'

'The Council will put a stop to this. It's not fair to spring a test on a potential. There are rules—'

'Unspoken ones, yes,' Nediah said. 'But the Council won't involve itself in something like this. People will mutter and think Alandred a touch cruel, but it will go no further.'

She knew he was right. She bit her lip when she thought of Kyndra being pulled from her bed and forced up onto that cliff, still blinking the sleep from her eyes. *This is my fault.*

'Brégenne –' Nediah's voice deepened – 'are you sure you're all right?' He took a step towards her and she shrank back, the thought of Alandred still cold in her stomach.

Hurt dimmed Nediah's face. He retreated swiftly, dropping his arms to his sides. Brégenne wrapped hers around her middle, hugging the cursed nightdress to her skin.

As if her movement had drawn his attention to it, Nediah glanced at the dress and then moved his eyes to her face. 'I didn't hear you ask me *why* Alandred has done this,' he said softly.

She gazed at him, her mind full of Alandred's petty revenge, but when she opened her mouth to answer, the words stuck in her throat.

12

They woke her before dawn.

She must have been too deeply asleep to hear the knocking and only struggled into consciousness when someone shook her roughly. The rude awakening was nothing to the shock of finding a dark figure bent over her, hooded against the pre-dawn chill.

Kyndra gasped and jerked upright, knocking her head on the wall behind. As she rubbed at the spot, the figure resolved into Alandred. Kyndra blinked and shielded her eyes from the flickering silver fire that danced above the Wielder's hand.

'Used to getting up later, are you?' Alandred spoke in the same condescending tone as yesterday.

'No,' she answered. 'Most of my town gets up before the sun.'

'Good. Novices rise two hours before dawn.'

Kyndra blinked, but said nothing.

'Oh yes,' Alandred said, evidently assuming he had unsettled her. 'A Wielder's road through life is not easy. Novices learn from an early age that a disciplined set of feet are essential. I hope you are up to it, Kyndra Vale.'

Kyndra didn't trust herself to speak, so she nodded curtly

and pushed back the blanket. 'I will leave you to dress,' Aland-red said, even though she had only removed her jerkin, belt and boots before sleeping. 'You'll not see me until the testing. Another will come and show you where to go.'

The door closed and Kyndra scowled at it. No lock. She yawned and rubbed the sleep from her eyes. She'd been dreaming, but Alandred's intrusion had melted the details. The only thing left was a feeling, and Jarand had always insisted that the feeling was more important than the dream itself.

She hoisted up the long trousers Nediah had given her and belted them tightly. Wishing for a mirror, Kyndra swept her hair out of her eyes and tried to pat it into some semblance of order.

The door opened without invitation and a man stood there, his unapologetic hand on the latch. Kyndra pulled on her boots and straightened, nerves rattling around her stomach. When would she be told what to do?

'Excuse me,' she said, 'I don't understand what I'm . . .' Her voice trailed off. Without a word, the man had turned his back and started away down the corridor. Kyndra swallowed, gave the room a last glance and followed him out.

It was obvious that most of Naris still slept. A rhythmic beating reached her, not unlike the one she'd heard in Murta. It was as if a heart pounded somewhere in the body of this black leviathan. Kyndra's guide halted outside a carved door and, in the silence, Kyndra heard her own heart thumping a counter-beat.

The Wielder knocked twice upon the door. It opened immediately; the man standing there had been expecting them. Equally wordless, he fell into place behind Kyndra and they continued on, wending a convoluted path through the passages of Naris. Fires hung, fitfully adrift, their silver flames throwing the walls into relief. Some stretches of stone bore the marks of chisels, Kyndra noticed, while others ran straight for many yards, ledges cut into them like steps.

The ritual, as she saw it, was repeated. Another door knocked upon, another man waiting behind it. She now had a retinue of three. The silver-clad Wielder walked out in front. Those directly behind him were members of the Solar Order, golden robes dull in the gloom.

After two more knocks and two more men, it seemed the party was complete, for they left the corridors, crossed the huge hall – now just dimly lit – and made for an archway at the opposite end. It was smaller than the one Kyndra had walked through yesterday and the mantel carried a pattern of runes.

The men walked in single file, following a path that narrowed steadily until it almost brushed their shoulders. The last two had fallen into step behind Kyndra, as if to stop her from turning and fleeing. When it grew so dark that Kyndra couldn't see her feet, the Lunar Wielder sculpted a flame and sent it up to hover like a moon above their heads. She tried again to ask about the test, but was met with stony silence.

The ceiling sloped down as the path sloped up, winding like a spiral stair, and there was barely enough room to stand. Kyndra strove to imagine herself beneath a cloudy night sky, but the rock was everywhere, solid and black in the false moonlight. It was rough to the touch, pitted like volcanic stone.

Her legs began to tire and the feeling left in the wake of her dream strengthened. It was a strange feeling, wholly unlike the foreboding before the Inheritance Ceremony. Kyndra might have called it resignation, except for the frenzied beating of her heart. In those twin chambers arose a sad certainty of *wrongness*. It wasn't a presentiment; it was a fact. The conviction pumping around her body told her the Wielders had made a terrible mistake.

Brégenne waited until the door closed outside her quarters and the shuffle of feet faded before she peered into the corridor. It was still night and the walls of Naris gleamed silver in her eyes. She threw a cloak over the plain clothes she now wore and drew up her hood. Then she slipped out of the room.

They'd come for Barrar, as she had guessed they would. Her neighbour was a fellow Lunar and one of Alandred's friends. Brégenne had listened to the knocks beyond her door, thinking of Kyndra, who stood mere feet away. She had to suppress the urge to spring out and grab her. It wasn't fair. Alandred's spite had robbed her of the chance to explain the test, to offer what reassurance she could. The place of testing alone would terrify the girl.

Brégenne hurried through the deserted corridors. Only four Wielders were allowed on the platform during a test – with two more to guard the passageway. It would do her no favours to be found up there and, with every step, prudence urged her back. She gritted her teeth and walked on.

She circled the atrium rather than crossing it directly. It took a lot longer and the small archway began to flicker in her vision. She cursed. Morning was near. From now until sunrise, her world would gradually blur until she was once again sightless.

The thought drove her to greater speed. She didn't have much time; the test could only be carried out in the short windows offered by dusk and dawn. And only then – halfway between night and day – were the cosmosethic powers equal. Both energies could be channelled.

Brégenne reached the sloping tunnel and her pace became harder to maintain. She'd taken part in the test several times, but found it unpleasant.

It was a simple procedure. Kyndra would stand in the centre of the platform under the changing sky. Four Wielders, two from each Order, would successively attack her with destructive energy until her latent affinity with one of those energies arose to protect her. If she turned out to be of the Lunar, she would take control of the Lunar beams directed at her and use them to create a shield to defend herself against the Solar. The longer it took for that to happen, Brégenne knew, the less chance Kyndra had of surviving.

Her breath came in short gasps. The test was brutal, but impossible to fail. Failure, after all, meant death. It was a rare outcome and none of Brégenne's finds had suffered it. But they'd had several days to prepare themselves mentally and physically, to rest after their journeys. She herself had taught them the basic principles before they were sent up here. Alandred's revenge could have more serious consequences than he realized.

The tunnel flickered regularly now – the moon was setting. Brégenne stumbled and in the moment of silence caused by her fall, she heard a scream. 'No,' she panted, dragging herself upright. Eyes wide against the darkness, she flew up the slope.

Another scream reached her, louder this time. Brégenne let out a growl of frustration and pushed herself faster. Her feet slapped the rock, sending the echoes of her passage and of Kyndra's cries down into Naris. The black walls flickered wildly now, but there was light ahead. Brégenne threw herself at it, her heartbeat thundering in her ears.

She rounded the final corner, shoved past the two startled

guards and emerged on the high, spike-ringed platform, cling-ing desperately to her sight. The Wielders stood in a semi-circle. Alandred wasn't facing her, but she noticed the Lunar glow around him fading. Then Brégenne saw Kyndra and bile bub-bled up into her throat.

The girl hung several inches off the ground, kept there by two Solar spears thrust between her ribs. The Wielders that held them stood to either side of her, lances braced against their shoulders. With every second that passed, those terrible weapons grew brighter. As Brégenne watched, the Lunar beams piercing Kyndra's shoulders faded, but the girl's screams did not. Torn from her throat, they were wet with the blood that dribbled from her lips and ran over her chin.

Propped up like some grotesque puppet, Kyndra raised her head. For the briefest of moments, her dark eyes met Bré-genne's and Brégenne felt the echo of a sharp pain rip through her belly, as if the lances pierced her too. She cried out.

The crest of the sun hit the horizon and the spears blazed into white-hot fire. Kyndra gave one last, agonized, shriek and then her head fell forward onto her chest.

She was blind. Brégenne stood in the thin air and felt the sun warm her face. The last moon-limned image lingered behind her eyes. She gasped and let out a sob.

'Brégenne?' Boots scraped over rock and an arm encircled her shoulders. She smelled Alandred and furiously shook him off. Then she stumbled forward. 'No, Brégenne,' Alandred said. He sounded shaken. 'Careful of the edge.'

She was almost certain she knew where the edge was, but she let him guide her. When he stopped, Brégenne dropped to her knees, hearing her own ragged breathing, and patted the ground around her. She found a leg and moved her hands up until her fingers sank into something soft and fleshy. Horrified, Brégenne snatched them away. They were wet and smelled sharply of iron.

'Brégenne . . .' Alandred laid his hand on her shoulder. 'You can't help.'

'Don't touch me! How could you, Alandred? How *dare* you?'

There was no response. She sensed the other Wielders shifting, beginning to mutter. 'Help!' she cried. 'Why didn't you stop when the sun rose? Why didn't you stop?'

'We can't help,' said a voice. 'None of us are healers, Brégenne.'

She let out a scream of frustration. 'Go! Quickly! Find someone!'

'Brégenne,' said Alandred's voice. 'It's too late. I'm sorry.'

'Sorry!' She heard her cry echo around the platform, climbing up the spire she couldn't see. 'This is your doing.'

'I am within my rights,' Alandred said, but he sounded unsure.

Nediah! Brégenne screamed silently, opening herself to the bond and sending a wave of urgency along it. Then she returned tentative hands to Kyndra, searching for a wrist. When she found one, it was warm, but lifeless. 'Why did you involve her?' she hissed, voice pitched for Alandred alone. 'What's between us *stays* between us. Kyndra was innocent!'

Alandred didn't reply. Brégenne couldn't find it, couldn't find a pulse. Her nostrils rejected the smell of burned skin. It made her gorge rise.

'I'm sorry,' Alandred said again. His voice was so quiet she almost missed it. 'This wasn't my intention. How could it have been? But it's not my fault, Brégenne. I agree the girl wasn't given the time to prepare and I regret it.'

'You *regret* it? You are Master of Novices. Your duty is to protect and guide them, not to make them pawns in your personal vendetta!'

'It's not a vendetta, Brégenne—'

'No. You don't deserve your office.'

There was silence and then Alandred said, 'I didn't intend it, Brégenne. But it would have ended like this anyway.'

'Dawn was too near!'

'Only because she didn't respond. Most potentials react at the first bolt and the rest at the second. We didn't expect to reach three, let alone four—'

'Just leave,' Brégenne growled. 'I can't stand you any more.' She didn't know how many Wielders remained to hear them, or even if Alandred had gone. She found Kyndra's chest and lowered her head to it, uncaring of the blood that smeared her. There was nothing, no heartbeat, though she strained her ears and tried to quiet her own breathing. A tear rolled down her cheek.

'Brégenne!'

She heard Nediah collapse beside her and gasped in relief.

'Are you all right?' His voice shook.

'It's not my blood, Nediah. Please help her.' She edged out of the way. Nediah made a sound like retching and for once she was glad she couldn't see what he could. She heard the small movements of his hands, as they examined Kyndra's body. Warmth came and she imagined golden light welling up between Nediah's fingers. He was arguably the citadel's most talented healer, but she knew she'd never be able to master the discipline. The healing she had done in Brenwym was the most complex she'd ever attempted and it had been far from perfect.

The warmth cut off and dawn blew cold against her face. 'Nediah?' she asked the wind, 'is it done?'

'Brégenne.' A hand took hers. She heard him swallow. 'I'm sorry,' Nediah said.

Countless lights shone around her. Between each, it was utterly dark. If she let that emptiness take her, she would be changed forever.

Gradually she became aware that one of the lights was moving. It beat rhythmically, shaking the others with its sound. She pushed towards it and the pounding light filled her vision, spreading to cover the four horizons. It reached over her head to clothe the spangled dark behind.

Drawn to its incessant beat, she opened her hand, vaster even than the light, and closed her fingers around it.

Her eyelids flew open. A ceiling crystallized, black, but clearly rock. There was no void to change her here. The air was cold and she sensed she was underground. Memories stirred slowly, each slotting into place like a puzzle. She lay unmoving, collecting as many pieces as she could. The picture was incomplete, but it hardly mattered. They must have put her here after the test.

Kyndra sat up, gasping, as dried blood flaked and settled. She drew her legs into her chest, clasping them, rocking forwards and backwards, squeezing her eyes shut against the horror of her broken body.

Except that it wasn't broken. It took her a long time to uncurl, but when she did, she saw skin – raw and pink, but whole. And blood had left a carnelian stain over her stomach and palms. *So it was real.*

Light welled from somewhere above and, in its weak glow,

Kyndra examined herself. Her feet were bare, her clothes in tatters. The shirt she wore was stiff and soiled, barely decent, and her trousers had fared little better.

Her own heart's rapid staccato returned her fully to herself and she tried to slow her breathing. *Where am I?* This room had to be somewhere in Naris; it was built of the same dark rock. Kyndra shivered. It was so cold – and her boots were nowhere to be seen.

The stone block on which she sat reminded her of a gravestone. They could have at least returned her to that tiny room, she thought. Kyndra looked over her shoulder and saw a path winding down into darkness. A musty smell crept from it and she hastily averted her gaze. Surely this wasn't still part of the test?

Kyndra slid off the block and almost fell. Trembling, she clutched at her chill bed, waiting for strength to return to her legs. When she felt able to move, she took a few tentative steps. The cave-like room wasn't large, and dim light flowed from an archway, over which a single phrase was carved: *May they sleep without dreaming.* Beyond it, shallow stairs led upwards. Kyndra tore her eyes away from the words before their meaning sank in fully.

A pile of folded cloth sat on the end of the slab. Kyndra unrolled it and found a black, robe-like coat. She slipped her arms gratefully into the sleeves. Although buttonless, it hung nearly to her ankles and hid most of the rips in her shirt.

Feet stinging from the cold flagstones, she made her slow way up the steps. There were a lot of them. Kyndra clutched her tender ribs as she climbed, out of breath after only one set. It took her ten minutes to reach the top, pausing at each small landing. The stairs opened up into a solemn corridor, almost as poorly lit as the room in which she'd woken.

Kyndra walked with one hand on the wall, trying not to stumble. It occurred to her that perhaps she ought not to be moving, but the thought of returning to the underground room was unbearable.

She reached the end of the passage and stopped, hearing footsteps rounding the corner. Dazedly, she recognized the novice, Irilin. Their talk last night seemed an age ago. She raised a hand in greeting.

Irilin shrieked and staggered back. Eyes wild, she clutched at something around her neck. Her mouth opened again, soundlessly.

'What's wrong?' Kyndra asked, alarmed. The girl looked awful. Every drop of blood had fled her cheeks and her pale eyes were wide with horror.

'You?' she whispered.

'It's Kyndra,' Kyndra said, worried that Irilin didn't recognize her. 'Remember, from last night?'

'I remember,' Irilin said faintly. She stared hard at Kyndra's face. Then she glanced down at the blood-encrusted shirt showing through the black coat. 'You're supposed to be dead,' she whispered.

Kyndra blinked. 'What?'

'I saw you. They carried you down from the platform. They laid you in the antechamber to the tombs.'

The hairs rose on Kyndra's arms. 'Tombs? That's where I woke up?'

Irilin nodded. 'I saw you,' she said again. 'They told us the testing killed you.'

'It nearly did,' Kyndra said, trying to lighten the mood, though the chill in her blood remained.

'You're really not dead?'

'Do I look it?'

The novice regained some of her colour. 'I guess not. But you do look terrible.'

Kyndra realized she was shaking. Her legs felt weak and her sides and shoulders ached. She had to lean against the wall. After a few deep breaths she said, 'You could have warned me.'

Irilin shook her head, still pale. 'That's the job of the Wielder who found you. Traditionally, it's their responsibility, but I don't think Master Brégenne got a chance. No one knows why the Master of Novices scheduled your test so soon.'

'Alandred,' Kyndra murmured. 'I don't think he likes me.'

Irilin tried a smile, but it wobbled feebly on her lips. 'He probably had no idea the test would go so wrong.'

'It did go wrong, then?' Kyndra asked, shifting from foot to foot on the stone floor. 'This didn't happen to you?'

Irilin stared at her. 'No.'

'What was I supposed to do?' Kyndra asked. 'I was defenceless – and they attacked me!'

'You weren't defenceless,' Irilin said, but her eyes flickered. 'A potential can only be awoken through an attack on their life. That's what the test is. You discover an affinity with one of the powers and it saves you . . . or you save yourself. Takes a while to learn to touch it again, though,' she added.

Kyndra looked away. 'I didn't feel an affinity with anything. They were trying to kill me.' She paused. 'Looks like everyone thought they succeeded.'

'They weren't trying to kill you,' Irilin insisted. Then, 'Well, they were, but only to awaken your power.'

'I don't have any power.'

'You must. Master Brégenne wouldn't have brought you here otherwise.'

'Brégenne made a mistake.'

'But you can see the citadel.'

'That doesn't prove anything,' Kyndra said bitterly with a shrug.

Neither spoke for a few moments. Then Irilin said quietly, 'You should have seen her.'

'Who?'

'Master Brégenne. She wouldn't leave your side, kept saying it was her fault. She was *crying*,' she added significantly.

Kyndra hesitated. 'Crying?'

Irilin nodded and clasped her elbows. 'I didn't think Master Brégenne *could* cry.'

'Then I need to let her know I'm all right.'

'You can't. She's in the big council chamber with Alandred and the other Wielders who witnessed your test. It's a hearing.'

'A hearing?'

'Yes. No one has died during a test for a while. It's rare, but has to be investigated. Sometimes the Wielder responsible for bringing the failed potential gets the blame. They have to explain why it happened.'

Kyndra's eyes widened. 'Brégenne will be blamed? But it's Alandred's fault!'

'If that's right, Master Brégenne has nothing to fear. Wait! Where are you going?'

Kyndra had dodged past the novice, walking as fast as she dared. 'To the council chamber. Where do you think?'

'You can't do that. You're not allowed.'

'Watch me.'

Irilin jogged to keep up. 'But you're wearing a funeral robe!'

Kyndra stopped and turned. The black coat turned with her. 'I think,' she said, her eyes glinting, 'that it's rather appropriate.'

13

Brégenne clenched her fists. Her nails dug into her flesh, but she didn't care. Although she couldn't see them, she turned her face towards the table where the Council sat and strove to remain calm. The other Wielders had left after giving their testimony and now the chamber was empty save for her, Alandred and the three Council members.

'It is an unfortunate event,' Loricus was saying. 'Master Brégenne has never been wrong before.'

'I do not believe I was wrong on this occasion.' A tiny quiver in her voice betrayed her anger. 'If Kyndra had been given the same opportunity as other potentials, this wouldn't have happened.'

'We cannot know that for sure,' Helira said firmly. 'But your case against Master Alandred stands. It is evident that the girl was not allowed the same courtesy as is generally shown to other potentials. Why was this so, Master Alandred?'

Brégenne couldn't see Alandred, but her sharp ears picked out the sound of fidgeting. 'It was an impulsive decision,' the Wielder said. 'I admit I didn't consider the consequences.'

'You willingly assume liability, then?' asked Gend in his deep voice.

'I do,' Alandred said, surprising Brégenne. 'But no one was more shocked than I at the outcome. All of Bré— Master Brégenne's finds have excelled during the test and are now promising novices.'

Brégenne couldn't help but grind her teeth at this. So Alandred would blame her own judgement for Kyndra's death?

'Members of the Council,' she spoke up hastily. 'I urge you to consider the facts. As the Master of Novices readily asserts, I have never yet been wrong in my judgement. I admit it was my responsibility to prepare Kyndra for the test, but the opportunity was taken from me!' Her anger at Alandred and the shock of Kyndra's awful death shattered her calm. She heard her voice crack and felt tears gather again in her eyes.

Maybe it was this that moved Helira, or perhaps Kyndra's blood that still stained Brégenne's cheek, for she said, 'The blame shall not be laid at your door, Brégenne. The situation would be different if the girl had lived. It is clear to me that the Master of Novices has been negligent in his duty, and for this he will be reprimanded.'

Somewhere to her right, Alandred spluttered.

'Have you anything to say to mitigate your actions, Master of Novices?' Helira's voice had lost its gentleness. Now it echoed with the iron law that beat in Naris's heart.

Brégenne heard Alandred shift again; it sounded as if he were smoothing down the front of his robes. Surely he wouldn't tell them about his intrusion into her quarters?

'No,' Alandred said finally.

'Then hear the terms of your punishment. You are relieved of your post for a year's duration. Furthermore, you are to—'

But what Alandred was to do, Brégenne never found out. She heard the double doors to the chamber swing inward and she turned towards them. A figure stood framed there, face obscured. It took Brégenne a long, bewildering moment to realize she was *seeing*. The sudden image unbalanced her. The figure was like an imprint that remained after one stared too long at a candle flame. For a wild moment, she thought she'd lost track of time, that night had come early, but the midday bell had just begun to chime.

The figure walked forward and details began to appear. It was a woman. She wore a long, dark coat, thin as a winding sheet. Underneath, Brégenne caught a glimpse of stained clothes. Thick tangles of hair framed her face, the ends matted and stuck together.

Brégenne stared, and as the woman neared her, she gave a cry of disbelief. When Kyndra raised her head, Brégenne could almost see blue in her eyes.

Finding and entering the council chamber had been easier than Kyndra had thought. Irilin trailed her to the huge hall they called the atrium, muttering about rules. Kyndra refused to listen. If the Council were blaming Brégenne for her death, she would stop them, and show them in the process that she was very much alive.

'Hey – you can't go in there!' a brown-robed young man shouted at her as she reached the chamber doors. Kyndra spared a glance for him. He looked at least five years her senior with a handsome face framed by curling blond hair. His belt was completely golden.

Perhaps her stark appearance unnerved him, for he stopped short, eyes travelling over the funeral robe that gaped to show the blood-encrusted shirt she wore beneath. Kyndra seized her chance, grabbed the door handles and pushed. The heavy panels swung inward. She'd half expected to find them locked.

The chamber was long and narrow and a grand table stood at the far end. Here sat three people: a woman in silver and two men, one dressed in gold and the other in silver. Their robes were the finest Kyndra had yet seen. Layers of silk, each a different shade of gold or silver, hung from their shoulders, belted at the waist with a bright cord of red. The bottoms of the robes were slashed with red too.

Kyndra advanced slowly and heard the doors close, but didn't turn to look. She kept her eyes fixed on Brégenne, who stared straight back, her mouth opening to cry out her shock. Unlike the others, she wore a plain grey tunic over trousers and her white-blond hair was twisted into its usual knot at the back of her neck. Dried blood stained one of her cheeks.

Alandred was there too, but without his patronizing smile. The Master of Novices looked pale and drawn. The woman at the table sat back in her chair and her eyes took in Kyndra's black coat and bare feet. Kyndra stopped walking.

'Brégenne.' She smiled, but the Wielder didn't return it. The intensity of her gaze gave Kyndra the impression that she could actually see her. *She was crying,* Irilin had said.

'I'm not dead,' Kyndra told her. 'I'm all right.'

As one, the Council stood, their amazement guarded. The man in gold stared at Kyndra, his eyes alight and calculating. They were hazel, set in a handsome, sculpted face. A moment passed before he smiled coldly. 'You must be the potential. I am Lord Loricus of the Solar. We were told you did not survive the testing.'

Kyndra's ribs throbbed and she curled a hand around them. 'You were told wrong,' she said, the pain rough in her voice.

Brégenne made a noise, but said nothing. Loricus raised an eyebrow. 'Clearly,' he said, 'we were misinformed.'

An uneasy silence spilled out into the room. Kyndra couldn't think of a suitable response. Either this was some vast joke – highly unlikely, given the people she was dealing with – or her state must truly have resembled death. She'd had a lucky escape.

The old woman who sat between the two men was white-haired and gaunt, and she watched Kyndra with a knife-sharp gaze. 'Loricus,' she said.

The gold-robed man moved so fast that he was back in his seat before Kyndra could draw breath. Her arm stung and a tiny drop of blood beaded on her skin. Shaken, she looked up at Loricus, who held a needle in his right hand. The tip gleamed red. She watched as he gave the needle a swift lick, made a face and deposited it in his robe. 'It's normal,' he said.

The horror Kyndra still felt at waking up in the tombs began to harden into anger. Before she could open her mouth, Brégenne laid a hand on the arm Loricus had pricked.

'Don't,' she whispered. 'They had to check.'

'Check what?' she asked loudly.

'We are decided,' the councilwoman announced, as if Kyndra hadn't spoken at all. 'Master Alandred's punishment is lifted.'

'What?' Events seemed to be moving too fast for Kyndra. No one had explained her situation, or offered an apology. '*This* is his fault!' She gestured at her blood-stained clothes. 'Are you saying he's forgiven for almost killing me?'

The woman observed her coolly. 'Master Alandred's conduct will be monitored. Your survival forces us to drop the charge of negligence, but presents another—'

'What difference does that make?'

'Do not interrupt me,' the woman snapped. 'Your survival presents us with a different problem. You failed the test, despite your Wielder's assurance that you would pass.' She addressed her next words to Brégenne. 'You who brought her here have risked exposing our secret for nothing. Your actions in the Far Valleys are unjustifiable – our ears in the east tell us the story has spread.'

Brégenne paled, but it was the only sign she gave of her unease. 'I have to disagree,' she said, and Kyndra admired her courage.

'Brégenne, no!' Alandred wore a peculiar expression, as if his face might break into pieces. 'Don't,' he said miserably. 'You'll only make it worse.'

Brégenne continued as if she hadn't heard him, her voice stronger now. 'Your conclusion is valid, as long as Kyndra indeed shows no potential.' She paused. 'But I don't believe it.'

'The test is failed. She barely escaped with her life,' Loricus said. 'What power do you think she has, Brégenne?' His eyes strayed to Kyndra and he stiffened. Then he shook his head and looked back at Brégenne. 'Are you so unwilling to admit defeat?'

'This is not about defeat,' Brégenne said evenly. 'This is not about me. You weren't there when the sun rose and turned those Solar beams to fire. How could anyone but a Wielder survive that?'

Her words temporarily silenced the Council. Kyndra stared at Brégenne, mind working feverishly. Was the blind woman doing this for her, or for herself? Kyndra thought back to the previous night, when she'd privately wondered what the Wielders would do if they found out she had no power. Her death, she realized now, purged the Council of responsibility. If the test had killed her, Brégenne's mistake could be laid to rest.

But she lived. For the first time, Kyndra wondered whether rushing to reassure Brégenne had been the wisest thing to do.

The Solar screen hummed gently, hiding the Council and their discussion from the room. They had talked for nearly twenty minutes, unheard and unseen behind the sunlit curtain. Brégenne didn't need to see it to be able to feel its heat upon her face.

She waited without speaking. She heard the occasional rustle of Alandred's robes, but he, too, said nothing. Even Kyndra passed the time in silence. Brégenne could still see her: a lonely figure standing amidst the usual blank greyish light which was the only thing visible to Brégenne during the day. The girl's eyes roamed the chamber.

It was not decorated as elaborately as Naris's recreational halls. This was the room in which justice was meted out, punishments decided, promotions given. Brégenne knew it well. It was an austere room, sculpted from black rock disfigured by the earth. She had always thought these four walls were the blackest in the whole citadel. Shadows amassed in channels where lava had once flowed and lurked behind chunks of stone that protruded untrimmed into the chamber. Novices who were unfortunate enough to be summoned here later told tales of sulphurous faces peering from the rock. Brégenne had not always laughed at those tales. At least in daylight, there were no walls for her to see.

She continued to stare at Kyndra. A presentiment had slept beneath her notice almost from the moment she'd spotted the girl, trapped in a circle of people, her face illumined by the mob's uneasy torchlight. Brégenne had known then that she belonged in Naris and that it was her task to bring her to the citadel. However, now that Kyndra was here, she began to wonder whether Naris really belonged within her. Could she be wrong? Becoming a Wielder wasn't only about harnessing your innate abilities; you learned to feel Naris itself in your blood. The great sunken citadel – its knowledge and the memories it chose to reveal – was as much a part of a Wielder's birthright as the energy he or she channelled.

'We have taken your words into account, Brégenne.'

The mention of her name brought Brégenne back to herself. The heat from the screen had vanished. 'Only the retrieval of a successful potential would have saved you from rebuke,' Helira said. 'You are well aware that our first law states no one outside the citadel may witness our power. You have justified your display in the town of Brenwym by claiming you protected this girl, a potential. The girl's failure to pass the test necessarily leaves you in an indefensible position.'

Brégenne resisted the urge to speak. An interruption would not endear her to the Council, especially not to Helira. She tried in vain to stop the galloping of her heart. She knew perfectly well that her actions contravened one of Naris's strictest laws.

Helira continued. 'Although your punishment is a consequence of the girl's survival, the same circumstance mitigates it. We accept that the girl must have some innate cosmosethic resistance. She will therefore take the test again.'

'What!' Kyndra burst out. 'You can't make me go through that again. I refuse!'

'You have no choice,' Loricus said. 'You will retake the test until you touch your power or you die. That is the Council's

201

will.' Brégenne heard a clap and then the sound of the double doors swinging inward. Several pairs of boots rang on the polished floor and Kyndra's arms were suddenly behind her back.

'Let me go!' she shouted, outrage clear in her voice. 'Get off me!'

'They are here to suppress any rash ideas,' Loricus said coolly. 'Your part in this interview is over.'

'I've failed your test. You can't stop me from leaving!'

Kyndra's words dropped into a silence that flowed from the black walls. 'You will find otherwise,' Loricus said, his silken tones sinister. 'And the Council does not wish to discuss it. The test will take place one week from now. Be sure to use the time wisely, Kyndra Vale. There is no guarantee you will wake from a second failure.'

Brégenne was certain she would shout at the Council and struggle against the arms that pulled her away, but Kyndra surprised her. Eyes blazing, she allowed herself to be led from the chamber and the doors slammed shut.

'This is monstrous.' Brégenne rounded on the Council. 'Her wounds are barely healed. How can that be your decision?'

'Isn't this the outcome you wanted, Brégenne?' Loricus asked, and she heard the smile in his voice. 'You believe she still has potential . . . and we agree.'

The guilt that had tormented Brégenne since that morning rose up anew in her throat. What had she done?

'The girl has been granted a period to recover,' Helira said, as if she sensed Brégenne's distress. 'During which time she will receive suitable preparation, but not from you.'

Brégenne felt a strange dread. 'It's my responsibility.'

'*Was* your responsibility,' Loricus said. 'You have lost the right.'

'It is a shame, Brégenne.' Gend's husky voice, seldom heard, resonated in her chest. 'You were one of our finest. Your actions disappoint us.'

Brégenne didn't miss his use of the past tense. 'I'd have liked to have seen you in my place. Would you have done any different?'

'Enough.' Helira's voice cracked across the chamber and Brégenne realized she already had the answer to her question. It was bitter. Not one of them would have stepped in to save Kyndra in Brenwym. Their rules were worth more than her life.

'You may keep your rank,' Helira said, 'but you will be stripped of certain privileges. You will not leave the citadel without our permission, not even to visit Murta.'

This was no more than she expected, Brégenne told herself. Her activities in the world would be curtailed, as would her search for new potentials. She tried to harden herself against the disappointment.

'You will no longer be attuned to Master Nediah.'

It took a moment for Helira's words to sink in. When they did, Brégenne felt a cold ripple of shock. 'What?'

'We feel you need to be linked to someone more disciplined,' Loricus said. 'Someone with a greater willingness to curb your . . . enthusiasm. You will therefore drop Nediah and take on Janus.'

'But Janus isn't even a master!' Brégenne cried. *Stop it*, she scolded herself. *Don't give him the satisfaction.*

'Correct,' Helira said. 'But he will be raised to the gold tomorrow morning. You will attune yourselves when his ceremony is complete.' She paused. 'We believe there is mutual benefit to this match. Janus will profit from your experience and you would do well to imitate his conduct in regard to Naris's laws. It seems you are in need of a reminder.'

Brégenne didn't trust herself to speak. It was an insult. She might not have lost her rank officially, but this pairing with a novice would lower her in the eyes of the citadel. And Nediah . . . A sickness rose in her chest and wrapped itself around her heart.

'The Council's decision is admirably fair.'

Until he spoke, Brégenne had forgotten Alandred was still in the room. The smug expression she could only imagine made her blood boil. She felt the heat in her cheeks. Her punishment was his reward; he had always despised Nediah. Nothing would please him more than to see them un-attuned.

'Be quiet, Alandred,' Helira said. 'Remember that you have behaved most unfittingly.'

'I regret my actions,' Alandred said smoothly. 'I will forfeit my post if the Council desires it.'

'That won't be necessary,' Helira replied, and Brégenne was too numb to feel outrage at this injustice. 'If you have nothing else to say, either of you, then consider yourselves dismissed.'

Brégenne let her body perform the honorific, and then fled from the chamber.

Brégenne stood high on one of Naris's dark spires, watching dusk sharpen the landscape beneath. Across the chasm, lights flared in the town and a snatch of singing came to her on the wind. She stretched out her arms, drinking in the twilight, taking the night into her body. This was her favourite time of day. Her power waxed, as the moon disembarked from the land. Brégenne could see its bright rim cresting the hills in the east. Soon it would be free of the earth, a galleon sailing solitary skies until dawn.

Thoughts crowded her mind and so she'd climbed up here – but whether to make sense of them or to run from them, she didn't know. Although she'd expected to be confined to the citadel, the reality was a bitter brew to swallow. Finding potentials was an integral part of her life as a Wielder. She had spent years searching this peaceful, settled world for the flickers of discord that tended to surround potentials. She'd saved a dozen children from homes that ostracized or feared them, or even – in Kyndra's case – tried to end them. And if some of those children didn't understand why they had to leave, she'd tell them the story of the pale-haired girl with eyes that saw too much, until those eyes were burned and blinded by people who said they loved her.

Brégenne felt the swell of her Lunar energy like a night tide. She let the moon rise under her skin, until her hands wore shining gauntlets of light.

Wielders had lived in secrecy for five hundred years, serving none but themselves. Their only concession to the world was the Breaking – they would monitor it, they would try to understand it and they would work to prevent deaths if possible. *But is that enough?* Brégenne found herself wondering. *If we became part of this world, potentials wouldn't have to suffer. It would take time, but eventually we could be accepted. Wasn't it like that before the war?*

Brégenne let her power fade. For the first time in all her years of service, she felt distanced from Naris and its laws. She had built her life around them, woven them into a cloak to protect her from . . . what? She breathed the night and gazed at the lonely moon. Those rules were there to guide, to safeguard. That they could betray her too was something she had never considered.

There'd been a ruling Council in Naris ever since the Deliverance. In the desolate wake of the war, the three surviving masters had taken charge, gathering in novices like lost sheep. Solinaris, the great fortress of the sun, had been utterly destroyed. Its subterranean tunnels were all that remained, and these were further excavated until they formed a labyrinthine complex. The first Council renamed it Naris and everyone in those broken days was thankful for their leadership. That leadership had turned to absolute authority was natural and inevitable – Naris needed authority and it needed structure. Successive Councils provided both, until the citadel was – if not restored to its former glory – again a place of strength. *But what was this strength founded upon?* Brégenne asked herself. *Despair*, she thought, sensing the depths beneath her feet, *and fear of the future.*

'Brégenne?'

She leapt at the voice, turned too quickly and had to grab at the spire's low parapet for balance. The open tower top looked more like a crag with its floor of rough stone and crumbling supports. Nediah stood at the top of steps that descended unevenly into the mountain. 'Curses,' Brégenne gasped, letting go of the parapet. 'Why must you sneak up on me?'

'Didn't you feel me coming?'

She looked at him. Knowing each other's location was the chief attribute of Attunement. Once she and Janus were paired, the Council would always know where she was. And Brégenne was under no illusions – Janus lived in the Council's pocket. She turned her face away from Nediah. 'You shouldn't be here,' she said quietly.

'Do you think they could stop me?'

She felt a brief flash of exultation at his words. 'No, but I could.'

Nediah shifted his weight and plunged his hands into his pockets, much like he'd done when he was younger and she was his mentor. 'Why do you do this to yourself, Brégenne?' he asked finally. 'Why do you isolate yourself? This involves me too.'

'Not for much longer,' she said.

'How can you say that? Has no one considered my feelings?'

'No,' she answered bluntly. 'Why would your feelings have any bearing on the Council's decision? You forget that this is a punishment.'

'I can't believe it,' Nediah said, finding comfort, it seemed, in righteous anger. 'Why would they—'

'They wish to monitor my movements without appearing to do so. I will not find an ally in Janus.' She sighed. 'Nothing has gone right since we arrived. First that earth is stolen, then Kyndra's test . . . And I keep thinking of that story Argat told – about the Breaking happening in two places at once. I know it's probably ridiculous, but I can't shake the feeling that there's a link.' She didn't mention the fourth thing – how she had begun to see Kyndra without needing to channel Lunar energy.

Nediah looked as if he couldn't care less about the Breaking. He opened his mouth and closed it, shifted his feet on the black stone.

'I'm not allowed to have anything to do with Kyndra,' Brégenne said. She swallowed. 'You must ensure she knows as much as possible before she takes the test again. I am counting on you, Nediah.'

The wind blew at her back and the darkness spread further

west. Nediah nodded and fixed her with his gaze, as if steeling himself for something. 'The Council can't stop me from seeing you,' he said. 'And I'll need to let you know if I find out anything about the earth.'

She studied him a while before replying. His face had firmed into the stubborn mask he wore whenever he was unsure of himself. Brégenne knew it would lead to trouble. 'You must be careful,' she told him. 'You are young and talented. Do not give them an excuse to restrain you.'

Nediah frowned and took his hands out of his pockets. 'You always say that,' he muttered. 'I'm not that young, Brégenne. Many years have passed since I came here . . . since I met you.'

She gazed at him and her heart began to beat more quickly. A crack appeared in the stubborn mask that covered his face and for a moment she saw a knot of emotions there. They frightened her.

'You know what I want to say, Brégenne.'

'Stop this.' It emerged as a whisper.

He hesitated and then raised his hand. She felt him brush a few pale strands of hair away from her face. His fingers were warm on her skin. 'I don't think I can,' he whispered.

Fire flashed through her, hot and terrifying, and she jerked away. His hand fell from her face, and with it died something wondrous, a fleeting joy she both feared and wanted.

'Then you will live in misery.'

The harsh words surprised even her. Nediah looked as if she had slapped him. His cheeks darkened. He stared at her, eyes wide, and sudden shame welled up in her throat. 'I'm sorry,' she stammered, 'I didn't mean—'

He turned away.

'Nediah, please—'

'Don't say that you're sorry,' he said to the darkness. 'I don't want to hear . . . Goodnight.'

She watched him descend the spiral stairs with an ache in her chest, half fear and half – she didn't know. The black rock of Naris swallowed him.

The wind teased out more strands of hair and Brégenne stood there for a long time, letting them blow across her face. Somewhere far below, the bell for evening repast would be ringing.

She climbed slowly down from the tower, wracked by a mingled tide of guilt and relief. Brégenne kept her head high and let the moon guide her back to her quarters. There, alone in the darkness, she also found regret.

14

Kyndra felt as if she had been in Naris for weeks already and had to remind herself that only two days had passed since she'd walked through the great iron gates. On her return from yesterday's hearing, she'd found some plain, ill-fitting clothes piled on the bed in the tiny room. A young novice had told her quite brusquely that she would not be moving to a dormitory. *I'm a prisoner then*, Kyndra thought, noting the new lock and bolt on the outside of the door.

As she followed Alandred down the veined passages, she tentatively touched her ribs. The wounds caused by the Solar beams still tingled painfully and it felt as if sparks of sunlight had lodged in her skin. Despite hours of sleep, her eyelids were heavy and her body ached all over. And on top of that, a constant, nagging fear had moved into the back of her throat.

She had almost died.

When those thugs tossed her out of yesterday's hearing, Nediah had appeared and seized her in a hug. Kyndra decided not to ask him what he'd witnessed up on the platform that morning. The unguarded relief on his face said plainly that he'd never expected to see her alive again.

Her wonder at setting foot in a secret citadel, magically

hidden from the world, had gone. She'd lost it up on the cliff when that same magic pierced her body and left her to choke on her own blood. Kyndra found herself thinking of the stories she loved, the ones that sang the glory of adventure. How wrong those stories were.

'Keep up,' Alandred snapped at her over his shoulder. It was the first day of Kyndra's 'preparation' and she had no idea what to expect. She trailed after the Master of Novices, listening to the deep quiet within the stone. It was a strange kind of quiet, a quiet that transported echoes of violence to her across the millennia. The mountain was ancient, pushed up from the low places of the earth by terrible pressure. Was she just imagining those subterranean cries? Kyndra tried to picture how the mountain had once looked with the great glass citadel rising from its slopes. And then, with a jolt, she remembered the dreams she'd had on her Inheritance day and the visions both here and in Market Primus. She didn't have to imagine what the mountain had looked like before the Deliverance – she had *seen* it.

Alandred stopped and Kyndra almost walked into him. Catching herself just in time, she stumbled and pulled her attention back to the present. They were standing outside a door set back in the stone. Alandred knocked once and then opened it without waiting for a response, and Kyndra peered warily over his shoulder.

The space beyond was more cave than room. Three long tables hosted a mixture of girls and boys, none of whom looked over the age of fifteen. Every eye stared at her as Alandred pushed her forward. 'This is Kyndra Vale,' the Master of Novices announced, and a gold-robed man rose from behind his desk at the front. 'Vale, this is Master Rush. He instructs the Initiated.'

Kyndra looked around the room and met the unabashed eyes of a little girl. They were huge and brown and they couldn't belong to a child older than eight. She blinked at Kyndra. Other children sat on either side of her, a girl of about twelve and a boy with ugly eyes that watered as he stared. 'Are you sure I'm supposed to be here?' she whispered to Alandred. 'They're all children.'

To her horror, Alandred gave a boisterous laugh and said loudly, 'Children they might be, Vale, but they know a lot more than you do.' His voice filled the chamber and Kyndra shrank away from it. Some of the eyes no longer looked as friendly and an older girl smirked at her from one of the tables.

Alandred turned to the other Wielder. 'Master Rush, the Council requests that this *girl* –' he placed heavy emphasis on the word – 'joins the Initiated for at least a couple of lessons. She must be better prepared for her test.'

'That is rather inappropriate,' Rush said, but Kyndra hardly heard him over the anger that bubbled up inside her. She stared at Alandred's grizzled face with burning eyes.

Alandred rubbed his cheek, frowned and dropped his arm. 'You understand that this instruction comes from the Council, Rush? I am well aware that the arrangement is unsuitable. The girl knows nothing, so she can't be put with the Inferiate Order and Master Brégenne –' his voice caught on her name – 'has been forbidden from preparing her.'

The two men stood in silent opposition for several moments before Rush sighed and laid his hands on the desk. 'Very well, Alandred,' he said.

Perhaps it was the missing appellation that darkened Alandred's face. 'I'll leave her in your capable hands, then, Rush.

I'll also need you to make a report to me at the end of today's session. For the Council.'

'It will be as you say.'

'Vale, find a place to sit,' Alandred said curtly. 'You are Master Rush's charge now.'

Kyndra opened her mouth to say that she was no one's charge, but Alandred turned on his heel and jerked the door shut behind him. Kyndra stood alone under the room's scrutiny.

'What's your name again?' Master Rush's voice was softer than Alandred's and Kyndra liked to think it sounded kind. She gave her name, trying to ignore the stares. Children could stare like no one else.

'Settle down, everyone. Once Kyndra finds a place — move up there, Cail — we will continue.'

There was nothing else to do but sit beside the watery-eyed boy. Cail pursed his lips and pointedly moved as far to the left as he could. Kyndra lowered herself onto the end of the bench and tried not to appear so tall.

'We were learning about the sources of cosmosethic energy,' Rush said to Kyndra, who nodded and looked down at the table. The wood had names burned into it. Old black ash had settled in the larger grooves, making some names darker than others. She wondered whether Nediah had sat here.

'Solar and Lunar are the twin manifestations of cosmo-sethic energy,' Rush said. He began to walk up and down behind his desk. 'There are some who claim the dominance of Solar, arguing that the Lunar power comes from the sun. True, Lunar is a reflection of Solar, but here the powers are equal. Solar Wielders can't channel the sun's energy in its reflected state, just as Lunar Wielders can't touch it in its primary state. The powers are balanced just as day balances night.'

Kyndra sat up straighter on the bench as Rush continued to pace, his eyes ranging over everyone. 'Cosmosethic energy affects all life,' he said. 'But only those destined to become Wielders are able to find an affinity with one of its two aspects. This is achieved through the test, as each of you knows from experience.'

Kyndra felt a chill and turned her head slowly to the left. The little girl with the brown eyes matched her stare with an intensity that didn't belong in an eight-year-old. Kyndra broke her gaze and faced the front, gooseflesh spreading up her arms. The test had given her scars she knew would never fade, and a sick horror seized her when she thought of the large-eyed child taking her place on the cliff. What marks did she bear from her own ordeal? What kind of people would have put her through that?

'At a basic level, Solar and Lunar energy can be used to heal or harm.' Rush turned his left palm up and his skin began to glow. A golden knife coalesced in his right fist. He gestured with it. 'This is *substantiation*, meaning giving physical form to something. It is much harder to do than *manipulation* –' the golden knife disappeared, the desk drawer shot open and a silver dagger flew into Rush's fist – 'like *so*.'

With a swift, steady slash, he opened the skin of his palm. Surprised gasps filled the room. Rush observed his dripping hand dispassionately. He held it up so that everyone could see; his brow creased and the wound sealed. There was scattered applause.

Master Rush pulled a cloth from his pocket, wiped his hand and the dagger and then tossed the bloody rag onto the desk. 'Healing is harder than harming,' he said and stuck the dagger in his belt. 'One must possess a detailed knowledge of human anatomy. And the energy used requires careful hand-ling. Too much and you could kill the patient. Too little and the wounds do not stay closed.'

Although Kyndra was impressed, a part of her couldn't help wondering why Rush kept a weapon in his desk drawer.

The Wielder spread his hands. 'But these things merely scratch the surface. Once you all have the ability to summon and hold energy, you'll be encouraged to use your imagination. New ways to channel cosmosethic power are often discovered. If any of you are lucky enough to speak with Master Brégenne, who is blind, you might ask her how she uses the Lunar power to imitate sight.'

It was strange to hear Brégenne's night vision discussed so openly. Kyndra had thought it something she kept to herself. She glanced at the novices. The diligent had taken notes, their fingers splotched with ink from the speed of Rush's lecture. Others fiddled with their brown robes or traced with a small finger the names burned into the table.

'Solars, divide into pairs. We'll work on some basic *manipulation*. Lunars, you'll have a chance to practise tonight with Master Juna. For now I'd like you to define in your own words the difference between *substantiation* and *manipulation*. Yes, Cail, what is it?'

The boy beside Kyndra had his hand in the air. 'What about the third aspect?' he asked, and, as one, the room sat up straight on their benches. 'What about the Starborn?'

'Starborn are not a topic for discussion,' Rush barked at Cail. The boy closed his mouth and dropped his eyes.

'But weren't they Wielders too?' a girl piped up.

Rush scowled. 'A Starborn is *not* a Wielder. The last Star-born aided the invaders during the war. He sneaked into the citadel and toppled it from the inside. Deservedly, he was then destroyed by the very enemy he'd helped.' Rush stopped again. 'But – though the cost was high – we drove that enemy back.'

. . . The air is fire, ash and fire. Molten, the walls fall fast like tears and their beauty is their undoing. She'd laugh, but for the screams of those caught in the liquid glass. It clings to their skin, a sparkling, fatal embrace. The enemy is beyond count. Like a severed artery, their forces spill towards the fortress, red armour bloody in the dying rays of the sun. They are beautiful, unstoppable. They are death . . .

'I saw them at Lycorash and at Kalast. And the crow-covered corpses of a thousand Kingswold Knights lay behind them in the dirt. Not with an army five times their size could you have driven them back.'

It wasn't until the lesson's quiet became absolute silence that Kyndra realized she had spoken. She found herself back on her bench, fists clenched under the table. She uncurled them and her heart began to beat more quickly. The unknown cities left char on her tongue, as if merely speaking their names could conjure a taste of their fate. And her voice sounded deeper, assured, not remotely like her own.

Between each blink, she could still see the doom that awaited Solinaris. She'd seen it before in Market Primus. She'd watched the red-plated army advance up the valley, their weapons of war powered by something other than cosmosethic energy. The Wielders had underestimated that power. She'd tried to warn Solinaris and now it was too late. She couldn't save them, but there *was* still a chance to save—

The pain was like a spear to the head, sudden and stabbing. Suppressing a gasp, Kyndra clenched her teeth and pulled her mind back to the classroom. Rush was looking at her. So was everyone else. Finally, the Wielder said, 'I will speak to you afterwards,' and his voice shattered the spellbound room. Whispers grew and lapped at Kyndra's back like the oncoming tide. She stared straight ahead, dimly aware that Rush had resumed his lecture. There was no Solinaris and no war, and she *hadn't* been there to witness the last and greatest march of the Sartyan Empire's army.

No, Kyndra thought, trying to rid her mind of the strange words. She didn't want to know what the Sartyan Empire was, or why it had laid siege to the citadel five hundred years ago. None of this had anything to do with her. What would Rush ask? The golden-robed man returned to his desk. Their eyes met briefly and Kyndra looked away. How could she explain what had just happened when she didn't understand it herself?

The end of the lesson arrived and Master Rush crooked a finger, beckoning Kyndra up to his desk. Once the room had emptied, he said calmly, 'Contradict me again in front of my class and I will submit a disciplinary note to the Council.'

His mild tone raised hairs on the back of Kyndra's neck. 'You are not yet one of us,' the Wielder continued, 'and I tolerate your presence here because I have to. You should be setting an example for the younger children instead of interrupting my lesson with things you know nothing about.'

Anger returned, but it wasn't all hers. She felt a pressure in her head, as if it lay against solid stone and a force were pushing down on it, trying to force it through. *How has the truth become so distorted? Is there no one alive who remembers?* And then on top of those strange thoughts came one of her own: *Remembers what?*

Rush opened a drawer and drew out a smooth sheet of paper. He scribbled down something she couldn't see, folded the paper and sealed it with wax. 'Give this to Master Alandred,' he said shortly.

Kyndra reached for the scroll. As she took it, her fingers brushed against the Wielder's palm.

Rush tore his hand away, as if her skin were heated metal. He cradled it to his chest and his eyes were wide and unfocused – but only for a moment. The Wielder blinked and lowered his hand, looking at it peculiarly, as if he'd forgotten why it was curled into a fist. Then he said, 'If you find yourself in this room again, you will keep your tales to yourself. Do you understand me?'

Uncertain what had happened, Kyndra nodded and beat a hasty retreat to the door. When she looked back, Rush was sitting at his desk, staring fixedly at the backs of his hands.

There was no sign of Alandred and Kyndra wondered whether she ought to wait for him. She leaned against the wall outside and let go of a breath she hadn't realized she was holding. The air was cool in the passage and had a whispering chill peculiar to caves. It reminded her of the ones back home, about a morning's walk east of town. A series of grottoes riddled the feet of the Feenfold Mountains, filled with stalagmites and their hanging sisters. The hollow darkness fascinated her, but Jhren and Colta weren't so comfortable in the caves, where only the slow dripping of water broke the silence.

Kyndra began to walk back the way Alandred had come, keeping one hand on the wall. She relished the rough stone beneath her fingers. It held secrets of a time before people, a time when the elements themselves were at war, and the war was one of reasonless nature. Something about that appealed to her.

She barely registered the feet standing in her path before

she tripped over them. Kyndra faltered and raised her head. A young man stood there. She recognized his haughty look from yesterday, when he'd tried to stop her entering the council chamber. He watched her with blue eyes the same colour as Jhren's and his curling hair fell to the side as he tilted his head.

'Who are you?' Kyndra asked guardedly.

'My name is Janus.' The young man crossed his arms over his chest. Only then did Kyndra register the colour of his robes, golden like his belt. Yesterday they'd been brown.

'Yes,' he said, anticipating her question. 'I was raised to the gold this morning. That means I'm a master now.'

'Good for you.' Kyndra tried to step around him, but Janus blocked her. 'Do you want something?' she asked.

He smiled. 'Only to make your acquaintance.'

Still plagued by the headache, Kyndra stared at him irritably. She wasn't in the mood for this. If only she could find her way back to her room, she could lie down awhile.

As if she'd spoken her thoughts aloud, Janus said, 'I could show you around the citadel, if you like. And you could tell me all about your journey here with Master Brégenne. She and I are going to be attuned later this evening.'

Kyndra frowned. 'But I thought Nediah—'

'The Council saw fit to separate them,' Janus said with a careless shrug that only increased her irritation. 'It's a turn of good luck for me, though. I'm sure I can learn a lot from Master Brégenne.'

Kyndra didn't care much for his tone. 'If you'll excuse me, then,' she said sharply, 'I ought to go and talk to Nediah.' She edged around him and took a few steps down the corridor. Suddenly Janus was in front of her again. She pulled up short with a gasp.

'Kyndra,' he said silkily, 'do you want to pass the test?'

She gazed at him, nettled. 'No. I don't want to stay here.'

Janus' handsome face grew serious. His features were delicate, almost feminine, Kyndra found herself thinking.

'The first test nearly killed you,' he told her softly. 'The second will be worse. I hope you haven't used up your luck, Kyndra.'

'What do you mean?'

Janus moved closer, but she held her ground. 'The second test will be different,' he said, his blue eyes full of concern. Kyndra wasn't sure whether it was genuine. 'Since you didn't respond to the level of force used in the first test, the Wielders will increase it. They will draw down more power against you.'

She shivered. 'I'm not afraid,' she said more to herself than to him.

'You ought to be.' His eyes dipped to her midriff, as if he could see the bandages under her shirt. 'But I would like to help you.'

Kyndra swallowed. 'Sounds more like you want to scare me.'

'I do,' Janus said and stepped back. There was something in the way he moved that reminded her of Jhren too. 'You're in great danger. Unless you find your affinity, the second test will kill you.'

Kyndra tried to ignore the fear that slithered down her spine. She didn't want to remember the high cliff or the terrible lances piercing her body, but most of all, she didn't want him to see that she was frightened. 'You can't be sure of that,' she said more confidently than she felt. 'The first one didn't.'

Janus shook his head, seeming exasperated. 'It should have,' he said. 'And you are in more trouble because it didn't. You attracted the Council's attention.'

She looked away. As much as Janus resembled Jhren, he wasn't her friend and she couldn't afford to trust him. He was one of them – a Wielder. *He's the enemy.* 'If you really want to help me,' she said, 'you can show me how to get out of here.'

'I can't do that, Kyndra.' This time, Janus' regret did seem genuine. 'I can't go against the Council.'

Kyndra released her breath in a sigh. 'Then I don't need your help, Janus.'

'What's going on?'

Janus spun at the new voice, a smile ready on his lips. 'Nediah. What are you doing here?'

'I could ask you the same question,' Nediah said, his face darkening.

'I've come to show Kyndra around the citadel.'

'No you haven't. Why are you really here?'

Janus frowned. 'I don't know what you mean, Nediah.'

Kyndra stood uncertainly between the two men, as they eyeballed each other. Nediah's eyes were narrowed in suspicion, Janus' wide and innocent. Finally, Nediah said, 'Go ahead and play your game, Janus. But don't expect me to join in. And leave Kyndra out of the stakes.'

Janus gave an airy laugh. 'You're so dramatic, Nediah. There is no game and certainly no stakes.' He paused. 'Rather, you should be glad you don't share Brégenne's punishment.' Then his smile turned crooked. 'Or perhaps you do.'

'She's Master Brégenne to you, novice.'

Janus flushed a deep red and Kyndra noticed little flickers of light escaping his clenched fists. Nediah glanced at them and raised an eyebrow. 'Don't be foolish, Janus. You and I both know the Council didn't raise you to the gold for your abilities.'

For a moment Kyndra was sure that the young man would

take it further, but he drew a few deep breaths and the fire faded. 'Very well,' he said. 'But, starting tomorrow, you'll find that Kyndra becomes my responsibility.' He flashed Kyndra a hot glance and then he was gone.

Kyndra spun to see him at the end of the passage, leaving a wisp of gold as he vanished around the corner. 'Won't he go to the Council?' she asked Nediah. The Wielder's eyes were fixed on the spot where Janus had just been standing.

'Probably,' he answered. 'And I don't doubt he will get what he wants. What were you talking to him about?'

'Nothing.'

Nediah gave her a searching look.

'He was offering to help me with the test,' she admitted. 'But I told him I wasn't interested.'

The Wielder scowled. 'Just be careful around him, Kyndra. He's not to be trusted.'

Kyndra hesitated. 'He said that you and Brégenne . . . Is it true?'

Nediah's green eyes blazed. He took her arm and marched her back down the passage, away from the one Janus had taken. Kyndra let herself be led, unwilling to have that emerald fire directed at her.

When they'd made enough turns and crossed enough intersections for her to have become utterly disoriented, Nediah relaxed his pace. There were fewer people here, Kyndra noticed. She wondered how Naris's citizens found their way through this black maze. True, not all passages looked the same and the hollowed-out chambers varied dramatically in size, but traversing the mountain must be like sailing without the stars. The black stone gave nothing away.

Nediah removed his hand and curled it into a fist. 'What

gives him the right to speak as if this Attunement is some sort of victory?'

'He didn't really—' she began, but stopped at the look on Nediah's face.

'A novice!' the Wielder continued. 'You have no idea of the insult, Kyndra. Brégenne has worked all her life in the furtherance of Naris. She has brought more potentials to this citadel than anyone else and *this* is her reward?'

'It's because of me,' Kyndra said quietly. She forced herself to meet Nediah's stormy gaze. 'This is my fault.'

Nediah jerked to a halt. 'Don't you ever think that,' he said harshly. He grasped her upper arms. 'Brégenne risked so much to bring you here. And look how Naris has treated you.' He released Kyndra and added quietly, 'I'm ashamed to be part of it.'

'So you agree I'm not a Wielder?' she asked hopefully. 'That it's all a mistake?'

Nediah turned a fresh glower upon her. 'I've already told you. Brégenne never makes mistakes.' His voice lost some of its fierceness. 'You have the ability, I'm sure of it.'

He ignored Kyndra's sigh and began walking again. When Kyndra didn't follow, he glanced over his shoulder. 'Come on. I seem to remember you like books?' When she nodded, he smiled and reached into a large pocket in his robes. 'I'm sure Hebrin, our archivist, would like to see this. Why don't we go and show him?'

When Kyndra saw what he held, a lump rose unbidden in her throat. She'd last seen it lying on a table in another life. Holding *Acre: Tales of the Lost World* tight to her chest, she followed Nediah down the passageway.

15

When imagining the archives, Kyndra had pictured a soaring, vaulted ceiling and a chamber so vast that a small army could comfortably fit inside it. There'd be row upon row of shelves, books and scrolls stashed in strict bibliographical order, circular mantels grasping the walls, lined with the spines of fraying tomes and a marble floor scuffed by the heels of eager scholars. And sunlight would be streaming from high windows, motes of dust hanging in the beams.

There was no sunlight here.

The archives of Naris were, in fact, so dark that Kyndra had trouble seeing at all. She also had trouble standing upright. The roof dipped often to brush her head and was studded with nubs of rock. She'd already bumped into several of these and now stood next to Nediah, rubbing her forehead while her eyes searched out the rest of the antechamber. It was about the size of The Nomos' common room, filled with square reading tables. Shelves ringed the dark walls, home to dozens of parchment bundles tied loosely together.

'Those are the archival catalogues,' Nediah told her.

'Why aren't they bound like proper books?'

'Because pages are constantly added.' Nediah eyed the low

ceiling before taking a few steps to his right to point at a dark archway. 'That leads down into the spiral galleries. To give you an idea of the size, there are nine levels below us and only around two thirds of the books housed there are recorded in the catalogues. Finding and shelving them correctly is an on-going task.'

Kyndra gazed at the ribbon-bound parchments. 'How long has it taken to compile those lists?'

'About two hundred years.'

'Two hundred!' Kyndra could hardly imagine it. 'And how many books are here?'

'I don't know exactly,' Nediah answered, spreading his hands. 'But less than before the war. Many didn't survive the fall of Solinaris. Cataloguing is a task passed down from one archivist to the next. There are actually a team of them who work under Master Hebrin — he's in charge of the archives.' Nediah fixed her with a stern eye. 'In here, his word is law.'

Kyndra looked at him enquiringly. 'Not the Council's word?'

'Don't be tiring.' Despite the rebuke, a tiny smile flickered in the corner of Nediah's mouth. Then the Wielder folded his arms. 'For someone who loves books as much as you do, I trust you understand the value of those kept here. The archives demand respect.'

'*Demand* is a strong word, Master Nediah.'

Kyndra wasn't the only one who jumped. Nediah hastily uncrossed his arms. 'Master Hebrin,' he said, flushing. 'I didn't hear you come in.'

The archivist moved into the light of the Solar fires that floated overhead. 'My,' he said, blinking at the empty chairs. 'Have you chased off all the novices?'

Nediah laughed and Hebrin smiled, deepening the creases

around his mouth. The archivist's eyes were green – not dark like Nediah's, but awash with pale light like the sky after rain. A shock of white hair betrayed his age and wrinkles meandered from the corners of his eyes into papery cheeks. Given that Wielders lived longer than ordinary people, Kyndra wondered just how old he was.

Hebrin held out his hand. 'You must be Kyndra Vale. It's always pleasant to meet a new potential.' He raised an eyebrow. 'Especially one who's created such a storm in the citadel.'

'I didn't mean to,' Kyndra said as she shook hands.

Hebrin chuckled drily. 'That makes little difference. Perhaps a squall is good for us.'

'That's why I asked your permission to bring her, Master Hebrin,' Nediah said. 'I thought she might find something here to help with the test, something that would explain to her what we are more clearly than the words we use ourselves.'

Hebrin studied Nediah approvingly. 'I understand. The Wielders of old were adept at conveying the essential truth of things. I sometimes fear we have lost the gift.'

Kyndra wasn't at all sure what they were talking about. She looked at the archway and saw that it, too, had symbols carved over its mantel. A solid darkness crept from it into the ante-chamber, darkness that lay unbroken all the way to the world's heart.

'Kyndra,' Nediah said then, breaking her reverie. 'Show Master Hebrin your book.'

Oddly reluctant to let it go now that she had it back, Kyndra handed over the book. 'It's about Acre,' she said. 'My stepfather bought it for me.'

As Hebrin took the slim volume, she felt a sudden sense of dislocation. Here she was, standing in the Wielders' city, showing a Wielder a book mainly about Wielders. What would the archivist make of that? She watched him carefully, but Hebrin only glanced at the inside page before giving it back to her. 'A charming storybook,' he said and Kyndra felt a ripple of resentment. She tucked her only relic of home safely inside her shirt.

'To business, then.' If Hebrin realized he'd offended her, he gave no outward sign of it. Perhaps he didn't care. 'Master Nediah can show you which books will further your understanding. Those texts are all on the upper spirals and there is no need to venture below the third.'

Kyndra didn't miss the warning. She only had time to nod before Hebrin continued.

'You must know the rules before you proceed. The seventh spiral is forbidden, as are those beneath. That level marks the end of free reading for *all* Wielders.' His gaze swept across Nediah, who shifted uncomfortably.

'There are shields in place that will stop you, should you think to test me,' Hebrin said. 'You will not be able to pass a shielded gate, or touch a shielded book. Should I find you attempting to do so, you will leave the archives and not be permitted to return. Do you understand?'

Kyndra nodded again. She watched Hebrin's eyebrows draw sternly together and added hastily, 'Yes, Master Hebrin.'

Her words banished his frown. 'Good,' Hebrin said. 'Now that the formalities are over, you may accompany Master Nediah. I hope the archives will be of aid.'

'Thank you, Master Archivist,' Nediah said quickly. 'I'll keep an eye on her.'

'I'm sure you will, Nediah,' Hebrin said as they crossed to the archway. 'But who's to keep an eye on you?'

Nediah chuckled, as if Hebrin had made a joke, but it fell

flat. He ushered Kyndra into the darkness, leaving the old man behind.

Kyndra waited until the solitary path they followed had taken them several minutes away from the antechamber. She watched Nediah curiously under the golden flames that the Wielder had conjured to light their way. 'What did Hebrin mean when he said there was no one to keep an eye on you?'

'*Master* Hebrin,' Nediah corrected. He paused. 'You could say I wasn't the most tractable of novices.'

'Does that mean you broke the rules?'

'I'm not proud of it,' Nediah said. 'I was stupid and courted trouble.' His face grew distant. 'It could have ended in disaster . . . I nearly destroyed my future forever.'

'How?'

Nediah didn't answer. When the silence began to build shadows between them, he said, 'After Brégenne became my mentor, I gave all that up. She opened my eyes.' He smiled faintly, ironically. 'I can never repay that debt.'

'I didn't know she was your mentor.'

'There wasn't a need for you to know.'

Kyndra frowned. 'But how could she teach you if you use opposite energies?'

Nediah glanced up at his flames and they strengthened, throwing fire against the creeping, black walls. 'A mentor isn't a teacher in that sense. Pupil and mentor often have different affinities. They guide you morally, intellectually. They are there to help with the issues all young people struggle with as they grow.'

Jarand's face came to Kyndra unbidden and she felt a wave of homesickness. Whether she'd been labelled as a bastard or not, Jarand had loved her like a father. She said nothing and stared at the rough fissures cut into the wall. Books lay there in various states of disrepair. 'Is this the first level?' she asked, looking at them.

'No. These books need some attention.' Nediah glanced at the niches and their shabby occupants. 'Most are just copies of common texts. They'll stay here until one of the novices who works in the archives has time to repair them.'

'So there aren't any forbidden ones here?'

Nediah looked sidelong at her. 'No.'

Kyndra hid her smile. 'According to Hebrin, I wouldn't be able to touch them anyway.'

'*Master* Hebrin,' Nediah said tiredly. 'And no, you wouldn't. I'll let you have a go at opening the second spiral.'

Quite suddenly a gate rose out of the darkness, barring their way. Nediah made a satisfied noise and let the golden fire spill over the elaborate portal. 'Ah. We're at the first spiral.'

Kyndra studied the gate. It stretched from floor to ceiling – a filigree of twisted metal. The bars looked like serpents and they coiled so tightly around each other that they almost blocked her view of the passage beyond. She poked them tentatively and when nothing happened, looked questioningly at Nediah. The Wielder smiled. 'The first spiral isn't shielded. Try the handle.'

She hadn't spotted it, hidden in the metalwork. The handle was a solid ring of iron and conjured up unpleasant images of dungeons. Kyndra turned it and they both stepped through. A large numeral glowed on the wall inside, welcoming them to the first spiral.

'Anyone can come here,' Nediah explained as they set off, following the tunnel that curved around to the right. 'You'll often find Initiated novices clustered together since most are too afraid to visit on their own.'

Kyndra thought of the children in Master Rush's class. She remembered the large brown eyes of the girl – the child who'd once stood alone in a circle of adults as they turned death upon her.

'What's wrong?'

Kyndra hesitated. 'Master Rush said that everyone in that classroom today had taken the test.' She looked up at Nediah. 'There was a girl, only a child. They were all children.'

Nediah stopped walking. 'You must think us monsters,' he said quietly. Kyndra didn't answer and the Wielder turned to face her. 'I wish you hadn't had to suffer,' he said. 'I wish you could have started out as I did. That first spark is a marvellous thing. You feel it burning in your veins and you think, at that moment, that there is nothing you cannot do.' Nediah's eyes were full of memory. 'Sharing the power of the cosmos connects you to everything. It's like touching life itself.'

Kyndra glanced down at her bandaged ribs and then up at Nediah. 'I don't think I ever thanked you for saving mine.'

The Wielder slowly shook his head. 'I repaired the damage to your body, but I didn't save your life.'

Kyndra stared at him, uneasy in the silence that had fallen between them. Finally, she said, 'I didn't heal myself. I'm thanking you anyway.'

Nediah smiled, though his face was tight with uncertainty. 'Come on,' he said. 'It's just around the next corner.'

When she rounded the bend, Kyndra's mouth fell open. She stood at the top of a slope – a path that clung without railings to the walls of a vertical gallery and wound a slow circle down to the floor. A starkly beautiful pillar pierced the middle of the cavern. It reminded Kyndra of a stalactite, its surface melted and then frozen in time. Veins of blue sparked through it, ghostly in the haze. Smaller pillars reached for the floor around it, some connecting and others tapering to a point in mid-air. However, none were as magnificent as their central cousin. It seemed to Kyndra as if the pillar disappeared into the ground like a tree root, possibly to emerge on the other side of the world.

'We call it the Spine,' Nediah said, watching her. 'It runs through the middle of each gallery, from ceiling to floor.'

'You mean there are more caverns like this *below* us?'

Nediah's eyes glittered. 'Eight more, each smaller than the one above it. The Spine narrows too. They say it's barely a hand's span across when it finally emerges in the ninth spiral and its tip is as sharp as a needle.'

'That would be something to see,' Kyndra said wistfully.

'Forget it. Nobody goes down that far.'

'Why not?'

Nediah frowned. 'Have you forgotten what Hebrin said? It's forbidden. And besides,' he added, 'you wouldn't be able to breathe.'

'What?'

'A natural deterrent. The lower you go, the less air there is. You have to be able to furnish your own and that's an extremely difficult thing to do, especially when there's not a lot to work with.'

'I can't believe that's even possible.' Kyndra stared at the subterranean space, catching the glimmer of quartz seams. 'Why is it so dark?'

'Darkness is good for the books.'

Tearing her eyes from the twisting pillar, Kyndra studied

the deep recesses set into the wall. Each was six feet high and contained four shelves, ingeniously carved to follow the irregular contours of the gallery. Words glowed faintly over each recess, citing field and subject.

'How do you get into the lower spirals?'

'I'll show you.'

She followed Nediah down the slope, taking care not to stray too close to the edge, but the drop gradually lessened as they neared the floor of the chamber. The Spine was even more intimidating at ground level. Kyndra's eyes strayed up its length, searching for the point where it disappeared into the roof far above. She stretched out her hand and touched it lightly with the tips of her fingers.

The pillar hummed, teasing the edges of her mind like a voice speaking in another room, a shade out of hearing. Instinctively, she listened.

'What's the matter?'

Nediah's words scattered the sound and Kyndra realized she stood as if frozen, hand glued to something that was now no more than a shard of rock. She shook her head and backed away. 'Nothing.'

Nediah turned towards a black tunnel that the curve of the wall had hidden from view. 'The way down to the second spiral is through here,' he said.

'Does each one have a gate?'

Nediah nodded. 'Like the one we just passed.'

Kyndra stole a last look over her shoulder and then followed the Wielder into the mouth of the tunnel. 'I suppose they aren't all as easy to open, though.'

'See for yourself.'

Another decorative gate awaited them ahead. Kyndra

walked up to it, trying and failing to follow the sinuous turns of its craftsmanship. She glanced at Nediah, who nodded encouragingly at the iron ring. Kyndra reached out and took it.

For a split second nothing happened. Then there was a crackle of light and the gate hurled her backwards. Kyndra staggered, grasping at the wall for balance. Nediah had prudently moved aside and she glared at him. 'You knew that was going to happen.'

'I thought you'd like to see the shield in action,' Nediah said lightly. He seized the iron ring and turned it with ease.

Kyndra eyed the handle cautiously as she stepped through. 'What's the trick?'

'The shields on the gates are a test,' Nediah said. 'If a novice can open the gate, they have earned the right to the books kept beyond it.'

'So why did it throw me halfway down the tunnel?'

'Because you don't share an affinity with either the Solar or Lunar power that created the shield.'

Kyndra felt a bit disgruntled. *Everything here is a test.* 'So that's all it takes to get through the second gate. You don't have to . . . *do* anything?'

Nediah shook his head. 'Having the affinity is enough.'

'What about the rest?'

'The real tests begin at the third gate and apply to all those that follow. It takes full Masters to open the sixth. As for the seventh, I doubt I could touch the handle.'

They started off down the gently sloping tunnel and Kyndra heard the gate swing shut behind them. She winced at the solid *clank* of the latch. Alone, she'd be trapped down here. 'How long do the gates stay open?' she asked.

'About half a minute.'

The passage wound in a large circle until Kyndra was sure that they would end up back where they'd begun. Then they passed another numeral and emerged at the top of an identical slope and an identical gallery, though smaller than its sister above. The Spine continued its dizzying plunge into the floor.

'This is as far as we go.'

Kyndra let out a disappointed sigh. Although her legs ached, she wanted to keep on walking. She wanted to go where the great pillar led, to see sights buried in the distant, pre-served past under the mountain. The air tasted of hidden chambers, rock and darkness.

'You'll have to hurry up and pass the test,' Nediah said, a bit too cheerfully. 'Become a Wielder.'

'I said I wasn't interested. And, according to you, even then I wouldn't be able to reach the lower spirals.'

Nediah dropped his smile. 'You wouldn't want to. That's where they keep the worst kinds of writing and the worst kinds of power.'

Kyndra tensed. 'Power?'

'Artefacts,' Nediah said shortly, 'left over from the war. Too dangerous to be kept near the surface where people might find and use them.'

'What kind of—'

The Wielder silenced her with a frown. 'That's not why I brought you here.' He crossed to one of the shelves and prised out a large tome. 'This,' Nediah said, hefting the book at Kyndra, 'is a new novice's closest companion. We made several copies due to its popularity. It's one of the few texts that sur-vived the war and though the language is a little dry, it may help to focus your mind.'

Kyndra clamped her fingers around the tome as it started to slip. 'Focus my mind on what?' she asked dubiously.

'Sensing your affinity. There is plenty in there about the nature of cosmosethic energy, where it comes from, how it's channelled. Immersing yourself in that knowledge may help to bring you closer to it before the – second test.'

Kyndra heard the pause and chewed her lip, wondering whether Janus had been telling the truth when he claimed that the next test would be worse. She awkwardly turned the huge book in her hands. 'What about Rush?' she asked Nediah. 'I thought I was supposed to be learning from him?'

The tall Wielder glanced around, eyes suspicious, as if he expected to see someone lurking nearby. Satisfied that they were alone for the moment, he said quietly, 'I suspect that Master Rush is under some duress. You've been put with the Initiated for a reason and I doubt you will hear anything to help you there. Rush might also refuse to answer any question concerning the test.'

Kyndra stared at the Wielder, ice trickling down her spine. The Council saw her as a problem, she realized, one that would best be solved by elimination. *They want me to fail.* She took a few deep breaths. Did Nediah know it too? Was that why he'd brought her here, to give her a fighting chance? She felt as if she were suffocating on the smell of old paper.

'Kyndra.' Nediah laid a hand on her shoulder. 'I'm not defending the Council's decision or what Alandred did, but I believe in you. *Brégenne* believes in you and she's never been wrong.'

Kyndra's throat tightened. Always it came back to Brégenne and her flawless record of finding potentials. Nediah couldn't see what was right in front of him. He couldn't see that she was an ordinary girl from an even more ordinary town, thrust into the middle of something so extraordinary, it would kill her.

Nediah's hand slipped from her shoulder. The Wielder stood quite still, as if listening to a distant voice. 'I have to go,' he said. 'They're ready.'

'Who are?'

He turned sharply without answering and retreated into the sloping tunnel. Kyndra hurried after him, thinking of the shielded gate. 'Nediah?' she panted, as the Wielder increased his pace. 'What is it?'

'The Attunement. I have to be there so that they can break my link with Brégenne.' His voice was inflectionless.

'I'm sorry,' Kyndra said quietly.

'Don't be. Maybe it's for the best.'

'But I thought you—'

'What I thought doesn't matter.' Nediah stopped so suddenly that Kyndra bumped into him. The golden flames above began to wane.

'Kyndra,' Nediah turned to face her, 'If Janus *is* to be your chaperone in the citadel, be careful around him. The Council can dress up his role in this Attunement as much as they want, but in reality he's no more than a spy. It's best if you stay away from Brégenne until you pass the test. And don't talk to Janus about her.'

'I wouldn't,' she said, seized by a memory of Janus' knowing blue eyes. Thrusting him from her thoughts, Kyndra followed Nediah back to the antechamber, which was empty save for a few older novices. 'I'm probably not allowed to leave you alone,' Nediah said in an undertone, 'but it's quiet here and you can make a start on that book. As soon as . . . it's done, I'll come for you.'

Kyndra nodded and then said awkwardly, 'Afterwards. If you want to talk about it, I can listen.'

The tall man gave her a look so bleak that Kyndra couldn't hold his gaze. When she raised her eyes from her study of the floor, Nediah had gone.

16

Alone in the antechamber, Kyndra sat at one of the tables with the book Nediah had insisted she read. Her left hand cradled her chin, while the right idly turned pages. Her concentration had begun to wane some few hundred words back. Now she stared at the heavy black lines, watching them swim out of focus.

This was impossible. Kyndra toyed with the top corner of page thirty-three, knowing she'd never finish before the test. She tried to concentrate on the book, rereading the same sentence five times. Surely there were other ways to do it. Why did the test have to be one of pain? It was savage. But a dozen children had done what she had not and Irilin claimed that none of them had been left for dead in the tombs.

Kyndra laid her palm on the page to keep her place and flipped to the cover. She stared at the scuffed title: *Laws of Energy*. It told her everything and nothing.

Reading was not going to be of any practical help. Her stomach rumbled and she rubbed it with her free hand, thinking. Perhaps belief was the key. Perhaps the power wouldn't come unless you really believed it would. Kyndra shivered. Deep down inside, where it mattered, she knew she could never be a Wielder. What if that conviction killed her?

Shrugging off the thought, Kyndra stared at someone's abandoned pen that lay on the table. She had watched the Solar novices trying to move ink bottles earlier. Cail had loosened the lid on his and sent it flying at a girl. This might have gone unnoticed if the girl in question hadn't already sent an ink bottle flying at him. The bottles had collided in mid-air, smashed and exploded their contents over Rush's back.

Kyndra swallowed her smile and stared harder at the pen. *You have no idea what you're doing,* a voice told her. *This is ridiculous.*

How difficult can it be, she silently replied, *if children half my age can do it?*

Move, Kyndra thought at the pen.

The pen didn't move.

Maybe it was because she hadn't found her affinity. She hadn't passed the test. But what was it Nediah had said? *Cosmosethic energy first manifests itself as a force of will.* Well, she was willing the pen to move, and it wasn't.

Voices reached her ears. Someone flung open the door to the antechamber and two young men came in. They stopped talking abruptly when they saw her. Kyndra spotted Irilin standing behind them and waved.

'Oh, hi, Kyndra,' Irilin said awkwardly. She stepped in front of one of the young men. 'Perhaps we should talk someplace else, Gareth. We don't want to disturb—'

'So this is her?' The novice called Gareth pushed past Irilin. He had arms almost as beefy as the blacksmith's back home, Kyndra noticed, and his brown robes strained across his shoulders. 'Pretty for a corpse, isn't she?'

Behind Gareth's back, Irilin flushed uncomfortably. 'Gareth,' she muttered.

'Well, she's not *my* type.' Another young man came to stand casually beside Gareth. He folded his arms. 'I like mine breathing.'

'Come on, Shika,' Irilin said to the other novice. 'Leave her be.'

Kyndra stared at the one called Shika. Although he wore the same robes and golden belt as Gareth, the similarity ended there. He was slender and a good deal shorter. His jaw-length black hair was streaked purple on one side and his eyes were an unusual mauve. A silken scarf wrapped his neck.

'Can I help you?' Kyndra asked with a roll of her eyes. Beneath the desk, however, her fists were clenched.

Gareth placed both hands on the tabletop and leaned in close to her. She could smell his breath, sour with food, and she pulled back as far as she could. 'Why don't you and I go somewhere a little quieter,' the big novice suggested. His eyes licked down her front. 'You can show me your scars.'

While Shika grinned appreciatively, Irilin made a sound of disgust. 'Don't be an idiot, Gareth.'

'It's all right, Iri,' Kyndra said. 'He can't help the way he was born.'

Gareth gave a bark of laughter and then he lunged for her.

Muscles already tensed, Kyndra scooted back and leapt out of her chair in one smooth movement. Gareth's grasping hands missed her by several inches. The novice grabbed the desk to steady himself and one flailing elbow knocked the book Kyndra had been reading to the floor. The tome crunched unpleasantly as it met the stone and pages spilled out of it.

There was a brief silence, as all four stared at it. Then, 'How clumsy of you, Gareth,' Shika said airily, waving a darkly bronzed hand. 'Poor Master Hebrin will not be happy. He treats his books as if they were his children.'

Gareth smirked. 'Then we had better put it out of its misery.' He raised his boot and stamped on the tome. Its spine popped and snapped and Kyndra gritted her teeth. 'Don't like that?' Gareth asked her. He crumpled some more pages under-foot. 'Are you going to stop me?'

Irilin wore a pained look, but she didn't move to restrain her friend. All she said was, 'Why are you being like this, Gareth? She's not done anything to you.'

Gareth rounded on her. 'Don't waste your breath, Iri. Can't you see? She's nothing. She's a stupid, ordinary human.'

'You're the stupid one,' Irilin retorted – rather weakly, Kyndra thought. How could a girl who seemed so nice be friends with these two?

There was an ugly flush to Gareth's cheeks now. Kyndra didn't like it and she didn't like the way he was looking at her. The novice gestured. Gold bands snapped around Kyndra's ankles, locking them together, and then the same force wrenched her arms behind her. Gareth gave her a push and she fell backwards onto a hard chair.

'Get these off me,' she gasped. The bands were hot. The pain in her wrists grew worse with every passing second. 'I said, get them off me!'

'It's speaking,' Shika remarked. He glanced at Gareth. 'I don't believe you gave it permission?' The big novice shook his head and grinned nastily. Shika's hands glowed.

Kyndra opened her mouth to yell, but her lips wouldn't part. She pulled in frantic breaths through her nose and strained against the force sealing her mouth shut. Shika laughed.

'Stop it, Shika,' Irilin said sharply, her tiny fists clenched. 'Leave her alone.'

'Listen, dead girl.' Ignoring Iri, Gareth straddled the chair and lowered himself until all his weight was on Kyndra's lap. She winced. He was *heavy*. The novice gripped the chair's high back, one hand either side of her head. Kyndra shrank away, but there was nowhere to go.

'You don't understand,' Gareth told her, his bulky face frighteningly close. 'I can do anything I want to you, *anything*. That's the difference between us: power.' His brown eyes were cold. 'You got lucky once, but that's all it was.'

Gareth leaned in and pressed his lips against her sealed mouth. She struggled, but he had her by the neck. Irilin gasped something. Kyndra saw her pale hands on Gareth's shoulders, trying to pull him away.

'Good luck with the test,' Gareth breathed in Kyndra's ear. He climbed off her, leaving her lips unpleasantly damp. Shika wore a strange expression, but he turned before she could work out what it meant. The force stopping her mouth vanished and Kyndra took a deep breath. The golden bands still held her pinned, however. Furious, unable to stand up, she watched all three novices leave. At the door, Irilin looked back. Then she glanced upwards, smiled slightly and gestured at Kyndra's manacles. Silver filaments crawled over the gold and dissolved them. As Kyndra dragged a rough sleeve across her mouth, Irilin shaped a silent apology and shut the door.

When she was satisfied that she had removed all trace of Gareth from her lips, Kyndra looked down at the book Nediah had given her. It was a mess. She crouched, gathered up all the pages and tried to fit them back into place. Many were creased

and marked by Gareth's boot. She felt too angry and humili-
ated to care about it.

A gasp sounded behind her and she straightened, arms full
of ruined book. Hebrin stood there, a look of horror blanching
his cheeks. Kyndra's heart sank. 'What . . . what have you
done?' the old man asked, staring at the remnants of *Laws of
Energy*.

'I'm sorry,' she said automatically. For a moment the book
became one of the Relic's lifeless shards. Kyndra was looking
at the Keeper, watching the horror melt into tears. She shook
her head, pulled herself together. 'It wasn't me. I would
never—'

'I should have known better than to let an outsider into the
archives.' Hebrin's tone was harsher than Iljin's had been. His
pale green eyes flickered. 'I wouldn't have permitted you to
come here except that Master Nediah vouched for you. I
trusted the judgement of that young man, just as he appeared
to trust you. I see he was mistaken.'

'You don't understand—'

'I understand perfectly.' He took the book from Kyndra's
hands and placed it on the desk. 'You will sit right here until
Master Nediah returns from the ceremony. Then you will
explain to him exactly why you have treated his help with such
contempt.'

Kyndra opened her mouth to protest again, but Hebrin
barked, '*Sit!*' and she found herself back in the chair, unable to
move. From the corner of her eye, she glimpsed a flicker of
silver about her body, but it vanished when she looked at it
directly. The book lay on the table in front of her, pages crumpled like perished blossoms.

'The bonds will remain until I return from supper.'

Mad at the injustice, Kyndra tried one last time to explain. 'Master Hebrin, I didn't do it. A novice did.'

The archivist paused in the entrance. 'You mistake me for a fool.' He snapped the door shut behind him.

Kyndra shouted at the walls in frustration. Why couldn't Hebrin have arrived a few moments earlier and put an end to Gareth's bullying? A thought occurred, which made her empty stomach churn. What if he had watched it all from his office and done nothing? Perhaps he'd only been nice to her in front of Nediah.

The minutes dragged by and her bonds did not loosen. Instead of dwelling on her humiliation, Kyndra wondered at the time. The light down here was always the same: no night, no day, only conjured flames and black walls. *It wasn't always like this*, she thought. Once the archives were filled with light and only the most precious and dangerous texts were kept below ground. The sun used to pour into the atrium too. Standing at the centre of that transparent dome, a person could survey each point of the compass. When night fell, the glass revealed the constellations, as clear as if they were riveted to the sky.

Kyndra's heart beat faster. Not another vision, not now. She tried to move her hands, but they wouldn't budge. She focused on one of the pages in front of her, mouthing the words, repeating them loudly in her head, but it was like trying to dam a river in flood. Her arms began to tremble. The tables dissolved, swept away before the wave. Kyndra filled her lungs as she went under, but the vision drowned her anyway.

. . . He has made it this far unnoticed. The archives are empty – Solinaris is more concerned with the army outside its gates.

Light slants across the marble floor from high windows and he feels the heat on his face. His eyes are fixed on a distant arch and a path that spirals down into depths untouched by the sun. He passes through the pitiful barrier erected to keep out errant novices and begins his descent.

Shields guard each level and grow stronger the deeper he goes. He stops at the entrance to the eighth spiral, gazing at an intricate web that blocks his path. It is a clever, tightly woven trap of Solar and Lunar power, and hums ominously in the silence.

He destroys it with a thought. The broken threads of energy settle on his shoulders like cobwebs and he walks on.

Soon the diminishing air sucks the moisture from his mouth and he runs a dry tongue over his lips. An uncomfortable deterrent, but a clever one; most people panic at a shortness of breath. He draws air from the cracks between the stone, from places even deeper than these galleries, from pockets trapped in the volcanic rock. And then he moves on, following the spiral as it coils upon itself.

It isn't until he feels a peculiar ache in his chest that he knows he has reached the final gauntlet. A howl of emotion waits to assail him. It wants to drown his heart in despair and flood his mind with senseless fear. He admires such ingenuity and smiles at how useless it is against him.

There is another shield. This is unexpected. Beyond its glow, he sees his destination: a tiny circular room with a solitary pedestal at its centre.

His eyes return to the shield. It is a marvel of engineering, but so flimsy that a mere breath disturbs it. There is something about it, though. The strands are charged with duty. There is a purpose to this web that goes beyond keeping him out.

No time. He flicks a finger and the web breaks. As he steps through, the frayed ends writhe in the air, as if alive. They drift towards him, seeking their destroyer. He ignores them and passes on into the chamber.

The book lies on the pedestal: the secret of the Wielders' greatest achievement. He tucks it into his robes. There is no time to lose. The citadel will soon be overrun.

When he turns, the broken web is waiting for him. Its glowing strands have grown thin – thin enough so that when he inhales, he pulls them into his nostrils. A sweaty note of panic cascades through him. He crushes it, reminding himself that he is far from defenceless. But he can feel the alien web in his mind. It has coiled itself there, serpent-like, and now lies quiescent.

There will be time enough to deal with it when he is out of here. There will be time enough to end this war. The killing will stop. He is the instrument of peace . . .

Kyndra couldn't breathe. She crouched in the darkness, smothered by the lack of air, by the desperate pounding of her heart. She gulped, but her lungs refused to fill. Her head felt odd, tingling in the manner of cramped limbs suddenly released from confinement. Confused images jostled her. *I am Kyndra Vale. I am the instrument of peace.*

She couldn't breathe.

Blind panic washed everything else away. Kyndra stumbled forward and there was light after all, a dim glow in the walls. She made out something pointed and terrible, a jut of needle-like stone that she skirted, scrabbling for the far side of the cavity. There had to be a way out, a door, something. Her lungs burned and her head spun with the lack of air.

Then her clawing fingers touched metal – a gate, and it was open. Sparks flashed in front of her eyes and Kyndra fell through it, landing on her back. She gasped and drew the barest breath of air into her lungs. Without knowing why, she pushed the gate closed with her feet and pulled in another tantalizing breath. It wasn't enough. She could feel herself slipping into unconsciousness, a black sleep that would last forever.

Something glowed high on the wall beyond the gate. Markings carved into the stone. She kept her waning gaze on them, drawn to their light. They grew to consume her, following her as she fell. And they were still there when her eyes closed, a blazing, chilling rebuke:

IX

Brégenne let herself be guided by Veeta's hand. The older woman was one of her closest friends and Brégenne nodded her thanks. The moon would be up soon and then she'd be able to see Veeta's face.

Veeta gave her shoulder a comforting pat and retreated. Brégenne heard her footsteps moving away. Everything was ready. She could sense Nediah through the bond, standing across from her. Anger rolled off him in waves and she hoped he wouldn't do anything rash.

They had only been attuned for a year, since his award of Master status, but to Brégenne that year seemed like forever. She had mentored Nediah for over a decade, watching the changes in this wayward novice from the Isles. Most Wielders achieved their title much faster, but Nediah's strength lay in healing, one of the hardest disciplines to master. It took Naris's few healers five to ten years longer to be raised to full status than those who leaned towards combat or craft.

Brégenne flexed her fingers as twilight approached. Day encased her Lunar energy in a blazing, golden cage that mentally dazzled her if she strove to break it. All novices tried a few times to touch their respective power when it slept. None succeeded. She'd once heard Solars compare the attempt to scaling a pitch-dark well, whose bricks were slick and impossible to grasp.

She made the familiar reach for the rising moon and the room flickered into being around her. It was another of the Council's chambers, a little less severe than the one in which they'd issued her punishment. Although the walls were as black as the rest of Naris, the floor was polished marble, streaked with a colour she couldn't distinguish.

A narrow carpet joined the door to a dais at the far end. Veeta had taken a position on the second of its three broad stairs. Tonight only one of the chairs up there was occupied.

Lord Loricus made the stiff seat look like a throne. He lounged on it, arms draped over the sides. Brégenne ground her teeth. Loricus was strong in his power, very strong, but she had never believed that a good enough reason to serve on the Council.

Janus stood poised behind Nediah. The young man's expression was perfectly neutral, but perhaps he'd caught Brégenne's glance and smothered his smile. His robes shone like burnished metal.

'Let us begin,' Veeta said. She glanced at Loricus, and the councilman nodded, smiling. Brégenne steeled herself. She must not give Loricus the satisfaction of seeing her upset.

Veeta began to speak and Brégenne let the words wash over her. Four decades in Naris. So much time had passed so quickly. What had she really done with the years? A stab of longing for Master Guiliel pierced her chest. Her own mentor had died a week before she was raised to the silver. She had grieved for him, as if for a father, but felt peculiarly strengthened by his death. She hoped she had been as good a mentor to Nediah. She hoped she had instilled in him some part of Guiliel's wisdom.

Brégenne finally allowed herself to look at her former pupil. She vividly remembered the day they were introduced. Even then he had towered over her, his eyes unerringly able to peer into her soul. Without warning, he'd taken her hands, placing them upon his face. He described himself in much the same way he described the rug in her room, emphasizing colour and shade, correctly guessing she could see neither. She'd snatched back her hands as if his touch had scalded her.

She only realized she was still staring at him when he turned his head to meet her gaze. Brégenne couldn't seem to look away. Trance-like she stood, letting the moonlight show her his face. Veeta addressed Janus, but Brégenne didn't hear what was said. Her feet tingled as if they longed to take her somewhere, but she couldn't move. The palms of her hands began to sweat.

'Master Brégenne.'

She blinked and slowly turned her head towards the old woman. Veeta watched her with a pale gaze, the folds of skin at her neck sagging in sympathy. Brégenne stared. Her friend's pity abruptly left her cold.

'Janus is ready. You must relinquish your bond with your former partner.'

Brégenne nodded. As the more experienced of the two, control of the bond rested with her. It was not within Nediah's power to dissolve it. She instinctively knew he wouldn't have complied with the Council's wishes.

'Brégenne.' Veeta's hand reached out and gently touched her chin. She felt the grain of the other woman's fingers. What was she waiting for? She concentrated on the link forged between herself and Nediah. She'd never truly examined it before. Remarkable, really, a twisting plait of Solar and Lunar energy, which drew from both to make it work. She stretched herself along it, marvelling at the way the powers were so neatly intertwined.

'Brégenne!'

Lord Loricus rose to his feet behind the table. In her moonlit sight, his eyes were like dark glass. 'I am here to ensure you are bonded to Master Janus. Play your part and all will be well. If you continue to hesitate, I shall intervene.' His fingers twitched.

'Of course,' Brégenne said smoothly. She didn't give herself time to think. She refocused on the bond and withered her Lunar strands. The link frayed and snapped like a boat torn from its mooring.

Footsteps echoed across the marble. She turned. Wordlessly, Nediah strode away. He didn't look at her, which pained her more than his silence. He flung open a door at the back of the chamber and stepped through, slamming it behind him.

'What a temper,' Loricus said. 'You should be relieved, Brégenne.'

She stood in awful silence, searching. She couldn't feel him, as hard as she tried.

'Touch your power,' Veeta said to Janus, 'before the sun disappears entirely. I will do the weaving.'

Brégenne opened herself to the Lunar when the old woman asked her to do so. Concentrating harder than ever, she finally felt something. She moved towards it, seeking Nediah, trying to pinpoint his location.

Looking for me?

The words smiled as they sidled into her head. Brégenne pulled back her awareness and slammed the door of her mind. She could feel Janus hovering capriciously outside and misery hit her in a foul wave.

Brégenne sought refuge in the persona she had worn like a second skin. She had crafted it so long ago, to protect her from the things she feared most. Tonight that chill façade felt different, even suffocating, but she pulled it around her like a cloak and pretended it was home.

'I'd really like to know how you managed to get there.' The words filtered down to Kyndra and she struggled to make sense of them and failed. 'That was too close. Are you making dying a habit?'

She couldn't place the voice, though it was vaguely familiar. Light flickered, surely bright enough to be the sun.

'That's right. Open your eyes.'

The flickering was caused by her eyelids, as they lifted and closed, striving to return her to wakefulness. The voice graciously waited.

Kyndra blinked at the gloom. The sunlight must have been an invention of her bruised mind, for nothing eased the shadows but a meagre hand lamp, leaning crookedly against the rock. A woman sat cross-legged beside her. Her elbows rested on her knees and her hands cupped her pointed chin. Long brown hair hung straight into her lap.

Shock jolted Kyndra upright. She'd last seen those almond-shaped eyes in a tavern back in Sky Port East. 'You!' she gasped.

'Me,' Kait said. She stretched like a cat. 'I'm glad you're awake. We can't stay down here forever.'

'Down here?' Kyndra repeated dazedly. She gave their immediate area a closer inspection. It seemed to be a tunnel. The lamplight reached only as far as the curving walls allowed. It reminded her of – 'The archives,' she said slowly.

'Very good,' Kait answered, as if it had been a test. 'Take a look through that fissure over there.' She yawned and clasped her knees. Shooting her a suspicious glance, Kyndra put her eye to the stone.

Huge, rectangular shapes loomed up and she jerked away before she realized what she was seeing. She must be behind one of the recesses that held the shelves. Between the books, she saw a slice of gallery, bluish and silent. The Spine was just visible, startlingly narrower than she remembered.

When she turned back, Kait was watching her. The woman's hair fell casually over one eye when she tilted her head. Kyndra looked at the strong lines of her jaw and swallowed nervously. 'I don't understand,' she said. 'What happened to me? Why are you here?'

Kait climbed to her feet. 'You're made of questions, aren't you? I'm afraid I can only answer the second.'

Kyndra's head felt light and her chest ached. A sharp intake of breath brought back the memory of floundering alone in that dark and airless space. 'Why am I alive?' she asked faintly.

Kait flashed her a sharp, white smile. 'Because of me. You're lucky these passages run parallel to the archives and that I found you *outside* the ninth. If you'd collapsed beyond that gate, we wouldn't be having this conversation.' She retrieved her lamp and headed up the tunnel. When Kyndra didn't follow, she glanced over her shoulder. 'Hurry. We're still a long way down.'

'Where are you taking me?'

Kait's look became withering. 'Back to civilization. I can't very well drop you off in the sixth gallery, can I?'

Kyndra stared at her, utterly lost, and Kait's expression softened. 'Come on. I'll explain on the way.'

Kyndra forced her legs to move. She could feel them trembling, like the rest of her. Memories of the last few hours seeped back with every step, and she tried to put them in order. The last thing she recalled was staring at the book, fighting the vision that threatened to sweep her away. Where had it taken her and why didn't she remember getting there? 'What's happening to me?'

She only realized she'd spoken the thought aloud when Kait said, 'Don't ask me. I've heard about your penchant for self-destruction, but didn't expect to encounter it first-hand. You know, I had to use a fair amount of air from my own body to save you and that is no mean feat down here.'

Something clicked into place. The lower you go, Nediah had claimed, the less air there was. 'I think I'm in trouble,' Kyndra said.

Kait smiled widely. She stopped beside a black hole in the wall, set close to the ground, and beckoned her over. Kyndra crouched down. Darkness flowed from the toothy fissure and she drew back, thinking of sunken ceilings and coffins. 'It's only a little way,' Kait promised, seeing Kyndra's face. 'Look, I'll go first.' She hunched over and disappeared into the hole like a ferret. 'Don't forget my lamp,' her muffled voice said.

Kyndra glanced at the tunnel. 'Why can't we carry on up?' she called.

Kait said something that sounded ominously like 'Rock fall', and Kyndra shuddered. She placed the lamp into the hole. After the first ring of stone incisors, the light showed her a smooth, black throat. 'I'm through,' Kait said from somewhere slightly up and to Kyndra's right. 'It doesn't take long.'

Swallowing her fear, Kyndra took a deep breath and wriggled into the crevice, pushing the lamp before her. Her clothes snagged every so often, causing her several moments of panic until they ripped free. The lamplight made her think of a miner's lantern, its paltry flame the only protection against the endless darkness of the earth. Finally, she could see another light ahead and Kait's face reappeared.

Kyndra popped out of the hole like a mole into sunlight, blinking in the cobalt glow of another gallery. When she straightened from examining the rips at her knees, Kait pointed at something on the wall. It was the numeral 'IV'. Kyndra stared at it in consternation and then scanned the chamber for witnesses. Thankfully, it was empty.

'Master Hebrin's going to kill me,' she said, feeling sick.

'If he finds out.'

Kyndra transferred her confused gaze to Kait. 'Well, you're a Wielder, aren't you? You'll tell him.'

All traces of Kait's smile disappeared. 'Not this time, Kyndra Vale.'

Kyndra studied the other woman silently. Now that they stood in the light of the gallery, she noticed Kait didn't wear the parted robes that seemed to be standard in Naris. Her clothes were similar to Kyndra's own: knee-high boots over dark trousers and a pale shirt. A belt, hung with several pouches, cinched her waist. 'Who are you?' she asked slowly.

Kait's look was level. 'I *am* a Wielder, but why do you think I'd betray you to Hebrin?'

The pouches on her belt reminded Kyndra of the one Nediah had asked about, the one stolen from Brégenne's room.

The events of the last two days had driven the mystery of the earth from her mind and she still owed Nediah that description.

'Why wouldn't you?' she asked. 'I can't go anywhere without you people watching me or bullying or threatening me. And I'm sure Hebrin is going to ban me from the archives because a novice tore up the book I was reading.'

It was hard to tell beneath that strange, subterranean light, but Kyndra thought a predatory glint entered Kait's eyes. The woman leaned forward. 'You say "you people", Kyndra. But they are not my people.'

The sentence hung in the air between them. 'What were you doing in Sky Port East that day?' Kyndra asked suddenly.

Kait turned away. She began to walk up the slope that spiralled into the higher galleries. 'I was looking for someone.'

Kyndra hurried after her. 'And did you find them?'

Kait didn't reply. She marched up through the ground in silence and soon Kyndra was too out of breath to ask her anything else. She followed her in and out of the gallery walls, using cunningly disguised crawl spaces. They avoided several gates that way and Kyndra marvelled at the illegal route, knowing she'd never be able to find it on her own.

'Who else knows about this?' she asked, as she and Kait cautiously emerged into the second gallery. She studied the slight movement of Kait's throat as she swallowed.

'My friends,' Kait said shortly. 'As far as the Council know, there is only one way into and out of the Deep.'

'*Kait?*'

Both of them jumped. Kyndra spun, expecting to meet Hebrin's stony stare, but it wasn't the archivist who stood there.

255

Kait gave a girlish laugh and leapt at the newcomer. 'Nediah,' she said, throwing her arms round his neck, 'you are far too handsome to go around with that scowl on your face. Why, it's making your cheeks red.'

Nediah flushed a deeper scarlet and swiftly disentangled himself. 'What are you doing to Kyndra?'

'*Doing* to her?' Kait arched a pointed brow. 'Nothing. You make it sound as if she's fallen foul of some villain.'

'She has,' Nediah growled, his cheeks still flaming. 'Your kind can't be trusted.'

An ugly glare dashed the smile from Kait's face. 'My *kind*? We are not animals, Nediah. I'd have thought you, of all people, knew that.'

Kyndra, watching the exchange with her mouth slightly open, saw the blood recede blotchily from Nediah's cheeks.

'I won't dredge up our past in front of the girl. I see by your face that you haven't forgotten a moment of me.'

Pale now, Nediah regarded her warily. 'I'll ask you again, Kait. What are you doing with Kyndra?'

The tall woman spun away. 'Saving her life, if you please, though I haven't yet heard a word of thanks from her mouth.'

'Thank you,' Kyndra muttered, uncomfortable at being caught in the middle of something she didn't quite understand.

'What nonsense is this?' Nediah demanded. He threw a quick look over his shoulder and lowered his voice. 'The archives are closed. I'm not supposed to be here, only I couldn't find Kyndra.'

'The years have dulled your sense of adventure,' Kait observed.

Nediah ignored her. His eyes travelled over Kyndra, noting

the tears in her clothes and the ashen cast to her skin. 'What happened?' he asked quietly.

'I found her expiring outside the ninth gate.'

Nediah shot Kait an incredulous look. 'That's impossible.'

'You really have been around that woman too long.' Kait folded her arms. 'If south seventh didn't run so close to that spiral, I'd never have heard her.'

'South what? Never mind.' He returned his gaze to Kyndra. 'Is this true? How did you get down there?'

Kyndra hugged herself. 'I don't know.' Her voice cracked. 'I think it was the visions.'

Both Wielders stared at her and Kait uncrossed her arms. 'What kind of visions?'

'I can't remember,' Kyndra lied, remembering all too well. It had been different this time. Even in the midst of the memories – if that's what they were – she'd known who she was: Kyndra Vale of Brenwym. Now she remembered how it felt to be someone else. She remembered being a *man*. She shook her head, suppressing a shudder. She had relived his journey to the archives to steal a book. A book that contained the secret of . . . there she failed.

'Nothing at all?' Nediah asked.

'It was to do with something that used to be in the archives,' Kyndra offered. She looked at the slope that led to the second gate. 'I don't remember anything between sitting in the ante-chamber and waking up in the dark. I couldn't breathe.'

'Sleepwalking through the archival gates is a rare talent,' Kait commented drily. 'But not one I envy. Lucky no one saw her, Nediah.'

'None of this makes sense,' Nediah muttered. 'She couldn't even open the second gate earlier, let alone the—'

'Ninth. Lack of air must finally have caught up with her.'

'I don't know enough about the lower shields. Maybe—'

'I was coming out, not going in.'

In the uncomfortable silence, both Wielders turned to stare at her. 'Coming out of the ninth spiral?' Kait asked, frowning. For the first time, she seemed uneasy.

Kyndra nodded. 'I remember it.'

Nediah's face darkened. 'This can't go any further,' he said fiercely to Kait. 'If it reaches the Council, whatever the circumstances, Kyndra won't live long enough to take a second test.'

'And why would I have dealings with the Council?' Kait answered acidly. 'Have you forgotten my fall from grace?'

Nediah shot her a silencing glare and then beckoned to Kyndra. 'I need to get you out of here in case you're missed.'

Kyndra nodded and looked sidelong at Kait. Obviously, Nediah knew something she didn't. 'Make yourself scarce,' Nediah told the woman tensely. 'Thank you for keeping her safe.'

Kait observed the flustered man. Beneath her lashes, her eyes seemed full of things unsaid. She stepped close to him, laid her hand upon his cheek and Nediah stiffened. 'She is a fool,' Kait breathed. She moved her hand to his chest. It lay there for the briefest of moments and then fell to her side. 'Don't close your heart, as she has.'

She spun on her heel then and strode away, returning into the earth. After a few seconds, her voice floated back to them, borne on the still air. 'I'm not finished with you, Kyndra Vale.'

17

Wordlessly, Nediah and Kyndra made their way out of the archives. The underground space was eerily quiet. Kyndra stared at the semi-precious veins strewn through the rock and caught a murmur of the Spine's drifting song.

When they reached the antechamber, the ruined book still lay on the desk. Kyndra wondered why Hebrin hadn't removed it. That was yet another question: how had she managed to break the archivist's Lunar binding? Perhaps the same way she'd walked through the gates. Kyndra shivered. *It's him*, she thought, shrinking away from the vision. *He did it.*

Nediah wasn't looking at the book. He was looking at her. 'You're pale,' he said with a sigh. 'I can't leave for a minute without you getting into trouble.'

'Sorry,' Kyndra mumbled. The vision was still in her head, but parts of it had begun to fade, leaving her to flounder in a welter of images. 'You do believe me, don't you?' she asked Nediah. 'About what happened?'

The Wielder said nothing. He fished a key from his pocket and unlocked the antechamber doors. 'Where'd you get that?' Kyndra asked.

'Stole it,' Nediah said shortly. He cracked open the door

259

and glanced out. 'Quick.' They darted into the dim corridor. Nediah closed the door and left the key in the lock. When Kyndra looked enquiringly at it, he said, 'Let Hebrin wonder.'

'What time is it?' she asked as they started through the silent halls.

'Well after midnight. I'm sorry I didn't come sooner, but something happened. It kept the higher-ranking masters busy for quite a while – Alandred, Hebrin, Myris. They sent for me because I'd encountered it before.'

So that was why Hebrin hadn't recovered the book. 'What was it?' she asked.

'Whatever happened to that man in Market Primus has happened again right here in the citadel.'

'What?' Kyndra felt plunged into icy water. 'To whom?'

'To Master Rush.'

'But he was fine earlier!'

'How much earlier?' Nediah searched her face. 'He wasn't found until supper.'

'This afternoon,' Kyndra said, trying to rub away the chill in her arms. 'You came for me, remember?'

'Of course,' Nediah said distractedly and for the first time Kyndra noticed the weary slant of his eyes. 'Until I get into Rush's mind, I won't know whether this affliction produces different symptoms in Wielders.' He shivered and Kyndra knew he was dreading the prospect.

'How is he now?' she asked.

'We gave him datura, so he's sleeping. It may help to slow the deterioration.' Nediah ran a hand through his hair and looked away. 'We found him . . . cradling his own filth. He was writing with it, chanting under his breath. His teaching room's a wreck.'

Kyndra didn't really want to know, but a macabre instinct urged her to ask, 'What was he writing?'

'Just nonsense. The same word over and over again.'

'What word?'

Nediah glanced at her. '*Rairam.*'

She frowned. 'I've never heard it before.'

'Nor have I.' Nediah paused. 'We could be in serious trouble. Until I work out what's causing this madness, it could happen again at any time to anyone. I don't think it's contagious, but just in case it is, Rush is being kept in one of the annexes beside the tombs.'

'That's where I woke up,' Kyndra said, swallowing back the memory of the stone slab and the passageway winding down into the lifeless earth.

'Short of the tombs themselves, the annexes are the best place to isolate someone.'

They reached the room Kyndra had come to see as her cell. Nediah opened the door. 'I'm sorry about this.' He nodded at the key in the lock with the bolt above it. 'But in light of recent events, it might actually be safer for you in here. Do you need anything?'

A few hours ago, Kyndra would have answered *food*. But her hunger had fled. 'That woman,' she said instead and watched Nediah's face tighten. 'Who is she?'

For a moment, Kyndra didn't think Nediah would reply. Then the Wielder sighed and raised a hand to his forehead. 'She belongs to a sect called the Nerian.'

'What's that?'

'*Nerian* is an Acrean word meaning "the saved". They're a group of people who preach an alternative history, a forgotten truth. They claim their leader is the unacknowledged saviour of this world.'

'Saviour?'

Nediah's mouth twisted. He leaned against the door frame and folded his arms. 'The Nerian believe that the Acrean wars were brought to an end through the efforts of just one man, who sacrificed everything to preserve our way of life. They are fanatics. They are kept in the Deep for their own protection.'

Kyndra gave him a sharp look. 'You mean they're prisoners.'

Nediah hesitated. His eyes flickered to the floor, as if he saw through the stone to something beneath. 'Yes,' he admitted. The Council doesn't want them peddling their ideas in Naris or – worse – the wider world. They don't care about keeping the citadel a secret. They'd set their madman up as a king.'

'If they're so dangerous, why doesn't the Council just wipe them out?'

Nediah raised an eyebrow at her cold suggestion. 'If the Council silenced the Nerian, it would send a message. It would give credence to the sect, make its members martyrs to an idea. The Council leaves them alone so that no one takes them seriously.'

'Seems like some people do, though,' Kyndra commented, matching him stare for stare.

Nediah's face darkened. 'I tried to stop Kait long ago, but it was too late. Their beliefs inflamed her. She was always impetuous and she hated the Council.' An old sadness misted his eyes, muted by time and acceptance. 'Once you join the Nerian, there is no returning. Kait is dangerous, strong in her power and her conviction, and she's devoted to the madman they call their leader. Stay away from her.'

Kyndra swallowed. 'I'm hardly going to go looking for her. What does she want with me, anyway?'

'I don't know,' Nediah said worriedly. 'The sect must have an interest in you, in your situation. Kait's timing in all this is very suspect. She may even have been sent to make contact. They don't expect you to know anything about them and you'll be lured in that way.'

Kyndra wondered whether she ought to tell Nediah that Kait had been in Sky Port East, but the Wielder looked anxious enough already. Talking about Kait had visibly aged him; sadness lingered in the lines around his mouth.

'You said that Medavle once tried to join a sect,' Kyndra recalled. 'Was it the Nerian?'

Nediah's eyes narrowed. 'For someone who looks dead on her feet, you're remarkably quick. Yes, it was. That's the only thing I know about Medavle.'

Kyndra nodded numbly. This day had lasted weeks already. She couldn't take it all in. Between poisonous sects, cases of madness and the visions that turned her into someone else, she hardly knew what was real any more.

'You don't need to worry about Medavle, Kyndra. Or the Nerian. Just concentrate on learning as much as you can before the test.'

'I would, but I think Hebrin's planning to ban me from the archives.'

'What?'

Wearier by the minute, she sketched a brief account of events in the antechamber. Kyndra studied the wall as she spoke, hoping Nediah wouldn't notice she was holding back. She had tried her best to forget about Gareth, but her pride wouldn't let her. 'I tried to tell Hebrin it wasn't me,' she finished, 'but he wouldn't listen.'

Nediah frowned and scratched his chin. 'That doesn't sound at all like Hebrin. I'll talk to him tomorrow, and I'm sorry about the novices.' He laid a light hand on her shoulder. 'I should have known there'd be some more than willing to give you a hard time.'

Kyndra looked away. 'It's not your fault, Nediah.'

'Did they hurt you?'

'No,' Kyndra said, remembering Gareth's weight pressing down on her. 'I'm fine.'

Nediah did not look convinced. 'If you have any problems, don't be afraid to come to me.'

He took his hand from her shoulder and she forced a smile. 'Thanks.'

Nediah closed the door and, a moment later, Kyndra heard the key turn in the lock. It was unnecessary, she thought. Where could she go that the Wielders wouldn't find her? She couldn't even remember the way to the entrance hall.

Kyndra lay back on the narrow bed and stared at the rock hanging oppressively over her head. *I can't give up*, she thought. *I promised Mother and Jarand I'd come home.* The memory of that night was always there and she saw again the look that deadened Jarand's eyes when he learned of the price Brégenne had set.

Kyndra turned her face to the wall. Once upon a time, she had recklessly wished that someone would take her away from the inn – away from idle talk and stilted days. But then the Breaking had come and, with it, the end of that life. Trapped inside the dark body of Naris and scarred by a power she didn't understand, Kyndra had never regretted any wish more fervently.

Unable to sleep, Nediah paced his quarters. His mind was a flotsam of thoughts and feelings, as changeable as spring weather. Lying in bed had only served to heighten his agitation, so now he wandered between his two cave-like rooms, half dressed, watching the lamplight flicker on the wall.

Again he saw Brégenne's face and remembered the way she had hesitated over unravelling the bond. Yet she'd played her part in the end – no one could stand against the Council. No one would dare. Kyndra would, he thought wryly. But Kyndra had not been raised in Naris and she didn't understand how much power and influence the Council had amassed.

Sometimes, when he looked at the girl, he felt a flicker of the same anger that had caused him to slam the door of the council chamber. If it wasn't for her, he'd still be paired with Brégenne. With time, he might have—

Nediah stopped the thought before it could go any further. Down that road lay only misery; Brégenne had said so herself. His anger was selfish and he'd sworn to redirect it into protecting Kyndra. Brégenne had paid dearly to bring her here.

The yellow lamplight slid over an array of glass sculptures. The partner of the wolf he'd given Brégenne crouched to leap, tiny fangs bared, and Nediah regarded it in silence. Fire sparked in its golden eyes and its fragile muscles appeared to ripple.

Kait. Fifteen years had passed since the night he'd watched her vanish into the Deep, a hot-eyed disciple at each shoulder. He recalled the moment she'd asked him to come with her, and all he'd felt was hate. He hated the Council who had driven her to abandon her future. He hated the sect whose pointless ideals had blinded her. Most of all, he hated himself for not being able to hold on to her.

The years had passed and sometimes he'd dreamed of her, waking with the feel of silken hair twined through his fingers. And now, to see her unchanged . . . Perhaps she was a little harder and there was a leanness in her voice, but when she'd stepped close and filled him with her scent, it all flooded back, the memories, the old pain. *Don't close your heart.* He clenched his fists. What gave Kait the right to speak those words to him, as if she didn't know she'd been the one to break it?

Nediah turned away from the wolf and caught a glimpse of his tired reflection. He shook his head ruefully. None of this would help him sleep – and especially not the memory of Alandred's satisfied smile. Working over poor Rush that evening had forced them together. The Master of Novices wore his triumph quite plainly and had no need of words to convey it. Nediah ground his teeth, remembering the smug creases in that craggy face.

He stopped pacing abruptly, riveted by a thought. What if Alandred had gone to see Brégenne the night before Kyndra's test? What if he had made another of his absurd advances and she'd refused him? Alandred would have left angry.

Nediah swore under his breath. He was a fool not to have seen it. Now he remembered Brégenne's distraction that night, her unease and the way she had flinched away from him. It was fear he'd seen in her face.

Before he knew what he was doing, Nediah pulled a tunic over his trousers, stuffed his feet into his boots and crossed to the door. It was there that common sense caught up with him.

What was he thinking? Brégenne wouldn't talk to him about it. She assiduously avoided the subject of Alandred.

Nediah stood with his hand on the door, hesitating. His anger at Brégenne still bubbled near the surface, but now it was tempered with concern. What had Alandred done to frighten her? The question drove him to open his door and to slip out into the passage.

His way lit by only a few dim fires, Nediah padded over the stone, heading for the Lunar Quarter. Naris was split roughly into four. Solars stayed in the east, Lunars in the west. North housed the novice dormitories and in the south were communal areas – the rooms given over for teaching, the refectory and the entrance to the archives. In the centre was the atrium, the ceiling of which spiralled up to Naris's distant peak.

The corridors were deserted, utterly silent, and it was eerie walking them alone. Of course, there would be Lunars about, probably in teaching rooms or up on one of the spires. Nediah guessed there were only a couple of hours until dawn. When he reached Brégenne's rooms, he stopped, wondering what he was doing here. He crossed his arms and leaned against the wall. Beyond making sure that she was all right, he hadn't thought of what to say to her.

Before he could reach a decision, the door opened and Brégenne stood there. Nediah stared at her. The hair she always tied back was loose and fell across her shoulders in pale waves. Lunar flames burned behind her, turning her skin silver. Her white eyes glowed softly. She looked ephemeral and cold, like a ghost. Only the rose in her lips and the slight flush in her cheeks showed that she was real.

He found his voice. 'How did you know I was here?'

'A feeling,' she said.

'Can I come in?' The late hour rasped in his throat. Silently, she stood back to let him pass and Nediah stepped through and spun to close the door before she could block it from view. The silver light showed him a dent in the middle of the soft wood, lines radiating out as if something had crashed against it. 'I thought so,' he whispered.

'Nediah –'

'I'm sorry for not realizing sooner.' He turned to look at her. Brégenne stood with her arms wrapped around her body, a silken shawl partly covering her nightgown.

'Did he hurt you?' he asked finally, striving to keep his voice level.

Brégenne looked away. 'No,' she said. 'He dented his pride more than the door.'

Nediah decided to let his anger simmer out of sight. It only upset her and she already looked upset, fragile even. He couldn't remember ever seeing her like this.

Brégenne drew a few breaths. 'I'm . . . I'm sorry about the Attunement.' She took a step nearer. 'And for those things I said to you yesterday evening on the spire.' Her voice emerged as barely more than a whisper. 'That was wrong of me.'

Nediah gazed at her without speaking.

'You said the Council couldn't stop you from seeing me,' she said, echoing his own vow back to him. Her voice dropped even lower. 'I hope you're right because – because I can't stand the thought of not seeing you.'

'Brégenne—' He broke off as she stepped very close. Shyly she put a hand on his chest and her palm was warm. She traced his collarbone with her fingertips, as if she had never seen it before. Nediah felt his heartbeat quicken and he tensed his body against her touch. 'Please don't do that, Brégenne. I mean I can't—'

She moved a finger to his lips. The light shone on a lock of hair that curled across her cheek and Nediah's blood pounded in his veins. She was so close; he could feel the heat from her body through his tunic. Fearfully, she touched his face, just where he had touched hers last night on the spire. Heat and cold swept through him. He couldn't move.

The brush of her lips across his was so light, like a moth's wings. She drew back and they gazed at each other in silence. Brégenne's chest rose and fell quickly with her breathing. Her cheeks were flushed and her lips slightly parted, as if she were surprised at herself.

His hesitation lasted only a moment. Desire swept hotly through his body and his skin tingled with it. Nediah let his arms pull her against him and she gasped, but didn't flinch away. He found his hands in her hair, the soft strands tangling round his fingers. Hers were against his chest, one clutching his tunic. The shawl tumbled to the floor as he brushed the smooth skin of her back, tracing the graceful Lunar filigree that curled over her shoulders.

When he kissed her neck, she gave a little moan and sought his lips again. Her second kiss was fierce and lingering, though she trembled in his arms. Nediah felt his control slipping and grasped at it half-heartedly, but all he could think about was her touch, the way her hands stroked the muscles of his back, her slender body pressed against his own.

He sank onto the rug, drawing her down with him. Brégenne came willingly, her lips hot on his skin. They threatened to burn away his caution, as if it had never been. The laces at the front of her gown were loose. While she kissed the same collarbone she had touched earlier, he pulled at the weak knot that tied her gown and it fell apart under his fingers.

Brégenne froze. Caught in his passion, he only noticed when her body went rigid and she pulled back. She grasped the open bodice of the gown and yanked it closed. Nediah stared at her, adrift for a long, bewildering moment, and then he snatched his hands away.

'I'm sorry,' he said. The words emerged as a whisper. He saw tears on her face and the sight chilled him. 'Please don't. I won't ever hurt you.'

She nodded mutely.

He reached for the dropped shawl and carefully draped it around her shoulders. Then with a sob, she fell against his chest and cried like a child. Her tears soaked through the thin cloth of his tunic. Gently, he put his arms around her, careful not to hold her too tight. They knelt there on the floor and Nediah let her cry, resting his chin on her head. He stroked her pale, beautiful hair, uneasy at the tears he'd so rarely seen. A desperate ache bound up his heart. 'I love you,' he said help-lessly.

The words made her cry harder. He was sorry for that, but not sorry he'd said them. The seconds wound into minutes, the minutes into an hour. Brégenne's tears slowed and stopped. When, finally, he sensed dawn nearing, she pulled away.

'I'm sorry,' she said, her voice choked. 'I need you to leave.'

'Brégenne –'

'Please.' She moved away, clutching the shawl about her, and rose unsteadily to her feet. 'I need to be alone.'

Nediah took a step towards her, his tunic still damp with her tears.

'No,' she said and backed away further, turning her head to

one side. 'Leave me, please. I should never have . . . I don't want you here.'

He felt a hot swell in his eyes. 'You don't mean that.'

'How dare you tell me what I do or don't mean?' she flared at him. Her face was blotched with crying and the mask she tried to pull over it kept splintering. 'You are not my keeper!'

'I never wanted to be,' he said quietly.

'Then go.'

Her glare drove Nediah to the door. He stared at her, chagrined, fighting the disappointment that dragged at him. 'Can you allow yourself to love anyone, Brégenne?'

Like a statue, she stood there, silent and sad.

18

Kyndra lay awake, staring listlessly at the ceiling. She hadn't caught much sleep. Her ribs tingled and itched and it took an enormous effort of will not to scratch them. She wished she could stay under the blanket indefinitely. Maybe if she closed her eyes again, she'd find herself back in The Nomos, where the only things she had to face were chores.

Kyndra let the daydream go. It was useless to lie here and wish. The test offered the only path out of Naris – she would die and escape that way, or she'd pass and be set free. She tried not to listen to a dark whisper that told her she'd become a different sort of prisoner if she lived: a novice.

There was a scratching at the door. She sat up sharply. It sounded like fingernails. Unsure whether to call out, Kyndra listened and caught stifled laughter. 'Who's there?'

More laughter. She threw off the blanket and crept closer. She heard a faint metallic scrape, as if something were being withdrawn. Abruptly realizing what it was, Kyndra banged on the door. 'Put the key back!'

There was a snort of glee. 'Throw it in the chasm, Shika,' said Gareth's voice. 'No one will find it there.'

'I said, put it back,' Kyndra growled, clenching her fists.

'Who'll make me?'

'I will,' said a new voice. There was silence beyond the door. 'Be good boys now and hand over the key, or Lord Loricus will hear of this.'

'We meant nothing by it,' Shika's voice said. 'Just a bit of fun.'

'Don't you have studies to attend?'

'Yes, Master,' Gareth replied sullenly.

'Go on, then. And don't let me catch you here again.'

Kyndra heard the key inserted into the lock and stepped hastily away from the door. When it opened, she saw Janus standing there, a tray of food in one hand. The young man gave her one of his radiant smiles, and – to her surprise – she found herself smiling back. Beyond his shoulder, Kyndra glimpsed the novices hurrying away, and was relieved to see that Irilin wasn't with them.

'Made friends, have you?' Janus said, coming into the room and closing the door.

'Not exactly.'

'Don't worry. They won't bother you again.'

Kyndra wasn't at all sure about that. She suspected Janus had made her situation ten times worse. She wasn't going to tell him, though. She watched him set the tray down and slip the key into his robes. 'I think I'd better hold on to this today,' he said, his blue eyes sweeping over her. Kyndra realized she was only wearing a short tunic and felt herself blush furiously. She snatched her shirt, leather jerkin and trousers from the floor and turned to put them on.

'What are you doing here?' she asked. She tugged her shirt down roughly and winced at the stabbing in her ribs. When she turned back, Janus was sitting on her bed. His golden robes suited him, coaxing a contrast from his eyes, and his hair was a different gold – paler, like cornsilk. She felt a passing urge to touch it.

'I've brought you your breakfast,' he said. 'You're in my care now.'

So Nediah had been right. 'Have you come to help me with the test?' Kyndra asked, unable to keep the suspicion from her voice. She wondered how long it would be before Janus started asking questions about Brégenne.

'Correct,' he answered briskly, 'and I've been busy this morning on your behalf.' He raised a sculpted eyebrow. 'You *have* upset Master Hebrin. But I persuaded him to give you another chance.'

'Another chance?' Kyndra asked. 'You mean I can go back to the archives?' The idea appealed to her more than she wished to admit. There was something about the hanging galleries, their blue silence and the enigmatic Spine that sang to her.

'Hebrin will allow you space to prepare for the test,' the young man said. 'And I will show you some books that'll prove far more useful than the old thing Nediah gave you.'

Kyndra narrowed her eyes. 'How do you know about that?'

'Master Hebrin seemed quite offended when I asked if you could be allowed back in. He showed me proof of your unsuitability.'

'I didn't—'

'It's nothing to me, Kyndra. What matters is that you can visit the archives again.'

'Thank you,' she said after a moment. She liked the way Janus said her name, his accent shortening the y sound to an

e. 'But, just so you know, I didn't wreck the book. It was those novices you chased off.' She attempted a wry smile. 'Master Hebrin said I mistook him for a fool.'

Janus laughed. 'An easy mistake to make.'

Kyndra felt another blush on her cheeks and, horrified, tried to hide it behind a casual hand. Was Janus really a spy, she found herself wondering, perhaps Nediah was just jealous that the young man was Brégenne's partner now?

Janus stood up, so that they were almost eye to eye and Kyndra hastily stepped back. But he merely scooped up a pastry from the tray and handed it to her with a flourish. 'Let's go, then,' he said. 'You can eat your breakfast on the way.'

Kyndra watched Janus in the perpetual twilight of the archives. His long hands looked delicate and soft-skinned. Markedly different to Jhren's, she found herself thinking. As much as he longed to be otherwise, Jhren was a Valleys boy and his palms were calloused with labour.

'Hold these for me a moment.' Janus deposited a stack of books in her arms and Kyndra staggered slightly under their weight.

'How am I going to get through all these in a week?'

The young man smiled knowingly. 'I'm arranging some help. In fact –' he glanced up the spiral path towards the second gate – 'it's time I fetched it. Why don't you see if you can reach *The Source*? That fat book up there. I'll be back in a few minutes.' He winked at her. 'Try not to wander off. If Hebrin sees you somewhere you shouldn't be, even I won't be able to talk him round again.'

Kyndra watched him go with a half-smile. Janus' easy company was a welcome change to the horror of the last few days, and her morning among the books had been almost pleasant. Yesterday, she'd thought him rather arrogant – *he is a little*, she conceded – but perhaps she'd judged too hastily. He'd already given her lots of advice on the test. And he hadn't asked anything about Brégenne or what had happened on their journey to Naris.

As they'd traded banter back and forth, Kyndra caught herself thinking of Jhren and the countless times she'd sat – dusty in the cellars of The Nomos, or on the roof of his parents' stable – and chatted with him in just the same way. But then a cloud would block the sun of her memories and she'd remember the Relic, the day it broke and those last awful words she'd spoken to Jhren.

Kyndra shook herself. She put down her books, crossed to the shelf and stretched up on tip-toe. She tried to prise out the bulky volume that Janus had indicated, but it was wedged tightly into one end of the shelf. Kyndra cursed under her breath and reached for the book beside it, intending to free up some wiggle room. This one was slimmer and fell into her hands in a ruffle of pages.

Kyndra came down on her heels. The book she held was called *Tools of Power*. Frowning slightly, she flipped it open to find a compendium of magical artefacts, each skilfully sketched above its own neat summary. About to close the book, Kyndra caught sight of a sub-heading: *Defence*. As she scanned the list of artefacts, words leapt out at her and she caught her breath: *cosmosethic shield, protection, barrier, the test*. Heart skipping, she reread the last sentence: *Indeed, akans are powerful enough to produce a barrier identical to those created by successful potentials during the test.*

Kyndra stood in the dry silence, her mind racing. What if

this was her answer? Quickly, she took down *The Source* and hid *Tools of Power* beneath it. Then she picked up her stack of books.

Janus was as good as his word. Barely ten minutes had passed before Kyndra spotted him at the top of the slope. Balancing the books against her shoulder, she made her way up to him. 'Let me take some of those,' Janus said, smiling, and before she could stop him, he scooped some titles off the top of the stack. Kyndra gritted her teeth. *Tools of Power* was one of them. 'Lead on,' he said, and she started out uneasily. Walking in front of him, she couldn't see whether he was looking at the books he carried.

Janus opened the gate and they made their way back up to the antechamber. 'Over there,' the young man said and gestured with his chin. Kyndra's stomach contracted. Irilin, Shika and Gareth sat round a large table, watching her. Shika and Gareth looked murderous.

'Hello, novices,' Janus said brightly. 'Thank you so much for helping. As you can see, Kyndra has a lot of books to read.' He placed his stack on the table and Kyndra couldn't tell whether he'd seen *Tools of Power* or not. Feeling a bit sick, she lowered her stack too and tried not to look at the novices. Why was Janus forcing her to sit with Gareth and Shika? He *knew* what they were like.

'I'll leave you four to get on with it,' Janus said. He smiled disarmingly at the two young men. 'Since your visit to Kyndra earlier was so much more important than your studies, I thought you wouldn't mind giving over your afternoon.' To Kyndra he said, 'I'll have a word with Hebrin. He'll keep an eye on you all until I return.'

Great, Kyndra thought. How would she be able to read

Tools of Power now? Perhaps she could stuff it down her shirt and sneak it back to her room for later.

'Hi,' Irilin said when Janus had left them alone.

'Hi,' Kyndra replied awkwardly. 'Why did you come too?'

'Because she's an idiot,' Shika said. 'Doesn't recognize a punishment when she sees one.'

'Look, you can just leave me alone,' Kyndra said. She paused, met Shika's eyes. 'This wasn't my idea.'

'I know,' Shika said, surprising her. 'Janus usually gets what he wants.'

'He's all right,' Kyndra said defensively. 'At least he's trying to help me.'

'How nice of him.'

She frowned. 'It is, actually. He's one of the only people here who doesn't make me feel like a prisoner, but I haven't done anything wrong. I just want to go home.' Her last words sounded plaintive and childish and she wished she hadn't said them.

'Home?' Irilin repeated. 'But you're a potential. That's why Master Brégenne brought you here.'

'Brégenne didn't tell *me* that.'

Shika leaned back in his chair, evidently confused. 'Then why would you come to Naris?'

'I didn't have a choice,' Kyndra said. She looked down. 'The Breaking destroyed my home.'

Into the sudden silence, Irilin whispered, 'You never said. I'm so sorry, Kyndra.'

Even Shika and Gareth seemed taken aback. 'The Breaking?' Shika asked. 'What was it like?'

'I don't want to talk about it,' Kyndra said shortly.

Irilin glanced at Hebrin's study. 'But how does Master Brégenne come into this?'

Kyndra swallowed. Why shouldn't they know? 'A mob tried to kill me. Brégenne saved my life.' Her voice sounded hollow.

Gareth folded beefy arms and finally met her eyes. 'There's a story here,' he said grudgingly. 'Let's hear it.'

Kyndra almost told him it was none of his business. She hadn't forgotten last night. But a part of her was sick of being almost entirely friendless, of being bullied and threatened and ordered about. So she took a deep breath and recounted the tale of her coming to Naris.

The novices listened silently. Kyndra told them about her disastrous Inheritance Ceremony, her departure from Brenwym and the journey to Sky Port East and Market Primus. She spoke uneasily of the potter, Mardon, and how the same thing might now have happened to Master Rush.

'His mind *disintegrated*?' Irilin asked, her pale eyes wide.

Kyndra nodded. 'Nediah seemed genuinely scared – said it might be too dangerous to examine him.'

Shika pulled distractedly at his scarf. 'Master Nediah doesn't think it's contagious?'

'He said it might be.'

'I talked to Master Rush the other day,' Shika said in a strained voice. 'Isn't there a cure?'

'Maybe, but Nediah didn't know it, or he'd have helped Mardon.' Kyndra paused. 'Besides, I spent a couple of hours listening to Rush yesterday, so I'm in as much danger as you. Probably more,' she added, remembering the vision that had prompted her to say those strange things during the class. What if she were going mad already?

'The Wielders will get to the bottom of it,' Gareth said confidently. 'I'm not frightened.'

'I am,' Irilin said fervently. 'But what happened after Market Primus, Kyndra?'

Kyndra looked at them all. Both Irilin and Shika were unashamedly hanging on her every word and even Gareth couldn't conceal his interest. Her story of the Breaking seemed to have softened the two boys – at least they'd stopped regarding her with open hostility. *Why should I tell them?* she thought, the memory of last night's humiliation fresh in her mind. Neither Gareth nor Shika had offered her an apology for the way they'd behaved, so why did they deserve her trust? But Irilin's face was alight with concern and curiosity, and Kyndra hadn't forgotten who had freed her from Gareth's manacles.

Addressing her words to Irilin, Kyndra recalled the night she'd trespassed in Argat's saloon. She told the tiny novice about the visions and the earth – about Brégenne taking it and Argat coming after them. 'Brégenne thinks the earth is somehow linked to the visions I keep seeing,' Kyndra concluded, 'but it was stolen the day we arrived here. Someone went into her room and took it.'

'What's so important about a handful of dirt,' Gareth said, 'even if it is magical?' His tone implied that he very much doubted the latter.

Before Kyndra could reply, Irilin asked the question she'd been dreading: 'What did you see in the visions?'

Kyndra wondered what to say. How could she tell them she had looked out of someone else's eyes? And not only looked. It was as if she'd *been* that man . . . the instrument of peace.

'Kyndra?' Irilin said, but the girl's voice was distant. Images were tumbling through Kyndra's mind: the red army marching on Solinaris's walls, the airless gallery with its shielded book and that unknown magic he'd foolishly taken inside him . . .

No, Kyndra thought, shocked back into herself. Her heart was thumping. *That man is not me.* She looked up to find Shika and Gareth eyeing her as if she really were mad.

'I don't hear reading,' Hebrin called from his study, making them all jump.

Irilin sighed and looked at the pile of books. 'We'd better get on with this.' She picked a book up and opened it, and after a moment's hesitation, Shika did the same. However, Gareth was staring at the table. Slowly he reached out and slid *Tools of Power* from beneath *The Source*. Kyndra tensed.

'Where did you find this?' the big novice asked, his voice barely above a whisper. He darted a look over his shoulder at Hebrin's study.

Kyndra frowned. 'I found it next to *that*.' She pointed at *The Source*. 'Why?'

'Do you know what we could do with this?' Gareth asked, eyes glinting. 'The seventh level isn't for books. It's where they keep all the stuff left over from the war – powerful amulets, staffs, things like that. This' – he tapped *Tools of Power* – 'is the definitive guide. I bet it would tell you what they are *and* how to use them.'

Shika snorted and then promptly looked horrified at the sound. 'Like we'd ever get down there to find out,' he said, and his words visibly reined in Gareth's excitement.

'I know,' the big novice agreed, continuing to hold the book in reverential hands. It was a strange sight to Kyndra, who vividly remembered him stamping on *Laws of Energy*.

'I thought it might help me with the test,' she admitted.

Shika looked at her sharply. 'So you were planning to cheat?'

'No, well—'

'I like it.' Shika's smile was devious. 'Shame it's impossible – you'd have to get into the lower spirals.'

'And no Wielder would help you,' Gareth added. He looked at the book in his hands. 'I'd give anything to go down there.'

Kyndra remembered what Nediah had told her about the lower spirals. *That's where they keep the worst kinds of writing and the worst kinds of power.* 'Nediah told me it was dangerous,' she said.

'Yeah,' Gareth replied wistfully.

He still had a few minutes before the meeting. Janus stopped by his new quarters to run a comb through his hair and study his face in the mirror, summoning a flame for extra light. When he turned his head, its golden glow gilded the bones of his cheeks, leaving his eyes in shadow.

The mirror showed him a slice of the room. Discarded brown robes spilled out of the wardrobe and all three of his dresser drawers hung open, disgorging a mix of scrolls, pens, ink and a few shirts. Several paintings and a small tapestry adorned a couch instead of the wall, awaiting the coming of order.

Janus had earned the room along with his master status and – small though it was – he loved it. He'd always resented the lack of privacy that came with sharing a dorm. The days of squashing his possessions into a chest at the foot of a hard pallet bed were past. Now he could scatter them across a softer mattress without fear of rebuke. Turning from the mirror, he strode recklessly across the littered floor, silently exulting.

Lord Loricus had placed his trust in *him*, not in Caius or Sylve, who thought they were so smart. *Me*, Janus thought fiercely. The councilman had brought forward the day of his dreams and Janus wouldn't let him down.

Leaving his new quarters, he wove comfortably through the citadel. It was the end of afternoon repast and Naris's main thoroughfares were teeming.

'Janus!'

Ranine dashed at him, brown robes flying. She skidded to a halt just inches from his toes. 'I still can't get used to it,' she panted, eyeing his new gold outfit. Janus heard jealousy in her voice and smiled to himself.

'I'm afraid I can't stop to talk,' he said with just a hint of loftiness. 'Lord Loricus is waiting for me.'

'You're so lucky.' Ranine rolled up her sleeves and fanned her face with both hands. 'To think a *councilman* is taking such an interest in you.'

Janus felt the familiar flutter in his stomach. 'Yes. I mustn't be late.'

'Of course not,' Ranine agreed. She paused. 'I'm happy for you.'

Janus touched her cheek and Ranine blushed scarlet. 'One day,' he said softly, 'the Council will see that you deserve to be raised too.' He moved his hand to her shoulder. 'Until then, work hard. I could even put in a good word for you.'

'You'd do that for me?' Ranine said breathlessly. 'I would be so grateful.'

'I know.' Janus smiled. 'See you later, Ranine. I really have to go now.'

'Good luck!'

Janus left her standing apple-red in the corridor. In truth, he felt a bit guilty for teasing her. She was his closest friend and they'd known each other since they were children. He sighed and brushed a curl of hair out of his eyes. He could catch up with Ranine later – now he had a more pressing appointment to keep.

His palms began to sweat when he neared Lord Loricus's quarters. Housed in one of Naris's spires, the three Council apartments each spanned two floors. Janus had never seen inside one. The corridors were quiet: perfect. Lord Loricus had told him to come at this hour. Masters were seldom invited here, let alone those of low rank, and Janus didn't want any awkward questions.

Without stopping, he turned to look behind him, but the hall was empty. Black marble lined the floor, its surface buffed to shine like a mirror. Busy scrutinizing his reflection, Janus didn't see the person in his path until he bumped into him.

'Lord Gend!' Janus took several steps back, awed by the councilman's height. Gend's quiet, dark face looked down into his. More mountain than man, his silver robes couldn't conceal the muscle that rippled beneath. He stood with huge arms folded, barring the way.

Janus thought fast. There was a roll of paper in his pocket and he seized upon it gratefully. 'I am to-to take this to Lord Loricus,' he stammered, producing the fake missive. Gend merely stared at him, his eyes flicking once to the paper. An age seemed to pass before the councilman unfolded his arms. 'Give it to me. I will take it from here.'

Janus knew he couldn't refuse, but the barest glance at the scroll would be his undoing. To his horror, he realized he held the sketch Ranine had given him last night, his own face expertly caught in inky strokes.

'Janus,' Lord Gend said firmly, 'you can go. I will deliver the missive.'

He was out of ideas. Already suspicion tightened the lines

around the councilman's mouth, as Janus extended his hand ever so slowly.

'There you are, Master. What kept you?'

Warm, wonderful relief surged through Janus. He swiftly retracted the scroll. Gend didn't turn at the new voice, but continued to observe him.

'I see,' Loricus said, his eyes alighting on the huge man. 'Why are you disturbing my messenger, Gend?'

Janus glanced at him. Loricus leaned against the door frame, arms folded and his golden robes rumpled, as if he'd recently been lying down. When the big man didn't answer, Loricus beckoned Janus over. 'Come on, you're late. Give me that scroll and then I'd like the report from your own lips.' His hazel eyes glittered.

Janus hurried over. Gend, he saw, had not stopped watching him. Only when he crossed the threshold did the councilman finally remove his gaze. 'Loricus,' he said, 'be careful.'

Lord Loricus shut the door crisply in the other Wielder's face then motioned the young man through to the sitting room. Janus gazed at the sumptuous furnishings, taking in the polished tables laden with fresh fruit, the marble sculptures and bookshelves. Intricate carpets blanketed the floor and tapestries softened the harsh, black walls. It was all so rich, so lavish.

Lord Loricus unfolded the scroll and held it up to the light of the golden fires that bathed the room in a cosy glow. Janus blushed. 'It's a good likeness,' the councilman observed. 'Who is the artist?'

'My friend. Novice Ranine.'

'She has captured the bones of your face exquisitely.' Loricus raised an eyebrow.

Hating his flaming cheeks, Janus studied the carpet. 'Would you like some wine?' he heard Loricus ask. The councilman swept up his own goblet from the table and Janus nodded eagerly. He realized his hands were trembling and hid them behind his back. Lord Loricus noticed and smiled. 'Did "the Mountain" give you a fright?' he asked.

'No,' Janus said hastily. 'I just . . . you said the corridors would be clear.'

'I can't account for the arbitrary movements of my fellows.' Lord Loricus sat down on a wide, backless divan and crooked a finger. Heart skipping, Janus went and sat nervously next to him and gulped some wine. The heat of it rushed down his throat and he looked at the goblet appreciatively.

'Yes, it's a good vintage,' Loricus said, taking a sip. Those hazel eyes and olive skin hid his years well, Janus thought, knowing the councilman was at least twice his age. It didn't trouble him, except to think how much more accomplished Lord Loricus was in wielding the Solar. He still had a long way to go.

'So,' Loricus said, giving him a look so predatory that it made him shiver, 'what have you to tell me?'

Janus drained his goblet and the wine sent a warm pulse through his body. 'She's a nice enough girl, but nothing special. She will definitely need your help.' He paused and met the councilman's gaze. 'If only she knew how generous you're being, my Lord—'

'Here you may call me Loricus.'

'Loricus,' he whispered, liking the sound of it in his mouth. The councilman poured more wine and Janus took a long drink. He licked his lips. 'She found the book just as you planned,' he said. 'The novices will tell her what it is – and what she could do with it.'

'Good. I see my trust was well placed.'

Janus drew in a breath. 'It is, my Lo— Loricus.'

'Above all, the girl must believe it her own idea,' Loricus told him. 'My hand cannot be seen in this. You know I act without my fellows' knowledge.'

Janus nodded. 'They don't have your compassion,' he said boldly. 'Kyndra's death would mean nothing to them.'

'Yes.' Lord Loricus sighed. 'I find that hard to swallow. It grieved me to speak so harshly to the girl in the hearing, but I couldn't let the others suspect. This way she will "pass" the test, be admitted to Naris, and then we may help her to escape later in secret.'

The wine was making his head fuzzy and Janus found he liked the feeling. He settled himself more comfortably on the divan. 'You would do all this for an ordinary girl?' he asked.

'I don't like deception,' Loricus answered with a shake of his head. 'But sometimes it is necessary to ensure justice is met. Brégenne did wrong by the girl in bringing her here and Kyndra has suffered for that mistake. She shouldn't have to die for it.'

Janus started on his third goblet of wine, relishing the chilled liquid as it slid down his throat. Dimly he noticed that Loricus wasn't drinking. 'What if she tells someone after she's left?' he asked. 'How will she explain where she's been?'

Lord Loricus waved an impatient hand. 'It is possible to alter memory. But from the little I've seen of the girl, I think gratitude may seal her lips quite effectively.'

Janus nodded again, distracted by the lazy glitter in those hazel eyes. 'What should I do next?' he asked.

'Go to my desk over there.'

Janus put down his wine and stood up unsteadily. The desk

was a huge piece of mahogany, which held neat stacks of paper and ink pots. 'In the first drawer,' Loricus instructed.

Janus opened it and found a single scroll, tied with red ribbon. 'It carries the Council's seal,' he heard Loricus say. 'Show that to Hebrin and he will grant you admittance to the seventh spiral.'

His back to the councilman, Janus slowly lifted the scroll. 'What is it?'

'It orders you to retrieve a certain artefact for use in deciphering the source of Master Rush's affliction. The girl must be given a chance to access that level.' Loricus paused. When he spoke again, his honeyed voice was tempered with ice. 'And your job is even more important. You have a week. Use that time to fan her fear of the test. She must be desperate. She must be searching for a lifeline. We will throw her one, and it's your responsibility to ensure she takes it. If all goes to plan, she'll be out of the way this time next week.'

'That is clever,' Janus said softly.

'It is necessary,' Loricus whispered and Janus spun around. The councilman was there, standing close behind him, framed by the room's golden light. Janus hadn't even heard him move. His breath caught. He gazed at Loricus and felt a stir in his groin.

'Will . . .' he stammered and coughed his voice free. 'Will Kyndra be able to use the object you plan for her to find?'

Loricus regarded him, his head on one side. 'I've made it easy for her,' he said. 'The object in question is the only one of its kind. And the book describes it in detail. All she has to do is hold it in her hand.'

'In her hand,' Janus whispered, still looking into his face. When Loricus stepped away, breaking their contact, he felt embarrassed and bereft all at once. He dropped his eyes.

'Approach Hebrin the day before the test and remember not to refer to me personally.' Lord Loricus turned his back. 'Don't fail me in this, Janus.' The councilman's voice was utterly cold now, all its honey gone. 'The girl's life depends on it.'

19

'Look at this,' Irilin said, hefting a book and pushing it towards Kyndra. It was called *The Test: A History of the Unfortunates*.

'Like that's going to help, Iri.' Shika made a swipe for the book and missed. 'She's trying to survive the test, not die from it.'

They were nearing the end of their fifth day in the archives and it had been no more promising than the ones before. 'I know,' Irilin said. She blew a floating strand of hair away from her mouth. 'But it might be useful to see where others went wrong.' Ignoring Shika's protests, she opened the volume on a random page. 'Aha! Listen to this: "If the potential, hereafter referred to as the unfortunate, was indeed possessed of an affinity, they failed to demonstrate it within the allotted span. A mortal body cannot sustain so violent an assault indefinitely, and prolonged exposure to the test's brand of cosmosethic energy results in the unfortunate's flesh blackening, their vital organs—"' Irilin stopped, flushing. 'I . . . uh, was sure that was leading somewhere else,' she said sheepishly. 'Sorry, Kyn.'

'Ümvast's balls, Iri.' Gareth's deep voice boomed in the dusty quiet of the antechamber. 'What's that book going to do for her morale?'

Irilin looked down. 'I just thought—'

'Don't worry,' Kyndra said. She'd been touching her ribs without realizing it and now dropped her hand. 'It doesn't matter.'

Shika slipped the book from the blonde girl's unresisting fingers and tossed it contemptuously onto the pile they had deemed useless. It was far larger than the one opposite, which consisted of a single small volume and a scroll. 'It's amazing how few books there are on the test,' Shika mused. 'Pretty much all of these assume that the reader's already passed it.'

'I told you this was a waste of time,' Gareth said, folding his arms. He scanned the antechamber for Hebrin and – assured of his absence – thumped his booted feet on the table.

'Janus just keeps bringing us more,' Irilin sighed.

Shika smoothed a crease out of his novice robe. 'He won't after tomorrow.' He glanced sidelong at Kyndra. 'Day of the test.'

'You've done enough,' Kyndra said. She tried to keep her voice steady. 'The test is my problem. All this reading is taking you away from your studies.'

Gareth snorted. 'We're not missing them.'

'All the same,' she said. 'If we haven't found anything help-ful by now, I don't think we ever will.'

Irilin made a sound of disagreement, but didn't put words to it. Kyndra knew they were thinking the same as she: that a person simply couldn't be taught how to pass the test. The experience differed for everyone and the novices had told her all they could. Nediah had also talked for an hour on the sub-ject and Janus, her almost constant companion now, had readily described his own test when she asked.

Now she realized that none of their answers would be

remotely useful. The best she could hope for was a sense of this *affinity* they kept talking about. Even then, it depended on the individual. Irilin described it as a kind of unfurling, as if she had wings, while Shika called it 'an infinitely graceful dawning of apprehension', a phrase which caused Gareth to snigger. When Kyndra asked the big novice about his own experience, Gareth waved the question away. 'You can't describe it,' he said flatly. Then, 'Maybe I'd compare it to the swell of courage a warrior feels in his blood before battle. The kind of courage that makes heroes of ordinary men.' He meticulously avoided Shika's eyes as he said this, but Kyndra saw the dark-haired young man look surprised and then oddly gratified.

'Why don't you come and have dinner with us?' Irilin suggested now. 'Too much time in this place will drive you mad.' The other three stared at her and Irilin shifted uneasily when she realized what she had said.

'I have to eat in my room,' Kyndra told her. 'Janus brings it.'

'Oh. I forgot.'

'Poor Master Rush.' Shika fiddled with the purple streak in his hair. 'Is he still getting worse?'

Gareth re-crossed his legs on the table. 'I heard that even Master Nediah can't stop whatever is eating away at his mind.' For the first time, Kyndra thought he looked apprehensive.

'Novice Hafgald.'

Gareth yanked his feet off the table. Hebrin stood behind them, obviously just returned from the galleries. His lips thinned as he observed Gareth and the scuffs on the table. 'The archives are not a place of leisure, Hafgald. Nor of idle chatter,' he added, pale eyes scanning the rest of them.

'We were talking about Master Rush,' Shika said soberly. 'I

was asking the others if there'd been any change in his condition.'

Hebrin sucked in his papery cheeks until he looked almost corpse-like. 'It is very serious,' he muttered. 'The citadel has not encountered the like in all its time.'

'Will they find a cure?' Irilin asked.

Hebrin didn't seem to hear her. He walked slowly back to his study, where he collapsed into a chair and sat unmoving, long fingers cradling his chin.

Kyndra and the novices shared a tense glance. Irilin reached for another book, but before she could open it, Janus came through the doors to the antechamber. He looked even more harried than when he'd come to wake Kyndra that morning. His curls were unkempt and a hint of stubble roughened his jaw.

'Janus has let himself go a bit,' Shika remarked to Gareth out of the corner of his mouth.

'He seems worried,' Kyndra hissed reproachfully. 'Maybe I should ask him what's wrong.' She gazed at Janus' rumpled form. For some reason, today's imperfections made him even more handsome in her eyes. She felt a blush coming on and looked quickly away.

'Don't get your hopes up,' Shika hissed back. 'Believe me when I say he's not interested in—'

'Shhh,' Irilin whispered. Janus had walked straight to Hebrin's study and was speaking to him.

'. . . a request from the Council,' they heard.

'Let's see it.'

Janus handed over a beribboned scroll sealed with red wax. Hebrin brought it close to his face before nodding and cracking it open. The novices were all watching as furtively as she, Kyndra noticed.

'This is a request to enter the seventh spiral,' Hebrin muttered after he'd finished reading.

Janus' shoulders tightened. 'Yes,' he said and coughed. 'An artefact kept there may be of help to the healers attending Master Rush.'

Hebrin shook his head. 'Terrible business,' he muttered. 'Terrible.' He tucked the scroll into his robes. 'I will give you a token that will allow you to pass the gate.' He rose from his chair and disappeared further into his study. When he returned, he carried something small in his hand.

Janus deposited it swiftly in a pocket. 'Thank you, Master Hebrin.'

'If it can wait just a little while, I would advise you to come back after hours, Master Janus.' Hebrin gave Kyndra's table a pointed stare. 'The archives will be closed then and you may enter the galleries undisturbed.'

'Yes. I'll come back a couple of hours after dinner.'

'This will unlock the antechamber.' Hebrin handed the young man a key that looked uncannily like the one Nediah had used the other night. 'You may return it tomorrow.'

'Thanks for your help, Master Archivist.' Janus turned on his heel and walked out. He looked rather pale.

There was silence around the table. Then Gareth whispered, 'Are you thinking what I'm thinking?'

Shika's eyes glittered. 'I'm thinking it.'

'What?' Irilin said. Gareth gave her a withering look and the girl inhaled sharply.

The big novice turned to Kyndra. 'This might just be your lucky day. You still got that book?'

*

Later that night, when Kyndra heard voices outside her room, she cracked open the door and smiled at the two startled novices. Shika, she saw, was brandishing a lock-pick. 'Janus hasn't been locking me in these past two nights,' Kyndra told them and Shika looked faintly disappointed. 'He said it was a reward for working hard and behaving myself in the archives.'

Gareth grinned. 'If only he could see you now.'

'Where's Irilin?' Kyndra said quickly, finding the thought of disappointing Janus unexpectedly painful. His smile had seemed a little brittle tonight when he'd brought her dinner, but she hadn't found the nerve to ask him what was wrong.

'She used her power to hide in the archives after old Hebrin shut up shop,' Shika said. 'If Janus locks the antechamber door behind him, she'll be able to open it for us from the inside.' He glanced at Gareth. 'I hope she's all right.'

'Don't worry,' the big novice said. 'When Iri doesn't want to be found, she won't be.' He checked that the coast was clear and then beckoned them down the corridor. Kyndra eased her door shut, hoping the late hour would discourage anyone from looking in on her.

They set off at a fast walk. 'Hurry it up,' Gareth hissed. 'Janus is about five minutes in front of us. If we're not careful, we'll lose the chance to follow him into the lower galleries.' But their pace was slowed by the fact that they had to hide from passing masters and by the time they reached the archives, Gareth's hands were curling and uncurling in impatience.

Irilin met them at the antechamber door. 'He didn't lock it,' she said, 'and he's already gone down to the galleries.'

Gareth swore roundly. 'We have to catch him before the fifth gate!'

Abandoning secrecy for speed, they threw themselves into

the tunnels. Kyndra gritted her teeth. It was hard to run *and* keep her boots quiet on a stone floor. Sweating with the effort, she glanced sideways at Gareth. 'Why are you doing this for me? Won't you be in big trouble if you're caught?'

'Not doing it for you,' Gareth rasped, now red in the face. 'We might never get another chance to see inside a forbidden spiral.' He gave a shark-like grin. 'And anyway, it's the most fun I've had in ages.'

Irilin scurried along beside Kyndra, faintly green and looking like she regretted ever agreeing to this. Kyndra didn't blame her – the whole idea was crazy – but it might also be her only chance.

They rounded another bend and there was Janus, pressing his palm to the fifth gate. Kyndra and the novices fell back out of sight. 'The gate stays open less than a minute,' Shika reminded them quietly and they peered around the curve of the tunnel and watched until Janus was safely through it. He wore a cloak over his robes, Kyndra saw, and he frequently turned his head from side to side, as if he knew he was being followed. Uneasily, she stole through the gate after the others, all of them now careful to keep to the shadows.

There was no shortage of shadows in the archives. With each downward spiral, the pools of darkness grew larger. The galleries became tighter, collapsing in on themselves like the conical end of a seashell.

Gareth's eyes sharpened once they passed the sixth gate. He gazed at the shelves with their silent occupants and Kyndra noticed his fingers twitching. What kinds of books did Hebrin keep down here? she wondered. What *were* the worst kinds of writing?

As they neared the seventh spiral, a pressure grew unpleasantly in their ears. Janus must have felt it too, for he slowed and put a hand to his head. Irilin groaned softly and Shika grimaced. 'My skull feels like it's going to explode,' he whispered. Gareth remained silent, but tiny beads of sweat stood out on his face. Kyndra agreed with Shika. Her head felt like a swollen fruit.

Janus opened the seventh gate, his hand tight around what must be Hebrin's token. They waited until he was out of sight before sneaking through after him. When the gate's invisible timer was up and it clanged shut behind them, Kyndra felt a sudden squeeze of claustrophobia. The tunnel they stood in was considerably smaller than the one directly above it. A low ceiling brushed the tops of their heads and black walls pressed in from either side. But at least the strange pressure had eased.

Kyndra's skin prickled as she followed Janus down the slope and into the green light of the seventh gallery. The vision must have led her through here, but she had no memory of it. Instead of shelves and books, lumps of rock jutted from the black floor, some tapering to spikes as thin as her arm. The larger monoliths menaced each other like opposing pieces on a game board. 'Perfect,' Gareth breathed when he saw them. 'He'll never spot us.'

Janus reached the bottom of the slope and disappeared behind a column. 'Now,' said Shika. He led them in a crouch, moving quickly until they came to the floor of the gallery. There was no sign of Janus.

'Are you really going to try and find this thing?' Irilin whispered to Kyndra. 'What's it called, anyway?'

Kyndra reached back and retrieved *Tools of Power* from where it sat secured in the waistband of her trousers. She flipped it open. 'The one that can produce a shield is called an *akan*. It looks like a statue of a sleeping child with wings.' In the strange green glow that seemed to come from everywhere and nowhere, she suddenly saw that the next page was missing. A sentence ended abruptly with the lines: *While any* akan *will shield its bearer from harm, one type – the white* akan *– was designed to do more. Its power—* And that was it. Kyndra shrugged and closed the book. 'It says any will do.'

'Spread out,' Gareth said. 'And don't be seen.'

Kyndra tucked the book away and darted between two stone monoliths. They were much bigger when viewed from ground level, and recesses carved into them held all sorts of objects. She saw polished stones, gems, gilded cups and – in one – something that looked grotesquely like a fossilized tongue. Another held a helmet and a black gauntlet; both glowed invitingly. Kyndra had a sudden urge to slip her hand into the gauntlet. When that ebony metal enveloped her wrist, she would be able to do anything. She swallowed the temptation with difficulty and moved on.

Janus materialized a few rows in front of her and Kyndra hastily ducked behind another recessed rock. In the unnatural silence, she could hear her own breathing and tried to calm it. As Janus swept past her hiding place, still darting glances to left and right, Kyndra caught a glimpse of his face. It was such a whirl of worry that she almost reached out to him.

A hand clamped down on her shoulder and Kyndra barely stifled a cry. 'I've got one,' Irilin whispered. She clutched a silk-wrapped bundle. When the novice unfolded it, Kyndra instinctively recoiled. A winged child glimmered corpse-pale in the gloom. Despite its beatific face, it made her flesh crawl. She nodded at Irilin, who smiled briefly and handed over the statue. The moment it touched her hand, Kyndra wanted to throw it away. Holding it was like feeling a spider's legs skitter unceasingly over her skin. She dropped it into her pocket and the sensation faded. *Let's go*, she mouthed.

Shika and Gareth were crouching by another rock. Irilin hissed through her teeth and they jumped up immediately. 'Where's Janus?' she whispered.

And then came the distant *creak* of hinges. Shika's eyes widened. 'The gate!'

As one, they dodged through the rocky maze and up the slope before sprinting into the tunnel. There was the gate swinging shut. 'Quick!' Shika gasped. He skidded through and Irilin and Gareth hurled themselves after him. The gate closed.

'No,' Irilin groaned when she'd picked herself up. 'Kyndra.'

Trapped on the other side, Kyndra slumped against the wall. She could see the novices' faces through the elaborate metalwork. They gazed back at her, horrified. Then Gareth folded his arms. 'Why'd you have to get yourself stuck like that?'

'I didn't mean to,' Kyndra growled. 'What were you two doing anyway? Weren't you supposed to be watching for Janus?'

'When did that become our job?' Shika asked.

'This was your idea,' Kyndra said. 'You wanted to see the seventh level.'

'And you wanted to cheat on your test,' Shika retorted. '*You* should have been watching him.'

'Children, children,' said a voice and the four of them froze. 'Argument is pointless and you'll miss your chance to get through the other gates.'

Kyndra spun around. 'Who's there?'

Kait melted out of the shadows beside her, long hair

framing her face. A silver knife gleamed behind her belt. 'Hello, Kyndra.' She smiled. 'Didn't I say I wasn't finished with you?'

Despite having the gate between them, the novices took a step back. 'That's one of the Nerian,' Irilin gasped. 'Kyn, be careful.'

Kait laughed. 'It's far too late for that.' She looked across at the novices. 'The young man you followed is almost at the sixth gate. If you don't hurry, you'll never get out of here unseen.'

'What about Kyndra?' Irilin said.

'You leave her with me. Only I can get her back to her room before Janus finds it empty.'

'Why would you help me?' Kyndra asked slowly.

'Did I not before?'

Shika frowned through the bars. 'What does that mean?'

'It's none of your business,' Kait snapped. 'So.' She returned her gaze to Kyndra. 'What's it to be?'

'Kyn, don't.' Irilin was shaking her head, pale eyes large in the gloom.

'Do you know what Hebrin will do to you if you're discovered here?' Kait asked her.

Irilin was silent.

'He will have you flogged. Nothing has changed in Naris,' Kait said and the shadow of memory darkened her face. 'The skin on your back will hang in tatters. No healer will be permitted to touch you. Are you still willing to stay here?'

Gareth cursed and grabbed Irilin's shoulder. 'Let's go.'

'But Gareth—'

'I said, let's *go*.' The novice bodily hauled Irilin away from the gate. Shika hesitated for a moment longer, looking at Kyndra.

'Go,' Kyndra said. 'If what she says is true, I don't want it on my conscience.'

Shika almost smiled. Then he nodded once and sprinted up the tunnel after the other two.

'That's better,' Kait said, stretching like a cat. 'Just you and me.'

'What do you want?' Kyndra asked her warily.

Kait turned and started back down the tunnel. When Kyndra didn't follow, she looked over her shoulder. 'Are you stupid? Do you want Janus to catch you?'

After a moment's pause, Kyndra followed her.

Just before they reached the top of the gallery, Kait put a hand on the wall and whispered under her breath. The solid rock melted, revealing a narrow hole leading into the mountain. Kyndra gazed at it, half astonished, half apprehensive. She vividly remembered her last crawl in the dark. 'No lamp this time.' Kait grinned. 'Better not lose me.'

The first hundred metres were the worst, as the black crevice seemed to double endlessly back on itself. Hysteria bubbled in Kyndra's chest, threatening to take her each time her body became stuck or she lost sight of Kait's feet. By the time she pushed herself out into a wider passage, she was trembling and covered in sweat.

'You did well,' Kait said, looking pleased. 'You've got more guts than I thought.'

Unable to speak, Kyndra simply stood there, drawing deep, calming breaths. She never wanted to go through that again.

'Think what it's like for us,' Kait said, as if she read her thoughts. 'You may vow never to enter the earth again, but if you live as I do, tunnels like the one we just passed are your only means of liberty.'

'Does the Council know that you can move around inside the citadel?'

'I told you before. These passages are known only to the Nerian. And only the Nerian can access them. We know the mountain better than anyone. It is our skin, our body. And the Deep is our heart.'

For a moment, Kait's words kindled the same desire as Nediah's had done on that first day in the archives. Kyndra wanted to see the deep places. She wanted to walk the valleys and the clefts in a world where the sky was solid rock, to lay hands on things no human hand had touched.

She shook herself. No. The mountain was crushing, suffocating. Wherever she went, she felt its immutability and drew its sulphurous age into her nostrils. How did the Nerian live without sunlight? Wouldn't the darkness send you mad? Kyndra looked at Kait, at the desperate whites of her eyes, and knew the answer.

'We've gained some time,' the woman said. 'Do you need to rest?'

Kyndra looked away. 'I'd rather not.'

Kait sighed. 'Nediah's been talking to you,' she said and slid dispiritedly down the tunnel wall to sit at its base.

Kyndra remained standing. 'What if he has? At least he tells me the truth.'

'He tells you less than you think,' Kait said. She paused, toying with a boot buckle. 'What did he say about me?'

'That you follow a madman,' Kyndra said without preamble. 'That you are dangerous and—'

'And . . . ?'

'I should keep away from you,' she finished uncomfortably.

Kait's smile returned like sunlight through whimsical clouds. 'Dangerous,' she murmured. 'That's quite a compliment.'

'It wasn't meant as one.'

Kait stretched her legs out in front of her. 'Naris is not your ally, Kyndra. Nor is it mine. Does that not give us something in common?' Her smile turned sad. 'Don't let a past lover's sour words turn your judgement.'

Kyndra gaped at her. Lover? Nediah's discomfort the last time they'd seen Kait took on a whole new meaning and she realized she didn't know him at all.

'You're shocked,' Kait said, sounding delighted. 'But it's the truth. If you doubt me, ask Nediah. He won't deny it.'

Kyndra forced down her curiosity. 'Why are you telling me this?'

'Because I want you to trust me,' Kait said simply.

'And why should I?'

'The Nerian can help you.'

Kyndra stared. 'How? With the test?'

The woman shook her head. 'Nediah won't be able to protect you from the Council,' she said. 'And when you're ready to accept the truth, he won't have the answers you'll seek. But the Nerian will. And we'll give them to you.'

'Riddles,' Kyndra said disgustedly. 'You sound like Brégenne.'

'*I am not Brégenne.*' Kait's voice was like the crack of a whip and Kyndra flinched. The other woman must have noticed, for she relaxed her snarl and said more calmly, 'I have no desire to withhold the truth, but you're not ready to hear it.'

'Fine,' Kyndra shrugged, 'then we have nothing else to say to each other.' Kait was more like Brégenne than she wanted to admit. Perhaps it was a Wielder thing, Kyndra thought angrily, remembering how Brégenne had refused to tell her anything that night she'd eavesdropped on Nediah and Argat.

Seemingly unfazed, Kait climbed to her feet. 'Let's go.'

And Kyndra was forced to follow her up the passage, hating the fact that she had no choice.

'I've been searching for a moment to speak with you for the past week.' Kait shot a look over her shoulder. 'But the Council aren't taking any chances. Meals are brought to your room, you're escorted to the archives and watched by Hebrin. And always that Janus hangs over you like a curse.'

'Janus?' Despite her anger, a blush settled stubbornly on Kyndra's cheeks. She was suddenly glad that Kait had no lamp. 'He's all right.'

'Why were you following him tonight?'

'That's my business.'

Kait huffed. 'I knew you were going to say that.'

The tunnel narrowed like a crevasse. Its walls were buckled here and stained yellow from an upwelling of minerals. 'Is it much further?' Kyndra asked.

'No.' Kait let her hand fall from the stone. Between one step and the next, she halted and turned. 'Before I let you out, I'll give you a warning.'

'Which is?' Kyndra asked diffidently.

Kait seized her forearm and Kyndra stiffened. 'Don't trust Janus. If you have acted tonight upon anything he has said or done, your life may be in danger. The Nerian do not wish to see you dead. Promise me.'

Kyndra jerked her arm back. 'It's none of your business whom I choose to trust.'

Kait's eyes flashed and Kyndra thought she would lash out, but instead she opened another piece of wall and pushed her hard. Kyndra tumbled through the gap and landed in a tangle of limbs. She scrambled furiously to her feet, but the wall was solid again.

Uttering some choice words, Kyndra took stock of her surroundings. Cautiously, she peered around the jut of stone that obscured the corridor. It was empty, but not silent. The mountain told her the story of its past in a rumble like coffined thunder, and she wondered how the Wielders endured it. Stopping her ears, she darted across the open space and ran down to her room. Slipping through the door, she closed it, threw off her cloak and boots and got into bed. The *akan* felt hot against her thigh, as if it were burning a hole in her pocket. She *had* done the right thing, hadn't she?

It wasn't until she heard footsteps outside that Kyndra realized her mistake. The lamp was still alight, throwing her guilty shadow on the wall. She'd forgotten to blow it out. Kyndra sat up, but it was too late. The door opened and Janus stood there. The tousled emotions he'd worn so plainly earlier in the day were gone, washed clean by something she couldn't fathom. Instead of seeming suspicious, he looked pleased to see her. The light dipped his hair in gold leaf. He was as unreal as a painting, Kyndra thought, feeling drab and unlovely by comparison, half covered by the blanket.

'Kyndra,' Janus said softly, 'could you not sleep?'

'Erm, no,' she managed.

Janus came to sit on the bed. 'Are you thinking about the test?'

She was acutely aware of his nearness and of the late hour. What was he doing here, anyway? Had he been coming to see her every night – after she'd gone to sleep? Kyndra looked quickly away from him, but her traitorous heart had already begun to beat faster. Belatedly remembering his question, she nodded.

'Everything will be all right,' Janus told her. 'You know what to do now.'

She glanced back at him. 'I do?'

He smiled gently and Kyndra felt her blush race euphorically down through her body. It settled in her belly, a blaze that fluttered and coaxed. *Ask him why he was upset earlier*, it urged her, and Kyndra drew breath to speak. But then she thought of Kait and what the woman had said about Nediah being her lover, and Kyndra recalled the unwelcome realization that she knew next to nothing about Nediah – and she knew even less about Janus. What if Kyndra was no more than a task to him, a task that could be dispensed with as soon as the test was done?

Unaware of her silent struggle, Janus stood up and her chance to ask him was gone. 'You need to rest,' he told her. 'You've a big day tomorrow.'

Feeling both reprieve and regret, she watched him open the door, step out and close it behind him. When his footsteps had faded, Kyndra plunged her hand into her pocket, seeking the *akan*. Its corpse-pallor was almost soothing and she let the child's spidery presence destroy the last of her blushes.

It was a few moments before she realized that Janus had distracted her from something she ought to have noticed straight away. Kyndra jumped up, her hand going to the back of her trousers. But whether she'd dropped it when Kait pushed her, or she'd lost it in her flight from the archives, her book, *Tools of Power*, was gone.

20

In an attempt to escape his own muddled thoughts, Nediah applied himself to what the higher masters had called, for the sake of convenience, the Madness. He hadn't forgotten his promise to investigate Brégenne's stolen bag of earth, but this malady of the mind was a far greater issue. Although the others cared only about Master Rush, as far as Nediah was concerned, Rush was the Madness's second victim. There was still the puzzle of Jim Mardon.

It isn't spread through contact. The only people who had been directly exposed to the Madness were himself, Hebrin, Myris and Alandred. And, as far as he knew, they were all well. So how did it strike? Was there a pattern he couldn't yet see?

Nediah wandered through the sixth level of the archives. It was quiet here and he found the dim, bluish light soothing. As a healer, there was nothing that irked him more than an illness he didn't understand. If only he could find a link between the cases. *Rush and Mardon*, he thought, idly trailing his fingers along the shelves. The Madness must have manifested in them both for a reason. What linked these two utterly disparate men? Why had Mardon collapsed so suddenly in the marketplace? According to Kyndra, the potter had been fine just moments before.

Nediah ground his teeth, sensing the ghost of an answer, but unable to grasp it. In all his time as a healer, he had never come across a disease that behaved remotely like this one. *Perhaps because it's not a disease.* But then, what was it?

Sick with questions, Nediah stopped walking. Kyndra's test was tonight. He ought to seek her out and offer what reassurance he could. He hadn't given an awful lot of consideration to her visions, or to Kait's claim that Kyndra had somehow managed to reach the ninth spiral of the archives. He raked a hand through his hair. Kyndra was as much of a mystery as the Madness.

Nediah turned to leave and a flash of white caught his eye. He spun in time to glimpse the flared hem of a cloak – and its wearer had vanished down the tunnel that led to the seventh gallery.

Before he knew it, Nediah was following, throwing himself into the tunnel's tightening spiral. He was rewarded with more glimpses and sped up, but so too did his quarry, remaining one tantalizing step ahead.

He knew he was near the seventh gate when the pressure built in his ears. Nediah cursed. He wouldn't be able to pass it. When he reached the tall metal portal, he jerked to a halt, staring. It was closed and there was no sign of the person in white. But they couldn't have opened the gate, not with him right on their heels. He breathed the still, close air of the archives and felt intensely alone. Only one path ran the length of the galleries, only one, apart from . . .

Nediah turned slowly on the spot, probing the rugged walls and remembering the words Kait had spoken on the night she'd found Kyndra outside the ninth gate. *If south seventh didn't run so close to that spiral, I'd never have heard her.* If passages did exist behind the unyielding stone, he couldn't begin to guess how to find them. Could that white cloak have belonged to a member of the Nerian? Although it was the only answer that made sense, Nediah didn't like it. What was so important that they'd risk being caught in Naris proper?

He turned away from the gate, feeling foolish. It was a long walk back to the antechamber.

Kyndra wasn't there and neither were the novices who usually sat with her. On his way to the door, Nediah caught a snatch of hushed conversation. A group of Initiated sat around a table discussing the object of his search.

'It's going to be tonight,' a boy said. 'Do you think she'll pass?'

'No,' said another flatly.

'Don't be mean.' This came from a young girl with brown eyes too big for her face. 'I think she will. She's had the same time to prepare as we did.'

'Excuse me,' Nediah said politely, and the novices jumped in their seats. 'You're talking about Kyndra Vale.'

The boy stared at Nediah, obviously appalled that the Wielder had overheard their conversation. None of them spoke. 'Do you know where she is?' Nediah tried. He kept his voice light and friendly, but an anxious fist squeezed his insides.

'No, Master,' the girl answered.

Nediah left the antechamber in a whirl of cloth. Where would Kyndra be at this time of day if not in the archives? He set off down the corridor, snapping sparks from his fingers. When he realized what he was doing, he stopped abruptly. It was an old habit he hadn't indulged for years.

Nediah headed down the short slope that led to Kyndra's room. Here the black walls bore signs of tunnelling, shaped by man rather than nature, and the low ceiling dampened echoes, which was why he only heard the footsteps coming up behind just before they reached him.

Nediah turned. Though a hooded cloak shrouded his pursuer, he knew who it was by the way she moved. She brought her hands up and pushed the cowl back from her face.

'Why are you here?' Nediah asked, striving to keep his tone neutral. It was the first time he'd seen Brégenne since the night in her quarters.

'Likely for the same reason you are,' she replied, one hand on the uneven wall. 'I'm worried. Janus has been suppressing the bond every day this week. There's something he doesn't want me to know.'

Nediah folded his arms. 'And why should this concern me?'

'Because it might have something to do with Kyndra's test.'

'What?' Nediah let his arms drop. 'Why would you think that?'

Brégenne shook her head. 'I don't know,' she said distractedly. 'But this isn't like Janus. The night we were first attuned, he didn't stop trying to talk to me. Now this long silence. I don't like it.'

'I warned Kyndra not to trust him.'

Brégenne looked stricken, without a hint of her usual calm. 'Perhaps I'm imagining things. There's nothing he could really do to affect the test, is there?'

The anxiety that clutched at Nediah's insides gave one sharp squeeze. 'I hope not.'

'What can we do?' Brégenne looked small against the dark stone, her white eyes dim and unseeing. 'This is my fault. I insisted on bringing Kyndra here. If she dies tonight, the blame will be mine.'

'No. It will be the Council's.'

Brégenne's shoulders sank miserably and all he wanted to do was to take her in his arms again and hold her. The echo of her lips upon his, the remembered feel of her skin, was a torment. Weighed down with regret, Nediah said, 'Let's check the room. She might not be with Janus.'

Brégenne nodded and they walked together to Kyndra's room. The door was unlocked and when they stepped inside, Kyndra wasn't there.

Kyndra stood in the hall they called the atrium, her gaze lost amidst its floating lights. Groups of novices and masters hovered nearby. Most appeared engrossed in conversation, but she caught several covert glances. They were here for her.

News of tonight's test had broken through the citadel on a wave of whispers, and now a kind of awful fame clung to her. Kyndra could sense its presence in the hushed voices and the startled, intrigued looks.

The end of the day was almost upon her. The four Wielders chosen to perform the test and the two customary guards stood just out of earshot, conversing in soft voices. Of the main four, two were women, two men. Alandred was not among them.

Janus hadn't come for her until almost midday. She'd spent the morning in her room, knees up to her chin, back to the wall. She held the child-like figurine balanced on her kneecaps, staring at its alabaster skin, and tried not to think about what had happened to *Tools of Power*. With a sinking feeling, she remembered that she'd folded the corner of the page down on *akans*. What if someone found it and put two and two together?

'Kyndra!'

Her name yanked her back to the present and she turned. Nediah hurried across the shining floor, Brégenne in his wake. Though both their faces were twisted anxiously, Kyndra smiled, pleased to see them. She hadn't found much time for either of them over the past week. Perhaps that was for the best, she thought grimly. If anything went wrong tonight, she didn't want them implicated.

Nediah gave her a wan smile. 'Are you all right?' he asked. 'We searched all over for you.'

'I'm sorry. I was with Janus this afternoon.'

Brégenne looked as if her worst fears had been confirmed. 'What were you doing?' she asked.

'He was teaching me how to clear my mind,' Kyndra answered truthfully. 'He said it would help.'

Brégenne narrowed her faintly glowing eyes. 'You're not planning on doing anything foolish?'

'No,' Kyndra said, thinking of the white *akan* in her pocket. And then suddenly she lost her grip on her fear. It crawled up her throat, drying her tongue. Afraid her face would betray her, she looked away.

Brégenne reached out and turned Kyndra's chin back towards her. 'Look inside yourself,' the Wielder said. 'You must believe, though it may seem impossible. I know I am not wrong.'

Surprised at her gentleness, Kyndra stared at Brégenne. She seemed somehow different, though she looked the same as ever, clad in velvety silver, pale hair gathered at the nape of her neck. But the difference was not in her appearance – it resided in the tense angle of her chin, the slight tremor in her voice. Unwilling to crush her faith, Kyndra said, 'I'm ready,' feeling anything but.

As if the Wielders had heard, they stopped talking and formed up around her in the same way as last time. The hall went quiet and people turned to watch. Kyndra spotted someone waving: Irilin. Shika and Gareth stood beside her and Kyndra felt a warm rush of relief. They surely wouldn't be here, smiling, had they been caught last night. She couldn't do more than give them the thumbs up, for the Wielders began a slow procession towards the distant dark archway Kyndra had come to fear.

It seemed as if it took them hours to cross the hall. The vast floor rolled away from her and, despite the presence of the four Wielders in front of her and the two behind, Kyndra felt hopelessly alone. She slipped a hand into her pocket, seeking the *akan*. When her fingers brushed against the smooth, white child, a sense of horror seized her and she snatched her hand back again.

Akans *provide a simple and effective defence against cosmo-sethic attack.* Kyndra had memorized the short section from *Tools of Power* and now recited it to herself, hoping to find some reassurance in the litany. *Unlike their sibling objects,* urkans, *an* akan's *power may freely be summoned by anyone. A clear mind and a clear intent are the only prerequisites.* It was that sentence in particular which had convinced Kyndra. When she'd shown it to Gareth, the novice had nodded sagely and said, 'I've heard of artefacts like that. If you can get your hands on one, you'll be laughing.'

Despite their plan's success, Kyndra didn't feel at all like laughing. All manner of things could go wrong.

The procession had almost reached the arch when a tumult broke out in the hall. The Wielders paused. Hearing cries of shock and anger, Kyndra turned to look.

Kait was upon her before she realized it. The tall woman dashed the last few yards and seized her collar. Kyndra gaped at her. What was she doing out in the open? Behind her, the hall erupted. Wielders yelled and a few novices spat in Kait's direction. She ignored them all, nose to nose with Kyndra. Kyndra tried to lean away, but Kait's grip only tightened.

'Where is it?' she hissed.

'I don't know what—'

'You mustn't use it, do you understand?' Though Kait's voice was low, almost too low to hear, the violence in it shocked Kyndra. 'No time to explain,' Kait said. Over her shoulder, Kyndra saw a group of Wielders coming towards them. Their expressions were thunderous.

'I have to,' she hissed back, wondering how Kait knew about the *akan*. 'It's my only chance.'

'Then you will die,' Kait snarled. Kyndra flinched at the saliva that hit her cheek. Again she tried to wrench out of her grasp, but Kait's thin fingers held on with unearthly strength.

The contingent of Wielders arrived. Hands reached for Kait, but stopped just short of touching her, as if she carried some contagion. The Nerian woman let go of Kyndra's collar and pushed her roughly away. 'I'm sorry,' she whispered.

Kait's long coat wrapped her as she spun around. 'Don't touch me!' she spat at the Wielders. Then she strode off without a backward glance, accompanied by jeers and angry shouts. Other Wielders formed up at her back, as if to ensure that she returned to the Deep without argument. No one asked why Kait had grabbed her. Perhaps they saw it as the senseless act of a madwoman, the act of one of the Nerian.

The line began moving again and, unsure what to feel, Kyndra followed them through the archway and up into the winding tunnel. Her last glimpse of the hall showed her a white-faced Janus, his expression obscured by distance. He stood by a marble pillar, clutching one of the carved gargoyles that gnawed at the stone.

Kyndra rubbed her neck, as Kait's grip had pulled her collar tight against her skin. The incident had happened so quickly that she didn't know what to think. Why would Kait risk coming up here unless she really believed the *akan* was dangerous? A sudden and dreadful certainty seized Kyndra: Kait must have found *Tools of Power*. But there was nothing in the book to say that *akans* did anything other than defend their user.

They were nearing the summit of the climb when Kyndra's hand again strayed to her pocket. When she couldn't find the *akan*, she simply put her hand in her other pocket, fingers already flinching away from the alabaster child.

Both pockets were empty. The white *akan* was gone. Kyndra's heart pounded against her ribcage, its frenzied beating almost painful. She wrapped her arms around herself, trying to stay calm, but all she felt was the ridged flesh of a scar through her shirt.

Two Wielders took up positions just inside the tunnel's mouth, their backs to the platform. Kyndra's footsteps dragged as she made herself follow the four in front. Last time she'd stood up here, pulled from her bed by Alandred whilst the sun still slept, she had been wholly ignorant of the horror that awaited her. Now she was wide awake and terrified. The ledge overwhelmed her with memories of the agony she had suffered, and great jagged spikes reared ominously around its edge.

Almost perfectly balanced between day and night, the sky was deceptively tranquil. Early summer softened the breeze, bringing to Kyndra the rustle of new leaves. She took deep gulps, wishing that the mild, aimless wind could carry her away. Heedless, it blew on across the chasm, taking its borrowed scents to town.

Only one person could have stolen the *akan*, someone with thin, light fingers – someone who believed Kyndra would use it, despite her warning. Kyndra felt numb at Kait's betrayal. Last night the woman had asked for her trust . . . and now this. Why had she done it? Without the *akan*, Kyndra had nothing. The dregs of her hope drained away.

Already the Wielders stood prepared. One of the women came to take her arm and Kyndra let herself be guided into place at the apex of the semi-circle, near to the cliff edge. For one wild moment, she considered squeezing between the spikes and flinging herself over the side. It was a black, awful fall, but at least it would be over quickly.

Precipice at her back, Kyndra faced the Wielders. *I can do this,* she tried to convince herself, *Brégenne never makes a mistake.* The woman let go of Kyndra's arm and took up her position. Her eyes were kind and Kyndra saw sympathy there. The gentle emotion sparked something in the pit of her stomach, heating fear to anger. She clenched her fists. These people would use their power against her, power enough to rip her body apart, for no other reason than that the Council wished it. Did they do so willingly, or had they been forced into it?

Kyndra fed those thoughts to the rage, trying to drive out her horror. The Wielders' hands began to glow.

'Don't.'

Her voice emerged as a croak, half plea, half command. One of the Wielders, a Solar, glanced worriedly at the sky. Only the sun's rim stood above the horizon. Soon it would dip beneath the world, taking the Solar power with it. The man looked to his fellow Wielder. They exchanged a nod and their expressions turned inward.

'I have no power!' Kyndra screamed at them, throwing out her arms. Both hands met a silvery barrier, much like the one Brégenne had used against her in Brenwym. She pushed at it and, just as before, it gave a little. A youngish man on Kyndra's right drew in his breath sharply and frowned. The barrier strengthened, forcing Kyndra's arms back.

The sudden compression broke some internal restraint, igniting the last of her fear and burning it from her. She surveyed the Wielders as if through a dark veil, watching as they summoned power and fashioned it into spears.

'Striking me down,' she said, unable to recognize her own voice, 'will be the last thing you ever do.'

The first lance slammed into her shoulder. The force of it staggered Kyndra and threw her back against the barrier. All the novices' advice disappeared. She couldn't remember a word of the books she'd read, or the illustrations that showed a potential successfully repelling attacks. Reeling in pain, she wasn't prepared when the second Solar lance pierced her other shoulder, sending an explosion of agony through her chest. She couldn't breathe, though she gasped for air, and it seemed she could hear the sizzle of her own flesh. She blinked and saw the Wielders' faces, stoic and grim and unforgiving.

When the third lance struck her thigh – Lunar this time – Kyndra screamed. And the fourth shredded the fury she clung to. Time lost substance and the moment was endless, a torture that seared to her bones. Something terrible was happening to her body. The Lunar beams were fire and moonlit snow. Pinpricks of light stared down at her, mocking her weakness, promising death, yet withholding it.

Please, she thought wildly, not knowing whether she spoke to them or not. With a raw wail, Kyndra threw herself against the barrier.

And it shattered.

Like a shockwave, the collision felled the Wielders and the lances in Kyndra's flesh snapped and died. Her head rang, as if she'd banged it against stone – just like that time in the market and again in Rush's classroom. But now it was stronger, so much stronger. And though the echoes in her head made her shriek anew with anguish, she could see another place overlaying the platform and its crumpled Wielders. It was the Nyka: the crystal tower of the Sentheon in Solinaris, but only a quarter of its seats were full . . .

. . . When has he commanded so little respect? He looks into the eyes of the nearest man and knows the truth: fear, the usurper, walks amongst them.

'Solinaris,' he calls, and his voice rings brazenly through the crystal space. Some flinch. 'Twice I have come before you and twice you have refused both my warning and alliance. The danger is now greater than ever. Sartya is at your door.'

'We have granted you an audience, despite your refusal to take a Wielder's Oath,' Realdon Shune says. 'Now what is it you want?'

He detects a tremor in Shune's voice. 'I am not the one you need fear,' he assures them all, turning up his patterned palms. 'We have a common enemy.'

'We are aware of the empire's position,' ancient Targon says, 'and we are prepared to stand against her.'

He curls his fingers and his palms become fists. 'You cannot win this fight – Sartya has gone uncontested too long. The army beyond your walls is here for one purpose: to raze this citadel to the rock.'

'Solinaris is strong,' Realdon Shune argues, the first hint of impatience in his face. 'We will not fall so easily.'

He takes a step forward and, as one, the Sentheon draw back. 'The Sartyans number in the tens of thousands. Remember Kingswold. Remember the defences at Baristogan and Lycorash and the rebels that lie dead there. They even killed the children, Shune.'

For a moment, Shune regards him in silence, as if working up the nerve to speak. Then he says, 'When has your kind ever cared about the deaths of ordinary people? Surely, they are nothing to you.'

He swallows. Anger swells, a hot kindling he has not felt in years. 'So you hate me,' he says, sweeping his gaze over the Sentheon, meeting those eyes that dare to meet his. 'But will you not put it aside when lives are at stake? I alone can help you. I have a vision, a vision of peace. Together we can build a world where all may live freely, a world without Sartya.'

'A world which you alone might rule.'

He stares at Realdon Shune, surprised at the shrewd words. 'You have less to fear from my rule than you do from Sartya's,' he answers.

Shock sweeps through the large, circular room. There are whispers – no doubt slanderous, he thinks. Were they perhaps expecting him to deny a desire to rule?

He holds up a finger and the murmurs cease. 'You have no friends. Not only did you refuse an alliance with me, but you also refused the aid of those who – with your support – could have turned this bloody tide. But you did nothing and now even surrender is no longer an option.' He pauses. 'I do not want to see Rairam – the last free land – in the empire's grip. And,' he adds heavily, 'if I cannot persuade you to join me, I will act alone.'

The Sentheon erupts. Some are on their feet. Others are too shocked, or too cautious to share their thoughts. He stands unthreatening but immovable. He watches Shune and he knows what the Wielder is thinking: what can one man do to stop a power that even Solinaris might not withstand?

'I can do more than you can dream,' he answers aloud and Realdon Shune's face hardens.

However, it is Targon who speaks and at his words, every-one in the Nyka falls silent. 'You talk of peace,' the old man says, 'yet plan to rule. You profess friendship, yet openly declare to act against our decisions. That is not friendship. Friendship is mutual regard and cooperation. It is the ability to show compassion and selflessness.' The old man meets his eyes. 'You cannot offer us something you do not understand.'

Fire dictates the next moment, as a flaming ball smashes into the glass. The Nyka's western wall turns yellow, orange and then black, and men and women scream. When it clears, he sees the stain of the empire's smoky claws and knows it is a promise of more to come.

'It has begun,' he says, amidst shouts of panic and the dis-believing gasps as tiny, terrible cracks are spotted in the glass. Out beyond Solinaris's walls, the siege engines belch their acrid fumes. The Sentheon is in turmoil and the time for talk-ing is done. He turns to go.

'Stop him!' Shune yells, but his words are lost in a clarion call to arms. Wielders leap from their seats and boots strike the marble floor as another fireball strikes the wall. The Nyka turns red.

'Master.' Anohin is there, dressed in his race's customary white. 'Are we alone, then?' the Yadin asks, his ageless features arranged in concern.

He nods. 'The Wielders cannot see beyond their fear of me.' They start off together – the inhuman and the non-human, he thinks wryly – walking side by side through the chaos. Up high on the western wall, glass splinters and he shakes his head. 'So much death, Anohin. But, the stars willing, peace will come.'

The Yadin pulls on a leather glove. 'You have the book?'

'Yes.' He draws it from his cloak and Anohin flinches. But of course he would – it is like showing a condemned man the rope that will hang him. How inconsiderate. He puts the book away. Anohin's face is pale and his eyes betray his agitation, but there has never been a Yadin more loyal. He has played his part and as a reward, Anohin will live to join him in the new world . . .

'Enough.'

There was a heavy blow and the crystal chamber shattered. She was Kyndra again, lying on a dark mountain in terrible pain. She cried out. Unconsciousness threatened and she wrestled with it, fearing worse would follow on its heels.

Someone stood over her – she could see the white leather of their boots. And there was moaning. *The Wielders*, she thought dazedly, *the test*. But there was also the empire and the war and the face of a trusted servant. It was all one and she didn't have the strength to separate it.

The deep voice spoke again and Kyndra had heard it somewhere before, but couldn't remember through the pain of breathing. Unable to raise her head, she stared at the pitted rock on which she lay. Her awareness began to fade and she struggled, knowing she couldn't hold on to it for long.

Tremors began to wrack her body and arms came around her and under her, lifting her into the air. The white-clad stranger had picked her up, as if she were a child, holding her easily in his strong arms. Kyndra let her head roll back against his shoulder and the stranger began to walk.

She glimpsed the scene through clouded eyes. The two guards were sprawled across the mouth of the tunnel, seemingly unconscious, and the four Wielders on the platform lay where they had fallen, whimpering and bleeding from their ears. The female Wielder's once-sympathetic face now hung slack and spittle flecked her lips. When the stranger turned to descend into Naris, Kyndra was glad to leave the sight behind.

Shadows fastened themselves to the corners of her eyes, but, anxious to see her rescuer's face, she used the last of her strength to keep them open. She tilted her head to look up into the white hood and at the same instant, the man glanced down at her.

'Rest now,' Medavle said and, after a faint lurch of surprise, Kyndra slid into darkness.

PART THREE

21

The first thing she saw was a face: Anohin with his white collar framing his neck. But no – the eyes were wrong. They were black, not grey and the chin was now unshaven. She heard a name – hers? – spoken gently, but it was muffled by sleep.

'Kyndra?'

It *was* her name. Memory flowed back, abrupt and all too vivid. Kyndra sat up and the room spun. But Medavle caught her shoulders and steadied her before she fell. *Medavle, not Anohin.* She had never known Anohin, she reminded herself forcefully.

Her mind was a jumble. What had happened? Where was she? Bits of the test returned to her – the lances, the shattered barrier. She remembered Kait and the missing *akan*. But Anohin was somehow there too. Kyndra could see his face as clearly as Medavle's, as if only a blink stood between them. She closed her eyes . . . and remembered the feeling of using a mind not her own, speaking with a man's accented tongue, seeing out of eyes that had not grown up watching the comings and goings of Brenwym. And still she couldn't picture him, this usurper of her self – not like she could picture Anohin or Realdon Shune or old Targon. She couldn't picture him because she *was* him. Kyndra shook her head and tried to slow her breathing.

'You're all right,' Medavle said, his deep voice breaking Kyndra's trance.

'Where am I?'

'Safe.'

She frowned. 'But the test—'

'It's over.' Medavle let go of her, moved away. 'You don't remember, do you?'

'Remember what?'

'What you did.'

Kyndra put a hand to her head, trying to halt the stream of images that only filled her with confusion. 'I remember Kait,' she said and found her fists clenched. 'She stole the *akan*.'

For the first time, Medavle's expression faltered. 'What *akan*?'

'My white *akan*.' Kyndra met his eyes. Medavle looked exactly as he had in Sky Port East. His garments were white from robes to belt to gloves and the same, tarnished flute hung at his hip. Kyndra recalled the last time they'd met – when Medavle had given her that ragged page of writing. A snatched echo of the poem returned to her and she remembered telling Nediah that the story was incomplete. How had Medavle come to be here? Was he enemy or friend?

'Kait told me I could trust her,' Kyndra said bitterly, 'but she lied. The *akan* was my only chance of passing the test. If she hadn't stolen it, all this would be over.'

Medavle turned as pale as his robes. In the light of the nearly featureless room, he knelt once again beside Kyndra and placed a hand on her shoulder. Kyndra glanced down at it, conscious that neither Brégenne nor Nediah trusted Medavle. She knew next to nothing about the man, but the hand on her shoulder was firm and warm. Trapped in a world where every movement hurt and her mind was no longer her own, it was the only comfort she had.

'How did you come by this *akan*?' Medavle asked.

And, numbly, Kyndra told him. She focused on speaking and tried not to look at her wounds. Waves of pain hit her, infrequent at first, but growing closer together the longer she spent sitting up. When the small room began to swim in her gaze, she paused to take several deep breaths, willing herself not to faint.

'Kait did not betray you,' Medavle said in a strained voice.

'What?'

'Was it Kait who led you to find this book? Was it Kait who gave you a chance to enter the archives? Was it Kait who made you believe that you would fail without help?'

'No,' Kyndra said slowly, shying away from the implied conclusion.

Medavle's face was grave. 'This goes further than you know. Many *akans* survived the collapse of Solinaris, but only one was white.'

Kyndra stared at him. 'Explain, please.'

Medavle stood up. 'The main purpose of *akans*', he said, 'is to shield a user from harm. During the Acrean wars, every Wielder carried one in case they needed to defend themselves when their respective power wasn't active.' He paused. 'But white *akans* are different. In the closing days of the war, the Sentheon' – Kyndra felt a small shock at the name – 'did some terrible things. Commissioning white *akans* was one of them. They were given to the citadel's non-Wielder servants, who were instructed to use them only in their hour of greatest need

– and only in defence of the citadel. When the enemies of Solinaris breached her walls, that need finally arose. Unlike regular *akans*, white *akans* have the ability to unleash a powerful counter-attack. But –' Medavle held up a finger – 'the servants were deceived. Concerned about bestowing any sort of cosmosethic power on those they considered unworthy of it, the Sentheon had built in a safeguard.'

Gooseflesh prickled along Kyndra's arms when she thought of the winged child's pallid face. Medavle's eyes were fixed and dark with memories. 'The cruelty of those days cannot be matched,' he whispered, one fist clenched. He uncurled it and turned his gaze on her. 'The power a white *akan* unleashes is drawn from its user's own life-force – enough to kill them outright.'

The silence in the small cave-like room was absolute. Then Kyndra whispered, 'That can't be right.' She stared at the black wall. 'Janus wouldn't do that to me, he couldn't.'

Medavle gave her a look and Kyndra felt a flush of humiliation. 'Pretty faces are best suited to deception,' he said. 'You let him get the better of you. And as much as I despise the Nerian, you owe Kait your life.'

Kyndra gazed at him. 'He said he wanted to help me. He wouldn't . . .'

Medavle shook his head. Away from the room's one weak lamp, his expression was unreadable. 'Janus planted that book,' he said quietly. 'He provided access to the archives. I suspect he also removed the regular *akans*, so that only the white remained. It was well done.'

Janus' face hovered before her, earnest, confident, his hands warm in hers. *Everything will be all right. You know what to do now.* She'd wondered at those words, but hadn't had the wit to suspect them.

Kyndra looked down at her legs and then wished she hadn't. Raw tissue showed through the tatters of her ruined trousers. For the first time she noticed the smell and almost gagged when she realized it was her own burned flesh.

'But I came up with the plan myself,' she said, holding desperately to denial.

'Yes. That way, the test could provide a cover for murder.'

Kyndra buried her face in her hands. Now in horror she remembered the missing page that Janus must have ripped out. *While any* akan *will shield its bearer from harm, one type – the white* akan *– was designed to do more. Its power—* How could she have been so stupid?

Medavle stroked his chin with white-gloved fingers. 'How much does he know,' he mused, 'to go to such lengths?'

'He could have let the test finish me,' Kyndra said numbly. Part of her couldn't believe Janus capable of murder. It didn't feel real. She'd never done him any harm.

'Perhaps he feared it wouldn't,' Medavle said. 'And he was right.' A smile of what might have been triumph flitted across his mouth, but was gone before Kyndra could be sure.

'I would be dead if you hadn't stopped them,' she said.

'I didn't stop them. You did.'

'You're not making sense.'

Medavle's face was grim. 'You don't remember?'

'Remember what?' The only thing about the test that Kyndra truly recalled was the pain. She raised a hand to sooth her aching head and gasped as the movement tugged at her wounds. Taking a breath, she chanced another look at them. The burns on her thighs were blistered and red with a bloody mess of yellow tissue at the centre. They didn't hurt as much as they should – the burns on her shoulders were far more painful, though they looked better. Her clothes hung on her by threads.

'Careful,' Medavle said, as Kyndra parted the cloth. 'I haven't been able to do much. You need a proper healer.'

She gave the bare room a more detailed study. For the first time, she realized there was no door. 'Where are we?'

'Safe, as I said.'

'What's that noise?' It was a low commotion, as if voices were calling to one another.

'They are searching for you. And me,' he added.

'Did anyone see you?'

Medavle shook his head. 'Not directly. I knocked out the Wielders guarding the platform and you did for the rest.'

Not understanding, Kyndra looked down. Heat radiated from her body, but she shivered in the airless space, trying to order her thoughts. 'What do you want with me?' she asked, letting her body lie back against the hard wall. 'Why did you help me?'

Medavle stared at her. At first his face seemed impassive, but gradually Kyndra made out a creasing around the dark eyes, a gnawing worry that reminded her of Jarand on the night Brégenne saved her life, the night it all started.

'Because you are my hope,' Medavle said. 'And someone tried to kill you.'

Kyndra opened her mouth to respond, but nothing came out. Then a shudder ran convulsively through her body, jerking her arms. Her throat was closing; she gasped for air. Dimly she saw Medavle wrench the flute from his belt and thought she heard a peal of notes like the rest-day bells in Brenwym. But they weren't calling her. They were sending her away.

22

'Nediah, is that—?'

'Yes, I've got her.'

'Has the Madness taken her too?'

'No, but she's badly injured.'

'Then they'll want to question her. Master Alandred said—'

'I don't care what he said. Kyndra is in no condition to talk. Open that door and then leave me alone with her.'

'Nediah, the girl must know something. Four masters—'

'Right now what she knows or doesn't know is irrelevant. I need time to heal her and silence to work in.'

Everything was pain. Nediah's face swam in and out of focus. Where was she? Where was Medavle? Somewhere beyond Nediah, she heard more words and the sound of a door closing. Nediah laid her down on a bed whose hardness she recognized: she was back in her room.

Golden fire climbed up the walls and ceiling – the only things Kyndra could see. It assaulted her eyes between each slow blink. Heat beat down on her body. She could almost pretend that she lay in lower Wym field with Jhren and Colta at her side, letting the sunlight coax her into a doze. Those summer mornings spent at idle, timeless play. Running through wood and meadow until their tired lungs demanded rest. And always the hot, teasing sun that watched them while they slept. She had known those years would end with the Inheritance Ceremony. But so too had her life in Brenwym.

Kyndra caught her breath, as sharp, skittering pains pulled her mind back to her burned body. Solar energy condensed on her skin, travelling through the broken flesh and into her bones. She gritted her teeth so that she wouldn't cry out, but then it stopped. The wall of heat receded and in its place washed a wonderful coolness. She let go of the breath she'd been holding and sighed.

'These wounds have been treated against infection,' Nediah murmured. Kyndra turned her head to look at the Wielder, whose sunlit corona had begun to fade. She had no idea how much time had passed, but if Nediah was able to heal her, it must be a new day.

Kyndra peered tentatively down at her legs, and her eyes widened. The burned skin was gone. New pink tissue covered what had not long ago been a ruin of blood and blisters. Her head was rapidly clearing too, each thought crystallizing with new intensity. She looked at Nediah, astonished. 'How did you do that?'

Nediah ran a hand through his hair. 'I only hastened your body's natural healing process. It seems you cope well with trauma.' Shadows gathered on his face and he came to sit on her bed. 'But, really, I should be asking you that.'

Kyndra frowned. 'Ask me what?'

'How it is that you're alive. I know my calling. You shouldn't be.' He paused. 'It's as if these injuries don't really touch you. They are real and they should, but something in you is stronger, something that makes mortal wounds behave like flesh wounds.

Healing you is too easy.' Nediah met her eyes and Kyndra flinched at a chill suspicion beginning to surface there. 'You still haven't found your affinity,' the Wielder concluded bleakly.

It wasn't really a question, but Kyndra shook her head.

'What happened on the platform?' Nediah asked.

'What do you mean?'

'Three Wielders are dead and the last is unlikely ever to wake up.'

Kyndra stared at him. 'I don't understand.'

'The Madness took them during the test,' Nediah said. The green barely showed in his eyes, so dark had they become. 'It was instantaneous, violent. Worse than either Mardon or Rush. Magat threw herself over the precipice. Two more were restrained before they could join her, but they didn't survive. The last is in the annexes.'

Kyndra's mouth was dry. 'I . . . I can't remember.'

'But you remember Medavle?'

She drew breath and eased up to a sitting position with her back against the rough wall. 'You know about him?'

'He was the one who told me where to find you. Begged me to help you.' Nediah shook his head. 'He didn't have to beg, of course. I came straightaway and carried you here.'

'He brought me down from the platform,' Kyndra said faintly.

'The Council don't know that. Well — they know *someone* brought you down, but the two Wielders he immobilized couldn't say who'd attacked them.' Nediah stared at the opposite wall. 'I wish I knew what all this was about. How is Medavle here in the citadel? Why did he help you?'

'He said —' Medavle's deep voice echoed back to her — 'I was his hope, or something.'

On the end of the bed, Nediah shifted uneasily. 'Or something?'

I have to tell him, Kyndra thought. But what if Medavle's story was just another lie? Janus surely didn't want her dead. She frowned. Something didn't sit right. When Janus had come to the archives, hadn't that scroll he'd shown Hebrin carried the Council's seal?

Kyndra bit her lip. Nediah had warned her about Janus and so had Kait and she'd chosen to ignore them both. Finally, she swallowed and began to speak. First, she told Nediah about the book she'd 'found' in the archives, the book with the missing page in which she'd read about *akans*. She described Janus' conversation with Hebrin, how the novices had suggested following him down to the seventh gallery. Kyndra inwardly winced. It all sounded so obvious now. And far too easy. She kept the part about meeting Kait in the archives to herself.

When she told Nediah what Medavle had said about the white *akan*, the Wielder stood up, alarm in the hunch of his shoulders. He glanced at the door and when he spoke, it was in a tight, doubtful voice. 'How do you know it's the truth?'

'I don't. But why else would Kait risk coming up here to take it off me?'

Nediah's look was sharp. 'So that's what she was doing when she grabbed you?'

'She warned me not to use it. And when I said the *akan* was my only chance, she stole it.'

The Wielder dropped back onto the bed, paler than before. 'And all of this so Janus could get rid of you without suspicion.'

'That's the thing, though.' Kyndra leaned forward. 'I can't make myself believe it was his idea. When he asked Hebrin for permission to visit that spiral, he showed him a scroll stamped with the Council's seal. Could he have forged it?'

Nediah shook his head. 'Those seals only work for Council members. The scroll at least will have been genuine.'

'Then he must have brought something back to help Rush,' Kyndra reasoned. She met Nediah's gaze. 'Have you seen anything like that?'

'Lord Loricus *did* visit with an artefact retrieved from the archives,' Nediah said, 'but it made no difference.'

'Then he was covering himself,' Kyndra insisted. Now that she had her theory, she was reluctant to let it go. *Because it makes sense*, she thought, but another voice – a voice she tried to crush – whispered that she just didn't want to think ill of Janus. *Even if it wasn't his idea, he knew what he was doing when he planted that book*, she argued back. Or did he? Perhaps Janus had truly believed he was helping her and they were both victims of manipulation. Before the silence became too impenetrable, Kyndra said, 'I think the Council gave Janus that scroll so I could follow him and find the *akan*.'

For the first time, Nediah seemed truly alarmed. Again he glanced at the door, as if frightened that someone had their ear pressed against it. 'That's a serious accusation.'

'And Medavle said that the *akan* unleashes a counter-attack.' Kyndra felt a shock of cold. 'Whoever meant for me to use it was prepared to hurt Wielders.'

Nediah didn't reply. She could see him struggling to even consider the possibility.

'Surely it's not impossible,' she said.

'No,' Nediah agreed after a reluctant pause. Then, 'If it's true, it might not involve the whole Council. All have use of that seal.'

'So you're saying one of them is acting alone?'

'I don't know what I'm saying.' Nediah stood, took a couple of distracted paces. 'Why would the Council risk harming their own? None of this makes sense.'

Kyndra looked down at her legs. 'I heard you talking to that man – before you healed me,' she said softly. 'They want to question me. They think I have something to do with those Wielders' deaths.'

'No,' Nediah said sharply, turning from his scrutiny of the wall. 'The Council want to know who managed to access the platform without being seen. And they want to know where that person took you and why.'

'As if I'd tell them,' Kyndra said, trying to seem unconcerned. 'Do they think I'm likely to betray the one who rescued me?'

'They don't see it as rescuing, Kyndra. The test is a necessary part of becoming a Wielder.'

Kyndra let that statement pass, though it stirred her anger. 'What if they're wrong?' she said, gazing fixedly at her new scars. 'What if I did have something to do with those Wielders dying?' A memory buried in her subconscious had resurfaced. She recalled feeling a black rage right before the test and she'd spoken to the Wielders, warned them not to touch her. *Striking me down will be the last thing you ever do.*

Kyndra clutched handfuls of blanket and squeezed her eyes shut, but the words expanded to fill that sable space, and, on top of them, echoed Medavle's and Nediah's. Each asked a question she couldn't and didn't want to answer.

You don't remember, do you? What you did.

How is it that you're alive?

Nediah had hold of her upper arms and was shaking her gently, but she couldn't open her eyes, couldn't look into his trusting face. *I don't know,* she answered him silently. *I don't even know who I am any more.* Because then there was the man whose memories she shared: the man who proclaimed himself the instrument of peace, who had stolen a book kept on the ninth spiral, who had stood in front of Solinaris's Sentheon and offered them his alliance. Who was he? Why did he haunt her? And what power did he have that allowed her to pass through shielded gates, to go where others could not?

'Kyndra,' Nediah said firmly, 'what's wrong?'

Finally she opened her eyes. 'Nothing,' she said. 'I think I'd like to rest now.'

Nediah considered her for a moment. 'It's what you need.'

What I need, Kyndra thought, *is to get out of here.* She nodded at Nediah and gave him a weak smile. 'Thank you,' she told the Wielder. *But perhaps you should have let me die.*

The lamp burned steadily through its wick and the dancing shadows danced unceasingly across the wall. She had slept, but now that sleep had left her, she felt alert, clear-headed – as she hadn't done in days. For the first time, she knew what she had to do.

And, like a well-laid plan, chance favoured her.

'Kyndra.' It came as a whisper through the door, a young woman's voice hissing her name. Gingerly, Kyndra climbed out of bed, but the pain wasn't as bad as she feared, just a dull ache in her shoulders and legs. Surprised to find the door unlocked, she cracked it open and saw Irilin's pale eyes staring at her.

The novice glanced back at the empty corridor and then slipped inside. She smiled at Kyndra. 'I'm making this a habit, aren't I?'

Kyndra smiled back and closed the door. 'So you didn't have any problems getting out of the archives the other night?'

'Never mind that now. What about you? Was it the Madness that killed those Wielders during the test? Did you use the *akan*?'

Kyndra didn't reply. The memory of the sinister threat she'd made whispered in her ear, refusing to be banished. She shook her head and met the novice's eyes. 'Irilin,' she said quietly, 'I need your help.'

'For what?'

Kyndra kept her gaze steady. 'To get out of the citadel.'

Irilin stared at her, mouth slightly open. 'I don't understand. Why would you want to leave? You belong here.'

'No I don't,' Kyndra said firmly. 'And by now, the Council will have realized that. They won't let me go, Irilin. I have to escape before . . . before they decide to get rid of me.' *And before anyone else dies because of me.*

Irilin's denial withered on her lips. She knew, Kyndra thought, what the Council would do. *What they may have already tried to do.* 'There's more,' she said aloud. Swiftly, she told Irilin what she'd learned about the white *akan*. Although she chided herself for it, she kept Janus' part to a minimum, making it sound as if the Council had planned it all.

Even before she'd finished speaking, Irilin was shooting fearful glances at the door, as if she half expected the Council to blast it apart at any moment. Nediah had been the same, Kyndra remembered. She watched Irilin's darting eyes and wondered how three people had managed to gain such control. Had the days when all Wielders ruled jointly died with Solinaris?

'I don't understand,' Irilin said finally in a hushed voice. 'Why give you another chance and then plot to kill you?'

Kyndra shook her head. 'Perhaps the second test was just a ruse. Perhaps they already knew I wasn't a Wielder.'

Irilin didn't look convinced. 'If they knew that, they wouldn't have gone to so much trouble. They have the authority to execute you anyway.'

Kyndra grimaced. 'Thanks.'

'Sorry. I was going to say you're crazy to run, but . . . I guess it's what I would do.'

Surprised, Kyndra looked up. 'So you'll help me?'

Irilin's face was sober. 'They'll punish us both if we're caught.'

'I'm not going to sit here and wait for whatever the Council has planned,' Kyndra said stubbornly. Besides,' she added, 'this is the last thing they'd expect. They're used to people doing what they tell them to.'

Irilin gave her a faintly sceptical nod. 'I suppose you want to go tonight.'

'I want to go now.'

'*Now?*' The novice took a step back. 'It's broad daylight, Kyndra. Are you sure you haven't lost your mind?'

'Nediah said they want to question me. They probably think I had something to do with what happened last night.'

Irilin shook her head. 'That's nonsense. The Madness killed those Wielders.'

Kyndra looked away. 'Even if it did, the Council will ask me about the person who rescued me from the platform. Would they believe me if I said I didn't remember?'

Irilin's silence was answer enough.

'And then I'll be locked up while they decide what to do about me – probably with more than just an ordinary key.' Kyndra gave the door a significant glance.

'They'd already locked you in just now and taken away the key,' Irilin said, a little colour returning to her cheeks. 'But I borrowed Shika's pick.'

Kyndra smothered her apprehension in a laugh. 'What happened to you, Iri?' she asked. 'I thought you followed the rules.'

'So did I,' the novice said with a rueful shake of her head. 'But that was before you came.'

The same fortune that had brought Irilin to Kyndra's room stayed with her as, head bent and disguised uncomfortably in a spare set of Irilin's tiny robes, she passed through Naris. Few Wielders spared a glance for two lowly novices hurrying about their studies, and hurry Irilin did, taking Kyndra on a convoluted route to one of the citadel's lower gates. Disaster almost struck when they bumped into Alandred backing out of a doorway. The Master of Novices, however, wore a rumpled, preoccupied air and spared them barely a glance. *Probably looking forward to my questioning*, Kyndra thought darkly.

It wasn't her only dark thought. She hated to leave Brégenne and Nediah without a word, but the success of her plan depended on speed and secrecy. Both would try to stop her, not because they wished her harm, but because they, too, were under the Council's control. She'd watched Nediah struggle to accept her story about the *akan* – she'd seen those doubtful, frightened glances. Kyndra knew that Nediah would never betray her, but she couldn't trust the Wielder to let her go.

'I'm taking you to the gate that the Murtan miners use,' Irilin whispered out of the corner of her mouth. 'It's the only one not usually watched. From there, the path winds up around the mountain until it reaches the bridge. That's the only way across the chasm.' They had already dropped a few

levels and Kyndra's ears popped at the steep gradient. Gradually the floating fires disappeared until only torches cast their
yellow eyes on the stone. 'No one comes down here,' Irilin said,
'except novices – Gareth sometimes tries to swipe food from
the kitchens when the Murtans aren't looking.'

'What's the arrangement with the Murtans?' Kyndra asked.
'I thought they couldn't see the citadel.'

'They can't. But they're given a token – I suppose it's a bit
like the one Master Hebrin gave Janus – that gets them across
the bridge and down the path into the citadel. Once they're
inside, they see the same as us, but they have to keep to the
under-levels.'

They scurried past the kitchens where the yeasty smell of
baking bread warmed the air, and Kyndra drew it deep into her
nose. It was a smell that stirred her familiar yearning for home,
a yearning that – with escape looking ever more possible –
grew stronger. She imagined walking down the road that led
to The Nomos. It was early summer . . . her mother would be
outside, whitewash in hand, and Jarand up on the roof, teasing
out some winter-welted thatch. She would wait for them to
pause in their work, to look up and see her where she stood
watching – just like before, as if nothing had ever happened.

The vision shattered when Irilin yanked her to a stop.
'Shhh,' the novice hissed. They stood in a narrow, curving passage that – in a few more steps – intersected with a much
larger one. Before Irilin pulled her back around the bend,
Kyndra felt a gust of fresh air and her heart leapt. Now she
could hear the unmistakable squeak of an axle in need of
grease and the irregular, puffing breaths of men at work.

'That wheel always squeaks,' Irilin whispered near Kyndra's

ear. 'I recognize it. They're taking away a cartload of ore. The Murtans mint the gold themselves.'

'These carts,' Kyndra said quietly, struck by the obvious. 'Is there space to hide, say, a person?'

Irilin smiled slowly. 'Why don't we wait and see?'

While Irilin covertly checked on the Murtans' progress as they loaded the cart, Kyndra leaned against the black stone and wondered what she would do when she reached the town. Her few coins wouldn't buy her a cabin on an airship, but perhaps there were caravans heading east who'd let her work for food and passage.

'Where will you go?' Irilin whispered.

'Home,' Kyndra answered immediately. 'Somehow.'

Irilin reached into her pocket and pulled out a small bag. 'Here,' she said, handing it to Kyndra, 'you'll need this.'

Kyndra squeezed the bag and metal clinked. 'Iri,' she said, staring at the young woman with wide eyes. 'You can't give me this.'

'I thought I just did.' The novice folded her arms. 'Take it, Kyn. Buy some clothes as soon as you can. You look like a beggar under those robes and you'll have to leave them behind here.'

'Iri, I can't take your money.'

'Don't be silly. I'll be given more next month.' She grinned. 'Anyway, what would Shika and Gareth say if they found out I'd let you go off with nothing?'

Kyndra sighed. 'You're going to have to tell them goodbye from me.' She glanced down at the bag of coins and then up at the young woman. 'Thank you, Iri,' she said sincerely. 'For everything.'

*

With Irilin's good luck ringing in her ears – luck she couldn't believe was still with her – Kyndra crouched under the cart's tarpaulin, uncomfortably squashed between small sacks of gold ore. There was probably enough here to rebuild Brenwym twice over and the thought had crossed her mind to stash a few nuggets away. But she wasn't a thief, she told herself, firmly squashing the temptation. And besides, she was richer than she'd ever been in her life, thanks to Iri. As if to punish her for being greedy, the cart's wooden wheels jolted over every stone and Kyndra winced, feeling wholly like the ragged stowaway she was.

She could only guess at the cart's progress. At first it trundled upwards at a steep angle, leaning always to the right. Then – when she couldn't take any more of being crushed by a particularly knobbly sack – it finally levelled out. She didn't know when they crossed the chasm, or when they reached the outlying farms. But when the tarpaulin grew sweltering under the sun, Kyndra knew that they'd left the shadow of Naris behind.

And though she was hot, thirsty and cramped, it was as if a fist uncurled from around her heart, letting the blood flow freely for the first time. She licked the sweat from her top lip and smiled.

Perhaps another half-hour passed before the cart rocked to a halt. Kyndra listened, but all she could hear were the sundry dealings of townsfolk. Where was the driver? She waited, but no hand came to unhook the tarpaulin. Kyndra took a chance and lifted up a corner. She was in a small, paved courtyard, enclosed on three sides by the stout Murtan buildings she remembered. Two doors stood open, black under the sun's glare. It was a late, bright afternoon, though clouds were massing in the south.

Muscles knotted and tingling unpleasantly, Kyndra eased out of the cart. No sooner had she gained her feet than a shout struck the stone courtyard and a man darted from one of the doorways. Kyndra didn't stop to think. Clutching Irilin's money bag, she broke into a run, hoping she looked like nothing more than a beggar on the scrounge.

Unfortunately, in neat, prosperous Murta, beggars were not a common sight. Dressed in rags that barely covered her healing flesh, Kyndra knew she cut a conspicuous figure. Despite Irilin's advice, she couldn't bring herself to waste coins on clothes, especially not when she saw an airship tied up at the dock. Kyndra weighed the money bag, wondering whether it might buy her a swift passage out of here. It wouldn't be long before the Wielders discovered her missing. She quickened her pace.

The streets of Murta welcomed her with smells of frying meat, wood smoke, tar and the distinctive musk of livestock. Occasionally she caught the fresh, subtle scent of new leaves. She tried to keep to the smaller lanes, but it seemed everyone's door was open. A skinny man with a broom was doing his best to chivvy some hens, and half a dozen children cluttered the other side of the path with a game. Kyndra opened her mouth to ask them to move, but after several startled glances that took in her battered appearance, they darted to one side, eyes downcast.

By the time she reached the steps to the airship dock, she was sweating and her heart thumped a protest in her chest. Kyndra forced herself to climb slowly, ignoring the stares she attracted. Men and women briskly passed her and a procession of handcarts creaked up a wooden slope to her left. The dock was laden with produce, some spilling out of barrels and sacks.

Kyndra looked automatically for the balls of wool she'd seen in Sky Port East, but it didn't seem that the Valleys had made it this far west. She smiled at the airship bumping gently in its berth – it looked just like the barge Argat had so disdained.

Scanning the deck for a quartermaster, Kyndra spotted a boy. He stood with his back to the railing, staring out at the country east of town. Kyndra moved closer. The boy wore dark woollen trousers – unsuitable in this sun – a shirt and short boots. His hair was blond and hung to his shoulders, but the wind whipped it up in a tangle of strands. Kyndra stopped, the breath catching in her throat.

As if sensing the gaze on the back of his head, the boy turned. Blue eyes blinked at Kyndra before they widened, mimicking the shape of the boy's astonished mouth.

The Valleys had made it west after all. She was looking at Jhren.

23

Shock rooted Kyndra to the spot. She couldn't stop staring at the boy who stood just steps away, dressed in those familiar Dales clothes. Jhren, too, stood unmoving and it seemed an age passed before Kyndra managed to cross the space between them.

Jhren made a strangled, incredulous sound. Still staring, he raised his hand dream-slow above the rail and Kyndra reached out and took it. 'How?' Jhren said and then he laughed. 'I can't believe it.'

Kyndra found herself laughing too. Jhren's mirth caught her up just as it always had done and for a moment nothing between them had changed. They could have been back in the cellars of The Nomos or crouching behind Ashley Gigg's house, up to their usual tricks, or racing – afterwards – cackling over the fields, drunk on their own daring.

Then the music of the dock reached a natural crescendo and broke the illusion. Kyndra stared at Jhren with the shadow of all that had happened in her eyes and pulled her hand back.

'I'm here on trader's business,' Jhren said a touch importantly. Then he sobered. 'The Breaking's disrupted trade from Sky Port North to the Eversea Isles. It wasn't just Brenwym that got hit. So many people have poured into the capital that the Assembly are thinking of closing the gates.' The speech had the ring of repetition about it. 'We've been scouting out new markets,' Jhren continued, 'and when we heard talk of a town that imports nearly everything, Aunt Hanna wanted to make some enquiries.' He blinked and seemed to take in her battered appearance for the first time. 'You look terrible. What happened to you?'

Kyndra's initial tide of shock had receded, leaving behind a jumble of feelings. 'Jhren,' she began and saw a ripple cross her friend's face. 'Sorry,' she amended hastily, 'Huran—'

'I prefer Jhren,' the boy said, shifting his weight from foot to foot. He didn't look at her.

'Oh. I thought that—'

'Everyone calls me Huran now,' Jhren said a touch bitterly. 'It was just odd, hearing you speak my name again.'

Kyndra stared at him, picturing a blond-haired boy coming from a tent crying, 'I am Huran!' She remembered Jhren's delight, his shining eyes, his pride. What had happened to strip that away?

'Things have changed since you left,' Jhren said.

'Are Reena and Jarand . . . ?' Kyndra faltered as the smile withered on Jhren's face.

'Fine,' Jhren said shortly. He gave her a sidelong look. 'But Brenwym was burned to the ground. There's nothing left.'

Kyndra swallowed the pain his news caused her. She'd seen the fires for herself. Feeling a prickle between her shoulders, she turned, but there was no one watching. New urgency seized her. 'Jhren,' she said, leaning in closer, 'help me get away from here.'

'Why did you do it, Kyndra?' Jhren spoke with a slow

despair that sent a chill through her blood. 'Why did you break the Relic? Why did you run away?'

'I didn't,' Kyndra said. 'You were there, weren't you? You saw what happened.'

'I saw you go with that witch,' Jhren said, his face darkening. 'I saw you leave your parents as they stood watching your home burn.'

'Then you must know that Brégenne healed—' Kyndra broke off. She didn't have time for this. 'Please, Jhren. I can explain everything later, once we're away.'

'No,' Jhren said. His hands shook, as if they wanted to ball into fists. 'You have no idea what it's like now, what you've done. Our home is gone, and it's because of you.' Something glittered in the corners of his eyes, tears or rage, Kyndra didn't know. She stared at Jhren, stunned, ice creeping through her at his words.

'Is that what you believe?' she asked eventually. 'Is that what everyone thinks?'

'Are you saying it's not true?'

Words tumbled inside her, words of denial, of anger. There were so many, she couldn't speak them – each wanted to be the first out of her mouth and they tripped each other up in their efforts. Beneath the silence that ensued from this soundless struggle, the ice worked through her. *Why deny it?* Jhren was right. She had broken the Relic and she had run away. No matter that neither was the complete truth. She looked at the boy who was once her best friend, unable to speak.

'I thought so,' Jhren said. Sadness tempered the disgust in his voice. 'I don't pretend to understand why you did it, Kyndra. I know those people stood against you, but you didn't have to run.' He met her eyes. 'You didn't have to run.'

'I'm sorry,' Kyndra said quietly. A peculiar emptiness drained her of feeling and she began to see a chasm between them, like the one that separated Naris from the world. She stood on one side, Jhren on the other. Perhaps Jhren saw it too and that was the source of his sadness.

'Is this about your father?' the boy asked suddenly.

'What?'

Jhren lifted an arm, swung it at Murta. 'This . . . whatever this is. Whatever you're doing here.'

It was the last question Kyndra expected. 'Why would you say that?' she asked, perplexed. 'I never knew my father.'

'Which is why you're here,' Jhren finished. 'You're of age now. Why wouldn't you want to know what became of him?'

Kyndra shook her head, feeling like the whole conversation was happening to someone else. 'I don't care what became of him,' she snapped. 'Jarand's my father now. And I don't have time to talk, Jhren. I need to go.'

Jhren's eyes narrowed. 'Why? What have you done?'

'It's too long a story. When does this ship leave?'

'You're not getting on this ship.'

Kyndra took a step forward. 'It's up to the captain,' she said, raising her bag of money. 'And I doubt he would turn down business.'

'I said *no*.' Jhren seized her arm. She flinched in his grip, remembering their quarrel on the stairs. Jhren was breathing heavily. The boyish ugliness in his face didn't suit him and Kyndra had never seen it there before.

'Why?' she asked, shooting another anxious glance over her shoulder. 'I want to come home. Isn't that what you want too?'

Jhren gazed at her. There was something else now, something in his look besides bitterness. 'No,' he said slowly, letting go of her. 'That's not what I want.' He paused. 'It's not what Colta wants.'

Kyndra felt that familiar stab of betrayal. 'How do you know what she wants?'

'Because we're to be married. When I return.'

The world slowed, so that Jhren's words hung against a still backdrop. 'What?' Kyndra said.

'You heard me.'

The present returned, so swiftly, so vividly that Kyndra's head spun. She put a hand on the dock's railing. 'It hasn't even been two months,' she heard herself say.

'You don't know what it was like for Colta, losing her Inheritance. It meant everything to her. For a while I was scared she would go off alone and I would never see her again.' Jhren looked once more to the east, as if his eyes could penetrate the leagues that separated him from the Valleys. 'I couldn't let that happen.'

'So she . . . so she said yes?'

Jhren returned his gaze to Kyndra's face and nodded.

Kyndra felt cold. It wasn't the rising wind that chilled her, though it blew straight through her ragged clothes. She realized now that a part of her had always believed she might marry Jhren one day. She remembered him that afternoon on the stairs, offering her a future. She had shaken him off, furious that he saw her as helpless. But what if she hadn't? What if she'd let him speak? Would he perhaps have ended the conversation on one knee – and what if she'd said yes?

Kyndra covered her face with her hands and squeezed her eyes shut. All these years and she hadn't seen it. *I don't care about Colta*, he'd said before she ran from him. Jhren had loved her, she had rejected him and Colta – consumed, perhaps, with jealousy – had denounced her to the town.

But Colta need not be jealous any more. Jhren was hers. *This* was the real reason he wanted to stop Kyndra going home.

'Jhren,' she said, dropping her hands. 'Please let me come back with you. You can marry Colta. I won't interfere.'

Jhren's cheeks flushed. *'I can marry Colta?'* There were tears in his voice. 'How can you say that to me? I don't need your *permission*. I don't need you to tell me—'

'I'm sorry, Jhren,' Kyndra interrupted. 'Please. I don't have much time. They're coming for me.'

Jhren opened his mouth to retort, but the words never arrived. Instead his gaze shifted to stare at something beyond her.

Kyndra spun around. A dark figure, cloaked and hooded, strode across the dock, scattering Murtans like a game of pins. The cloak billowed out in the wind, revealing familiar golden robes beneath. Women gasped and yanked children away by their collars. Grown men stumbled back, arms raised as if to ward off a demon.

Panic took Kyndra. She wouldn't go back there, not now, not when escape was so close. She could still get away before the Wielder saw her. She could hide aboard the ship. She launched herself at the rail, hooked one leg over it and swung the other off the dock. It was at this point – frightened, desperate and only precariously balanced – that Jhren pushed her.

She could see black rock. Black rock, a cloak's hem and boot heels moving steadily back and forth. She was being carried, slung over someone's shoulder like a sack of grain. One of her wrists hurt, but the pain in the back of her head was worse. She reached up and gingerly touched the spot. Already an alarmingly large lump swelled beneath her hair.

'As long as you're awake,' said a voice tersely, 'you can walk.'

Kyndra's feet met solid ground and her head gave an angry throb. Memories were returning, but not fast enough. It took her several long, befuddled moments to realize that she was standing on the bridge that spanned the chasm to Naris and looking at Nediah. And several more to realize exactly what that meant.

'No,' Kyndra gasped, once again in the cold shadow of the mountain. She made to turn back, but Nediah caught her.

'Don't make me use it,' the Wielder growled. 'I don't want to restrain you, but if you try to run off, I will.'

'Why, Nediah?' Kyndra asked roughly. 'Why can't you let me go?'

'You're a fool,' the Wielder said through clenched teeth. 'I made your mother a promise to keep you safe and you almost saw that promise broken.' He seized her arm, pulling her on across the bridge.

Kyndra struggled. 'Then why are you taking me back to die?' she cried.

Nediah turned to look at her. Clouds had blown up from the south and rain slid down the Wielder's bare, fierce face. 'I'm taking you back before the Council discovers you're missing,' he hissed. 'At least, this way, there's a chance you might survive. Why give them a legitimate reason to hunt you down?'

Kyndra looked at distant Murta, veiled behind a drizzling sheet. Rain slicked the near lip of the chasm and streams trickled through little gullies in the rock to fall spinning out of sight. The weeping sky washed her clean of hope. 'What happened to my head?' she asked bleakly.

'When that boy pushed you, you lost your balance. You fell and hit your head on the edge of some crates.' Nediah's grim expression flickered. 'I'm beginning to wonder why I waste time healing you.'

'Jhren,' Kyndra muttered under her breath.

'A friend of yours?'

'Not any more.' Kyndra dropped her eyes, watching the bottomless chasm pass to either side, as Nediah dragged her on across the bridge. A scant hour ago, she'd been full of joy at her escape. She'd put the mountain at her back and consigned Naris to her past forever. But then, inexplicably, Jhren had come and told her she could never go home.

'Wait.' Nediah stopped walking and held up a hand. 'Did you hear that?'

The sound came again and this time Kyndra did hear it: a murmur of thunder. Apprehension seized her – she recognized that thunder. She'd heard it before on another night of rain in another place. The murmur grew to a continuous rumble. And now it wasn't just in the sky, but thrumming through the stone beneath them. Nediah frowned at the small pebbles skipping across the rock and took a few steps forward.

There was a mighty *crack* – and they were hurled from their feet. Kyndra rolled and found herself face to face with a sick, endless drop. She scrambled backwards, palms sweating. Part of the parapet had fallen away. 'What was—?' The rest of her sentence was lost in a series of sonorous booms immediately followed by a flash so bright that it blinded her. When she blinked her eyes open, spotted with after-images, she cried, 'Nediah!' and flung out her arm to their left. 'There!'

The circular chasm that made an island of Naris had ruptured. Before Kyndra's horrified gaze, the ground broke open and a tear zigzagged southwards. As the solid rock divided with an awful groan, Nediah pulled her up. 'Go in front,' he yelled. 'Make for the citadel.'

'This side's closer!' Kyndra screamed over the tumult. 'We'll never get across in time.' She tried to turn around, but Nediah tightened his grip and forced her into a run, his face set.

Another tremor nearly tumbled them again. The sky lit up and this time Kyndra saw the fork of lightning as it hit. It was a jagged bar of fire, impossibly thick, and, where it struck, an identical fissure opened to the north of the fortress, so that Naris seemed like the pupil of a terrible, widening eye. They'd never make it. The stone bridge was heaving and bucking as if the lightning had given it life, and blind terror pumped through her veins. She was going to die here, falling endlessly into the dark.

Desperately, Kyndra fixed her gaze on the far side of the trembling bridge, but couldn't help noticing the cracks that spider-webbed through the stone beneath her. Every footfall seemed like it would be her last – the next could send her screaming into the abyss.

There was an ominous creak and Kyndra glanced over her shoulder. The buttresses that connected the bridge to the Murtan side of the chasm wall had dropped away, leaving behind a bare whisker of stone. It crumbled in a rapid crescendo and chunks of the bridge collapsed. Wracking growls preceded their fall, as if from a giant's throat.

They had almost reached Naris when the supports on the near side failed too. The bridge dropped a few inches and panic flooded through Kyndra. The cracks beneath her feet were no longer spider-thin and she could see the chasm's gaping mouth beneath her, feel its cold breath. She leapt as the buttress gave way, landing on solid ground and rolling to a stop. Then, grazed, her breath coming in shuddering gasps, she scrambled up and looked for Nediah.

The gap was now too wide to jump. Kyndra's heart clenched. Little flashes of gold erupted from the Wielder's hands, but it was evening now and his power was fading. In an agony of slowness, Nediah began to fall. Kyndra saw the rock slide out from beneath his feet, the fat raindrops tumbling a curtain between them. 'No!' she screamed, throwing out a useless hand. Nediah's eyes were wide, disbelieving. Then his face firmed.

The Wielder leapt into space and Kyndra yelled his name. Nediah slammed into the mountainside below her, his hands and feet scrabbling ineffectually for purchase on the wet stone. Not pausing to think, Kyndra wrapped one arm around the ornamental pillar beside her and launched her body towards Nediah. 'Take my hand!' she screamed. The Wielder made one wild swing and Kyndra caught his grasping fingers.

She wasn't prepared for the lurch of pain as she took Nediah's weight. Her shoulder wrenched and it felt as if her arm would be pulled from its socket. Nediah's hand was slippery with blood and rain and Kyndra could feel her grip loosening, as she pulled upwards. The effort tore a scream from her lips. Nediah tried to get his feet under him, but the rock face was too smooth.

Then light flared like a miner's torch striking a vein of silver and Kyndra heard the same night song that had hypnotized her in Brenwym. This time it sounded like owl wings or a breeze through dark grass. It conjured images of gleaming, tilted eyes and of trees rendered in black and silver. Nediah's weight lessened – there was a filmy coalescence beneath his feet, moonlight made solid. Kyndra immediately pulled the Wielder up over the lip of rock and Nediah collapsed beside her, whey-faced and trembling.

A gasp sounded behind them. Wearily, Kyndra looked around. Brégenne stood there, the Lunar light fading from her skin. Wind had pulled her hair loose and rain dripped from its long, pale ends. Her robes clung to her and she was shaking almost as much as Nediah, who had raised himself onto hands and knees. His hair hung over his face as he took deep, steadying breaths. Brégenne hurried over and, ignoring the dirt that smeared her silver robe, dropped down beside him. Nediah knelt back and she put her arms around him, wet hair against his cheek. 'I thought,' Kyndra heard her whisper, 'oh, I thought . . .'

There were other witnesses to the scene. A crowd had come out to stare at the empty space where the bridge had been. Alandred was one of them, but he was not looking at the chasm. His hot eyes lingered on Brégenne and Nediah still kneeling on the rock.

Kyndra watched the shock ripple back towards the gates of Naris. The thunder boomed and the lightning came again, directly overhead this time. The rain beat down on Naris, as furiously as it had upon Brenwym, and though there were no houses here to topple and nothing to burn but bare rock, the Breaking did not abate. It had come without warning, as abruptly as a spring squall. Murmuring swept through the Wielders and Kyndra heard her own thoughts echoed back to her.

As if awakening from a trance, Brégenne let go of Nediah. Their gazes locked for a few seconds then Brégenne dropped her eyes. 'Your hands,' she said, examining the torn flesh, 'they're hurt.'

'It doesn't matter,' Nediah replied. He did not take his gaze from her face. 'I'll see to them in the morning.'

Brégenne shook her head, picked up both his hands in hers and frowned at them. Lunar light climbed out of her skin once more. As Kyndra watched, chips of stone began to wriggle free from Nediah's flesh and he winced. Slowly, the wounds knitted and closed.

Nediah looked over his hands critically. 'A fair job,' he said, his smile teasing, but Kyndra noted his bloodless cheeks and ragged eyes. Perhaps Brégenne noticed them too, for she dropped his hands and rose swiftly to her feet.

'What were you doing out here?' she demanded.

Instead of answering, Nediah looked at Kyndra. 'You saved my life,' he said quietly, wonderingly, as if he couldn't quite believe it had ever been in danger.

Kyndra shook her head, thinking that she'd spoken the same words to Nediah only a week or so before. 'If it wasn't for Brégenne—'

'No,' Brégenne said. 'You bought me time. If you hadn't caught him . . .' She trailed off, obviously unwilling to voice the alternative.

More Wielders came out to swell the crowd. Now cries of dismay rang under the stormy sky and, for the first time, Kyndra fully appreciated the situation. She was trapped. They were all trapped. 'Isn't there another way across?' she asked, aware that Irilin had already told her there wasn't.

Nediah shook his head. His green eyes darkened as they looked back over the impassable chasm. Kyndra turned her gaze towards distant Murta and, unbidden, an image came to her of Solinaris under siege, ringed not by an abyss, but by an army clad in blood. An eerie feeling of history repeating itself seeped through her and she tried to throw it off. There was no war now, no hungry empire branding the world with its fire. But, Kyndra thought with a shudder, the citadel was faced with a different kind of fire – a threat that attacked the Wielders in their very home. Where had the Madness come from and why? Staring into the endless dark of the chasm, a terrible suspicion began to close around her heart. She thought about Mardon and Rush and the Wielders who'd died during the test. Kyndra could see only one thing that linked them together – herself. And it wouldn't be long until someone else came to the same conclusion.

Rubble now fringed the ground around the mountain, shaken loose from the heights. Another crack of lightning sent a flurry of small rocks down into the gathered Wielders. There were cries of pain and Lunar shields bloomed in the dusk. Then a boulder the size of a cider cask hit the edge of one too hastily erected and it broke in a shatter of sparks. The rock struck the Wielder beneath a glancing blow on the shoulder, hard enough to knock him back and he shrieked in pain as he fell amongst his fellows.

There was almost pandemonium – almost. But then Kyndra heard a crisp voice start to issue orders. 'Solars, you're of no use here. Get the novices inside and anyone else who's been injured. Lunars, cover them.'

The Council had arrived. Lords Loricus and Gend stood behind Lady Helira, who watched with chilly blue eyes as her orders were carried out. An impressively large silver shield with curving sides hovered over her head. One of her fists glowed, feeding it a constant stream of energy.

Nediah rose to stand beside Brégenne and Helira eyed his blood-stained hands. 'All three of you will come with us,' she said, and without waiting for a response, she turned on her heel. Loricus and Gend fell silently into position around the three of them and Kyndra keenly felt the danger of their proximity. Taking a deep breath, trusting to Brégenne and Nediah, she let herself be herded back up the slope and under the great lintel of Naris.

24

A peculiar sense came over Kyndra when she entered the citadel for the second time. At first she couldn't tell whether it came from within or without. Perhaps something in Naris responded to something in her that hadn't been there earlier in the day. What had changed? Kyndra wondered, searching herself, but all she could think of was Jhren and his chill, hopeless words.

Brenwym would never take her back. Even her friends had turned against her, turned to *each other* in an attempt to forget she was ever one of them. Kyndra clenched her fists. This was the Relic's fault. It had been nothing but a stupid old bowl that – as Brégenne had said so rightly – stripped people of choice. Surely all she had done was end centuries of enslavement.

Surely all he had done was to end the war.

Kyndra's thoughts stopped cold. Her feet kept moving and she let them, mentally searching for the presence that again had so suddenly usurped her. It was the first time she had done so, she realized. Before, she had shrunk from it, terrified of the stranger whose eyes allowed her access to the past. Now she wanted to know – she *had* to know. Who was he, and what part had he and the Yadin, Anohin, played in ending the war?

The Wielder Realdon Shune had asked the same, silent question all those years ago: *What can one man do to stop a power that even Solinaris might not withstand?*

'I can do more than you can dream,' Kyndra breathed, remembering the stranger's answer.

'Sorry?' asked Nediah who walked beside her.

'Nothing.'

Kyndra seemed to recall a passage on Yadin in *Acre: Tales of the Lost World*. The book claimed that they were a race of people created to be the Wielders' servants in Solinaris. They looked human – they could bleed and die like humans – but they didn't age and the power they were granted was finite. And they served their masters with a love and loyalty that went beyond simple duty. Or had that information come with the visions? Kyndra wasn't at all certain.

They reached a corridor noticeably grander than the others she had seen within Naris, its floor overlaid with polished marble. Helira made to stop, but Loricus gestured her on. 'Please feel free to use my quarters,' he said. Helira glanced at him and nodded curtly. Brégenne and Nediah, Kyndra saw, gazed at their surroundings in surprise.

'You are wondering why I chose to bring you here,' Helira said, guessing their thoughts. 'Simply, we must hold a meeting after we deal with the girl, a practice usually undertaken in the privacy of our quarters.'

Kyndra did not miss the worried face Brégenne turned her way. Quite obviously, the Wielder had little to no idea what to expect. *That makes two of us*, she thought.

Loricus placed one hand against a tall set of doors and they swung inward. With Brégenne and Nediah beside her, Kyndra stepped through and gaped at the room beyond.

Glazed Talarun tiles made a mosaic of the floor, which was spread with an unnecessary number of fine rugs. Silken drapes screened murals. Piles of fresh fruit – too much for one person – languished on elegant tables. The room reminded Kyndra of the vain and wasteful monarchs who always seemed to be the enemies in children's tales.

Coolly solicitous, the councilman pulled out a chair for Brégenne. She looked at it for a moment and then sat down. Helira sat too, as did Loricus and Gend, but both Kyndra and Nediah remained standing. Kyndra cast a surreptitious glance at the Wielder beside her. She had the impression that this was Nediah's way of showing some sort of solidarity.

'Master Nediah,' Helira said then. 'You placed yourself in harm's way this evening whilst in our service. You will be suitably rewarded.'

Nediah's mouth twitched, as if he found the idea of being rewarded distasteful. He bowed silently and when he raised his head, his face was again unreadable.

'How did you leave the citadel, girl?'

Kyndra didn't answer. The old woman's dogged use of the word *girl* set her teeth on edge. Brégenne turned sharply and fixed glowing eyes upon her.

'I urge you to cooperate,' Helira said coldly, as if she didn't care whether Kyndra did so or not. 'You will find the alternative less pleasant.'

Minutely, Brégenne lowered her chin and Kyndra remembered the words she had spoken on board Argat's airship. *We have ways to examine a person's mind by means unavailable to others.* 'I hid in a miner's cart,' she said shortly.

'How did you know about the miners' gate?' Helira pressed. 'Not only are those levels off limits to most, they are also extensive. Someone must have helped you.'

They'll punish us both if we're caught. Kyndra steeled herself. If there was to be punishment, she would take it alone. Escaping had been her idea.

'Very well.' Lunar light coalesced on Helira's skin. She raised a hand and the next moment, Kyndra found herself floating in a sea of silver. *Lie back,* a voice seemed to be saying, *lie back and let me in.* The gentle waves buoyed her limbs and lapped over her skin in a calm luminescence. *Sink beneath me, lie back in me.* All she had to do was relax and submerge her body completely. If she put her head beneath the waves, everything would be all right.

Mentally, she sighed and let go.

The waves closed over her face and there was darkness, terrible, wailing darkness. And there were hands, dozens of aged claws that grasped her and pierced her skin as she struggled helplessly. An image of Irilin's face rose out of the black depths and she tried to push it down, to hide it in the crushing water, but the hands snatched and triumphantly pulled it into the light.

'No!' The voice was hers. She was standing once again in Loricus' quarters, hands riveted to her head. Helira was no longer glowing. Instead she stared irritably at Brégenne, who had risen to stand close beside Kyndra, touching her shoulder. Brégenne's face was hard and sheathed in Lunar energy. In her heavy robes she looked like a gleaming, quicksilver statue, implacable as death.

'Sit down, Brégenne,' the usually silent Gend commanded. 'Do not interfere.'

Helira waved a hand. 'No matter. I have what I sought.' She turned her pale blue eyes on Kyndra and smiled unpleasantly.

'I think twenty strokes are requisite for such a serious breach in discipline. Make a note of the novice's name – Irilin Straa.'

Kyndra wanted to lash out, to tear the sagging, careless smile from Helira's mouth. She swallowed her rage with difficulty, thinking of Irilin. She *wouldn't* let them hurt her.

'The situation is grave,' Helira said, addressing them all now. 'Between the Breaking and the Madness, we are besieged. A cause *must* be found, or better – a cure. I expect you to make it your top priority, Master Nediah. Moreover, with the bridge gone, we have no means of monitoring the Breaking or discovering the reason for its intensification. We have people outside the citadel who will be unable to return.' Her voice turned flat. 'Brégenne, I saw what you did to save Master Nediah. Few have your command of *substantiation*. You took the weight of a man. Do you think you could take heavier?'

The hostility Brégenne had worn like a second skin when Helira invaded Kyndra's mind had gone. Now she regarded the councilwoman impassively. 'I expect so.'

Helira did not seem pleased by Brégenne's casual response and Kyndra had a sudden suspicion that the old woman wasn't able to emulate whatever it was that Brégenne had done. The thought brought her a fierce satisfaction.

'Plans will be made to reconstruct the bridge as a matter of urgency and we may require your help.'

'As the Council commands,' Brégenne said, still in the voice that gave nothing away.

Helira nodded. 'Now I ask both of you to leave us. We wish to question the girl over the events of last night.'

'Is our absence strictly necessary?' Nediah asked and although Kyndra was dreading the return of the irresistible silver sea, she was relieved to hear the alarm in Nediah's voice.

Perhaps the Wielder believed her warning about the Council after all.

'It is,' Gend declared huskily. 'The matter is sensitive.'

'If I may,' Loricus said. He spread conciliatory hands and rose to his feet. 'I see no reason to intimidate Kyndra. I will take this matter upon myself.' He looked pointedly at Helira. 'I would prefer to work without the use of force.'

Nediah, Kyndra noticed, appeared to share her own uncertainty at this unexpected development. The Wielder regarded the councilman with stiff, suspicious eyes. Helira and Gend stared at Loricus too and Kyndra imagined some silent exchange passing between the three of them. Then Gend rose to his feet. 'Let him handle it, then,' he said in his deep voice. 'We reconvene in an hour.' He strode to the door.

Helira gave Loricus a piercing, speculative glance before she, too, swept from the room. 'I will not keep her long,' Loricus told Brégenne and Nediah. 'You may even wait outside if you wish.'

With a weight in her stomach like a sack of stones, Kyndra watched the two Wielders leave. Nediah turned as he shut the door and his look said quite plainly that he wouldn't be far away.

When they were alone in the opulent room, Loricus gestured her to a seat. Despite knowing that the councilman's power was currently bound, Kyndra sat warily. Medavle's revelation of the white *akan*'s true nature had taught her not to take anything or anyone at face value again.

'Now that they are gone, we may speak openly.' The councilman seated himself on a slim divan opposite Kyndra. There was a decanter of red wine at his elbow, but he made no move to touch it. His eyes did not leave her face. 'Why were you out-side the citadel today?' he asked.

The question was not the one Kyndra expected. 'I planned to go home,' she said, seeing no reason to lie. 'You've kept me here against my will. I've already told you I don't want to be, and can't be, a Wielder.'

Scepticism twisted Loricus' mouth. 'You were running away?'

Despite herself, Kyndra winced. It hadn't felt like that at the time. 'Yes,' she said a touch defiantly, as much to herself as to the councilman. *But where to?* a voice chided her. *You haven't got a home any more.*

'You didn't strike me as the type.' Loricus shrugged. 'Per-haps I was wrong.'

Kyndra said nothing.

The councilman rose to his feet and began to pace the room. Kyndra's eyes moved beyond him to a large and beautiful map that seemed to be part of the wall. It was a mosaic, she realized, squinting at the tiny blue tiles that formed the sea. The whole continent was there, picked out by the delicate plac-ing of the stones. The light from the room's candelabra fell across it and set the colours sparkling. In the top left-hand corner, onyx letters spelled out 'MARIAR'.

'I understand you may find this hard to believe.' Loricus stopped and looked at her, his gaze unwavering. 'But I want us to be friends.'

She was instantly suspicious. 'Why?'

'Naris faces a difficult time, the most difficult, certainly, since that event men call the Deliverance. The Breaking is increasing in power and frequency. Wielders are losing their minds to some nameless malady. And then there's you – the first person ever to fail the test and live. Your coming is not the work of chance.' Loricus took a few steps closer, light catching in the folds of his golden robe. 'There are those who stand to profit from such a situation, Kyndra, those who seek to impose chaos, to glorify insanity. What do you know of the Nerian?'

So this is where he's heading, Kyndra thought. She had expected an interrogation about the test. 'Not much,' she answered carefully. 'Just that they're a group of people living below Naris.'

Loricus' eyes narrowed. 'And what of Kierik?'

She felt the name like a lash across the back of her mind, sharp with memory and pain. She shook her head, breathless, hoping that nothing showed on her face.

The councilman studied her, his own face a practised blank. 'But the Nerian are watching out for you, no? One of them helped you after the second test and they overpowered two of my Wielders to do it.'

So he didn't know it was Medavle who'd rescued her. *But he obviously thinks I'm friends with the Nerian.* Kyndra's bruised mind raced – she would have to tread cautiously. One wrong word and Loricus would have a better, more legitimate reason to kill her.

'If they *are* watching out for me,' Kyndra said, knowing that a simple denial would not suffice, 'I didn't ask them to.'

The councilman seemed to turn over her words, searching for something buried therein. Then he sighed. 'Let me be blunt, Kyndra. Times, as I say, are difficult. But I am a man who finds advantage in such times and Helira and Gend may not be around for very much longer. Their ideas are staid, narrow-minded.' His hazel eyes glittered. 'They contrive to . . . eradicate rather than elucidate. Are you with me?'

Kyndra nodded faintly, wondering whether Loricus meant that Helira and Gend were the ones behind the *akan*.

'You must choose your allies now, Kyndra Vale,' Loricus continued. 'And choose them carefully. When this storm blows over, you don't want to find yourself stranded out at sea. The Nerian are not only dangerous, but unpredictable. With one hand, they would offer you friendship, and with the other, they would seek out means to destroy you.'

This didn't feel right. There was something Loricus knew, some vital piece of information that lay behind all this manoeuvring. Stirred finally to anger, Kyndra said, 'And how are your hands any different?'

'My hands?' Loricus asked, smiling slightly. 'Mine seek power, as most do. I have worked long and hard in pursuit of it. You cannot know just how long.' His eyes strayed to the map, lingering on the topaz plains of Hrosst. His reverie lasted only a moment before he looked back at her. 'These hands —' he clenched them — 'do not wish to share the rewards of that journey with Helira and Gend.' His lip curled briefly, revealing a glimpse of teeth. 'And the Naris they will rule will be mercifully simpler. A Council of one, a compulsory programme of study for all novices and a Deep swept clean of the rebellious mouthings of the Nerian.' He held up a finger. 'And a world that knows us, that respects our power. We have lived in the shadow of the past for too long.'

Kyndra sat immobile, shocked by his open duplicity. Why was Loricus revealing his intentions and how could he ensure that Kyndra would keep them to herself? She watched the councilman's cold, zealous reflection in the mirror that hung opposite the great map. His robed figure hid almost all of it save for the top two corners. She was about to look away when something caught her eye. In the mirror, as on the wall, were the black stones that spelled out the name of the world. But that name was not Mariar. As in the nature of mirrors, the word was reversed. 'MARIAR,' she read on the wall. And then, in the mirror, 'ЯAIЯAM'.

Rairam.

That time in the corridor, she'd asked Nediah what Rush had been writing in his madness. *Just nonsense*, Nediah had replied. *The same word over and over again. Rairam.*

Kyndra sat stock still, remembering. *I do not want to see Rairam – the last free land – in the empire's grip.* His voice echoed in her head – the man who had witnessed the last days of Solinaris. Five hundred years stood between the day those words were spoken and Rush's mindless scrawling. But the scrawl was not mindless. It was excruciatingly simple. Kyndra felt as if she was teetering on the edge of a vast truth, a truth that reached back to the time of the war, something to explain exactly what had happened to the lost world – to Acre and the empire.

The councilman was watching her, waiting, perhaps, for her reaction to the traitorous plans discussed so openly in this room. Despite his show of friendship, Kyndra did not trust him. Of all people, why had Loricus chosen *her* to be the bearer of his secrets? What place did Kyndra have in his vision of a new Naris? She looked into the councilman's narrowed eyes and was suddenly afraid of the answer.

Hammering on the door made her jump. Even Loricus started, so great had the tension in the room become. Without waiting for an invitation, the double doors opened, revealing Helira, Nediah and a Wielder Kyndra didn't know. Kyndra thought she glimpsed the silver-clad forms of Brégenne and Gend hurrying away down the corridor.

'Loricus,' Helira barked, 'the meeting will have to wait. Soryn says that the Breaking is growing worse. If those lightning strikes bring down the ledge over the main gates, we'll be buried alive. Gend and I will go up there ourselves. Send every Lunar in the citadel to join us.' She paused. 'Superiate novices too. We'll weave a *khetah* and hold it in shifts until the Breaking abates.' Turning to go, she shot Kyndra an inimical look, which Kyndra interpreted as a promise of unpleasant things to come. Then she and the Wielder called Soryn disappeared down the same corridor that Brégenne and Gend had taken.

'Events are moving faster than anticipated,' Loricus said to Kyndra. 'I hope you'll give my words careful consideration. And remember what I said about the Nerian.'

Nediah still stood in the doorway, his eyes on the councilman. When Loricus made a dismissive gesture, Nediah took it as an opportunity to seize Kyndra's elbow and steer her out of the door and down the passage. When they'd put some distance behind them, he asked, 'What did he want?'

'I don't know,' Kyndra answered slowly, still trying to understand exactly what Loricus intended, both for her and for the citadel. 'I'll tell you about it when we're alone.'

In point of fact, they were alone. The black, curving corridors were empty of people, despite the early evening hour. The Breaking had called all the Lunar Wielders away. *This is the second time*, Kyndra thought, and had to crush the unwelcome suspicion that the Breaking was following her. She listened to the isolated thud of their footsteps. 'There must be a way to stop the Madness,' she muttered.

'In order to find the cure, you have to understand the disease,' Nediah said. 'And that's the problem. I don't understand it.' He shivered visibly. 'I'm beginning to think it can't be cured. The damage could be compared to a powerful impact, but mental rather than physical.'

Kyndra kept her eyes ahead, unwilling to voice her certainty that the Madness was somehow linked to her visions. *It can't be cured.* But the visions could strike at any moment. If one came now, she could kill Nediah just like she had the Wielders during the test. And what about Brégenne and the novices? It could only be a matter of time before she hurt one of them.

When the door of her cell-like room stood closed between them and the corridor, Kyndra turned to Nediah. 'Loricus plans to kill the other councilmembers and make himself sole ruler of Naris.'

Nediah's reaction was exactly as she expected: shock followed swiftly by disbelief. 'Why would I lie to you?' Kyndra asked him soberly. 'It sounds as if Loricus has been planning this for years.'

'Then why tell you about it?' Nediah asked in consternation.

'Perhaps because he doesn't intend to keep it a secret for very much longer.'

'But why *you*?'

'I don't know,' Kyndra said honestly, shaking her head. 'He kept saying I ought to choose my friends carefully – if I didn't want to find myself on the wrong side.'

'Side?' Nediah asked, frowning. 'What other side did he mean?'

'The Nerian. He seems to think they're friends of mine.'

Nediah gave her a narrow look. 'Are they?'

'Maybe,' Kyndra answered. 'Kait came to see me again. She

was the one who helped me get out of the archives after I took the *akan*.'

Nediah made a few spluttering sounds. 'Why didn't you tell me about this before?'

'I've seen the effect she has on you,' Kyndra said bluntly. 'I didn't want to mention it.'

Nediah looked away and his face bore a kind of bitter chiding that Kyndra didn't think was aimed at her. 'Kait said that the Nerian could help me,' she added quietly, remembering the woman's evasive words. *Nediah won't be able to protect you from the Council. And when you're ready to accept the truth, he won't have the answers you'll seek. But the Nerian will. And we'll give them to you.*

Nediah's face was dark. 'Don't trust her, Kyndra.'

The anger Kyndra had felt earlier in the councilman's quarters rumbled to the surface and she didn't try to hold it back. 'Whom should I trust, then? Loricus?'

'Until we have the situation under control, the question is irrelevant.'

'No one can control the Breaking. And you said yourself that you didn't understand the Madness and that there might not be a cure.' She paused, but Nediah said nothing. 'The only place left to search for answers,' Kyndra finished, voicing her decision aloud, 'is with the Nerian.'

'No,' the Wielder said. 'It's what Loricus wants.'

Kyndra shook her head. 'He warned me away from them. He wants me on his side.'

'You can't,' Nediah said painfully. 'The Nerian are . . . You don't understand.'

'Maybe not,' she conceded, 'but aside from you and Brégenne, Kait is the only person who seems to care whether I live or die.' *And Medavle*, she added silently. He was another piece to add to this vast puzzle.

While Nediah looked at her helplessly, Kyndra steeled herself. 'Do you know how to contact them?' she asked.

The tall Wielder turned his back. 'I can't believe you're even considering this.'

'Something much bigger is happening, Nediah. Bigger than the Nerian, bigger than Naris.' Kyndra took a deep breath. 'What if my visions, the Madness and the Breaking are linked together? Remember what Argat said about the Breaking being in two places at once? It's only ever struck in one place at a time, from what I've heard. And it could be responsible for that mountain range collapsing – you saw how it destroyed the bridge today. It's getting worse and it's happening all over the world. Jhren said that Market Primus is full of people whose homes have been destroyed.' She paused and then said more bravely than she felt, 'I thought I didn't run away from things, but since I left Brenwym, I haven't stopped running. If I'm right and all of this is linked together, then surely we have a duty to try and stop it. Isn't that what Wielders are supposed to do?'

'Anything,' Nediah said to the wall. There was a stillness about him that spoke of an animal backed, despite all its efforts, into a corner. 'I will do anything else you ask. You know that. But not this.'

And then Kyndra did something she had never done before. She moved to stand in front of Nediah and took his hands in both of hers. 'I'm sorry, Nediah,' she whispered. 'I think I know what I'm asking you. But I wouldn't ask unless I believed there was no other way forward.'

Nediah closed his eyes. Moments passed. When at last he

opened them and pulled back his hands, there was a shaky kind of resolution in his face. 'I was there when Kait spoke the rite that new converts have to recite,' he said bleakly. 'Some members of the Nerian came and when they left, they took her away with them.'

Kyndra said nothing.

'I don't think I could forget those words even if I tried.'

'And the Nerian will come?'

'Yes.'

'I've wasted enough time,' Kyndra said. 'When I asked Irilin to show me a way out, I was thinking only of myself. If Kait's right and the Nerian know something that can help me make sense of all of this, then I have to find out what.'

Nediah took a few deep breaths and then he knelt, closing his eyes. 'Show me the way,' he whispered and stopped. His face contorted as if somewhere in his body, a knife twisted and a wound, which had half healed, reopened. 'I am a seeker of truth . . . I am a servant of light willing to share the darkness to which our saviour is condemned. Thus will I lessen it.' Nediah paused again, eyes still screwed shut. 'I renounce position and place to take up the banner. Until death will I hold it, or the day comes when the people no longer have need of it. Show me the way.'

Nediah's voice dwindled to a whisper. He opened his eyes and the tears that stood in them fell to stain his cheeks. There were no more. Kyndra looked away.

Minutes passed as minutes do, marching to their hourly purpose. Both of them sat in silence, knowing that nothing could be said to lighten the wait. At last, Nediah stirred. 'Perhaps I said it wrong,' he suggested flatly. 'Perhaps you have to mean it.'

'In that case, we're going to have to find another way.'

'Short of walking blindly into the Deep, there isn't—' Nediah broke off. He held up a hand, motioned Kyndra to keep quiet. There was a pair of voices beyond the door, coming closer.

'The order came from Lady Helira.'

'Yes, but surely the girl isn't more important than the Breaking. Why aren't you up there helping?'

'I was, but Lady Helira ordered the girl brought to her directly and discreetly. She's taking a break to question her. I suppose she has her reasons.'

'Pressing reasons to warrant putting the girl to the question tonight? Why can't it wait till morning?'

'Rhekka, Simmon and now Josef are dead, Gerrick. And Magat —'

There was a pause. Then, 'I'm sorry,' said the second voice. 'Wasn't she . . . I'm sorry.' Another pause. 'So you think Lady Helira suspects the girl might somehow be involved?'

'Yes.'

'She certainly survived again where everyone believed she couldn't.'

'But did she do it alone? The Council still haven't discovered who brought her down from the testing platform.' The voice lowered. 'Others say the Nerian are helping her.'

'Wait. Did you hear that?'

'What?'

'Stay here a second.'

One set of footsteps moved off down the corridor. A few moments passed while Kyndra and Nediah listened intently.

'Gerrick?' the other Wielder called. 'What's going on?'

There was a gasp, quickly stifled, and then silence. Nediah

shot Kyndra a look of alarm and pulled open the door. The Wielder lay on the floor outside, limp as an unmanned marionette. A lump had already begun to swell at his temple. A figure stood over him, swathed in black. Though the nose and mouth were covered, Kyndra recognized the almond eyes.

Kait bent to examine the man on the floor. She tapped his skull with the pommel of her dagger. 'Take his legs,' she commanded, hefting his shoulders. Nediah didn't move, so Kyndra grabbed the trailing legs and together she and Kait bundled the Wielder into the room.

There wasn't a lot of space, what with the man slumped against the wall. Kait shut the door and tugged down her black scarf. Her almond eyes found Nediah's face. 'You have no idea how much I longed to hear you speak those words,' she said.

Nediah flinched. Kait's voice was not soft with nostalgia. It was laced with regret that the years had soured. Kyndra heard bitterness, even resentment – and yet there was also a vicious kind of satisfaction in her smile.

'Is that why you came?' Nediah asked finally.

'That and other reasons. Anohin was worried I couldn't handle trouble.' Kait directed a scornful glance at the unconscious man. 'A Solar taking out a Lunar at night,' she declared, fingering her knife. 'Sometimes the old ways are best.'

Kyndra had started at the name. Now she stared at Kait and a tremor ran through her body. 'Anohin?' she whispered.

Kait's cheeks bore their usual high spots of colour and her eyes were fiery. She nodded.

'But that's impossible.'

'Anohin is one of the Yadin, Kyndra, and doesn't age. He founded the Nerian.'

'I know he's a Yadin,' Kyndra whispered, remembering how

she'd learned of Anohin from the last vision. 'But what—'

Kait jammed the knife in her belt. 'If you want answers, you will come with me.' She looked at Nediah. 'Isn't that why you called?'

'Who is Anohin, Kyndra?' he asked. 'How do you know this person?'

Kyndra began to describe her most recent vision, but Kait let out a growl. 'Not now. If these cretins don't return with Kyndra soon, they'll send someone to find out why. Let's go.'

Kyndra looked at her uneasily. If Anohin really was still alive, he'd know the truth of what had happened at the end of the war. He would also know the identity of the man whose memories she shared. At that thought, Kyndra felt an awful premonition – once she went with Kait, things would never be the same again.

She could still refuse. Kait wouldn't be able to force her. She could stay here and wait for Loricus to wrest power from Helira and Gend, or for the Breaking to destroy the citadel a second time – to say nothing of what it was doing to the rest of the world. She could wait until the Madness struck down her friends, or until Loricus reached the same conclusion as she – that Kyndra and her visions were causing the Madness and only her death would stop it.

Kyndra took a deep breath. 'I'm ready,' she told Kait. 'Take me to see the Nerian.'

25

Brégenne walked the passageways of Naris. It was three hours before midnight and the citadel gleamed starkly in her eyes. There were many shadows tonight – resting in corners and dropping upon her from vaulted ceilings. They suited her mood. The Breaking still raged above, but down here, muffled by the mountain's dark layers, all was still. She'd been holding the *khetah*, feeding the great shield with as much Lunar power as she could draw from the sky. Now it was her turn to rest, but instead she was combing the citadel with all the other available Wielders, searching for the missing potential.

What have you done, Kyndra? she asked silently, remembering the chagrin on Helira's face when Gerrick and Davion had been found unconscious near the girl's room. *Where are you?* And Kyndra wasn't the only one missing – Brégenne hadn't been able to find Nediah anywhere.

She briefly closed her eyes, but he was there in the darkness too with his wild, rain-streaked face and hands scraped raw from the mountain. Brégenne snapped her eyes open, chiding herself. Thinking of the bridge rallied the feelings she had tried unsuccessfully to rout. Her heart had almost stopped when she saw him leap into space. And when she had reached for the Lunar, she had never reached more desperately, or more fiercely. But Nediah was safe now. How was it, then, that her mind played out the episode again and again?

Consumed by her thoughts, Brégenne almost walked straight into the three people standing in her path. With a gasp, she pulled up short, staring at them.

'Brégenne?' Kyndra said, obviously startled.

She looked around. The corridor they stood in was empty, but it wouldn't be for long. Brégenne opened her mouth to warn the young woman – and then she saw who stood beside Kyndra.

'Hello, Brégenne,' Kait said pleasantly. A scarf covered most of her face, but no one else had those almond eyes. Brown hair pooled on her shoulders and fell straight beyond them halfway to her waist. Fifteen years had passed since she had last looked into that face. Nediah, she saw, stood on Kyndra's other side.

'Kait.' Brégenne heard the cold creeping into her voice of its own accord. She took a quick glance around, but they were alone. 'What are you doing here?'

'The answer's none of your business,' Kait said airily. 'You ought to forget you ever saw us.'

'Kyndra,' Brégenne appealed to the young woman. 'What is going on?'

Kait planted her hands on her hips and Brégenne noticed a dagger sheathed there. *Let her try*, she thought, flexing her fingers.

'I'm sorry, Brégenne,' Kyndra said and she looked away. 'I have to go to the Nerian.'

Brégenne stared at her, aghast. 'Kyndra, no,' she said, imploring the young woman to meet her gaze. 'The Nerian can't help you. How has she convinced you to trust her?'

'How?' Kait repeated angrily. 'By saving her life, Brégenne, when *your* Council tried to murder her, by offering her another way. That's more than you've done, with your rules and your unflinching obedience. Tell Kyndra why you're out in the corridors tonight, Brégenne.'

Brégenne felt herself pale. 'Kyndra, I wasn't—' she began, but Kait overrode her.

'You've been searching for the missing potential like a good girl – like one of the Council's faithful. And who knows, if you're the one who finds her, maybe there'll be a little something in it for you – a partner who isn't a novice, perhaps.'

'Enough.'

His voice was quiet, but it froze Kait's tirade. Nediah's gaze was steely. 'That was cruel,' he said softly. He didn't look at Brégenne. 'You were never a cruel person.'

They were of a height, Brégenne saw. Before she could smother it, a loathsome little voice hissed, *They are a good match.*

'Come to take her side?' Kait said. 'Go ahead, Nediah, but remember. Once the words are spoken, they cannot be taken back.'

Some of the steel left Nediah's eyes. 'What?'

Kait smiled triumphantly. 'You didn't know? Those words you so carelessly recited are infused with an oath of Anohin's making. Should you think to use your power against me or any of your new brethren, you will find it impossible.'

An abiding horror swarmed Brégenne. She stared at Nediah. 'You didn't,' she whispered.

Nediah's face flickered before he schooled it to stillness. 'I had to. For everyone's sake.'

'No,' Brégenne gasped. She raised a trembling finger and pointed it at Kait. 'Make him unsay it. Let him go.'

'I can't,' Kait said simply. 'It's as irreversible as time.'

A howl was building inside Brégenne. She tried to swallow it and choked. Not now, not after all these years. She had brought Nediah back from the brink . . . and Kait had returned to chase him over it.

'He won't be going alone.' Kyndra looked at her, and in her eyes, Brégenne saw a consuming kind of purpose. 'I asked him to do it, Brégenne.'

She clenched her fists. 'Why?' she almost sobbed. 'Neither of you can ever come back.'

'If I don't find some answers, there won't be anything to come back *to*.' The resolution in Kyndra's face burned stronger. 'Nediah understands.' She paused. 'You could come with us, Brégenne.'

Tears of anger pricked her eyes. She couldn't look at Kait, didn't want to see the pleased little smile she knew was there. Her heart thumped horribly in her chest and it was suddenly very hard to breathe. 'If you are set on this,' she heard herself say, 'then go. And hurry – the Wielders are searching for you.' She forced herself to look at Nediah. 'You've made your choice,' she whispered.

For a moment so brief that she thought she'd imagined it, Nediah's face changed and Brégenne recoiled from the turmoil she saw there. Then it was gone, stifled by the stubborn mask he wore to hide his feelings. *I taught him that*, she thought, trying to flee from a terrible wrenching inside her. *I didn't mean to, but I did*. It was that realization which finally let loose the tears she had dammed. She felt one roll shamefully down her cheek and turned her face away.

'We've wasted enough time here,' Kait said harshly.

381

A hand tentatively touched Brégenne's shoulder and she looked up into Kyndra's face. When had she gained that extra inch? The young woman regarded her with a steady gaze. 'I will look out for him,' she said so quietly that Brégenne knew she spoke for her alone. 'And everything will work out – I have to believe it will.'

The girl she had plucked from the murderous hands of her town was gone. Someone else stood in her place, someone Brégenne didn't know. And in the face of her anguish, it was a strange comfort.

She watched them take the path to the Deep. It was a path she had always abhorred, unable to understand the reasons that spurred others down it. Although she watched him until he was out of sight, Nediah did not look back.

Janus crouched, concealed in the deep shadows through which he had followed Brégenne. It was risky being so close to her, as she could easily sense him if she chose to. But Lord Loricus had given him orders to watch Kyndra closely, and now Janus understood why.

The Nerian. He ground his teeth. Bad enough that she hadn't used the *akan* after Loricus had gone to such trouble for her. She'd been lucky, Janus thought. If the Madness hadn't taken those Wielders during the test, she would surely be dead.

Lord Loricus must have suspected that Kyndra would turn to the Nerian. Why else would he ask Janus to keep such a close eye on her? The councilman had been short with him tonight – not only had they failed to help Kyndra, but now the Breaking was trying to bring down the mountain on their heads. And there was still no way to know when or if the Madness would strike again.

Perhaps Kyndra thought she could escape it. Perhaps that was why she wanted to go to the Nerian. Janus felt a stab of nerves in his belly. Or was it fear? He had grown up with tales of the sect and their heresy. He'd heard about their carnal rituals and their worship of a mad saviour. Besides voicing his disgust alongside the other novices, he hadn't spared much thought for the Nerian. Now he faced the dark journey into the Deep and realized with a lurch that he was frightened.

Janus steeled himself. He would do this for Loricus, he decided, remembering his own hot need when those hazel eyes had raked his body. *I must* do this.

Taking a deep breath, he left the shadows and scurried down the passage that Kyndra had taken. He reached a junction and looked around. In the distance to his right, just before the corridor turned a corner, he caught a flash of movement. With the bright thought of the councilman's gratitude as a shield against his fear, Janus swallowed his apprehension and broke into a stooping run.

Kyndra's certainty that she was doing the right thing grew with every step she took, as she followed Kait into the Deep, Nediah at her back. The current passage was now too narrow to walk abreast and its walls grew rougher – bulging and contorting, showing signs of the terrible pressure that had wrought them. Sweat streaked Kyndra's face, but she ignored it. The complaints of her recovering body seemed muted.

Once they'd left the upper citadel behind, she'd felt a tugging, as if something or someone were drawing her on. It was that same premonition – the one she'd sensed earlier in her room with Kait – but now its urgency was all-consuming. She had hardly spoken, leaving the others to their scant talk. For the most part, all three walked in silence, watching the path change beneath their feet.

Kait held a lamp and its fitful light threw their lurching shadows against the stone, now more yellow than black. Water dripped somewhere beyond the light's reach and a prickle of unease worked its way into the gap between Kyndra's shoulders. The mountain was a honeycomb. It was easy to imagine that it housed the tunnellings of an ancient wyrm.

There was a change in the air and she sensed rather than saw the ceiling fall away from them, following the bones of the mountain. Kait's flame danced in the sudden space, as they stepped out of the tunnel and onto the strangest floor Kyndra had ever seen. The rock beneath their feet was a solid sea, its swirling waters coiled around strings of what looked like fossilized ropes. Kyndra gazed at it in wonder. The flows were dark and bunched, but stretched away into the distance as if the rock had once been alive and moving.

The wall nearest to them was rounded, curving towards the cavern's ceiling, its façade uneven and yellowish. Kait held her lamp high and, as the light spread, Kyndra saw the shape of another wall far to her left. But facing them was a darkness found only in the deep places of the world. Rather than reflecting, it absorbed Kait's light, hinting at nothing but itself.

'This is a lava tube.' Kait's voice sounded flat. 'One of the largest. We measured it at twenty metres wide and a whole league long.'

'You measured it?' Kyndra asked, astounded.

'Of course,' the woman said casually. 'It lies on the doorstep of our home. And we have among our number some keenly interested in the earth's secrets. Since we must live among those secrets, it is better to know them than to fear them.'

Nediah stared at Kait, a peculiar look in his eyes. His complexion had paled with their descent into the ground and perspiration beaded his brow.

'You see, Nediah,' Kait said, noticing his look. 'Our Saviour is not our only concern. The Nerian have never stopped being Wielders, or faltered in pursuit of knowledge. True, our priorities differ from yours, but we have not forgotten who we are.'

She waited for Nediah's reply and sighed when it didn't come. 'We're near. Follow me.' Keeping the lamp high, Kait marched into the darkness.

A league . . . Kyndra marvelled at the distance and her imagined wyrm resized itself in her mind. This enclosed pathway must coil around and through the rock, joined by other smaller tubes like the one they'd just left. How many years had passed since fire had raged here, carving out the mountain's heart?

'You see those ledges?'

Kyndra looked to where Kait was pointing. The side of the tunnel had several step marks etched into it.

'They show the levels of the lava that once flowed here.'

Kyndra nodded and let her eyes drift back to the floor. She was mesmerized by its raised coils and turns, the earth's primordial shifting captured forever. Kait did not speak again and they walked in silence. Not one word had passed Nediah's lips in the last hour. His face was introspective and he didn't seem to see the fascinating rock sculptures they passed. Though Kait pointed out pillars, lava falls and roofs of lavacicles, Nediah's eyes ghosted over them without seeing. Kyndra stuck close behind Kait, thankful that she knew the way. As for herself, she'd long since lost track of their passage. Alone she could die here, wandering the dark caverns until her strength failed.

It was the chanting that finally broke Nediah's reverie. The tunnel they followed sloped down yet again and turned, bringing the low murmur closer. Kait increased her pace. 'They are ready,' she hissed.

'Ready for what?' Kyndra asked uneasily.

'For you.'

When it became clear that Kait would say no more, Kyndra concentrated on her feet. Jogging over the uneven coils of rock was somewhat hazardous. She felt the ends of Kait's long hair brush her face, as the woman sped in front of her. The chanting grew louder and there was a light flickering in the distance. The tugging inside Kyndra increased; it seemed strong enough to work her legs, to drive her on until she met whatever awaited her here in the Deep.

The chanting had an unnerving effect upon Kait. She was moving so fast now that Kyndra was sure she would trip, but her booted feet were as nimble as a goat's. She had begun to chant under her breath too. Unable to match her agility, Kyndra and Nediah fell back. There was light all around them now. Torches burned in brackets, some of natural, yellow flame and others eerily silver. The voices intoned louder and Kyndra felt as if she were about to intrude on some primitive ceremony. She shared a glance with Nediah. The Lunar torches limned his face in hoary silver, and he kept turning his head, as if he sensed someone behind them.

One more corner and their journey was done. Kyndra looked out over a room of kneeling people, each one dressed, not in matching robes as she expected, but in a ragtag collection of garments. Some wore their Wielder raiment, but the silver or gold silk had been ripped into different styles. The sleeves were generally missing and several people had cut away the bottom half of the robe and wore loose trousers instead. The only thing they all had in common was a band of black fabric worn on the upper arm. Kait hastily donned hers. Without any explanation, she hurried them to an empty patch of carpeted floor and pulled them down beside her. The nearest people shot Kyndra several nervous glances before increasing the volume of their chanting, as if the droning mantra somehow warded her off. A small dais occupied the front of the chamber. For the moment, it was empty.

Uncomfortably aware of Kait's chanting, Kyndra tried to appear inconspicuous and noticed Nediah doing the same. Nediah's face had thawed somewhat after Kait's assertion that the Nerian were still Wielders. But, confronted with this bizarre gathering, his expression was once again chill, and every unintelligible syllable stiffened his body further.

And then it stopped. The room held its breath. From beneath an archway, two hooded men appeared, one leading the other by the hand. Kyndra studied them as they climbed onto the dais. The man guiding his companion was garbed in white and a large cowl hid his face from the crowd. The garments reminded her of Medavle, but this man was slighter. He did not have Medavle's height or the breadth in his shoulders.

Kyndra's eyes strayed to the other man. His clothes were black, and a low keening came from his throat, which the man in white ignored. Still holding the other's hand, he nodded once and Kait stood up.

'Nerian,' she called and all heads turned to her. 'You are gathered here this night to welcome others into our company.' Muttering rippled through the crowd, murmurs of interest and curiosity. The man in white nodded again.

Kyndra tried to sink into the floor. Some eyes had already

fixed upon her, though she noticed Nediah had attracted his fair share too. Kait lifted a hand and silence resumed. 'She began as a simple potential, but after sore treatment from the Council – treatment we are all too familiar with – she has turned from them. She has come to us.'

The muttering became a low cheer. Kyndra choked and tried to catch Kait's attention, but she couldn't do so without standing up.

'Twice she has survived where others would not. Twice she has defied the Council. Brothers, sisters, I say that we unite behind her. I say we should welcome her to the Nerian, to the people of the Saviour – he who removed our world from the brink of destruction, who brought us peace!'

A roar greeted her speech and beside Kyndra, Nediah groaned softly. All heads turned to the dais and the nearest people stretched their arms towards the keening, black-clad man. His guide gently moved him out of their reach.

'Kyndra.' Kait was looking down at her, eyes shining with fervour. 'Please stand up.'

Kyndra hesitated, torn between wanting to hide from the crowd and obeying the compulsion that had brought her here. Taking a deep breath, she rose unsteadily to her feet.

All eyes were instantly upon her and there was something savage in their regard. Avoiding them, she looked at the dais, as the white-cowled man stepped forward. He lifted his gloved hands and drew back the hood that hid his charge's face.

It was like a blow and Kyndra staggered, the breath searing her lungs. She couldn't tear her gaze from the man who stood revealed in the brutal Lunar light. Black lines scarred his cheeks, running down his neck in a pattern that might once have been enchanting. It disappeared into his clothes and hairline, suggesting it also covered his body. Kyndra stared at the ugly channels. She blinked, seeing fire roar through and die, leaving them dark.

The man's hair was tangled and most of it was grey like his short beard. His face was narrow and so familiar that Kyndra simply stared, unable to move. She breathed the cave-damp air and felt herself fragment as the stranger's eyes seized her own. They were dark blue, almost black. Kyndra looked into them and saw a memory there, a memory of stars . . .

. . . Where is Anohin?

He waits in the dying daylight, his patience fraying. The sounds of battle filter up to him, borne on a wind that carries death. The cannons continue their ceaseless barrage, and wave after wave of red-metalled men break against Solinaris's walls. Will their ranks never diminish? He knows this battle has been planned for decades and these forces meticulously prepared, schooled in the art of ruin.

Where is Anohin? Already the sun fails, dropping behind the mountains that cap the valley. The book from the archives rests on the stone at his feet. Some lingering instinct troubles him, instinct that could once have been emotion. Anohin must stand beside him. Only by touching the Yadin could he ensure his safety. He sighs. Feeling is foreign to him.

'Kierik: Master.'

It is Anohin at last. He turns to him and lays a hand on his shoulder. 'I must begin before all is lost. Stay near me, Anohin.' The Yadin nods, his face as white as his robes.

The pages of the book flip open to his silent instruction. He will prepare the stripping now, so that the Yadin's life-energy will be ready to use when the time comes. A wind rises from the book, a black wind, capable of harvesting the raw energy contained within the bodies of all the Yadin in the citadel. Anohin flinches as it swirls about his ankles. To him, it is death.

He opens his mind to the stars. Their power is his to command and he is adept at bringing it into himself, sculpting it and then releasing it in the form of his will. But this time its form will be vaster than anything he has ever attempted. Should he succeed, his name will echo down the centuries, woven into the fabric of rock and tree and the turn of the foaming tide.

He reaches out to the Watchers – the stars of North, South, East and West: Noruri, Soruri, Austri and Vestri. Their stable light will help him hold Rairam steady in his mind. But first he must draw a line under the past and, to do that, he needs the star, Sigel. It fills him with a power so huge that even he trembles at it. The blow must be decisive: the land of Acre and the Sartyan disease cut away like a gangrenous limb. From now on the continent of Rairam will exist as a world in its own right. And he will be its master.

His awareness of Acre recedes. All he has left of that vast world is a handful of earth, taken from the red valley. It will serve as both memento and warning – the one piece of evidence to prove that Rairam was once part of a greater land, a land torn apart by war.

He draws on the knowledge of the stars, weaving a barrier of gigantic proportions. Without the physical laws of Acre to govern it, Rairam will need new laws and new boundaries. The ocean in the south is one such boundary. Its waves will never again lap another coast. Guided by the Watchers, he makes mountains grow in the west to match their sisters in the east: strong arms to cradle his new world. Then he lets the deep bank of forest in the north run unchecked for many leagues before using the star, Thurn, to persuade the trees to grow gnarled and dark. Their limbs are knotted, impenetrable, and a chill lies on them like death. This place where day meets night must have a name, so he calls it Chort: the Rib Wall. Once upon a time, it would have abutted the Acrean ice fields, but now the Rib Wall will serve as his northernmost boundary.

He doesn't know how long it has taken him to craft the skeleton of a new world, but it is done and he is weary and there is only one thing left to do. The book's black wind still wails at his feet, striving for release. He releases it.

A sharply indrawn breath; it is Anohin feeling the wind pass over him and on, seeking out every other Yadin. They are unnecessary things, these Yadin. He considers them mere constructs, the result of the Wielders playing at being gods. He doesn't want them in his world, not these abominations that walk and talk like human beings. Except for Anohin, of course. Anohin is different. They have been together for so long. Anohin helps to keep the human part of him alive and the deep irony of this thought makes him smile.

The black wind unravels the Yadin, returning their energy to him. It is unfamiliar, but not unusable. He lets it remain in its simplest form and – from up on high – begins to smash the Sartyan army still on his soil. Their screams mingle with the metallic shrieks of their engines, which he bursts one by one.

The slaughter bores him after a while. He gazes with both eyes and mind at the continent he has stolen from Acre. It is not perfect, he silently tells the people of Rairam, but it is peace. Almost as an afterthought, he calms the protesting sea with the star, Lagus, and sends his mind out through the world, checking for lesions and knitting those he finds.

He already has a name for his new world. 'Good morning, Mariar,' he whispers. And as the sun rises to spill its golden warmth across the hills, while his mind is still linked with the land and with the stars, a black agony gusts into him, and rips his soul apart.

The blow flung him to his knees. He was screaming, clutching his head as the wind tore away his sanity. It stripped him of his self, trying to get to the very heart of him.

Then a voice cried, 'Kyndra!' and that name was enough. *I am me,* she thought wildly, *not him, never him.* She was on the ground and so were the Nerian, as if a great wind had roared through and swept them violently against the walls. Her head had surely split open at the impact – the agony made her ears ring. And those pinpricks of light were staring down at her, closer now than they'd ever been before. If she could just reach them, the pain would stop.

But that now-familiar wall was there again and Kyndra hurt too much to push against it.

Dimly she realized that none of the Nerian were seriously hurt, despite the violence of the vision. Surely the Madness should have taken everyone in the room, but the only one who seemed disturbed was the man with the cratered face. He was on the floor too, hands fisted against his skull. As Kyndra watched, his companion picked himself up and hurried to calm him, stroking his back and whispering what sounded like soothing words. They had no effect. The black-clad man's keening grew louder, until it turned into an expression of unutterable horror. The sound echoed around the chamber and those gathered there flinched, as if it hurt them.

But Kyndra drew an odd kind of strength from the man's wailing and she found herself climbing stiffly to her feet and walking through the scattered Nerian towards the dais. The distraught man was the lodestone that had brought her here and she could not fight the pull any longer. She was at the platform and then climbing the steps, the man was within reach of her hand—

An arm blocked her. It sat hard against her stomach, barring her way.

'I'm sorry,' the man in white said. With his free hand, he reached up and tugged down his cowl. The face beneath was unlined, but tired, as if it had seen more years than it cared to. 'I cannot let you come any closer.'

Behind Anohin, Kierik started to howl.

26

No one moved, and a religious silence formed around the madman's cries. Kyndra stared at Anohin, recognizing him from the visions. The hood had mussed his straw-coloured hair and stray locks hung to a chin roughened with stubble. Although his grey eyes were wan, the arm against her stomach was as solid and unyielding as iron.

The tension in Anohin's body was strung to breaking point. Every muscle was taut and coiled, ready to act. Kyndra slowly raised her hands and stepped back. Only when she had put the steps between them did Anohin relax.

'I must see to my friend and master,' he said. His was a clear voice, but its bell-like tones couldn't disguise a weariness as deep and old as the earth. 'You will be allowed to remain here so long as you swear fealty.'

'Fealty?'

'Your companion has already spoken the vow. Now it is your turn, Kyndra Vale.'

'Don't, Kyndra,' Nediah said from somewhere behind her. 'It will bind you to them.'

Kyndra looked past Anohin to the trembling man that the

Nerian called saviour and raised her voice over his howling. 'I don't want to hurt him.'

'Then swear it.'

'Show me the way,' Kait called.

She didn't have any choice. All the answers lay here in this primitive chamber of hollowed-out rock. *It's true,* she thought, as her battered mind began to turn over this latest vision, *the Nerian are right about the war.*

'Show me the way,' Kyndra murmured.

'I am a seeker of truth. I am a servant of light . . .'

She repeated verbatim the words Kait spoke and imagined their coiled power unfurling to bind her into the service of this strange crew. Kierik's noise did not cease and each piteous wail jarred her spine.

The awful sound didn't seem to affect Anohin, who gazed at his master with sad eyes. Seemingly satisfied with her vow, he took up his charge's arm and the madman's howling quietened a little. 'I must calm him,' Anohin said. 'He's more agitated than usual.'

Leaning on his guide, the madman lurched through the archway and his uneven gait caused something around his neck to swing wildly. Kyndra squinted. It was a pouch, strung on a worn cord. The cracked leather looked uncannily like the one she'd found on the airship, the one later stolen from Brégenne's room. But if it was the same, why did it now swing from a madman's neck?

Kierik disappeared from view, taking the pouch with him. *I'd have to get closer to make sure,* Kyndra thought and shuddered. The prospect of approaching the Nerian's saviour again turned her stomach. And yet she wanted it. She both wanted and feared to look into those eyes.

The noise in the chamber grew and Kyndra turned at a touch on her arm. It was Kait and her smile was sunlit. 'Welcome!' she cried. 'I knew you would swear. I knew you would become one of us!'

Kyndra tried to speak, but more of the Nerian joined Kait, eager to offer their greetings. She shook hands, smiling shallowly, and wondered what she'd got herself into. Someone slipped a plain black band over her shirt sleeve and between the bobbing heads of the crowd, she caught sight of Nediah trying to remain inconspicuous.

'Who is this?'

A finger was pointing at Nediah. It belonged to a thickset man with a suspicious, craggy face. He reminded Kyndra alarmingly of Alandred.

Kait pushed her way through the crowd to stand in front of Nediah. 'He is the one whose words brought Kyndra to us.'

'Then he is welcome,' the man answered, suspicion abandoned. He moved forward and without preamble worked an identical black band over Nediah's sleeve. The Wielder didn't resist, but watched with empty eyes.

Trying her best to avoid the jubilant stares of the crowd, Kyndra studied the room more closely. Torch brackets hung on the walls and murals brightened the gloomy stone. The largest depicted a man standing tall against a night sky, arms thrown forward. In the space between his hands, a world spun into being. Stars glimmered in his eyes and a stark tattoo blazed over his face and shoulders, racing down across his bare chest like a fan of comets.

'It is our history,' Kait said, coming to stand beside her. Together they gazed at the godlike man sculpting a world. 'It is the moment of Deliverance. The true Deliverance.'

'That is Kierik?'

Adoration warmed Kait's eyes. 'Are you not proud?' she whispered.

Kyndra stared at the mural. The tattoos on the face matched those on the madman's, but where these were beautiful, the madman's were black and dead-looking. 'What happened to him?' she asked softly.

'That is Anohin's tale,' Kait said. 'He will tell it when he returns.'

Kyndra looked at her sidelong. Kait seemed as unaffected by the aftermath of the vision as everyone else in the room. Either Kyndra was wrong and the Madness had nothing to do with her, or the sect had some protection she couldn't see. Anohin would know.

The commotion abruptly ceased and, as if he had heard his name in her thoughts, Anohin appeared in the archway. He began to walk through the gathered people and they bent before him like grass before a wind. His garments glimmered palely under the torchlight.

When he reached Kyndra, he stopped. 'Come.' The command was quiet, insistent.

'She's not going anywhere without me,' Nediah said, moving to stand at Kyndra's shoulder.

'She doesn't need you,' Kait said. 'She is one of us now. We do not harm our own.'

Nediah folded his arms. Anohin regarded the Wielder's stubborn stance and a smile flickered across his lips. 'Your dedication is applauded, disciple. But I would like to speak to your young friend alone and beg your indulgence. It is as Kait says. No harm shall come to either of you.'

'I want to hear what he has to say, Nediah,' Kyndra said,

desperate to ask Anohin about her latest vision and what it meant – and whether it had anything to do with the Madness. 'Isn't this why we came?'

Nediah glowered at Anohin, but eventually let his arms fall.

'You have done well,' the Yadin said then to Kait. 'Stay and induct our new member into the truths of our people.' Kait did not look happy at being left behind, but said nothing. Instead she shared a meaningful glance with Anohin and Kyndra thought she gave him the whisker of a nod.

Then the Yadin turned and led Kyndra out of the chamber. Thick walls soon muffled the chatter behind them, as Anohin led her through a series of honeycombed corridors. The ceiling dipped low in places, forcing them to stoop. She kept an eye on the Yadin, whose body still showed signs of tension. Perhaps it never left him. What did he guard against down here, Kyndra wondered, far from the light of the sun?

When the path diverged, Anohin did not hesitate. They went left, right and left again. The turns grew too many to remember. A reddish glow lit their way, tinted by the ochre of the stone and there was a smooth channel worn in the floor – possibly formed by generations of feet. They passed openings hung with cloth, which Kyndra guessed might be living quarters. Anohin said nothing until they reached a similar opening where a heavy curtain served as a door. He flipped it aside and beckoned her in.

The space beyond more closely resembled a cell than a room. It was barely larger than the one Kyndra had up in the citadel. The only furniture was a simple pallet that lacked any impression of a body, a small chest, a chair and a chipped wooden desk. No furnishings softened the bare stone. The uncarpeted floor was worn smooth from pacing feet, much like the one outside.

Anohin gestured her to the chair and then crossed to lean against the wall. They looked at each other for a few silent moments. 'You know me,' the man said. It wasn't a question.

Kyndra studied him. No wrinkles marred his cheeks, or spots of age. His back was straight and his legs strong. Only one other wore timelessness like a second skin: Medavle.

'I see at least some of the truth in your eyes,' Anohin continued. 'You were destined to learn it, after all, and I knew it would lead you here. What have the visions shown you?'

She did not ask how Anohin knew about the visions, but said instead, 'Rairam.' The word tasted strange on her tongue. For the first time, she allowed herself to fully consider the vision that had revealed the fate of Acre. The old world was still there. It had been hidden, not destroyed. And her world – Mariar – wasn't a world at all, but a continent called Rairam that had once been part of Acre, a land full of the wonders in her story books. Kyndra's hands trembled. She knew Kierik for what he was now. 'Starborn,' she whispered.

'Yes,' Anohin said. 'The last.' Grey eyes watched her closely. 'But . . . how is it even possible, what he did?'

'When he first told me of his plan, I said the same. No one can hide a whole continent, its people, its rivers and mountains – even its sea.' Anohin's gaze strayed. He stared at the wall, but Kyndra was sure he saw more than the rough stone. 'I underestimated him. I underestimated his ambition.'

Anohin looked back at her. 'To one who wasn't there, it is difficult to explain how desperate the situation had become. The Sartyans had grown fat on the spoils of war. Any who resisted were cut down by an army too great to withstand, an army wearing the scarlet plates of the empire. Many cities surrendered and were spared, their people converted and their cultures absorbed. Kierik knew he couldn't stop it. What power does one man – even a Starborn – have against the combined might of a world united under one banner? Even Solinaris, the ancestral seat of the Wielders, had begun to rupture, turned from within. The fortress of the sun had always been a beacon of hope to the people it governed, but some foresaw its fall and defected to the empire.'

He paused. 'I became increasingly estranged from the citadel. My first loyalty was to Kierik and he was not welcome in Solinaris. The Wielders feared him almost as much as they feared the empire, though he gave them no cause to do so.'

Remembering the frightened faces of the Sentheon, Kyndra disagreed. Kierik had not disguised his desire to rule. And who there could have stopped him?

'All Kierik wanted was peace,' Anohin continued with a catch in his voice. 'To create a world where no one power could grow to dominate another. He saw it as his destiny. Was that so wrong?'

'I am the instrument of peace,' Kyndra murmured, remembering. She didn't know what she felt at finally learning the identity of the man on the mountain, the man who had altered the flow of history. And the question remained: why was she sharing his memories? She glanced up at Anohin to find the Yadin white-faced. He was staring at her, as if seeing her clearly for the first time. 'What's wrong?' she asked.

'Nothing,' Anohin said, visibly collecting himself. 'For a moment you reminded me of— Never mind. Talking of this has dredged up memories.'

'I'm sorry.'

Anohin held up a hand. 'Don't be. I have lived too long to permit myself such weaknesses.'

'So if Kierik's plan worked,' Kyndra said after a moment, 'why is he the way he is?'

'Medavle.' The colour returned to Anohin's cheeks in a rush. He began to pace, constricted by the small room. 'Kierik knew that separating Rairam from Acre would take all he could draw from the stars without killing himself. He needed another source of power to destroy the Sartyan army on his soil.'

Anohin stopped, staring straight ahead. 'I agreed,' he whispered, as if reminding himself of the fact. When he looked back at Kyndra, wetness gleamed in the corners of his eyes. 'Though we are creatures of flesh, the Yadin lack the spark of life. We were a race created from cosmosethic energy and it is that energy which lives in our blood and keeps our hearts beating.'

They are unnecessary things, these Yadin . . . mere constructs, the result of the Wielders playing at being gods. Kierik's cold thoughts came rushing back to Kyndra. *Except for Anohin, of course . . .* She looked at the Yadin standing across from her. What had Kierik meant when he'd said that Anohin helped to keep the human part of him alive? And did Anohin realize just how much Kierik had despised the rest of the Yadin race?

'How many of you were there?' she forced herself to ask.

'We were five hundred,' Anohin answered. 'Men and women. We came to consciousness fully grown and our only purpose was to serve the Wielders, our masters.'

'But you served Kierik.'

'I was different.'

'In what way?'

'I only ever served Kierik,' Anohin said. A shudder ran through him. 'I . . . I was drawn to him, to his strength and his vision. And even though he was a Starborn, he let me stay, he

401

didn't send me away. It was then that I realized I could never leave his side. And I never have,' he added softly.

Kyndra swallowed. 'So you knew what Kierik planned to do with that book. You knew it would—'

'I knew it would destroy us.'

'And yet you still stood by him?'

'I was willing to give up my life to see Kierik's purpose through.'

'But the others,' Kyndra demanded. 'Were the other Yadin as willing to die?'

She watched the answer slide like dark poison between Anohin's lips. 'No,' the Yadin said tonelessly. 'They didn't know; not until it was too late.'

Disgust and disbelief drove Kyndra to her feet. 'So you let him kill them? How could you? They were your own people!'

Anohin watched her. 'After five hundred years,' he said, 'the regret has not left me. And yet . . .' His expression became distant. 'Kierik used their power to destroy the army outside the walls of Solinaris. Without their sacrifice, he might not have had the strength, and the killing would have continued.'

It was too much for Kyndra. She gazed at the man before her, unable to grasp the horrible depths of his loyalty to Kierik, to a person so unfeeling. 'The people living in Rairam weren't given a choice either, were they?' she asked. 'Kierik treated them just like the Yadin. What if they didn't want to be separated from Acre, from the rest of the world?'

'You don't understand,' Anohin said sharply. 'If you had seen the empire and the practices enforced, you would not say such a thing. Kierik sacrificed himself for the greater good.'

'He didn't intend to sacrifice himself, though – he built

himself a world to rule. The only things he chose to sacrifice were the lives of innocent people.'

They faced each other across the small room. Anger had chased the shadows away from Anohin's eyes. 'You haven't answered my question,' Kyndra said. 'Why is Kierik the way he is? You said Medavle had something to do with it.'

'Medavle overheard us discussing the plan. He thought, much like you –' Anohin's voice was bitter – 'that separating Rairam from Acre was too drastic a course.'

'What could he do to stop it?'

'Nothing,' Anohin said bluntly. 'He was strong, but he couldn't defeat a Starborn. And when he heard about the fate Kierik had planned for the Yadin, he knew his own life was soon to end.' He clenched his fists. 'I did not know,' he grated. 'I saw him near the archives, after he'd planted his revenge. He was agitated, but I did not guess why. If only I had—'

'His revenge?' Kyndra interrupted.

'Medavle is cleverer than me,' Anohin admitted. 'I had not realized the extent to which he'd explored his own abilities. He laid a trap for Kierik in the archives, a trap made of the same energy that Kierik planned to siphon from the Yadin. He drew it from his own veins and set it to seize on the first person who walked through it, knowing it would be Kierik.'

'What did the trap do?'

'Medavle used his own life force to bind himself to Kierik. It was risky, but I don't think Medavle cared whether he lived or died, as long as he brought Kierik down. When Kierik set the book's instructions in motion, the Yadin began to die. A black wind they couldn't see stripped away the power that gave them form. Afterwards, I found nothing left of them, just empty clothes. It was as if they had never been.'

Anohin spoke harshly, a shield against his memories. 'But when that wind touched Medavle, it couldn't take him. Kierik was absorbed in his new world, in killing the Sartyans. He didn't see that the wind, unable to consume Medavle without first consuming him, had turned. I was there.'

Kyndra stilled. This was where the vision had left her.

'I was there,' Anohin said again. A tremor shivered through his body. 'I knew something was wrong, for I had felt the touch of the wind upon me, though Kierik's protection prevented me from being destroyed. It should have faded after consuming the Yadin, but it did not. It returned to Kierik, seeking Medavle, and tore through his mind – shattered it.'

Anohin's voice broke. 'He fell to his knees. I can still hear his screams, like echoes down the years. The wind ripped him apart, scattering his reason beyond recovery. And he was still tied to Rairam, tied to his new world. What happened to one, happened to the other. The breaking of Kierik's mind still resonates across the land, even to this day.'

'What?' Kyndra whispered, stunned. 'Do you mean the Breaking?'

Anohin smiled bleakly. 'The Breaking is Medavle's legacy, his curse upon a world whose creation he opposed. He has had his revenge.'

As if on cue, a familiar wailing started up close by. Anohin moved quickly to the curtain. 'Excuse me just a moment,' he said, 'I must go to him – I keep him near me these days.' He looked back at her from the doorway and his gaze sharpened to a threat. 'Now that you know Medavle's history and the things he is capable of, follow my example. Stay away from him.'

The curtain fell back into place behind the Yadin, its loose threads brushing the floor. Kyndra sat alone in the bleak cell and wondered whether the years had wreaked the same damage upon Anohin as Medavle had upon his master.

27

Brégenne turned her face to the light.

She stood in the day chamber, a small space bathed by tied Solar energy. Even at midnight, the heat here was like the noon sun. Exotic plants spewed their fronds across her path, forcing her to tread carefully. The fashion of collecting flora had become so popular that storing it and growing it was now the day chamber's sole purpose.

Brégenne tilted her head and imagined a playful wind shaking light into leaves, chasing the ever-changing dappling on the boughs. She imagined a swift, or some bright bird, riding the thermals, circling into the sun. In her mind she saw a meadow, a town and a water mill lazily turning. She saw a mother bid a pale-haired daughter take care, to be back in the house before the afternoon's end. She watched the daughter head alone into woodland, hands wrapping each tree, scooping flowers from the ground. The small group that followed her had darkness in their eyes.

She felt a sharp scratch on her arm. Brégenne looked down, grateful for the thorns that had broken her trance. Memories of summer were abhorrent, for they always led her back to the playful wind and the wildflowers. She inhaled the chamber's sour greenery and tried to put the sunlight away, but it turned with her, clung to her and sank into hibiscus and rose, until all she could smell was its ripe truth.

The blood on her hands the night she returned for revenge had not been cleansing. It had felt gritty with self-disgust. She had thought it would bring her peace. But their screams had not satisfied, their pleas for mercy not warmed. They were her kin, they'd said, they had only done what was best for her, they'd said. Taking her sight, they'd said, would cure her of witchcraft. She wouldn't have to worry about the moon, or how – under its light – she could sometimes do things other people couldn't. They'd make sure she didn't see the moon and all of that strangeness would stop. And so they followed her to the woods and they ignored her screams and they tore away all the beauty in the world.

Brégenne didn't forget and she didn't forgive, but in the end their deaths meant nothing. The only thing vengeance had given her was a prison, barred with memory, where the hot summer wind blew all year long and the wood beckoned and her torturers lived on.

She clenched her fists, but felt no pain from her short nails. A hot jumble of thoughts coaxed her back to the present.

I have failed her.

Kyndra had gone to the Nerian – Kyndra, whom she had brought here against her will. And with her had gone Nediah.

Brégenne screamed at the plants. It was a quick, stifled cry and she hated it as soon as it left her mouth. She pressed her lips together. That distant day was still with her, alongside the girl she had been, her anger and horror hammered into hard, foolish armour. Brégenne closed her eyes and felt a single tear on her cheek.

Time passed. The false sun slowly dimmed, granting the plants their few hours of darkness. *Enough*, she thought, the shade of the girl stirring inside her. She wondered what was happening in the Deep. What questions had Kyndra chased there and had she found answers with the Nerian?

Brégenne turned to leave.

A wave of force hit her without warning. If she hadn't been holding the Lunar, it would have thrown her from her feet. As it was, she staggered, seeing the air ripple before her face. Almost immediately, a scream sounded, somewhere beyond the door. Strengthening her Lunar sight, Brégenne rushed from the day chamber, leaving its doors – heavily beaded with condensation – gaping open behind her. The scene that greeted her was one born from a nightmare.

Kyndra felt as if she'd awakened from a long, strange dream. Surely, if she pulled aside the curtain, she would find the steep staircase leading down from the attic to The Nomos. Reena would be there, chiding her for sleeping so late, red hair tied up in a kerchief to start the day's chores. Jarand would appear from the cellar, dusty and smiling, a wink for Kyndra creasing his eyelid. Perhaps her mother would ruffle her hair, as she sometimes did, taking the bite from her reprimand.

An ache arose in Kyndra's heart. Discovering the Breaking's true nature would not reverse the destruction it had wreaked upon Brenwym. And how would that knowledge help her to stop its continued destruction of Mariar?

Alone in Anohin's cell, she remembered the pouch she'd seen swinging from Kierik's neck and her palms tingled. She wanted to touch the red earth again – it was yet another mystery and she added it to her list of questions to ask Anohin.

Impatient, Kyndra pulled aside the curtain and followed the whimpering that echoed about the corridors.

She didn't have far to go. The sounds came from behind a door, the first proper door she'd seen down here. It was fitted with a lock and stood ajar. Knowing she would have to face the madman again, Kyndra bit her lip and gently poked the door open.

Anohin knelt beside a large bed, but whirled immediately. His expression was so fierce that Kyndra stepped back despite herself. She tried to look unthreatening and slowly Anohin's snarl faded. 'No closer,' he growled.

Kyndra nodded and looked around. This room was larger and far more comfortable than the Yadin's. The bed had a soft-looking mattress, stuffed thickly with feathers, and two heavy bolsters lay on the carpeted floor. She noticed there were no sharp edges anywhere. The bedside table had blunted corners, as had the chairs and the small desk. What use was a desk to a madman? The lack of sharp objects and the furniture's rounded edges were the only clues that hinted at the state of the room's occupant. Kyndra looked at Kierik and wondered whether he had ever tried to kill himself.

Anohin turned back to his charge. One hand soothed Kierik's back, stroking in large circles. The other held one of the madman's curled fists. It seemed that the outburst was over, but then Kierik raised his eyes and saw Kyndra standing motionless in the doorway.

His gaze pinned her with the same intensity as earlier. And then Kierik let out a howl and thrashed about, kicking the quilt off the bed. Anohin shot her a glare, but Kyndra found she could not leave. The pouch hung in plain view on Kierik's chest, jostled by his flailing. It *was* the same one – she was sure of it. She recognized the old, cracked leather and moth-eaten drawstring. Kyndra felt the earth as if she held it once more, bloody grains burning her palm.

Kierik stilled. His gaze had not left her. An expression, almost lucid, sharpened his scarred face. Then one hand rose and closed protectively around the pouch, hiding it from view. Without realizing it, Kyndra started forward, but Anohin was there, blocking her way. 'Stay back,' he ordered.

'You stole that from Brégenne,' she accused. 'Why?'

Anohin shooed her out of the room and Kierik's howling started up again. This time Anohin ignored it and closed the door behind them. 'Do not go in there again.'

'I don't want to hurt him,' Kyndra insisted. 'I swore not to.'

Anohin's shoulders lost a little of their tension. 'Your presence here upsets him.'

Kyndra folded her arms. 'Why did you steal the pouch from Brégenne's room?' she asked again.

'I didn't steal it. Kait retrieved it for me. The earth belongs to Kierik and was stolen by Medavle twenty years ago.'

'So Medavle was here, then.'

'Briefly, but I was careful to conceal myself from him. I wanted to be able to watch him without his realizing it. When he turned up here, I could hardly believe it.' His eyes hardened. 'You see, I had not known until then that Medavle had survived the fracture of Kierik's mind – he's linked to Kierik by the strands of his own life-energy.'

Anohin pulled off his gloves and tucked them behind his belt. 'It is because of Medavle that I had to smuggle Kait out of Naris. I sent her to follow you on your journey here, to make sure he didn't try to harm you.'

Kyndra stared at him. 'You . . . ?'

'Yes. I think Medavle came here for one reason – the bag of earth. After he escaped with it, I tried to track him using my own brand of power, but he managed to disappear. It's been only a few months since he resurfaced, and on the other side of the continent.' Anohin's look sharpened. 'A farming community in the Far Valleys.'

Kyndra's heart thumped in the silence. She remembered Medavle's black eyes piercing her during the Inheritance Ceremony. She'd dreamed of them too.

'What had he found to interest him in so distant a place? I wondered. It wasn't until later that I knew the answer: *you*.'

Kyndra's mouth dried. When she didn't speak, Anohin continued. 'I don't know what Medavle's plans for you are, Kyndra, but he is the chief reason why I've chosen to help you – why I've offered you asylum amongst the Nerian. Medavle is dangerous, unstable and still consumed with hatred for Kierik. At least while you're with us, you won't encounter him again.'

Kyndra kept her face neutral with difficulty. Was Anohin unaware of Medavle's role in rescuing her from the second test? Didn't he know Medavle was once again in the citadel? *You are my hope*, the dark-eyed Yadin had told her. But hope for what?

'Why did Medavle steal the bag of earth?' Kyndra asked slowly.

'I don't know.' From the frustrated set of his face, she guessed it was a question that had troubled Anohin for a long time. 'But the earth could be dangerous in the wrong hands.' The Yadin's eyes were suddenly sharp on her face. 'It must stay with Kierik.'

'Why?'

'It is time to return to the hall,' the Yadin said curtly. He

411

strode off down the passage, leaving her in his wake. Startled, Kyndra stared at his retreating back.

'Do you know why Medavle was at my Inheritance Ceremony?' she asked, hurrying after him.

Anohin stared straight ahead. 'I have suspicions, but nothing certain.'

He was lying. Kyndra could tell by the way he refused to look at her. She ground her teeth. She'd come here for answers and it felt as if all she'd received so far were more questions.

'Kait told me about Janus,' the Yadin said before she could press the issue. 'She also gave me this.' He reached into the high-collared coat and pulled out a small object. Kyndra recoiled. The white *akan* sat on Anohin's palm, both as innocent-seeming and as sinister as she remembered it.

'A treacherous thing,' Anohin commented mildly before returning the *akan* to his pocket. 'Lucky you dropped that book and Kait worked out what you were planning. Otherwise we wouldn't be having this conversation.'

So Kait *had* found *Tools of Power*. Kyndra stared at the Yadin, hearing an edge to his voice that she didn't much like. Time to try another question. 'You might pretend to know nothing about Medavle's interest in me,' she said boldly, 'but what about the visions I keep having – and the Madness?'

When she caught a glimpse of the Yadin's grey eyes, they were opaque. 'What about it?' he asked.

So he'd make her work for every word. 'Where does the Madness come from?' she asked, frustrated. 'Can it be stopped and –' she steeled herself – 'is it linked to my visions?' She thought of the vision – the *memory*, she corrected herself – that she'd witnessed tonight and how a huge wave of force had tumbled the Nerian, as if they were leaves in a gale. That same force had struck the Wielders during the test. 'Has anyone here been affected?' she asked.

'As long as we remain in the Deep, the Madness cannot touch us,' Anohin said.

'Why? Is there some kind of protection here?'

The Yadin looked at her. 'Kierik.'

Kyndra almost didn't catch his answer, for a drum started beating somewhere up ahead. Resonating through the stone, it was joined a moment later by a fiddle, which spun out a frenzied tune to the patter of feet. When the crowd in the meeting hall caught sight of her, they surged forward, dancing and clapping. Before Kyndra knew what was happening, they'd swept her up, encircled her. Someone stuffed a cup into her hand and Kyndra had to close her fingers or drop it. Her eyes began to smart from the smoking torches that were now the room's only source of light.

Confused by the feverish celebration, she tried and failed to extricate herself. Anohin had melted away from her and the crowd seemed intent on preventing her from reaching him. People came to clasp Kyndra's black-banded arm as if it were somehow talismanic, but Nediah — who was trying unsuccessfully to reach her through the crowd — received no notice at all. There was an edge to the Nerian's excitement, an undertide that flowed through the gathering. Kyndra could see it in their eyes and smell it in acrid air. It was anticipation; it was readiness. They circled her until she began to feel like a rallying point on a battlefield, the last hope of fading victory. What was going on? Surely all this wasn't just to celebrate her initiation into the sect?

Kyndra made a concerted effort to break free of the melee and managed to reach Nediah, who was standing seemingly

forgotten against a mural. This one depicted a shining structure, afternoon light blazing on its glass spires. Kyndra
recognized it at once; she had seen it so often in Kierik's memories. It was Solinaris, the fortress of the sun. Looking at it,
ephemeral on the ragged stone, she could hardly believe that
such a place had existed, that she was standing deep beneath
the ground from which it had once risen.

'Do *you* know what's going on?' Kyndra asked Nediah in a
low voice. 'Anohin wouldn't tell me anything and now they're
stopping me from getting to him.'

Nediah looked at her, green eyes sharp despite his clear
fatigue. 'If I didn't know better, I would say revolution.'

'Revolution?' Kyndra repeated uneasily. 'Meaning what
exactly?'

Nediah unfolded his arms. 'I don't know, Kyndra. The
Nerian have never tried to force their way into the citadel.
They've never been violent, as far as I know. But this –' He
paused, scanning the rhapsodic crowd. 'I didn't realize the sect
had grown so large.'

Kyndra watched them. The crowd showed no signs of weariness. As they banged their cups together, she heard her name
more than once on their lips. 'Why would they invade Naris?'

'I didn't appreciate until I came here tonight what life must
be like in the Deep,' Nediah said pensively. 'It is always dark.
The only form of sunlight they have is Solar energy. Every day,
if you can call it day, is spent surrounded by stone. These corridors are airless and stuffy and they never feel the wind on
their faces.' Nediah shifted his gaze to her. 'To live like this for
years would drive anyone mad.'

'Then why have they?' Kyndra asked, feeling Nediah's words
open a gulf inside her. 'Why haven't they risen up before now?'

Nediah didn't answer for a moment. He stared at her until Kyndra began to feel uncomfortable under his close scrutiny. 'Perhaps because they didn't have a reason to do so,' the Wielder said slowly.

'And you think they have a reason now?'

'Yes.'

Kyndra spotted a small knot of people coming towards them. 'What reason?' she asked quickly.

'You.'

At a loss, Kyndra stared at him, but before she could respond, they had company. Five members of the Nerian stood in front of them and amongst their number was the man who looked like Alandred. Impulsively she asked, 'Are you related to the Master of Novices?'

Disgust darkened the man's face. 'My brother,' he growled and spat on the floor. 'A sanctimonious fool who pretends he has no sibling. The shame I brought upon Alandred is too great for him to bear.'

'Sorry,' Kyndra said hastily. 'I only asked because you look alike.'

The man dismissed her apology. 'My name is Caendred,' he said. 'I sense you are no friend to my brother either.' His lips pulled back in a grin. A few of his teeth were missing.

'You could say that.'

'I'm glad,' Caendred replied. 'You belong here with us, with the true people of Naris.'

'Thank you,' Kyndra said cautiously, feeling awkward under their stares. Nediah remained silent beside her.

'We wanted you to know that we stand with you,' a woman next to Caendred spoke up. 'You have taken the vow and are now our sister.'

Her words raised hairs on the back of Kyndra's neck. Could Nediah be right? What were the Nerian planning? And why did her presence make the slightest difference?

'Thank you,' she said again when she realized her silence might sound rude. The five Nerian gazed at her without speaking. Then each touched the black band on her arm and melted back into the crowd.

'What was that about?' Kyndra whispered to Nediah when they were once again alone.

'I don't know,' Nediah said slowly, 'but I don't like it.'

Kyndra didn't either. She had the sense of something overlooked, something just on the verge of being realized. First Loricus with his speech about taking sides, now Anohin with his evasive knowledge of her visions and the Madness. Both men knew something she didn't and they seemed to be going out of their way to ensure she didn't find out what.

'It must be late,' she muttered. Though her mind constantly turned over the conversation with Anohin, her body felt heavy, still healing from the last test. She wondered whether she should tell Nediah everything – that the Nerian's version of history, labelled by the Council as delusion, was in fact true. Would Nediah believe her? He had been schooled to see the Nerian as an unstable cult, one whose preposterous ideas must be confined underground.

What Kierik had done was in the past, Kyndra decided. It could not be changed. Finding a way to stop both the Breaking and the Madness was, however, essential. And Anohin knew far more than he was willing to tell.

'Nerian!' Kait's voice sliced through the celebration. 'The hour is almost at hand.'

Kyndra hadn't seen Kait for some time. Now, as the tall

woman led her into the centre of the chamber, the flush across her high cheekbones was darker and her eyes were belladonna-bright. 'By the time dawn has broken, my friends,' she called, 'Naris will see the world as the Nerian see it!'

The cries of the crowd welled up to him and the drum thudded in his chest. A wild waltz spun from the fiddle, its strings screeching in the dingy space.

Janus crouched, body stiff from long inactivity. Through a crack in the stone, he looked down on the chamber below. Although the smoking torches made his eyes water, he didn't move away, frightened to miss something. However, for the last half-hour, the chamber had descended into raucous carousal. He saw drink passed around and curled his lip in disgust. *They really are savages*, he thought, wiping his stinging eyes. Torches instead of Lunar light, hard stone bereft of furnishings – no wonder the Council kept them penned here. The Nerian were an embarrassment.

He'd discovered the crawl space by accident, while searching for a way to observe the chamber surreptitiously. Janus had followed Kyndra and her companions as far as the corridor by which they'd entered, but it was too dangerous to remain crouched there. Anyone could discover him. Better by far was this space, tiny though it was. From here, he could see everything.

Janus clenched a fist. He could see everything, he reminded himself, except the corridor down which Kyndra had vanished with the man in white. He knew he couldn't search for them – the danger of becoming lost was too great. He could end up wandering in the dark until he died, or be discovered by one of the Nerian and imprisoned. Janus wouldn't risk either fate, not when Lord Loricus relied on him.

Now he stared at Kyndra as she stood beside Nediah. Her eyes roved distractedly and he wondered what thoughts chased each other behind them. Her face was a peculiar mix of relief and burden, as if the solving of one problem had raised another.

An unwelcome feeling arose in Janus' chest, which he recognized a moment later as jealousy. If it weren't for this girl, he might not be wearing the gold. Had Loricus raised him solely because of her? *No*, he reminded himself, *the full Council has to vote on whether to raise a novice to master status.* But it was Loricus who'd put his name forward, Loricus who'd suggested he should be paired with Brégenne when – surely – any other Superiate novice would do. Instead of enjoying his first week as a master, he'd spent every day with a talentless girl, a job which he'd been *flattered* to undertake. Janus swallowed the sour taste in his mouth. What was she to Loricus? And what, now he thought about it, was he?

The noise levels in the chamber abruptly lowered and the music stopped. Janus watched the man in white beckon Kyndra into the centre of the room. She went reluctantly, the tall woman from earlier at her shoulder and Nediah on her heels.

'The hour is almost at hand,' the woman announced. Shouts rose in the wake of her words, no longer cries of celebration, but righteous and unafraid. Janus pressed his face closer to the gap. The woman let the clamour subside before she continued. 'By the time dawn has broken, my friends, Naris will see the world as the Nerian see it! Kierik and his deeds will be recognized. We will rise into the light!'

A roar greeted these words. People threw their fists in the air and hands reached out to touch Kyndra, who tried to edge away from them. 'We have all seen . . .' The rest of the sentence was lost to Janus, as the woman lowered her voice. Though he grimaced and strained his ears, he couldn't make out the words. 'Too many years,' he heard, and 'never before'. He beat his fist against the stone in frustration, but he'd already heard enough to feel the first stirrings of fear. The Nerian were planning something, something *big*.

And though it all revolved around Kyndra, Janus could tell by her face that it was not of her making. He watched her lips move, but her voice was too quiet to make out. It didn't matter. He'd seen enough now and his report was too vital to delay. Lord Loricus had to be warned.

Inch by inch, Janus backed out of the gap, his body clumsy and cold. When he could stand, he held on to the wall for a few moments, rolling his shoulders and flexing his arms and legs, waiting for the blood to return to them.

Dawn was still a good four hours away and he'd need light to find the way back. Janus pulled a Lunar stone from his pocket and, in the darkness, it burst immediately to life.

A face flared in front of him and he yelled, but nothing came out. A gloved hand covered his mouth. Janus thrashed and the Lunar stone fell from his hand. Its light flickered and began to wane as he looked through huge eyes at his captor. A white hood hid the man's face and he wore a high-collared coat over white robes.

Janus drew frantic breaths through his nose, hearing nothing now but his own muffled sounds of terror. How had the man in white found him and climbed up here so fast? He gathered his strength and aimed a kick at the man's shins, but his captor turned his body aside.

'I don't think so,' came a deep voice.

Janus saw a fist coil and then it was flying towards his temple, too fast, far too fast. There was an explosion of light, pain, and then darkness.

28

He had no real wish to kill the young man, but what else could he do? Rendering him unconscious was an imperfect solution. Janus hung over Medavle's shoulder, a dead weight, as the Yadin stalked through the darkness of the earth. Medavle adjusted his grip and scowled.

Janus was a loose thread in the tapestry of his plan. He did not care to let him go. After all, he had been instrumental in giving Kyndra access to the white *akan*. But if Medavle was to take advantage of this opportunity, he couldn't bring Janus with him.

He ground his teeth. If only the captain had kept his end of the deal. Medavle had paid the man well: three gold pieces for a small favour. Perhaps that generosity had been his undoing, he mused. Three gold pieces to ensure the pouch of earth reached Kyndra, but the rat had kept it, no doubt thinking it valuable.

It's worthless in your hands. But in Kyndra's, it was priceless. And now it would no doubt be attached to the madman, guarded by his howls.

Janus started to slip again, but Medavle couldn't afford to stop. He needed to be out of the Nerian's range. *I ought to leave him here to die*, he thought.

When he spied a likely pillar, he dumped Janus beside it and then pulled the young man into a sitting position. He slipped the silver flute from its bag and blew two notes, stark and cold. They writhed like snakes in the gloom before forming a shining chain that bound Janus to the pillar.

Medavle smiled and lowered the flute. The young Solar Wielder would not be escaping from a Lunar binding for some time. A Yadin's energy was finite, but could be used at any time of day. The flute wasn't necessary, but it augmented his power. Medavle had crafted it long ago, based on plans he'd filched from Solinaris's archives.

He turned away. The madman's guards would be few, he thought, mentally mapping out his next moves. If the Nerian intended to force their way into Naris, they would need the bulk of their forces. He could lie low until they were well out of the way, steal into the complex, take out the guards and help himself to the earth. Kyndra needed it. Perhaps he might even slit the madman's throat while he was at it, just to see that polluted blood pool uselessly on the stone. Medavle let himself savour the prospect before letting it go with a sigh. He should probably reserve that act for another.

Kyndra returned to the citadel – much to her horror – at the head of a small army.

Anohin marched on her right, Kait on her left and Nediah was behind her. The Nerian were going to war. Only a few remained in the Deep to watch over Kierik while the rest moved inexorably up through the rock, mouthing their talismanic chant. Although they planned to reach Naris well before dawn, every Lunar clutched a dark-hued *akan* to aid them once the sun had risen. Others carried staffs, scrolls and bits of mismatched armour that glowed softly in the gloom.

Anohin did not seem concerned about their diminutive force. Nediah had pointed out that Naris's Wielders outnumbered them at least three to one, but the Yadin had shrugged off his argument, pale face alight with anticipation. Kyndra's heart kept up an anxious beat. Why would the Nerian, who had lived peaceably in the Deep for years, choose this night to throw off their oppression?

The answer became dreadfully clear as they approached the citadel's lower floors. When the screams reached their ears, Nediah stiffened and both Kait and Anohin smiled and increased the pace. The torturous cries roused the Nerian like a tonic. Their voices grew louder and this time, Kierik's name could be heard in the fabric of their chant.

The chaos that greeted them when they emerged from the Deep seemed only to surprise Kyndra and Nediah. The Nerian whooped and grinned at each other, as if everything were going to plan. Kyndra watched a Wielder come staggering down the passage towards them, his mouth gaping soundlessly. Bloodshot eyes looked at them without comprehension. Caendred took the opportunity to shoot a couple of Lunar darts into his unprotected neck and he toppled, blood running from his punctured throat.

Nediah gave a horrified yell and launched himself at Caendred, but the Nerian man shoved him scornfully aside. 'No.' Kait caught Nediah's uplifted arm. Her voice was wintry. 'You are one of us now. Your loyalty is to the Nerian.'

Nediah stared at her, as if seeing her clearly for the first time. 'These people are helpless,' he said. 'You can't just murder them – they're victims of the Madness.'

'*Defenceless* victims,' Caendred said, as he coolly stepped over the dead Wielder.

Aghast, Nediah shook his head and then Kyndra saw a light dawn slowly in his eyes. 'You *knew* this would happen,' he said to Kait. 'Somehow this is your doing.'

'Hers, actually.'

Anohin was staring at Kyndra and – once again – she was the focus of all eyes.

'What?' Nediah said.

'She knows the truth.' The Yadin's smile hardened. 'She's suspected it herself.'

Kyndra's breath came fast and shallow. All she could see was the fallen Wielder with his blood spilled out around him. That vacant look in his eyes before Caendred killed him – the same look that Mardon had and the female Wielder after the test – that look was the Madness and it *was* her fault. She'd known it, but tried to bury it under a deluge of questions that now seemed meaningless. She was as much of a murderer as Caendred and Kierik.

Nediah's face was ashen. 'It can't be her,' he said, but his voice wobbled uncertainly and Kyndra couldn't bear to meet his eyes. She couldn't bear to meet any of their eyes, except those of the dead man, fixed and unknowing in his head.

'You aided her,' Anohin said to Nediah amid the Nerian's hoots of glee. 'You brought her to us – to Kierik. And the meeting of their minds caused a shock powerful enough to sweep through the whole citadel. You have our thanks, healer, for helping to even the odds in this conflict. Consider yourself fortunate that you had our protection too.'

Nediah turned slowly to look at Kyndra. 'The meeting of their minds?' he repeated. 'You can't mean—?'

'Master Nediah?' came a woman's voice. 'What's going on here? Why are you—' She broke off at Anohin's baleful glare. Recognizing the voice, Kyndra looked up and saw Master Juna, the Wielder who had taken over Rush's classes. 'Nediah?' Juna asked again, her eyes travelling over the Nerian. 'What are you doing with *them*? The Madness is—'

This time it was the woman beside Caendred who moved. She bared her teeth and a knife of moonlight appeared in her fist. Then she lunged forward and slashed it across Juna's throat.

But the Wielder was too quick. She jumped back out of reach and the knife left a thin trail of blood on her skin. A silver glow enveloped her.

'Take her down,' Anohin said contemptuously and a dozen Nerian rushed Juna, who threw out a barrage of Lunar strikes. She managed to injure a couple, but Kyndra knew it was useless.

'Nediah!' Juna screamed as a blast of energy hurled her to the floor. 'Help me!'

Nediah's face was terrible. He let out a sob and tried to rush to her aid, but three men caught him roughly across the chest and held him back. Juna let out one last shriek and then her shield collapsed and the Nerian were on her like a pack of wild dogs.

Shaking, Kyndra turned away, only to look straight into Anohin's eyes. The Yadin smiled at her and then with a shouted command swept up the Nerian and advanced down the corridor with Kyndra and Nediah penned in their midst.

They encountered dozens more victims of the Madness and the killing continued relentlessly. Blood flecked the Nerian's faces and Kyndra looked for remorse in their eyes, but all she saw was fervour and a terrible, determined joy.

They met their first concerted resistance just before they reached the atrium. It was led by Alandred, and Kyndra was hugely relieved to see him – it meant that at least some Wielders had escaped the Madness. His craggy face was creased with fear and Lunar light sheathed his body. There was a shout behind Kyndra and then a hand grabbed her shoulder and pulled her back. Caendred leapt past, straight into Alandred's path. 'Brother,' he growled. 'It's been too long.'

Kyndra watched Alandred's fear harden into rage. 'I have no brother,' he spat, his bulging eyes looking as demented as Caendred's. The silver light strengthened around his body and Caendred called upon his own power to shield him too. Shining and evenly matched, the brothers faced each other like armoured knights squared off for a duel. As they began to fight, each holding a pulsing fistful of splinters, other Nerian leapt into the fray, engaging those behind Alandred. Kyndra found herself pushed further back, away from the fighting.

Blood began to streak robes and skin, dripping from gashed faces. The sharp reek of burned flesh – so morbidly familiar to Kyndra – rose from the melee. Anohin and Kait held back, letting the bulk of the Nerian loose on the Council's Wielders. The fifty or so rebels attacked in a bestial pack, their blows driven by the promise of a freedom long denied. Slowly the Wielders gave ground, edging back towards the great entrance hall and dragging their injured with them. Sensing victory, the Nerian's onslaught intensified until at last the Wielders turned and broke for the atrium.

The first thing Kyndra saw upon entering the now shadow-draped hall was Loricus. The councilman spearheaded a phalanx of Wielders, behind which Alandred's broken group recovered. Loricus' face was black and the eyes he turned on Kyndra full of hatred. She unwittingly took a step back, such was the force emanating from that gaze.

'Thank you for bringing me the Nerian,' the councilman said to her. 'I would never have been able to defeat them on their own ground, but this –' he swept a hand at the open space around them – 'this is my field.'

'Where are the rest of your Wielders?' Anohin called then, striding forward. 'Surely you can't expect to rout us with so few?'

'An unexpected hindrance,' Loricus agreed coldly. 'But most of these are Solars. I don't see quite as many in your ranks.'

'The morning hasn't yet come, councilman,' Caendred shouted. 'And you will fall before it does.'

'Silence.'

It was Helira. The wizened old woman strode wearily out into the centre of the hall to stand next to Loricus. Brégenne was with her and so profound a relief flooded Kyndra that she wanted to cry. Brégenne was all right. Both women looked as if they hadn't slept, but the circles surrounding Helira's eyes were deeper. Her face seemed wholly composed of veins and shadows.

'What do you do here?' Helira asked Loricus, gesturing to the battle-ready Wielders ranged behind him.

'I should think it perfectly clear, Lady Helira,' Loricus answered. 'There is an uprising to be put down.'

'What about the girl?' Helira pointed a claw-like hand at Kyndra. 'Have you forgotten her?'

'She has made her choice,' Loricus answered. When the old woman didn't reply, he said with a raise of his eyebrows, 'Come,

Helira. Has age finally stolen your wits? You must have realized by now what she is, what she will become.'

Helira's tongue had just begun to form an affront when her gaze met Kyndra's and the words died. Kyndra looked into the old woman's faded eyes and, as she stared, their colour deepened into blue midnight, becoming depthless and cold, until it was the madman Kierik that gazed out at her from the councilwoman's face.

Kyndra blinked and broke the gaze in the same moment that Helira gasped. Kyndra shook her head. There was no madman, no piercing scrutiny, only an old woman, clutching her shaking hands to her face. Helira had never looked so small to Kyndra. Her hair was scraped up too tightly and the red-slashed robes hung on her thin frame. Kyndra tried to concentrate on those things, but Kierik's eyes would not leave her alone. They were there in the brief darkness behind each blink, asking her, acknowledging her.

'What are you?' Helira said, horror rasping her voice. The atrium was now completely silent. Kyndra stood with the bloodied Nerian behind her and Loricus' hostile Wielders in front. Caught between the two, she felt intensely alone. It was Brenwym all over again, the whole town arrayed against her while the Breaking rained down chaos upon them all.

Loricus smiled at her. 'Why don't you tell her, Starborn?' he said.

29

The walls resounded with her laughter.

In a silent hall full of silent people, all of whom stared at her in open shock, Kyndra laughed. It was a dark noise, and reminded her of the time she'd stood brazen under the crystal ceiling and laughed at Realdon Shune. That man had made outrageous claims too, chiefly that the Sartyan Empire could be resisted. *For how long?* she'd asked mockingly, sweeping out a hand through a ray of sunlight, feeling it upon her skin. *Will you sit behind these walls until the empire covers all Acre like a fetid sea? What then? The tide will not stay out forever.*

Now she stared at the two before her and their Wielders behind. She stared at the opaque black walls and the high, indifferent windows through which the stars could still be seen. Much was lost, many perished, but through her efforts Solinaris had survived.

No, Kyndra thought desperately, pushing Kierik's overbearing presence away, *I am not you.*

'No,' she said aloud and took several steps forward. Helira drew back. 'You really believe this,' Kyndra said wonderingly, looking at her nervous face. 'It's crazy. I don't have any power, I failed the test twice.'

'Yes,' Loricus said. 'And you would continue to fail it, at least until the madman dies.'

'Madman,' Kyndra muttered. She raised her voice. 'You mean Kierik?' When Loricus nodded, she said, 'What's he got to do with me being . . . with what you claim?'

'Only a single Starborn can exist at any one time,' Helira answered her, thin fingers clasped tightly. 'Kierik's mind and power may be lost, but that doesn't change what he is. While he lives, you cannot inherit.' She paused, evidently thinking it through for the first time. 'It explains how you are able to survive such blasts of cosmosethic energy. Even in this state, you have some resistance.'

'The situation is irregular,' Loricus cut in. 'Starborn do not usually lose their minds to age or infirmity.' His hazel eyes swept over the Nerian, lingering on Anohin's face. 'The madman's fate was engineered many years ago. He must have had enemies. As to how he gave them the opportunity to strike, and why he was unable to prevent their actions, we remain ignorant.'

Kyndra stared at the councilman, wondering how much he knew. Was Loricus aware of Medavle's role in Kierik's downfall? Did he realize just how far Kierik had gone to end the killing? She grimaced at the paradox: killing to end killing. Although Kierik's use of the Yadin had backfired, she reminded herself, thinking of the madman's blackened cheeks. There was always a price.

Standing alone between the two opposing forces, Kyndra suddenly understood why the Nerian existed and why they had endured a stunted life in the Deep. A group of people brought together by shared knowledge, united in the conviction that they were right. She looked at the smudged, resolute faces behind her. The truth was powerful, they'd said, and important enough to uphold through the years, to defend from indifference. It was the vow of fealty she had taken. Not only did the Nerian honour Kierik's sacrifice, they *acknowledged* it. They bore it as a matter of fact.

'Enough of this,' Helira said loudly. She straightened her back. 'The girl must take a Wielder's Oath. I see no other recourse.'

Loricus looked at her sharply, but said nothing.

'What's a Wielder's Oath?' Kyndra asked, sensing she would not like the answer.

'Simply that you will bind yourself into the service of the citadel,' Helira told her. 'You will dedicate your life to the furtherance of Naris and to her ruling Council. You will never bring harm here.'

Two vows in one night, Kyndra thought. This, she knew, was the oath Kierik had thrice refused to swear, each time he had appeared before the Sentheon; it was the root of their distrust of him. For the first time, Kyndra felt an unwelcome kinship with the man who had once perhaps been the most powerful individual in the world.

'Why must I swear an oath,' she asked, 'if I can't even use this power you believe I have?'

'You cannot use it only so long as the madman lives,' Loricus said, 'and Kierik is old. Even Starborn are mortal.'

'You think he'll die soon?'

'Who can say?' Helira answered. 'Perhaps he'll pass in your lifetime, perhaps not. Without the ability to become a true Starborn, your own life may be as short as an ordinary person's.'

Kyndra clenched her fists against the cold rising in her

stomach. She drew a breath with difficulty. 'You are telling me that I have to stay here and dedicate my life to Naris, to a place where I've been tortured and kept prisoner, *just in case* Kierik dies? A man who's lived for centuries?'

'You will be given certain freedoms,' Helira said. 'Supervised, of course.'

'What about my family?'

There was a pause and then Helira said, 'You must sever all ties with your home. You will live here, be properly instructed.'

'Instructed?' The cold wave of fear and anger rose higher, closing over her. 'I am not one of you. You've said so yourself. There is no one here who could teach me anything.'

Silence answered her. Brégenne and Nediah looked strange to Kyndra, as if they had only lent her their familiarity.

'Once you take the oath,' Helira said finally, 'you are bound by its terms. You must swear before all gathered.'

Kyndra looked challengingly at her. 'And if I don't?'

The old woman returned her gaze, unflinching now. 'Then you will die. Here.'

While Kyndra stood frozen, the hall erupted. She saw Brégenne confront Helira, shock in her face. Nediah seemed ready to leap to her defence, but Kait clamped a warning hand on his arm. Kyndra heard protest in the hall, even from Loricus' Wielders – maybe she had some allies in Naris after all. Others, however, stood adamant. Kyndra spotted Hebrin, haggard but silent. She watched agreement blossom in the archivist's pale eyes and looked away.

She hadn't meant to meet Alandred's eyes, but the Master of Novices stood at Loricus' shoulder. The condescension he'd always worn before in her presence wasn't there. Now his face was troubled and more serious than Kyndra had ever seen it.

When their eyes met for that one second, it was the Wielder who looked away first.

'Quiet!' Helira cried. The hall subsided, but the atmosphere had changed and the silence wasn't as deep as before. Both the Wielders and the Nerian shifted restlessly.

'So I have no choice,' Kyndra said to Helira.

The old woman's face was grave. 'There is always a choice,' she said.

Kyndra let her gaze drift out over the crowd. Their features blurred together, much like they had at her Inheritance Ceremony. She could choose to die. She would be free of it, at least: free from Kierik, the Nerian and from the citadel with its brutal justice. She would be free from the guilt of leaving Brenwym to its fate and from the pain of losing her two best friends.

But as these thoughts chased each other through her head, she saw Reena's face in her mind. Her mother's voice seemed to ring in her ears and the familiar sound of it gave Kyndra heart. She blinked and the blur of the crowd resolved into people. She saw Brégenne's wide, white eyes and Nediah's darker, apprehensive ones.

'Death is not a choice,' she said to Helira.

'So all the young believe,' the old woman answered. 'But if you had seen as many years as I have, you would understand that there is always a choice and that death is the last and greatest.'

'Enough.' Loricus advanced a few steps towards Kyndra. 'I offered you the chance to work with me,' the councilman said to her, extending his hand. 'If you do as Helira says, that offer remains open.'

Helira slowly turned her head to look at Loricus, eyes narrow and questioning.

'Swear the oath,' Loricus continued, 'and stand beside me. Then when the time comes and everything is as it should be, you may ask a boon. Consider, Kyndra. I won't keep you from seeing your family.'

He was choosing his words carefully, Kyndra thought. Judging from Helira's uncertain face, she knew nothing of Loricus' plans for power. *So this is the reason he told me, why he wants me on his side. He thinks I'm a—* Even in the privacy of her mind, Kyndra couldn't say the word, not when it meant her.

'You don't have to do this,' she told the hall. 'I've never wanted to hurt anyone. I don't want power, or authority. Or to take Kierik's place,' she added to the Nerian. They alone had been unsurprised when Loricus told everyone what she was. Kyndra didn't want to think too closely about what that meant.

'You are not a full Starborn,' Loricus countered. 'You are untouched by the power and its corruption. But once it marks you, it will set you apart forever. It is the price that those who walk the void must pay.'

And it seemed to Kyndra that the hall darkened at his words. She shivered and closed her eyes against the truth, knowing it came for her. When she'd gathered enough shreds of courage to open them again, she saw Loricus watching, waiting for her answer.

'No.'

A collective sigh passed over those gathered and Loricus' face tightened. 'You refuse me?'

Kyndra drew breath, feeling the strength of her conviction waver. If she chose to side with Loricus and the councilman successfully seized power, she could see her family again . . . Her heart beat hard in her chest, as if it knew it could soon stop forever.

'I do,' she whispered.

Helira looked up at the slices of windowed sky, which were only just beginning to pale. And then she began to glow. She cupped her hands in front of her, as if she held a ball, and Lunar energy, like ragged silk, flowed down her arms. Something grew between her palms: a sleek, silver head, featureless save for two black eyes that compelled Kyndra to look into them. The thing pulled itself into existence, drawing more energy, and Helira trembled as she struggled to hold it back. A crack split below its eyes and a mouth opened, full of tongues that writhed like tentacles. Reptilian claws scratched at the air, drew back into light then re-emerged, scrabbling more vigorously.

It was hideous and Kyndra stared at it, unable to escape the hypnotic pull of its eyes. She sensed something terrible about Helira's creation and knew she would die in the next few moments. The test's searing lances were nothing to this. Its purpose was solely to destroy.

She heard shouting, but couldn't turn her head. 'No, Helira!' someone yelled and Kyndra thought it was Brégenne. '*Executis* are forbidden by our own laws. If you lose control of it—'

'I will not,' Helira barked, but her brow was beaded with sweat. And then the thing broke from her grasp with a wail and screamed towards Kyndra.

A low boom shook the hall and sparks stung Kyndra's face, as a shining lattice expanded around her. The creature had broken against it, but was swiftly reforming. Loosed from the grip of its eyes, Kyndra looked around.

Brégenne shone like the winter moon. Her arms were thrown forward, and though they shook, the determination in her face did not. She bared her teeth at the creature, as it threw itself against the lattice. The shield held, but Kyndra saw the effort it cost Brégenne. She could not hold it back forever, not with morning drawing ever closer.

Helira stared at Brégenne, mouth twisted as if the Wielder's interference was a mere irritation. 'Restrain her,' she snapped.

Loricus clicked his fingers and several Lunar Wielders broke from the phalanx, but before they reached Brégenne, chaos erupted. The Nerian obviously considered the stalemate at an end and bolts of power flew across the hall, smashing into the front rank of Loricus' Wielders. Kyndra watched Caendred spring from behind Kait to hurl a cascade of Lunar fire.

Helira ignored the surrounding conflict. She extended both hands in front of her and clenched them, and the creature gnashed more viciously against Brégenne's silver bars. Kyndra heard a gasp and saw the blind Wielder down on one knee, teeth gritted. Her chest heaved and the creature's tongues latched on to the silver bars and began to prise them apart. If it reached her, Kyndra knew she was dead.

It was all-out battle. The Wielders had recovered enough to counter the Nerian's attack and there were screams as Lunar bolts struck flesh, burning through cloth and skin. Here and there, golden shields erupted and Kyndra guessed that some of Loricus' Wielders must be using *akans*, too, while they waited for the sun to rise.

And then she saw the novices. A group of them had pressed themselves back against the wall, but now they came forward to aid the Wielders. With a shock, Kyndra saw Irilin, ablaze with light, her tiny arms held protectively in front of Shika and Gareth, who was busy pulling something from behind his belt. Shika made to stop him, but Gareth shook his friend off and stuffed his hand into a dull, black metal gauntlet that looked unerringly like the one Kyndra had longed to put on in the archives. She watched his face tighten briefly in pain, but then it cleared and Gareth clenched his fist inside the gauntlet.

A weakness in the Wielders' line broke under the Nerian's onslaught and a man blasted his way through the gap. He smiled when he saw Irilin. But Gareth pushed Irilin aside, lifted his gauntleted fist and swept it through the air – and the man from the Nerian was thrown screaming to smash into the atrium wall. He did not get up again. Gareth looked wonderingly at his own hand then gave a yell and leapt unreservedly into the fray, slashing the gauntlet to left and right, but Kyndra noticed that each strike was less powerful than the one before.

Kait spun into her peripheral vision and then Anohin, whose white robes flew in the wind of his passage. 'For Kierik!' he cried. 'Nerian, this is your moment! Take back what was yours!' And the Nerian's attacks became ferocious. The cold marble beneath their feet began to warm, the air shimmered and more Wielders fell.

Kyndra watched it all through her thinning silver bars. The faces of the Nerian were twisted in rage and triumph. After so many years spent in the Deep, they fought with the strength of slaves promised freedom. Naris's remaining Lunar Wielders – already exhausted from a night of trying to control the Breaking – were no match for them.

Loricus' expression was terrible to behold. When the Nerian's concerted efforts broke his phalanx apart, he drew out two glowing rods – weapons that must also have come from the archives. In his hands, they lengthened into whips and the councilman began laying about him, his rage easily matching that of the Nerian's. A black-banded woman shot a fistful of darts at him, but Loricus flicked the whip, swept them aside and then he brought back his arm and lashed the woman. She caught the blow full in the face and screamed, blood pouring from her ruined eyes. Sickened, Kyndra looked away.

The tongues of Helira's beast were now tearing apart the lattice faster than Brégenne could knit it together. Her skin was ashen, both knees hard on the stone. And then one tongue smashed aside a silver bar and wrapped itself around Kyndra's wrist. She shrieked. It was pain beyond anything she'd ever known, beyond even the test. Needles pierced her skin like fangs, pumping agony into her arm. She thrashed in the creature's hold, but the tongue just latched tighter, drawing another shriek from her lungs.

Blackness gathered at the corners of her eyes and pinpricks of light glimmered at her across a distance. Kyndra knew them for what they were now – the as-yet nameless stars. If their power was really hers, why wouldn't they aid her now? *Because of Kierik. Kierik is still their master.*

But the madman is weak. She wasn't sure whether that last thought was hers or not. It didn't matter – Kierik *was* weak. The pain of the *executis* receded as she probed the familiar black wall in her mind. Again it stopped her as effectively as solid stone, holding her back. But what if it wasn't really a wall at all, but a person? What if she was sensing Kierik himself?

Mentally, Kyndra tapped at the black wall . . . and a fragment came away. It wasn't the stars, but it *was* something she could use. She watched dispassionately as black ice crackled down her arms and she chipped further at the wall. She thought she heard an agonized cry from somewhere beyond her, but she ignored it. The ice sank into her chest, burying her fear and her pain, even her anger.

It shattered what remained of Brégenne's shield and – when it touched the creature – the thing burst into powdery light. Helira staggered and her eyes were huge as she looked on Kyndra. Obeying some dark instinct, Kyndra extended her hand, her lips curving into a mirthless smile. The dark ice dripped from her fingers and flowed across the marble floor. It covered Helira's feet, climbed up her legs and caressed her arms like a lover. Then it entered her body through her open, shrieking mouth. Kyndra watched emotionlessly as the old woman's screams ceased. For a moment, Helira stood still, rooted to the floor by the dark tendril. Then blood began to seep from her eyes, her nose and ears. It ran in rivulets down her face, soaking into her silver robes.

Wonderingly, Kyndra turned her palm up – the black substance coated her fingers and somewhere, far below her, that voice was still crying out its agony. Then Helira crumpled like an empty sack and Kyndra switched her gaze to Loricus.

'Stop.' The command was Anohin's. Kyndra looked at the Yadin and Anohin took a step back, despite the resolve in his face. 'You have gone too far, Kyndra. This should not have been possible. You will kill Kierik!'

She said nothing, filled with the brutal awe of power.

'And you could destroy everyone here,' Anohin said desperately. 'What you call the Madness is caused by the shock of your mind colliding with Kierik's, and that's been happening every time you've inherited one of his memories. Starborn cannot coexist. If you stop hurting him, I can explain it all to you – I promise.'

'Why should I stop?' Kyndra asked. The ice was in her throat too, so that it sounded as if she spoke with multiple voices. 'He is in my way. Once he is dead, all this will end.' The gaze she fixed on Anohin was utterly chill. 'And he deserves to die for what he's done.'

The Yadin's expression darkened. 'He is damaged, Kyndra. Defenceless. You'll kill a defenceless man?'

'Isn't that what he did to your people?' Kyndra said, but Anohin's words had caused a crack to spider through the black layer that encased her. *I don't want to hurt anyone else,* she thought. *So many are dead already because of me.* But the cold power fought to keep her – as long as she held on to it, no pain could reach her.

'Kyndra.' Brégenne knelt on the floor, weakened by her struggle with Helira's creature. 'Hurting those that hurt you won't bring comfort.' The blind woman's eyes glowed brightly, as they looked into Kyndra's own. 'And vengeance is a prison. Don't make my mistake.'

The crack widened and Kyndra stared through it at Brégenne's face beyond. *No,* she thought and forced the cracks wider, causing black to slough from her body like dried clay.

This is not me! With a scream of effort, Kyndra tore herself away from the chill, dark wall and, as she'd feared it would, agonizing pain seized her. She retched and the room spun and Kyndra fell to her knees, thinking she would vomit. Heat rushed into her, boiling her insides, and her chest tightened so that she couldn't breathe.

Then Anohin was there. He placed a cool hand that glowed silver against Kyndra's forehead and the pain in her body lessened.

'Anohin!' Kait cried then. 'Sef's talking to me across the bond. She said something's happened to Kierik – he's not in his room.' Her face clouded. 'And Evan is dead.'

'*No!*' Anohin clenched his fists and his feverish gaze roamed

440

the hall. Bodies lay here and there, some belonging to the
Nerian, but a great deal more to the Wielders of Naris – a large
contingent had already yielded, comprising mostly novices and
a few gold-robed masters. Only one pocket was still fighting.

'Come.' The Yadin hauled Kyndra roughly to her feet. 'This
is your doing and you will put it right.' His fierce eyes roved
over the scene of battle. 'Nerian!' he called. 'Hold the atrium.
I go to our master!'

'Brégenne!' Kyndra cried and stumbled as Anohin pulled
her towards a narrow corridor at the back of the hall. A shout
went up from those Wielders still fighting and they dashed
after the small group fleeing for the corridor. The Nerian
flanked them on every side, but a black-banded man went
down and a gap opened in the Nerian's defence. Then Caendred was there, darting forward to fill the man's place and
buying time for Anohin and the others to escape. Cords flew
from his fingers like silver spider webs to tangle around the
nearest Wielders, who cursed and spat at the sticky strings.
Caendred grinned and cast a handful of lances, but they
bounced harmlessly off a Lunar wall that had appeared out of
nowhere. Then other walls sprang up around Caendred until
he was enclosed in a shimmering box.

'You're not going anywhere,' Alandred said, stepping out of
the crowd, a tiny replica of the silver box glowing between his
hands.

Kait shouted and made to rush forward, but Nediah
grabbed her arms, tugging her away from the brothers.

The box shattered and Caendred reappeared, fists aglow
with flickering energy. At that moment, the brothers were so
alike that Kyndra couldn't tell the difference between them.
Then a bend in the corridor hid them from view.

'What about the others?' she gasped at Anohin.

'They can look out for themselves,' the Yadin said harshly. 'The atrium is taken.'

Not if Loricus has any say, Kyndra thought. She felt weak from her use of whatever dark power she'd channelled and Anohin had her wrist in an iron grip. She was forced to run with him down the passage, Nediah and Kait hard on her heels.

'Anohin, the councilman will follow us,' Kait panted, as if she had read Kyndra's mind. 'The drop behind the kitchens is too risky.'

'I don't care,' Anohin growled back. 'We'll take the quickest way.'

He led them through the citadel at an exhausting pace. Initially, Kyndra thought the Wielders were right on their heels, but the Nerian had done their work well. *Everything was planned*, she thought. *All they needed was me.*

Anohin stopped at an unremarkable piece of wall, which melted at his touch. He crouched and crawled into the hole beyond. Thankfully, the space quickly opened out into a steep tunnel and Kyndra placed one hand on the wall for guidance, straining to see by the small flame that hovered over Anohin's head.

'You used me,' she said to the Yadin's back. 'You knew that if I came face to face with Kierik, the shock of our meeting would strike down dozens of Wielders.'

The tunnel widened further and Anohin yanked her roughly up to run beside him. The conjured flame cast flickering shadows across his face. 'Yes,' he said stonily. 'The Nerian owe you a debt of gratitude.'

'But those people were innocent!' Kyndra said, hiding her

terrible guilt beneath her anger. The plan might have been Anohin's, but he wasn't the one who'd destroyed those Wielders' minds.

'How conveniently you forget the agonies that they and their Council put you through.' Anohin looked at her. 'But justice is never without cost.'

'You've known all along what I am.' Kyndra forced herself to say it. 'That's why you made me take your vow – so that if I came into my power, I couldn't hurt Kierik. Well, it didn't work, did it?' she said harshly, donning her anger like armour. 'It turned out that I *could* hurt him and I did hurt him, Anohin. I could hear him screaming.'

The Yadin's grip tightened to the point where it forced a yelp of pain from her lips. 'You knew,' she continued relentlessly. 'So why didn't you tell me when you had the chance?'

'Why would I tell you?' Anohin snarled at her. 'I needed you quiet, compliant. You have no idea of the danger you pose. Telling you would hardly make you less of a threat. And you had the facts in front of you – you asked me all the right questions. I couldn't believe you hadn't worked it out.'

Kyndra realized that she hadn't *wanted* to work it out. Anohin was right – she'd already guessed that a link existed between herself and the Madness. She'd finally grasped that the visions were memories, and that someone had tried to kill her covertly with the *akan*. And then there was Loricus with his offer of an alliance. As a Starborn, she was a major threat to his coup and he'd want to make an ally of her – after he'd failed to get rid of her quietly, of course.

She only had herself to blame for her blindness.

'It shouldn't be possible for Starborn to coexist,' Anohin said, still hauling her bodily along. 'Your situation is utterly unique.' He increased his pace and Kyndra struggled to keep up. 'About a month before you came here, Kierik started to decline – he grew weaker and was more confused than usual. It took me a while to work out exactly what was happening to him. When a Starborn comes of age – as you have done – they begin to inherit the memories of their immediate predecessor, along with the names of the stars. Kierik once said it forms an unbroken link back to the very first Starborn that ever lived. But you and he are different.'

He spared Kyndra a penetrating glance. 'I don't know how you came to be. Perhaps the laws of the cosmos no longer consider Kierik a Starborn. Every time you inherited a memory from him, or some threat gave you cause to reach out unknowingly to the stars, the impact of your mind colliding with Kierik's caused a shockwave strong enough to harm those nearby. Not knowing any better, the Wielders called it the Madness after the mental deterioration it produced.' The Yadin paused. 'Eventually, I realized I could use the situation to my advantage.'

Kyndra suddenly remembered Helira's face and the old woman's raspy screams echoed once more in her ears. *I killed her.* Revulsion curdled her stomach, almost too awful to bear, except that underneath it, something dark ground its teeth in satisfaction. Kyndra recoiled from it. 'You have what you wanted, then,' she said aloud, hearing the bitterness in her voice. Anohin was no better than Loricus – both would use her to further their own ends. 'Why do you need me?'

'To *help* Kierik,' Anohin said, his eyes hard. 'We will search for a way to heal him. You might be a travesty of a Starborn, but you can still be of use.' He ignored Kyndra's attempt to speak. 'And then, when Kierik and I are together again and he is restored to his rightful place, we will hunt down Medavle and bring him, likewise, to justice.'

30

The moment she neared the Nerian's complex, Kyndra sensed something amiss.

Anohin's anxiety was palpable and Kyndra felt her own heart beat faster in response. They had taken a quicker path to the Deep than the one Kait had led her down earlier and now, barely an hour since leaving the atrium, their passage fractured into a series of shafts. Anohin went straight to a black fissure in the floor, crouched and dropped inside. Kyndra peered cautiously over the edge and the light showed her a smooth-sided chute, which seemed to level out about two metres down.

'Sit with your legs over the hole and let go,' Kait said shortly. Her face was strained and smudged with dirt – she obviously shared Anohin's worry. Kyndra did as she said and, after a brief but exhilarating slide, found herself in a wide passage. Anohin was waiting for her and again he seized her wrist and dragged her off down the tunnel. Thumps sounded from behind, as Kait and then Nediah landed too.

The air began to smell more lived in and Anohin broke into a run. 'Sef! Bryn!' he shouted. He turned right down the corridor that led to Kierik's room and stopped sharply. A body lay face down on the floor. Beyond it, the door stood open. 'No,'

Anohin panted. He let go of Kyndra and dashed up to the room, almost tripping over the body in his haste.

The madman's room was an empty wreck. Split pillows spilled their feathers like snow over the broken furniture and the desk was battered and upended. The chair had lost one of its legs. Anohin gazed at the chaos, grey eyes wild.

Kait elbowed her way past Kyndra. 'Anohin.' Tentatively she laid a hand on the Yadin's shoulder. 'It might not be what it looks like.'

Faster than seemed possible, Anohin spun, grabbed Kait by the neck and slammed her against the wall. Kait struggled for air and her legs kicked uselessly, as the Yadin gripped her by the throat. 'You are wrong,' he spat. 'This is *his* doing!'

'Let her go!' Nediah yelled, springing forward. Anohin bared his teeth at the Wielder, but removed his hand and Kait slid down the wall. Nediah knelt beside her, as she coughed and gasped for air. Her neck was livid with the marks of the Yadin's fingers.

Anohin ignored them both and his eyes were terrible: burning, sunken pits that Kyndra couldn't meet. Deliberately, it seemed, the Yadin stepped on the body outside the door. 'Evan,' Kait rasped. She brushed Nediah's hand aside, shuffled over to the body and began to turn it.

Anohin didn't look at her. 'Leave him,' he said coldly. 'He failed in his duty.' He turned to Kyndra. 'You. Stay with me.'

The Yadin reminded her forcefully of Medavle, as he glared at her. 'Do you know where Kierik is?' she asked cautiously, afraid of provoking him further.

Anohin tipped up his face and sniffed the air. 'Medavle's stink is easy to follow. If we find him, we find Kierik.'

They came across another body shortly after they'd left the

main corridor, turning into a narrow passage that climbed upwards into the mountain. But Anohin didn't stop. Kyndra looked back to see Nediah and Kait kneeling beside it, checking for a pulse, before the Yadin increased his pace and left them behind. Just when Kyndra thought they would surely lose them, she heard hurried footsteps and both Wielders emerged from the gloom. Anohin was a white shape, surging ahead.

Kyndra lost track of time. Her legs ached from their earlier flight and she began to stumble. Desperately thirsty, she stared into the darkness, thinking of underground streams and the hollow trickle of liquid on stone, but the tunnel remained dry and continued to climb mercilessly upwards.

When the unexpected noise came, it was not the dripping of water. The slope had begun to level out and the low ceiling curved away from their heads. Anohin stood motionless several yards ahead, listening to the whine that curled from the throat of a woman lying across their path. As she neared, Kyndra realized there were words interspersed between each moan of pain.

'Sef,' Anohin said tonelessly, looking down at the woman.

'He was . . . too strong.'

'Evidently.'

'Sorry, Mast—' The rest of the word ended in a strangled gasp as Anohin calmly placed his boot on the woman's neck and began to press down.

'Anohin, no.' There were tears in Kait's voice. One arm held Nediah back, but the other stretched out towards the Yadin. 'Please don't. Sef's my attuned partner – we've been bonded for years.'

Anohin ignored her, his eyes never leaving the woman who

thrashed weakly on the ground. 'I don't want to hear your apologies,' he said to her. Sef's eyes bulged. She tried to speak, but Anohin pressed harder and the words died with her. Only when her struggles had ceased did he remove his boot. His gaze raked over the three gathered behind him, daring them to say something. No one did, though Kait's tear-streaked face spoke plainly. Anohin turned away and Kyndra stared at his back, horrified by his heedless cruelty. He'd murdered a woman in cold blood right before their eyes, seemingly without a second thought.

Kait's quiet sobs accompanied them as they followed in the Yadin's wake. Kyndra tried desperately to forget the image of Anohin's boot crushing the woman's fragile neck, but she couldn't because a dreadful part of her whispered that she was no different. *I'm not like him,* she thought back fiercely, *I couldn't kill anyone like that.*

But you wanted to, there in the atrium. You were ready to kill a defenceless man.

Kyndra remembered her own words, spoken under the influence of that terrible, icy power. She *had* wanted to kill Kierik – a man as helpless as the woman Anohin had just murdered. She felt sickened. No matter what he'd done in the past, he didn't deserve such a death. No one did.

The freshening of the air was a merciful distraction. Occasional gusts of wind cooled Kyndra's brow, a wind that tasted of morning. A renewed desperation to be free of the mountain seized her, propelling her tired legs towards the light that crept stealthily over the walls, sliding its fingers down into the earth. And though she feared what she would find at the tunnel's end, her pace did not falter.

The light grew brighter and Anohin let his flame fade. They rounded a tight bend and there was the sky, a still morning grey. Kyndra clambered out of the mountain and looked around. She stood on a small plateau on Naris's western face. Piles of rock and shattered stones were the only evidence that the Breaking had left behind. The sun had not yet climbed above the mountain's peak and the rugged area lay in shadow. Steep cliffs fell away on three sides, as if some great hand had torn away the earth there. And beyond the misty chasm, split asunder by the Breaking, the land sloped up into a litany of peaks. Their white-capped summits marched to the horizon.

At first the plateau seemed empty, but then Kyndra caught movement at its far edge. Someone stood on the dangerous rim: a man, his face turned outwards to gaze across the airy space.

A stone crunched beneath Kyndra's boot and the figure turned.

It was Kierik.

Janus surfaced slowly from a groggy, delirious sleep. His head ached and he felt drained, exhausted from straining against the Lunar chain that bound him. Disgust at his carelessness had sharpened to a terror of dying here alone.

There it was again. A noise. Janus liked to think it was boots on stone. He moistened his dry tongue to call out and managed a rasping squeak. He swallowed painfully and tried again. He thought about dying undiscovered in the dark and shouted louder, over and over, until the footsteps came closer.

He heard a voice, no, *felt* a voice calling his name. Confused, he concentrated and the voice grew stronger. Janus gasped. It was coming along the bond. The call was Brégenne's. Tearful with relief, he answered, sending the woman a picture of his surroundings. Brégenne's presence comforted him, though he would have scorned it a few days ago. Voices, real this time, reached his ears and light threw his trussed shadow against the far wall.

'There!'

Six Wielders materialized at the edge of the light and swiftly crossed to his pillar. Janus felt a ripple of surprise. Two held Brégenne prisoner, each gripping a coil of glowing, golden chain. He looked down at his own chain and flushed uncomfortably.

'So there you are.'

Lord Loricus came to stand over Janus, his resplendent robes ashen with dust and a look of disgust on his face. 'Did a Nerian dog do this to you?'

Janus hung his head. The thought he was trying so desperately to avoid wormed its way to the surface: the Nerian had been planning to invade the citadel and he, instead of issuing a warning, had passed the hours trussed up like game. Shame bubbled in his stomach. If only he'd been more alert.

'Someone untie him.'

One of the Solars holding Brégenne merely looked at the chain and it vanished, making Janus feel more ashamed than ever. He was like a useless novice. Left to scramble to his feet unaided, he made to brush himself down, but Loricus seized his chin, jerking his head up painfully.

Janus stared at the floor.

'Look at me,' Loricus said softly in the voice he used when they were alone and Janus glanced up. The councilman's face was too close. All he could see were the hazel eyes and the disappointment that muddied them. 'All this time you were here,' Loricus said, still in the soft voice. 'You alone could have warned us of the Nerian's uprising. We could have saved some of our strength instead of exhausting every Lunar Wielder on the Breaking. But you did not have the competence. I am disappointed, Janus.'

'Please, Loricus. I tried.'

'You'll address me by my title.' Still he held Janus' chin.

'Leave the boy alone,' Brégenne's voice chimed from the shadows.

'Silence,' Loricus snapped. He didn't turn his head.

Humiliating tears threatened Janus' cheeks. 'Please, my Lord.' He swallowed hard. 'I've only ever wanted to help you.'

He thought he heard Brégenne speak again, but the Wielder's words were smothered by one of her guards.

'I know you have,' Loricus said pleasantly, coldly. He brushed Janus' face with the back of his hand. 'But my patience is not infinite. You owe Brégenne your life, Janus. Think on that. It is the only reason we brought the traitor along.'

Despite being unable to see, Brégenne looked serene and unconcerned, and Janus wished he could muster the same control.

'Give him something to drink before he falls over,' Loricus said dismissively, turning away. Janus took the skin thrust at him and drank greedily, the water pouring down his throat like liquid life.

'We have a way to go yet,' Lord Loricus told him. 'I hope you can keep up, as you may yet have a chance to redeem yourself.'

'Where are we going?' Janus asked hesitantly, wiping his mouth.

'To finish what we started.'

*

'No!' Anohin yelled. He broke into a heedless run, dashing across the uneven ground with arms outstretched, as if to snatch Kierik before he fell.

A shimmer in the air was his only warning that someone waited there, unseen, and Anohin stopped short. He pulled back his right arm, attempted a desperate punch and a tremor shook the ground. Kyndra clutched at the rock wall behind her and Kierik stumbled perilously to his knees.

When she looked up, two men in white were visible, locking arms against the sky. Kyndra stared at them, mesmerized. She watched Medavle's dark eyes widen, a flood of emotions breaking clear across his face. 'I knew it,' he whispered into Anohin's glare. 'I knew you lived.'

Anohin screamed in frustration and broke the deadlock. He made to rush forward, but Medavle's arm shot out, slamming into his stomach. As the other man doubled over, Medavle's expression hardened, belying the shine of tears in his eyes. 'I am sorry, brother,' he said, looking at the wheezing Anohin, 'but I cannot let you pass.'

'We . . . are not . . . brothers,' Anohin gasped, winded. He straightened with one arm held protectively in front of his stomach. 'You are a murderer.'

Medavle shook his head. 'Murder is not my province, but his.' He gestured at Kierik crouched on the rock.

Anohin's face flushed an ugly red. 'You killed three of my people.'

'No,' Medavle said again and a grim smile shaded his lips. '*He* did most of my work for me, though I admit his methods are more final than my own.'

'You lie.'

Medavle's smile withered. 'He is dangerous, Anohin. The

Nerian do not fear him as they should. Trust allowed him to take their lives.'

'He wouldn't hurt them. He couldn't.'

'You no longer have any idea of his capabilities.' Medavle paused. 'Those hands of his, for example, are perfectly capable of crushing the breath from an unsuspecting throat.'

Anohin snarled and sprang out of Medavle's reach. 'If he is as you say, then it is *you* who made him so!'

'I haven't touched him. I merely want the bag of earth hanging around his neck.'

'And he knew it!' Anohin cried shrilly. 'That's why he fled.'

'Perhaps.' Medavle took a few steps to his right, hiding Kierik from view. He gazed at Anohin, and Kyndra shrank from the maelstrom of hurt and fury in his black eyes. 'Why?' Medavle asked the other Yadin. 'Why did you let him kill our people?'

Anohin didn't speak for several moments. When he did, his voice was bitter. 'After all this time, you still cling uselessly to the past.'

Medavle raised his fist and a sudden shock of light lit the plateau in answer. 'You think I have any choice?' he roared. When the light faded, he stood there, his broad chest heaving. 'Do you even remember them, Anohin?' he asked then, his voice much softer. 'Do you remember their faces? I see them every night in my waking, restless sleep. Tarin, Duelo, Lukas, Quent . . . Isla.' The last name emerged as a whisper. 'I cannot rest. They urge me onward. They cry for revenge.'

'It is not their revenge you pursue, but your own, Medavle,' Anohin said. 'They helped purge this world of war. They live on as . . . as keepers of the peace.'

'They are *nowhere*!' Medavle screamed. 'No more. They are

dead, gone. You weren't there to see them die, your brothers and sisters, your friends, your people. But I was. I should have died with them, as you and the Starborn planned.' His voice shook. 'You betrayed your own race, Anohin. You gave them into *his* hands and you left them to perish while you walked free.'

Anohin's face went corpse white, almost the colour of his robes. 'I was ready to die,' he shouted back. 'I would gladly have given my life to the cause of freedom.'

'Freedom,' Medavle spat. 'What has freedom done for you, Anohin? Five hundred years chained to a mindless monster, squatting in the dark. Forgive me if I scorn the word.'

Anohin's eyes blazed. He threw out a shaking arm, gesturing at Kyndra, at Kait and Nediah. '*They* have freedom. That's what matters. They and all those before them were born into a world free from tyranny. That was Kierik's vision. That's what I would have given my life for, had he allowed it.'

'You disgust me,' Medavle said, his face dark against the lightening sky. 'How have you lived with the blood of your kinsmen on your hands? *You* are the monster, Anohin. You even knew I was alive, didn't you? Yet you never sought me out, not even to exact revenge. You let me believe I was the only survivor. For years I wandered this *free* world searching for any the wind had missed. I found nothing.' He slowly closed a white-gloved fist. 'But I didn't give up. A tiny part of me is still within him, Anohin, so I knew he'd survived and I planned vengeance for all those he killed – for those voices you helped to silence.'

Medavle raised an arm and pointed at Kyndra. 'Beautiful, isn't she? Look at her, Anohin. Look at her eyes. They are the shape of my revenge.'

With a scream, Anohin lunged for Medavle, but the other

man flipped his flute into his fingers and blew a sharp note. Writhing beams wrapped Anohin's body and he struggled and bit against them. Kyndra could only stare, confused by Medavle's words.

'Oh my friend,' Medavle said, stepping closer to the bound Yadin. His laugh carried notes of hysteria. 'Even you must appreciate this flawless retribution.'

Anohin's hair hung down around his face. He shook it back and struggled harder. Medavle bent so that they were eye to eye. 'It is all to do with the ruin of the Starborn's mind,' he said.

Kyndra shut her eyes, remembering the white filaments that Kierik had inhaled when he'd gone to fetch the book from the archives. She felt their sinuous tails quieten as they settled in her mind . . . no, in Kierik's mind. She snapped her eyes open, recoiling from the Starborn's memories.

With a roar of effort, Anohin snapped his bonds. He grabbed Medavle's collar, crafting a gleaming bolt in his other hand, but Medavle snatched a fistful of cloth and bodily threw the other Yadin away. The bolt flew wide.

Anohin landed heavily and something rolled out of his robes. It was the white *akan*. Kyndra watched him scramble up, leaving the winged child where it had fallen. With a roar, he sent a volley of glowing arrows straight at Medavle's face. Medavle waved the hand that held the flute, and the arrows burst into harmless light. 'The years have made you soft,' he mocked.

Anohin's glare could have seared stone. He raised both hands and stabbed them forwards and thick, golden lances flew at Medavle. The dark-eyed Yadin deflected one of them, but the other skimmed his side, tearing his coat. Blood, shockingly red, blossomed against the white cloth. Medavle gritted his teeth and blew a long, low note. A glowing net tangled Anohin's limbs and he crashed to the ground.

Medavle was not aiming to kill, Kyndra noticed. The same could not be said of Anohin. Hatred smouldered in his eyes and he constantly darted glances at Kierik, who squatted still and quiet on the cliff edge.

'He won't jump,' Medavle said. One hand held the wound in his side. 'Not unless I tell him to.'

'What do you mean?' Anohin panted, straining against the net that bound him.

'The strands of my life force are still there,' Medavle answered. 'When I felt his mind break, I used my remaining strength to flee the citadel. Though I spent years recovering, the pain was worth it. I realized I could still feel him. I could touch that mind, though it boiled like a storm.' He made a disgusted sound in his throat. 'His madness prevented any prolonged form of control – an ironic protection. However, I hypothesized that he might be susceptible to . . . suggestion.'

Anohin's struggles had temporarily ceased. 'What sort of suggestion?'

'All manner of it,' Medavle said, taking a slow walk around the trussed Yadin. 'What do you think stops him from throwing himself over as we speak?'

Anohin's eyes widened. 'Impossible.'

'No,' Medavle said. He continued to circle Anohin, though his eyes now strayed to Kierik. 'You have no idea what touching his mind is like.' A shadow passed over his face. 'I admit this kind of control tires me. Your lucky hit is proof. But there are other ways of manipulation, Anohin, subtler ways. *She –*'

Medavle again pointed at Kyndra – 'is the result of a suggestion I planted twenty years ago.'

Kyndra felt the world fall away from her, as she gazed at Medavle without breathing. The Yadin met her eyes.

'Two decades ago, I approached the Nerian,' he said. 'I posed as an interested party. And if Anohin knew I was there, he didn't show himself.'

Kyndra frowned. 'But Anohin recognized you. Why didn't he just kill you when he had the chance?'

Medavle looked at the other Yadin. 'Perhaps because he couldn't bring himself to do it,' he said softly. 'As I cannot. We are the last of our kind.'

'Those sentiments are dead,' Anohin said coldly.

Medavle ignored him and turned back to Kyndra. 'I needed to be near the madman,' he said, picking up where he left off, 'to plant an impulse so contrary to his natural state.'

The plateau grew silent, save for the chill morning wind that stirred hair and clothes. All eyes were on Medavle. 'It took two years to manifest,' the Yadin said. 'Longer than I had hoped. But in the end the desire to escape, to sow the seeds of his demise, was too great to ignore.' He glanced at Anohin. 'I left many things to chance, and I confess I am amazed that he managed to evade his watchdog and escape the citadel.'

'An oversight,' Anohin growled, 'that was not repeated.'

'Oh it didn't need to be repeated,' Medavle said, smiling. 'The damage – apologies, Kyndra – was done. I even managed to steal that bag of earth before I left – though due to a certain airship captain's dishonesty, it didn't reach its intended recipient.' He nodded at Kyndra. 'I will rectify that soon enough.'

Kyndra took a few steps forward. 'I don't understand.' Her

gaze darted between Medavle and Kierik. The madman began a hum deep in his throat, rocking at the cliff edge.

Medavle looked at her and his dark eyes were sober. 'I am sorry that you have endured so much because of me.' He held out an arm towards Kierik. 'But today, at last, I can give you your Inheritance.'

31

Kyndra's ears rang. She blinked against the rough stone, stunned by the force of the sudden blast that had flung her across the plateau. Hoisting herself onto all fours, she looked over her shoulder. The small hole leading to the tunnel was gone and the stone was rent asunder – now light poured into the mountain through a jagged gash and debris littered the area.

Medavle climbed to his feet, his face scraped and bloody, clutching the silver flute tightly to his chest. Kyndra stood up too. Dust hung thickly and sounds of coughing reached her through the haze. When it cleared, she saw that the others were unharmed, if a little bruised. Anohin's bonds were gone, but he made no move towards Medavle. Instead he frantically searched the small plateau for Kierik. Kyndra spotted the madman first, flat on his back, thrown mercifully away from the edge of the cliff.

Loricus stepped out of the rubble, shimmering with Solar energy. His robe was torn at the shoulders and his tattoo gleamed in the dim morning. The sun had not yet cleared the mountain behind them and Naris cast its huge shadow over the plateau.

The councilman gestured and six Wielders emerged to join him. Kyndra's heart clenched when she saw that two of them held Brégenne prisoner.

'You. Keep hold of her,' Loricus instructed one gold-robed man. His eyes raked the small plateau. 'The rest of you restrain the Solars.'

As the Wielders fanned out around Nediah and Kait, Kyndra saw both of them blaze defensively gold.

'Who are you?' Loricus asked Medavle. His eyes skimmed Medavle's wound and then flicked to Anohin. 'Not friends, I see.'

Medavle's face darkened. 'I have not come this far to be stopped by the likes of you.'

'I care nothing for how far you've come,' Loricus said. 'I only want the girl.'

Kyndra took a step back and the councilman smiled at her. 'You've led us on quite a chase.' His hazel eyes flicked to the chasm. 'But there's nowhere left to run, Kyndra.'

In the next moment, a shrieking ball of light hurtled at Loricus. The councilman disappeared in its fury, robbed of even a scream, and Anohin's hands dripped with flame. He panted in the aftermath of the fireball, and the glow around him faded.

For a moment there was silence. Then a tremor rocked the plateau and Loricus stepped from the fire unmarked. He snuffed its flames between finger and thumb and turned a contemptuous gaze upon Anohin. Almost lazily, he lifted a hand and flung the Yadin against the side of the mountain. Bone splintered.

'Anohin!' Medavle screamed. Anohin lay nearby in a crumpled heap, stirring feebly as blood trickled down his face and into his eyes.

Loricus looked on without interest. 'I thought I might have saved you the trouble of killing him,' he commented to Medavle.

The dark-eyed Yadin clenched his teeth. 'Pitiful man, you know nothing of me.'

'I know enough,' Loricus said, unsmiling now. He looked at Kyndra. 'Are you content to let your friends take my blows?'

Another battle was unfolding near the blasted tunnel, Kyndra saw, as Kait and Nediah fought the Wielders sent to subdue them. Energy crackled over the combatants' heads and the mêlée was almost too fast to follow. Kait held a flaming rapier in each hand. Her lips curled in savage concentration and her brown hair whirled across her face, as she parried and dodged.

Two of her opponents also bore weapons. The remaining three crooked their fingers and attacked with blasts of energy. Kait's blades stopped these as effectively as they stopped the wide sweep of the flaming broadsword, and the Wielder who held it stepped back for another swing.

As Kyndra looked on, a scorching trio of bolts roared towards Kait from the left, the sword swung in from the right and a glowing web snared her feet. Kait staggered and fell into the path of the sword.

An inch from Kait's nose, the blade stopped and the bolts burst into sparks. Beyond Kait, who strove to break the net around her legs, Kyndra saw Nediah, fingertips pressed against a burnished shield that he was struggling to maintain. It reached over both their heads and down to the ground behind. Kait's bonds dissipated and she stood, but neither could do anything further inside the shield. As the Wielders turned their attacks upon the shining dome, Nediah's face grew more strained. They wouldn't last, Kyndra realized. Nediah's talents lay in healing, not in offence, which left Kait against the five Solars. No matter how fast she was, one of them would eventually break through her guard.

Something tugged at Kyndra's ankles and, tearing her eyes from the battle, she looked down. A golden serpent tightened its coils around her legs, sliding inexorably upwards. She jerked and cried out in disgust, but the snake hissed and constricted, binding her legs together.

'A nice touch,' Loricus said.

Janus stood several yards away, a miniature version coiled in his palm. Each tiny scale pulsed with Solar energy. Tasting the air, the snake now writhed around her hips and Kyndra tensed, breathing shallowly.

'Keep still,' Janus said. Dirt smeared his robe, his hair hung in listless knots and there was a grey cast to his skin, as if from exhaustion. 'Why did you not just use the *akan*?' he asked her regretfully. 'This need never have happened.'

'Please, Janus,' Kyndra said, moving her lips as little as possible. The serpent pinned both arms now, heavy coils sliding up her chest. She couldn't repress a shudder. Why had she let her guard down?

Loricus stood behind the young man, watching intently. A possessive smile darkened his lips.

'Janus,' Kyndra tried. 'The *akan* was a trap. Whatever Loricus has told you, it's not true. It's him – he meant to kill me.'

Janus' fixed expression wavered, and for an instant she glimpsed someone very young looking out at her, confused and frightened. She saw horror there and a terrible, twisted desire to be of value, but then his face hardened and those emotions disappeared. Kyndra's heart pounded sickly: Jhren had worn a similar expression when he'd told her he was marrying Colta.

'The snake will bite if she feels you move,' Janus said hollowly. 'Her poison is very potent. It will be a quick end, if you choose it.' He stepped back to join Loricus and Kyndra felt a dreadful hopelessness.

'You will not find me as merciful,' Loricus told her. 'You are going to die, Vale, one way or another. You cannot say I haven't been fair. I gave you a chance to stand with me.'

'Only after trying to kill me,' Kyndra said, her voice roughened by fear. Janus' snake continued its sinuous advance up her body. 'How is that fair?'

'I believe I have been over-generous,' Loricus said, his eyes darkening. 'Not only do you threaten everything *I* have worked towards, but you also pose a greater threat to the rest of Mariar.'

'What are you talking about?'

Loricus cast a contemptuous look at Anohin. 'I have known the truth for some time, but it changes nothing. The Nerian can sing the madman's praises while he rots in the Deep. I have no desire to harm him. In fact, I applaud his achievement. Acre was a world full of unpredictable elements and conflicting powers vying for control. Mariar, however, is – as you so like to put it – a place of peace.' His eyes narrowed. 'And Naris can rule a peaceful land unchallenged.'

'Solinaris – was not – supposed to rule,' Anohin gasped, one bloodied hand outstretched as he hauled himself towards them across the rock. 'Kierik's Mariar is a free land.'

'*Kierik's* Mariar?' Loricus raised an eyebrow. 'That does not sound like a free land to me. The Starborn may have cloaked his desire for power in platitudes of peace, but he intended to rule from the outset. I am merely finishing what he began. And to do that –' he looked back at Kyndra – 'I must first eliminate you.'

'Why?' Kyndra asked desperately. 'You said I might not ever be a true Starborn, so what harm can I do you or anyone?'

Loricus' gaze sharpened. '*If* you ever inherit – a great deal. Only another Starborn has the ability to reunite this land with Acre.'

All Kyndra could do was stare at him, wondering if she had heard correctly.

Loricus circled her. 'Yes, as long as Kierik is alive, you pose little threat. But why take the chance? As soon as you inherit, you will be beyond my control. If you won't swear a Wielder's Oath and join me, how can I – in good conscience – leave you to roam free, knowing full well what you are capable of?'

'You believe I can bring Acre back?' Kyndra hadn't even thought it was possible, let alone that *she* could do such a thing.

'Enough talk.' Loricus returned to stand in front of her. 'You have one choice left to make. Accept Janus' offer of a quick death and I will allow it.' A glowing ball, golden this time, surged between his hands. Then the feared sleek head emerged and claws dug at the air. Kyndra stared at the new *executis* and felt an echo of pain in her wrist.

'You think this one will act as Helira's did?' Loricus grimaced as his creation struggled to free itself. 'But she, too, wanted to grant you a quick end. I, however, am interested in seeing just how resilient a Starborn's body is on the inside.' He held out the writhing bundle of claws. 'The *executis* may seem in a hurry, but it will tunnel a slow path through your organs if I command it to.'

Frozen by the squeezing snake, Kyndra stared at the

creature, terrified of feeling that agony again. Its golden light fell on Janus' cheek and he turned his face away. Kyndra tried to think of a plan, a distraction, anything that might give her a chance to escape the snake.

'Remember, girl. One little move.' Loricus paused, his gaze roving over her face. 'But that would disappoint me.'

Kyndra flicked her eyes, the only things she could safely shift, to Medavle. The Yadin was staring intensely at Loricus, as if he, too, searched for an answer. Anohin was still trying to crawl over the rock, his blood-rimmed eyes now fixed on a point to Kyndra's right, away from the others. A moan issued from his throat, rising to a horrified wail.

'Things could have been different between us, Kyndra Vale,' Loricus said. 'I am sorry they are not.'

A vortex of silence ripped across the plateau and Anohin's mouth opened wider, as he screamed soundlessly. Without thinking, Kyndra turned, and the snake bit her.

She howled at the sharp puncture, feeling the venom pump unstoppably into her body. She tried to wriggle free from the coils that bound her arms and legs, but they wouldn't budge. The beast had become a dead weight, its Solar energy spent. Kyndra blinked at the scene before her, but a mist clung to her eyes and she couldn't seem to catch her breath.

Forgotten amidst the separate battles, Kierik stood, one hand outstretched. The white *akan* blazed on his palm.

'No,' Anohin moaned and tore his fingers on the sharp rock, striving to reach Kierik, who stood mesmerized by the statue's unfolding wings. The silent pressure in the air increased and, like an omen of doom, Kierik's gaze fell on Loricus.

The statue of the child leapt from his fingers, its eyes opening as its feathered wings expanded. In that moment, Loricus seemed to recognize it, for he stumbled back, face drained of colour, and set free the *executis*. But the child's mouth stretched wide and its fat, white lips sucked the creature inside with a wail. Loricus staggered and backed away further, furiously tearing a pendant from his neck. He hurled it into the *akan*'s path and a wall of flame roared up. There were faces in the fire, screaming and tortuous, and when the bulbous child neared them, they cried at it with one deathly voice. Again, the *akan* did not slow, but shook its now vast wings and the flames shrank beneath their wind. The child passed through the fire and though it shuddered violently, it came on.

Kyndra's chest tightened and she could feel the irregular beats of her heart, as it began to fail. Her blood carried the venom around her body and a hot, panicked despair rushed with it. She didn't want to die, not here on this wasted cliff.

The attacks on Nediah's shield diminished, as the five Wielders turned to watch the *akan*. One of the older men made to join Loricus, but the woman beside him seized his arm. Naked terror moistened her eyes.

The child was now so huge that its wings screened the sky. One of them knocked Janus aside. The young man shrieked, as if his skin were aflame, and began tearing at it, leaving dreadful gashes down his cheeks, neck and arms.

Loricus paid him no heed, his fury changing to panic. He turned his face towards Kyndra and desperation made it grotesque. Hazel eyes took in the dead snake and he smiled wildly before falling to his knees. His arms lurched up over his head, as if pulled by a great force and he screamed as his shoulders dislocated. The scream went on and on while a golden mist rose from his skin. The white *akan* beat its wings, stripping the energy from the councilman. Kyndra wished it would stop.

Finally, the tattoo on Loricus' back fractured and bled and the blood ran down over his shoulders and chest to soak into the silken robes. When every shred of power had left him, the child wrapped both wings around the kneeling man. Only then did the tortured screams die. His skin blackened and cracked, flesh sliding from bone like overcooked meat. A stench clogged Kyndra's nostrils and filled her spinning head with death.

When it was done and nothing remained of the man, the *akan* spun with one sweep of its wings. They were stained black now and glittered golden at their tips. Shrinking, it returned to Kierik.

'No!' Anohin screamed, still too far from his master. As the child reached Kierik, Medavle threw out a hand, fear heating his dark eyes. Whitish filaments crawled from the Starborn's nose and Kierik clutched his head, his cries a mirror of Anohin's. Kyndra's legs finally crumpled and she sank to her knees, still wrapped in the snake.

The child fluttered in front of Kierik, tiny once more. For one long, agonizing moment, Kierik stared at it and then his head sagged and the white *akan* fell at his feet.

All sound ceased. Kierik's chin sat on his chest. Then a fan of light burst from his shoulders, as if someone had thrown up a handful of stars. Each speck shone with cold brilliance. They formed, broke, reformed and separated in an ageless dance. It was a beautiful, terrible sequence. The summer air turned cold and a sharp scent rent the wind. The stars hung momentarily around Kierik, making him part of their constellation. Then they began to flow away from him in earnest, spinning and dancing until the sky took them back.

Released, Kierik fell to his knees and tears appeared on his cheeks. He touched them, peering at the salty moisture that silvered his fingers. He raised his head, eyes clear and unguarded, and looked at Kyndra.

Kyndra gasped as a force slammed into her back. Clarity shredded the poison's fog, as ice splintered through her body and razed the snake's venom from her blood.

Behind her closed eyelids, countless suns exploded into being, scattering their light across infinity. The wind was a thousand voices, lifting her, filling her hands and head. Constellations rolled beneath her feet. They hammered her with names and it was as if they had known her all her life. Among them was *Sigel*, massive and incandescent, and around it spun its errant siblings, *Wynn* and *Lagus*. *Isa* showed her how to bridge the void, and *Yeras* how to claim it. Mysterious *Pyrth* acknowledged her from its dark corner of the sky, and she shuddered at *Hagal*'s demonic regard.

She glimpsed a vast imagination and recoiled at the awful power they told her was theirs. They showed her the void and the dark reaches where there was no life, but a frozen and timeless waste. Crossing it would change her, but to be one with the stars was to dwell where they dwelled, and they burned in isolation. A strange pain grew in her heart, which she knew a moment later as sadness. They did not understand tears or laughter, love or sympathy. They would share with her only what they could: the third and greatest power of the cosmos, a power which in the end would destroy her.

'Why,' she cried, '*why me?*'

What would satisfy you as an answer?

Pain lanced from the force that bent her, as if a fine knife scored fire across her back. It climbed up her neck, cutting her scalp and forehead. It flowed beneath her eyes, down both cheeks and over her breasts until it covered her whole body.

The pattern pulsed in her skin and she knew it for a map, a constellatory route she could follow home.

No, she thought, *you are not my home.*

She felt something from them – in a human, it might have been humour. As swiftly as it had come, the force left her and Kyndra straightened. Flexing her fingers, she reached up and wrenched the snake's fangs from her neck. The coils loosened and the dead serpent collapsed into ash.

Her face stung. She raised a hand to her cheek and followed the curving scars, unwilling to see what damage they had wrought. She remembered the black chasms that made a horror of Kierik's face.

The touch of the stars had emptied her, hollowed her out like a fruit divested of its pulp. It made the terror of the *executis* a distant memory. Kyndra looked at the sooty pile that minutes ago had been a living man and felt nothing. Janus lay where the *akan's* wing had knocked him, face down on the rock. She couldn't tell whether he lived.

Kyndra stared at Kierik. His face was unmarked now, and the straggling beard that hung over his chin and the long, tangled hair gave him the look of a vagrant. His eyes, a blue that was almost black, regarded her clearly for the first time. *My eyes,* she thought.

The wind swept the plateau, laid claim to the councilman's ashes and bore them away.

'You remind me of her,' Kierik whispered. He crumpled. Finally at his side, Anohin caught him and clasped his friend to his chest. They crouched on the rock and Anohin's blood smeared Kierik's skin. 'Hini,' Kierik acknowledged, his eyes beginning to glaze. Anohin sobbed and clutched him tighter, as if his grip alone held death at bay.

'You have . . . what you wanted,' Kierik breathed and Kyndra realized he was speaking to Medavle.

The Yadin regarded the dying man, pity and disgust in his face. 'No,' he said. 'I wanted only one thing, and you took her from me many years ago.'

'So,' Kierik's voice grew weaker, 'you will make the world pay . . . for my crime.'

Medavle towered against the morning sky, and a hush lay thick on the land, as if all life waited for the sun to crest the mountain's shoulder. His gaze moved to the pouch around Kierik's neck. 'It is not my world,' he said.

'But it is hers.' Kierik looked at Kyndra. 'I do not even know your name,' he whispered.

'Kyndra,' she said reluctantly.

'Daughter of Reena,' Kierik whispered, and Kyndra flinched to hear her mother's name on those terrible, unlikely lips. 'I wish you had never been born.'

Chilled, Kyndra waited for more, but Kierik's eyes held only remorse. They rolled up in his head, the whites showed for a brief instant and then his eyelids closed.

Anohin's grieving wail hit the plateau like a bleak wind. He clasped the dead man and moaned, rocking back and forth. His shattered legs lolled at obscene angles, and the blood flaked on his lips.

'Leave him, Anohin.'

Medavle spoke harshly. When the other Yadin didn't respond, he repeated his command and Anohin looked up with a face that was wracked and senseless. 'It is over,' Medavle told him.

Anohin screamed. He dropped Kierik and tried to throw himself at Medavle, but instead rolled helplessly across the rock. Immediately, Medavle knelt down beside him. He ignored Anohin's curses to keep away and placed his hands on the broken body. After a moment he withdrew them, pale-faced, and turned to look over his shoulder. 'Nediah!' he called.

Kyndra followed his gaze. Loricus' death had ended Kait and Nediah's struggle and the councilman's Wielders now stood loosely together, stunned and frightened. Kait knelt on the ground, her hands over her mouth, with tears falling thickly from her wide, disbelieving eyes. Brégenne still hovered near the shattered tunnel. Her expression was guarded, as the high wind whipped up her hair, and Kyndra realized that day had taken her sight.

Nediah made his way hesitantly to Medavle's side. 'His injuries are great,' the Yadin said, gesturing to Anohin. 'Please heal him.'

Nediah knelt mechanically and laid his hands on Anohin's body, but his face was grave. 'This is very serious,' he muttered.

'You *must* heal him.' Medavle's hands balled into fists.

'Why?' Nediah asked quietly.

It seemed as if Medavle would lash out, but Nediah held his ground, one hand resting on Anohin, and the moment passed. Then Medavle's fists uncurled. His shoulders slumped, as he looked down at the bleeding man. 'We are the last,' he whispered. 'I don't want to carry that burden alone again.'

Nediah's face was unreadable, but he nodded. He placed both hands on Anohin's chest and a glow seeped between his fingers.

'No!' The force that burst from Anohin knocked Nediah sprawling and the light around his hands faded.

'Let him heal you, Anohin,' Medavle said. 'You are dying.' His deep voice caught on the word.

A mist drifted across Anohin's grey eyes. He gazed at Medavle, as if he saw through him to the empty sky beyond. 'No . . .' he sighed, his voice little louder than wind over stone. 'I will not live for you.'

Medavle seized Anohin's hands and gripped them so tightly that a spasm of pain crossed the other Yadin's face. 'Live,' he said fiercely, the command roughened by fear. 'You cannot leave me alone. *I won't allow it!*'

He shouted the last words and shook him, careless, it seemed, of the pain he caused. Anohin's eyes clouded and his face whitened beneath the bloodstains. 'Make my last moments unbearable,' he breathed.

Medavle stopped his desperate shaking, staring at Anohin with wet eyes. 'You would be a traitor to the last,' he murmured.

'I served.' Anohin coughed up blood. It trickled from the corner of his mouth and Medavle wiped it gently away with a sleeve. Kyndra could not bear to look at his face. It was a maelstrom of hatred, fury and grief that she knew she would never understand.

Anohin died with his eyes open. When the last breath had left his lungs, Medavle rose. Death had swept his face clean of expression. 'What do the young people of Brenwym learn during their Inheritance Ceremony?' he asked Kyndra.

Kyndra stared at him, dazed by the question. 'Their true name and calling,' she answered slowly.

'And what was your calling?'

'I don't know.' That afternoon was so distant now. 'The Relic broke before it showed me.'

Medavle's eyes glittered. 'Are you sure it didn't show you?' He lifted a white-clad arm and pointed. 'There is your calling.'

The finger pointed at Kierik, at the pouch still hanging around his neck. Hesitantly, Kyndra crossed the open ground to the Starborn's body. She would never think of him as anything more, she decided. The dead man was a stranger whose life had been lived long ago in a world recalled on crumbling paper.

She tried to touch the corpse as little as possible, but the pouch's string was tangled in Kierik's matted hair and Kyndra had to break a few strands to free it. Shuddering, she returned to Medavle, the pouch on her palm, but the Yadin shook his head. 'It's yours,' he said, 'and yours alone. Remember the Ceremony. Remember what the Relic showed you.'

'It didn't show me anything,' Kyndra began and then she stopped, staring wide-eyed at Medavle. 'Are you saying . . . it was supposed to break?'

Medavle smiled.

Kyndra thought back to the Ceremony. She remembered the weightlessness of the Relic and its freezing, searing touch. She remembered the lights spinning in its depths. Most starkly of all, she remembered the crack as it shattered. 'What is my calling?' she whispered.

'Open the bag.'

Her fingers trembled. As she loosened the neck of the pouch, Kierik's memories soared and sang within her. The fortress of the sun; a phalanx of Lleu-yelin, ribbons whipping the wind; great cities heaving with people; the Cargarac Ocean's stormy swells that drove the warships of the south.

The earth pooled on her hand, each grain seemingly infused with a drop of blood, and Kyndra saw the red valley once more, but this time it wasn't in the earth or a memory. She took a few astonished steps towards the precipice on which Kierik had crouched and, blinking, tried to strip the mirage from her eyes.

Beyond the circular chasm, there had only been mountains, but now she saw the red valley too, stretching away west and bearing the pockmarks of war. The mountains were still there, but they looked fragile, as if drawn on paper, and the longer she looked, the clearer the valley grew.

Medavle caught her arm. 'If you can see it, don't trust your sight just yet. The Starborn's death has brought it closer, but only you can reunite this continent with Acre. You'll need the earth. It is the soil of the old world, of the true world.'

Kyndra gazed at him, unseeing, too stunned to speak. Kierik had spent years in study and, as a result, had shaped concepts few could comprehend. She remembered that final vision, when she'd looked out of Kierik's eyes. She remembered the feel of Rairam in her hands and the chill touch of the stars.

'Acre is your calling,' Medavle said.

Kyndra watched the double landscapes that only she could see. How could she undo what had been done? How could she break the barrier that Kierik had forged between worlds? 'Why should I?' she asked aloud.

'It's the only way to protect Mariar and its people from the Breaking.'

Kyndra looked sharply at Medavle. 'What do you mean?'

'The Breaking is a force that can't be controlled – even by you,' the Yadin said. 'And now that Kierik is gone, it will grow wilder. You saw how it worsened as the Starborn declined. But it only exists so long as Mariar remains separate from Acre. Once Kierik's laws are destroyed and the last of his power fades, so, too, will the Breaking.' He held out a hand. 'Your path is clear, Kyndra. Restore the continent of Rairam to Acre. Make the world whole again.' Medavle briefly closed his eyes. 'Enough people have died for a madman's dream.'

'What about the empire?' she asked the Yadin. 'What about the war?'

'Five hundred years have passed,' Medavle answered, staring out at the mountains. 'The empire may be no more. It is, however, a risk you have to take.'

Kyndra turned away from him and a cold whisper touched her mind. At first she recoiled, but the whisper became a voice speaking and Kyndra started to listen. Other voices joined the first and she forgot Medavle and the people who stood behind her. A freezing core hardened in her chest. She saw it as a door, a black, shining portal to the void. The great star, *Sigel*, beckoned her and she felt an instant of terror before she passed through.

The sun finally crested the mountain and Kyndra threw up her hand. The red earth left her palm in a scatter of light and each grain hung in the air, turning slowly. Standing on the black path that ran between the stars, she saw the power that separated Rairam from Acre. It was Kierik's law and it wrenched at the margins of time. The world would not fight her – it struggled to be whole.

Sigel's heat poured into her. She let it flow in her veins like blood, relishing the sensation. It wasn't the black ice she had used to kill Helira. This was clean, brutal energy capable of ruinous things. It took all her will to hold it back until she felt saturated – a being of fire. And, in a moment, that fire would obliterate her. *No*, Kyndra thought, and she brought the power crashing down on the strained cords that kept Rairam and Acre apart.

Red earth fell like a curtain, and to those watching, it seemed as if it pulled the endless mountains down with it. Thunder shook the plateau and cracks splintered across the surface of the rock. Everyone except Kyndra was thrown from their feet, as the quake rumbled on, spreading north and south, dragging down the mountains known as the Infinite Hills. Great choking plumes rocketed into the air, rising in a dark cloud.

Kyndra used the four cardinal stars called the Watchers to witness Kierik's bonds unravel across the world. The southern ocean heaved, as it crashed against a new land, sending a mile-high wave towards the coast. She reached for *Sigel* again and a gust of power broke the wave before it hit. The Great Northern Forest breached the Rib Wall to straggle onto a vast, icy plain, where the ground hissed and water boiled in deep troughs. Then Acre rose in the west like a flawed sun, a yawning, end-less earth whose distant corners lay beyond her sight.

Overwhelmed, Kyndra pulled her mind away from the stars and dropped to her knees, hands flat on the rock. It was history repeating itself once again, she realized, gazing at the pitted surface. This spot – sunken by the force of the Deliverance – was where Kierik had first stood to create his world.

The sun shone, the wind blew and the scent of summer grew strong in her nose. Ahead, the desolate valley glowed, as if it were made of countless rubies, or the bright red blood of the slain. Somewhere, unconcerned, a bird began to sing.

32

'Long ago, when the Starborn were still acknowledged as part of the cosmosethic triad, they traditionally wore black.'

Kyndra looked up from her packing to see Medavle leaning idly against the chamber wall. The Yadin's white outfit was once again pristine, cleansed of the blood that had stained it a month ago. Though his wound had been healed, he still favoured his right side when he walked.

'Nediah got these for me,' Kyndra said, plucking at a black sleeve. 'It's nice not to wear rags.'

'You're nearly finished, I see.'

She nodded. 'I don't have much to pack. There wasn't time to take anything from home.'

Events had moved forward so quickly, Kyndra thought, as she tucked a spare shirt into the bag. She scanned the room — at least five times the size of her previous cell — for anything she'd missed. The walls bore a myriad collection of tapestries and paintings, and bright rugs hid the unforgiving stone. Despite the opulence, or perhaps because of it, Kyndra keenly felt the presence of the mountain surrounding her here. She would almost have preferred to stay in her tiny room, but that had been deemed inappropriate.

Kyndra grimaced. If she had attracted attention before, it was nothing to the kind of attention she attracted now. Some faces wore awe, others curiosity. But she also caught poorly veiled disgust, especially from some of the older Wielders. And fear.

'What are you thinking about?'

'How much has changed,' Kyndra answered after a moment. 'In a way, I feel like I'll wake up any day now, and everything will be as it was.'

Medavle watched her with intent, dark eyes. 'Do you want it to be?'

Kyndra hesitated. 'I suppose not,' she said wistfully. 'But . . . did I make the right decision? What if the war starts again?'

'Kierik's world was never going to last forever,' Medavle said. 'Even the greatest power gifted to an individual cannot be used to change the fabric of what is.'

'Cannot or should not?'

'That is a matter of opinion,' the Yadin answered. 'Had Kierik's idea to separate Rairam from Acre ever been put to a vote, I would have stood against it.'

'Why?'

'My people's demise aside, it came at a high cost.'

Kyndra waited, hands paused on the pack's fastenings.

'Yes,' Medavle said, 'Sartyan rule was violent and autocratic, but it also brought order. And by separating us from Acre, Kierik deprived Rairam of all sorts of Acrean inventions. The empire was wealthy beyond imagining. Not only from plundering its enemies' towns, which it did without mercy, but also from developing a host of advancements.'

'Advancements?'

'Contraptions to improve farming, designed to lighten the ploughman's load, devices to streamline domestic and agricultural processes.' Medavle gestured as he spoke. 'Dangerous yet necessary jobs like mining and building could be made safer and more efficient.' He paused. 'For a price, of course. The empire's technology wasn't cheap, but it could be used by anyone. Solinaris and its Wielders weren't in the practice of mixing with ordinary people. Though their abilities were widely known, very few used them to better a person's lot. The empire's rule was strict – and I'm not condoning its practices – but once a land agreed to be governed, it generally prospered.'

'I wonder what we're going to find,' Kyndra said. She imagined walking through the red valley, boots coated in the bloody earth. What lay beyond the forested hills at its end?

They lapsed into an unexpected silence and Kyndra kept her hands busy, trying to disguise the thoughts that tumbled about her head. One loomed larger than the rest, a question she'd striven to ignore. But Medavle's quiet presence drew it out, and she realized that if she didn't ask now, she never would.

'You knew, didn't you?' she said, staring at the pack's fastened straps. 'You knew as soon as you saw me that I was his . . .'

'Yes,' Medavle said. 'Your eyes, the shape of your face. Yes, I knew.'

'But that was what you planned, wasn't it?' Kyndra made herself continue, gaze still fixed on the bag. 'You wanted him to father a child, another Starborn.'

Medavle pushed himself off the wall and took a step closer. 'It was a theory,' he said, 'based on legend. No more than a gamble. You even know the legend.'

Kyndra looked up. 'I do?'

'I gave you part of it in Sky Port East.'

She stared at Medavle for a few puzzled moments before the memory of the poem returned. 'The dragon-riders,' she said wonderingly. 'It was about a woman . . . and a Starborn.'

'More importantly, it was about the love they bore for each other,' Medavle said. His expression grew distant. 'Their love is the reason why the story became legend. Starborn are not given to love.'

Kyndra shifted uncomfortably. 'So what made this one different?'

'Nobody knows. The story is remarkable because the dragon-rider also chose him. They never take partners outside of their society, a custom based on an ancient law.'

'What happened to them?'

'They had a child,' Medavle said, his face serious. 'A daughter. She was as wild as her mother, they say, but possessed of her father's terrible power.'

'She was a Starborn too?'

'Yes, the birthright was there. The moment her father died, she would come into her own. But her father was young then, unlike Kierik, and had centuries of life left to him. As is the case with many legends, tragedy struck. The Lleu-yelin, incensed at the woman's crime of mating outside of her society, finally tracked down the family where they lived in exile, hidden high in the mountains. It was the rider's dragon that betrayed her, mad with jealousy and rage. You see, in Lleu-yelin society, a rider's dragon is their mate.'

Kyndra blinked, uncertain she had heard correctly. 'What?'

'Though few realize it, the dragon-riders and their dragons

are one people. All have the ability to become dragons. Even if they do not, they share certain features.'

'But how do they . . . ?'

Medavle smiled a small, wicked smile. 'I don't know,' he said. 'The world never knew much about them.'

'So what happened when the Lleu-yelin turned up?' Kyndra asked, trying unsuccessfully to rid her mind of several disturbing images.

'The rider was killed, of course. Her dragon ate her heart.'

'And the Starborn stood by and watched?'

'Yes,' Medavle said soberly. 'That was the true tragedy. Though he called on his power to protect her, he couldn't touch it. He couldn't find his way back to the stars – they had become so alien to him. Loving her destroyed his ability to recognize them in his soul.'

Kyndra was silent, hearing her heart thump uneasily.

'Wracked with grief over his lover's death and at his failure to protect her, he threw himself over the precipice.'

'That's horrible,' Kyndra said, shuddering. 'What about his daughter? Didn't he think of her?'

'Evidently not,' Medavle said, spreading his hands. 'The child was by then a young woman, probably around your age. She watched her parents die from the window of her home and heard the Lleu-yelin order her own death. They dispatched two riders to finish her, but they didn't return.'

'The girl killed them?'

Medavle nodded. 'She had inherited her father's power at the moment of his death. It's said she became one of the greatest and most feared Starborn that ever lived, half dragon as she was. She walked Acre alone and didn't emulate her father's mistake.'

'You tried to achieve the same outcome with me,' Kyndra

said after a moment, her unease at the story turning to anger. 'You used my mother.'

'I wanted to see whether a Starborn really could sire another Starborn,' Medavle said honestly. 'When Wielders mate, there is no guarantee that their offspring will share their affinity – that's the main reason why most choose not to. But Starborn, it seems, are different.'

'So my life was just an experiment to you,' Kyndra said bitterly. She looked up at the Yadin. 'You wanted a Starborn to reverse what Kierik had done. Killing him wasn't vengeance enough.'

Medavle was silent.

'What about my mother?' she asked, clenching her fists. 'You didn't give her a choice!'

'She had a choice,' Medavle said, dark eyes penetrating. 'What she did, she did of her own free will.'

Disgust curdled her outrage. 'She would never have—'

'You cannot say what she would or would not have done,' the Yadin said loudly. Then he lowered his voice. 'Kierik didn't hurt her. I made sure of that.'

Suddenly the whole subject was too much. Kyndra couldn't bring herself to think of her mother with Kierik, couldn't imagine a scenario in which they had met. Whenever she'd asked about her father, Reena's eyes had clouded with a strange, bittersweet memory, the truth of which Kyndra would never know. She looked back down at the pack and wondered how she would ever understand.

'It would only be for a moment.'

'My answer is no.'

'I'm leaving soon. Please let me see him.'

'There's nothing to see. His face is bandaged. And he already has a visitor.'

Kyndra stood outside Janus' quarters, arguing with the gold-robed Wielder who guarded the door. Wrinkles ringed the woman's stubborn mouth and Kyndra felt a flutter of respect. Facing down a Starborn or not, the Wielder stood with arms folded, blocking the way. 'I won't disturb him,' Kyndra said. 'I only wanted to say goodbye.'

The woman's face wavered. 'He still hasn't woken,' she said dismissively. 'He probably won't hear you.'

'That doesn't matter.' Kyndra pressed her advantage. 'Please. You can watch me.'

The Wielder pursed her lips. 'Two minutes,' she said finally, 'and I *will* be watching.'

'Thank you,' Kyndra said. The woman gave her a look, but opened the door. Kyndra recognized the round-faced girl who sat in a chair beside Janus. Her name was Ranine and she'd visited Janus every day for the last month.

Ranine looked round at Kyndra's entrance, but didn't speak. Kyndra nodded at her and the novice turned back to the still figure in the bed. Janus was unrecognizable. Only his head, neck and shoulders showed above the coverlet. All were heavily bandaged and Kyndra saw nothing of his face. One golden curl escaped close to his ear and she stared at it, conflicted. The sadness she had felt a month ago returned to her alongside the hurt of Janus' betrayal.

The young man's shallow breathing barely stirred the blanket. Did he deserve this fate? Kyndra asked herself, gazing at the face she couldn't see. That morning on the plateau had changed them both forever. She glanced at the mirror above the bed. From this distance, the constellations in her skin could barely be seen. They were flesh-coloured, but glinted in light. One mark was slightly darker than the rest – a souvenir of *Sigel*. That was the star she'd used to destroy Kierik's bindings. Kyndra knew that the more she touched them, the more the stars would mark her.

'Goodbye, Janus,' she whispered to the inert body in the bed. 'I'm sorry.'

Later, Kyndra stood outside the gates of Naris, watching the sky deepen into afternoon. She was surrounded by Medavle, Nediah and Kait, hooded against the bright sunlight, and the three novices. All were dressed for travel except Gareth, who stood sullenly, the sleeve of his robe pulled down over one hand. Horses brought carefully across the makeshift bridge from Murta stood ready in the courtyard nearby, their reins held by another young novice.

'I can't believe I'm not coming with you,' Gareth said for the umpteenth time, fiddling irritably with his sleeve. The other was pushed right back to his elbow in the summer heat.

'Master Brégenne says she needs you,' Irilin reminded him yet again. 'How many other Wielders do you know from Ümvast?'

'Just because I was born there, doesn't mean they won't bury an axe in my skull as soon as look at me,' Gareth retorted. He tried to scratch unobtrusively at his right forearm, and Kyndra saw the glint of metal.

'Well, you didn't leave yourself much choice, idiot,' Irilin hissed. 'You're lucky that only Master Brégenne knows about that gauntlet *and* that she found a perfect excuse to take you with her when she leaves the citadel.'

'It could have been me,' Shika said in his velvet voice. 'I was *this* close to slipping it on, but then Gareth had it off me.' He smirked. 'I am so glad he did. That gauntlet might be handy in a night-fight, but I like to take my armour off afterwards.'

'I didn't know it wasn't going to come off again!' Gareth said loudly and then looked around in case anyone had heard. 'And it itches like crazy.'

'I'm sure Master Brégenne will find a way to remove it,' Shika said breezily, but the humour was beginning to fade from his face.

'Don't know why they're letting you two go,' Gareth muttered. 'You're not even in the Superiate.'

'We're going because we want to help Kyndra,' Irilin said and Kyndra winced. She'd tried to talk the novices out of coming with her as many times as Gareth had complained about the stuck gauntlet. But Irilin was determined to stop Kyndra venturing into the unknown with only Nediah to protect her – she didn't trust Medavle or Kait. And then Shika had insisted he needed to come to protect Irilin. The irony of the situation was not lost on Kyndra: why should a Starborn need a half-trained novice as protection? *But I don't want this power,* she thought vehemently, *and I won't use it.*

A month ago, all three novices had stood beside her and watched as the pyre consumed the bodies of Kierik and Anohin, up on the plateau within sight of Acre. They'd listened to Medavle's deep voice, as he spoke words of parting in the spiky Acrean tongue and in the language of Mariar. Kyndra had marvelled at the Yadin's composure, at the respect he showed to people who had caused him such pain in life. When the flames began to lick over Anohin's white garments, a single tear had rolled down his cheek.

Now Kyndra turned to Irilin and Shika. 'You realize we could be walking into a war, don't you?'

Instead of falling back on his usual sarcasm, Shika nodded. 'We've made our choice, Kyndra, and we're happy with it.'

'I don't think Alandred is,' Kyndra replied wryly.

The Master of Novices had made it clear that both Irilin and Shika – if they left –would forfeit their right to further instruction in Naris. 'I have no control over masters or Star-born or members of the Nerian,' Alandred had lectured them sternly, 'but as Master of Novices, you two are my charges. If you choose to leave now, you will not be permitted to return to your studies.' He'd given Shika and Irilin a look that Kyndra knew well. 'Past laws would have kept you here whether you willed it or not.' The look said plainly that he wished those laws still held. 'But no longer. We face new challenges.' His eyes had flickered briefly to Kyndra before fixing once again upon the novices. 'Remember, you are still only at Inferiate level. You have many years of study ahead of you before you'll be ready to face the threat this girl has forced upon the world.'

Kyndra clenched her fists at the memory. As if she'd had any real choice.

Nediah approached her. 'Messengers have left for Market Primus and Mariar's largest kingdoms with news of Acre. Until we know what we face, the defence of our home must be our first consideration.'

'That's good,' Kyndra said awkwardly. She wasn't at all com-fortable being the leader of their group. Medavle would make a better choice, as the Yadin had lived in Acre. He knew the world and the history of the empire that had once ruled it.

Kyndra shivered in the sunlight. Whenever she thought of the Sartyans, foreboding built up in her chest. Some of it was Kierik, she realized. She might not want them, but she had his memories of the empire and she recoiled at the horrors he'd witnessed. She'd had so little time to think before reuniting Rairam with Acre, and she'd had very little choice, if she wanted to stop the Breaking from destroying more lives.

Nobody knew what was out there. Even if the empire no longer ruled, there would be others to contend with, those who might seek to harm Rairam and its people. She looked down at her hands and then wished she hadn't. Where the fingernails of Wielders were either silver or gold, hers were now black. They looked rotten.

'I hope you weren't thinking of leaving without saying good-bye.'

Kyndra turned at the voice. Brégenne walked carefully down the entrance hall, one hand on the wall for guidance. The sunlight flooding up to the wide double doors gleamed in her hair. 'You are like a blaze of starlight,' she told Kyndra, white eyes fixed on her face. 'Even at noon.'

Kyndra swallowed. 'Are you sure you won't come?'

Brégenne left the shelter of the doors and moved outside. 'There's work to do here. Naris has hidden itself for too long.' She paused and the thin, high clouds blew their shadows across her face. 'It is time we left secrecy behind.'

Kyndra nodded. Brégenne, she saw, now wore silver robes slashed with red. She and another Wielder, Veeta, had agreed to serve on the Council beside Gend – the only surviving member of the previous Council. A victim of the Madness, Gend had been one of a handful of Wielders that Nediah had finally managed to cure. Despite his recovery, the tall man was not unchanged. Kyndra had sat in on their first meetings and noticed that Gend now spoke more often, though a shadow lingered in his eyes.

Although it was good to see Brégenne on the Council, it

was a shame that Naris wasn't ready to go back to the more democratic days of the Sentheon. At least Brégenne had ordered the Deep sealed and the Nerian given their own space in the upper citadel. Naris had suffered heavy losses and – in the uncertain future that loomed – needed all the able Wielders it could get. Naris's residents had protested, of course – centuries of prejudice were not easily erased and both sides had lost friends in the Long Night, as the evening of the Breaking had come to be called. The Nerian still wore their black bands and moved around the citadel listless and hollow-eyed. Kierik had been everything to them and now he was dead.

Kyndra looked at Brégenne and remembered the cold sorceress who had torn her away on the night of the Breaking in Brenwym. Another life, she thought, another person. She left the others and walked over to the blind woman, offering her hand. Brégenne took it without hesitation and held it, as Kyndra looked into the white eyes that once had so unnerved her. 'Goodbye, Brégenne,' she said quietly.

'Farewell for now, Kyndra Vale,' Brégenne said and smiled. 'I knew I was right about you.'

Kyndra heard footsteps behind her and turned. Nediah stood there, grim-faced. Kyndra nodded at Brégenne and returned to the others, but all were in earshot of the pair. Nediah stared at Brégenne, his eyes unfathomable and Kait watched him narrowly.

'I have a gift for you,' Nediah said, 'and I'm sorry that it's taken me so long.'

Perhaps Brégenne heard something in those words to frighten her, for she took a step back. 'Nediah,' she began, but in one swift movement, the Wielder took her head in his hands. Golden light welled between them.

Brégenne gasped. 'No!' She tried to pull free of his grip. 'Nediah, please!'

Such was the tumult of horror and hope in her voice that Kyndra nearly rushed to her side. Nediah lowered his forehead to Brégenne's. His lips moved, but the words were too soft to hear. Then he raised his head and closed his eyes. His face tightened in concentration.

'No!' Brégenne cried. 'Nediah, they tried, they tried. Not again, please not again. Let me go!'

Her words had no effect on Nediah, who gritted his teeth and pulled down energy from the hot sun. His hands grew incandescent, hiding Brégenne in their light. She screamed, and though Nediah looked stricken, still he didn't let her go.

Brégenne screamed again and then the light around her face diminished. Nediah released her and she fell to her knees, chest heaving. Nediah took a step back, staggered and almost fell too. When he straightened wearily, Kyndra noticed his hands trembling. Brégenne's were pressed against the black stone, her eyes screwed shut.

'Look at me,' Nediah said, but Brégenne didn't move.

'Look at me,' he repeated.

Head still bent, Brégenne's eyelids fluttered. Pain flashed across her face and puckered the thin skin beneath her eyes. She blinked quickly, tears flowing over her cheeks.

It seemed an age passed before she looked up and, as she did so, Medavle swore under his breath. Kait let out a low gasp and astonishment lit the faces of the three novices. Kyndra stared at Brégenne.

She looked back with storm-grey, slightly bloodshot eyes. Her gaze swung to each of them, to her own hands, the sky, to the volcanic stone beneath her knees and to the smoke curling up from distant Murta. Her breath came fast. Finally, she moved her gaze to Nediah and her face was changed, softened, as if her tears were washing away some long-held hurt.

He had watched her with an unreadable expression, but when their eyes met, his face crumpled and he turned away. 'Come,' he said to the others, gaze hard and brittle, 'we ought to be going.'

Wielders emerged from the doors behind Brégenne, who still knelt on the ground. Some gathered around her and there were shocked exclamations and questions babbled into her ears. Brégenne ignored them all. Her eyes did not leave Nediah.

Kyndra's horse stamped impatiently and she patted it, grimacing at the memory of her journey to Naris with Brégenne and Nediah – she wasn't looking forward to whole days spent in the saddle again.

She put a foot in the stirrup and swung up unsteadily. Her horse was a great black stallion – really too big for her – and she wondered drily whether Medavle had chosen it. She glanced at the others. All sat atop their horses except Shika, who looked like he was on his third attempt at mounting. Gareth laughed as the slim young man scrabbled gracelessly into the saddle, but his laugh carried a nervous edge. As Shika eyed the animal beneath him with distrust, Gareth said gruffly, 'Don't get yourself killed, Shik.'

Shika gave him a brief smile and, once he was settled, leaned down and grasped his friend's gauntleted arm. Their eyes met. 'And don't you do anything I wouldn't,' he said.

They were waiting on her, Kyndra realized. She took a last look at the dark mountain that had forever altered her life. The many faces of Naris looked back and she felt the weight of their implacable scrutiny. Drawing in a lungful of summer air, she wheeled her horse around to face the chasm. Its black reaches warned her that the journey had barely begun.

The six horses crossed the bridge and broke into a canter. They would need to head north to circle the citadel and its chasm before they could turn west into the old world. *Strange ambassadors*, Brégenne thought, watching them go.

She ignored the hands touching her shoulders and the voices asking their questions over and over again. With the eyes he had restored to her, she watched Nediah leave. Only when he was out of sight did the squall in her chest burst free.

'Leave me alone!' she screamed and the hands flew off her. She screamed again, wordless now, each cry ripping through the remnants of the person she had been. She screamed at what Nediah had done to her, at his gift – the most beautiful and terrible she had ever been given. She cried at his leaving and that she had forced him to do so.

When her throat was raw, the madness subsided and she found herself alone at the gates of Naris. The wind brought her honeysuckle and the sun beat hot on her hair. Her eyes stung and watered with the novelty of light. She stared at the blue sky and felt a great tide rising in her. She saw the trees waving below in the town, verdant green – and when a cloud passed above them, they darkened into forest, the colour of his eyes.

Brégenne rose stiffly, tears and light still misting her gaze. Beneath the shade of her hand, she saw a dark speck winging out of Mariar's lands to the east. It soared towards the citadel and over, a black hawk, carried high on the thermals.

She was about to return to the citadel when a shriek split the air and Brégenne craned her neck to look. Above her head, two birds now tore at each other, wings slapping the sky. One was the black hawk. She watched it lurch, as it screeched in pain and began to fall. Torn wings flapping uselessly, it crashed to earth and lay still, only feet from the chasm.

The other bird followed it down in wide, lazy circles and Brégenne caught her breath. It was huge, its wingspan twice that of the hawk's. With a curved, serrated beak, it tore open its meal and began to feed. When Brégenne took a few steps closer, it raised its head and regarded her with malevolent yellow pupils.

She retreated as the bird ripped off another dangling mouthful, and in a few short minutes, the hawk was gone. Blood and feathers smeared the stone. The butcher raised its head, shrieked at the sky and, with a parting glance for Brégenne, it took off. The wind from its passage reached her where she stood and carried a smell of fetid meat.

Brégenne watched it wheel away onwards into the east, casting an alien shadow on the ground. There was no doubt in her mind where the bird had come from. The scouts of Acre had found them at last.

EPILOGUE

. . . The mountain fades and the morning sky is as grey as a wolfhound's coat. His eyes are failing, as his life ebbs, so he follows them into darkness. Sorrow, too, has no place here, in the last rich seconds of existence.

In his memory, her face is frightened. I ran away from them, she says, skin flushed red as her unbound hair. Are you running too?

He cannot remember. Is he hurt? she asks, sitting close, tracing the dark scars on his face with her eyes. Yes, he answers, many years ago. Why is she running?

Anger and tears spill down her cheeks. Tomorrow my life will be decided for me, she tells him. He watches her fists curl, as she trembles in outrage, in fear.

Only you can decide, he tells her, and she beats the ground. No! The still-drowsy night birds are startled and there's a flurry of wings overhead. No, the Ceremony decides, she says. My true name and calling are given me and so my choice is taken away.

He already knows her true name. He will tell her, if she wants. She gazes at him, astonished and suspicious, yet still curious. She nods slowly.

You are called Reena, he says, and a small sigh tumbles from her lips. The words scare her, he sees, but she draws nearer. Her coarse clothes rasp pleasantly. And who are you, she asks, to tell me this?

I don't remember, he answers and it is the truth. He tells her of the shadow that hunts him, a shadow that descends upon his mind and twists it so that he cannot think. He has evaded it, but eventually it will claim him once more. Please, he says, suddenly afraid. Stay with me until it comes.

It won't come, she tells him, setting his head upon her shoulder. He knows she is wrong, but doesn't say so. Her hair smells of wind and her skin of her run through the night. He feels her heart reaching up to him, strong beats in her chest.

They lie on the forest floor, face to face. His scars hold no horror for her; neither does her youth for him. The night opens around them. None of this is real, she says. None of this is real.

He curls a lock of her hair around his fingers.

Tell me, she whispers, what does Reena mean?

It means, he says, that your hair is beautiful like flame. It means that you come alone through darkness. It means that you found me, as no one ever has.

Her eyes are liquid, grey-blue.

It means a colour, he whispers, as he holds her. The brilliant rim of the setting sun. The sands of a valley I will never walk again.